About the Author

NICOLA UPSON is the author of *An Expert in Murder*, her first mystery featuring Josephine Tey, and two works of nonfiction. She has worked in theater and as a freelance journalist. She is the recipient of an Escalator Award from Arts Council England, and she splits her time between Cambridge and Cornwall.

ANGEL WITH TWO FACES

A Mystery Featuring Josephine Tey

Nicola Upson

HARPER

NEW YORK • LONDON • TORONTO • SYDNEY

HARPER

First published in Great Britain in 2009 by Faber and Faber Ltd.

ISBN 978-1-61664-573-1

For Hettie, with love from us both

Death is an angel with two faces –
To us he turns
A face of terrors, blighting all things fair.
The other burns
With glory of the stars, a love is there.

—T. C. WILLIAMS

The horse hit the water at a gallop, fracturing the early morning peace which hung about the lake. Still breathless from the race across the sand and the shock of what had happened, Harry ran his hand the length of Shilling's neck, trying to calm him down, but the horse was already beyond reassurance. Suddenly, the bed of the lake fell away beneath them and water swirled up to Harry's waist. Shilling twisted his head round in fear, and Harry could see the panic in his eyes and feel the tension in the powerful muscles of his back. He leaned forward in the saddle, noticing how the smell of horse sweat mixed with the dank odour of the water, and spoke gentle words of encouragement, but Shilling seemed to sense the uncertainty in his voice and grew more frightened than ever. The spirit and defiance were entirely gone from him, and the fierce joy which Harry had always found in his bond with the horse was replaced by an intense sadness: the moment to let go had come. Knowing that Shilling would stand more chance without any weight on his back, Harry loosened his feet from the stirrups and slid from the saddle for the last time.

The water was ice-cold but the shock of it brought confusion rather than clarity. Disoriented, Harry felt himself pulled downwards, separated from the dawn by a dark mass of water. The strengthening light of the day disappeared entirely, and the water stabbed at his eyes and rushed in his ears, making it impossible to see or even to think. The pressure in his throat and chest told him to breathe but made it impossible to do so, and he tried to fight a choking sensation which threatened to overwhelm him. His whole body was a magnet for unimaginable pain and he knew that he was dying, but where was the euphoria that people spoke about? Where was the peace? He wanted to stay calm, to accept his fate, but his feet struggled desperately for a surface to kick against and the frantic search for something to hold on to became more than a physical need: without Shilling, he felt so alone.

Time expanded, turning seconds into hours, but at last he felt the bed of the lake beneath him. He thrashed wildly with his legs, but only succeeded in making the water solid with mud and tangling himself in a mass of dead branches and weed. His limbs were impossibly heavy now, and slime clung to his face. Unable to bear the suffocation any longer, Harry opened his mouth and screamed against a silent wall of water.

Chapter One

The sun beat down on Harry Pinching's coffin, and Archie Penrose shifted the weight on his shoulder in a vain attempt to alleviate his discomfort. Instead, the oak seemed to press harder against his neck, and every time he breathed in he caught a faint whiff of polish from the wood, its sweet, house-proud scent jarring sharply with the mood of the day. The heat was extreme for the time of year, and that alone would have been oppressive; combined with the other demands on his senses, it was almost unbearable and he was glad when he heard the stable clock strike noon, a signal for the small group of men to move towards the waiting hearse.

A funeral was not how he had intended to spend the first day of his holiday: this fortnight on his family's Cornish estate was supposed to be a much-needed break from the professional interest which he took in death. More importantly, he had made a promise to himself that these few days would mark a fresh start to his long, difficult and precious friendship with Josephine Tey. They had known each other now for twenty years, but eighteen of those had been clouded by secrets and guilt, and only the tragic events of the previous year had allowed them to clear the air once and for all. Since then, they had seen each other a few times in London, but this would be the first chance they had had to spend any length of time together, and to enjoy a new ease and honesty in their friendship. Admittedly, they were supposed to have travelled down together and the fact that a corpse had already changed their plans could be seen as an ill omen but, with summer here early and Josephine due on the afternoon train, Archie was optimistic that death and sadness would soon be behind them. It wasn't possible to forget the past – and neither of them would have wanted to – but perhaps from now on it would strengthen their bond instead of creating an awkwardness that both of them had tried to avoid.

The wooden hearse which stood just a few feet away was an open, no-nonsense affair, appropriate to the young man whose body it was to carry and – in a gesture of remarkable forgiveness, Archie thought – drawn by the horse which had killed him. It had been painstakingly decorated in the glorious assortment of flowers that Cornwall offered up at this time of year, all gathered from local gardens by friends who were glad of a simple way to express their sorrow. The bearers walked slowly forward, careful to keep in step, and Archie was close enough to the man in front to see the muscles in his neck tighten with the strain of weight and responsibility. As they lowered the coffin gently onto the cart, he could see his own relief reflected in the faces of the others. They had stood for just a short time with Harry's body on their shoulders, but it had been long enough for the midday sun to soak their funeral clothes with sweat. Archie's shirt stuck uncomfortably to his back and the dark, well-cut suit felt awkward and restrictive, as alien to him as it was to those around him whose daily lives required less fastidious tailoring. There ought to be a law against burying someone in temperatures like these, he thought. When his turn came, he hoped for rain, or at least for weather which was less of an affront to grief.

The coffin was fixed securely in place, and Archie glanced round at the other bearers – five men of varying ages and professions but all, to some degree, familiar to him. He had grown up on this estate, sixteen hundred acres of stunning wood and farmland on the south coast, but he returned home rarely now that his parents were dead. His uncle, William Motley, had inherited Loe just before the war and Archie admired the resourceful and spirited way in which he had kept the land and house going ever since, but that life was not for him and, like his cousins, Lettice and Ronnie, who had quite literally fashioned themselves a successful career in theatre design, he preferred to call London his home. Holidays were one thing, but he hated these public occasions which required him to play a more formal part in his family's life. Everyone was always polite and seemed genuinely pleased to see him, but no one at Loe had any use for an inspector from Scotland Yard, and he found it hard to relinquish that role – a matter of behaviour, rather than uniform. Being out of place was not something he experienced very often, and it made him irrationally annoyed that he should feel it most strongly amongst the men and women he had known since his childhood.

Today, though, formality could not be avoided. It was a long-standing tradition at Loe that whenever a member of the estate's community died, a representative from each of the families resident there would be chosen to carry the coffin. As they took their positions, ready to escort the body to the cliff-top church, it seemed to Archie that there could hardly have been a more appropriate expression of respect: among those present, it was possible to build a picture of daily life in this part of Cornwall which had probably not changed very much in three hundred years. For a few hours, these men were

5

symbols of the Cornish landscape as much as they were individuals and friends, and each brought his own testament to the
contribution that the dead man had made towards that whole.
Archie was moved to be a part of it, whilst always questioning
his right to belong.

They were ready to move off now, and the undertaker, Jago
Snipe – a well-built, pleasant-looking man in his fifties, whose
only stereotypical trait was a reassuring certainty in the face of
grief – walked over to two young women who waited by the
door of Loe House, hanging back from the scene as if reluctant
to engage. Archie recognised Harry's sisters – his twin,
Morwenna, and a much younger girl, Loveday, whom he
supposed must be thirteen or fourteen by now. Both seemed at
a loss to know what to do, Morwenna even more so than her
little sister, and they were obviously grateful when Jago put
an arm comfortingly around each of them and led them over
to the hearse. Archie watched as Harry's only remaining family
added their personal tributes to the flowers: Morwenna held
his best riding boots, which she laid carefully on top of the
coffin; Loveday's offering was a horseshoe – not a real one, but
a replica carved from wood and beautifully decorated with
long braids and flowers. Neither would have been obvious gifts
for a man who had died in a riding accident, but Harry had
worked with horses all his life and Archie was not surprised
that these should be regarded as the things he would wish to
take with him. Loveday struggled to reach the top of the coffin
and Archie – standing close by – automatically stepped
forward to help. As he lifted the girl up, he caught Morwenna's
eye and was shocked at how pale and tired she looked, even for
someone in mourning. Then he considered how long she had
been living a nightmare: the lake in which Harry had drowned

had been slow to give up his body, and several weeks had passed between his death and his funeral. The relentless coupling of hope and fear must have been exhausting, particularly as the inevitable outcome would make her head of the family and responsible for a sister who was generally acknowledged to be 'difficult'. It was little wonder that Morwenna Pinching bore scant resemblance to the young woman he remembered with such affection.

The funeral party headed slowly away from the house, through thick walls of rhododendron and towards the track which would take them to the small church on the cliff. Rounding the bend of the drive, they got their first glimpse of the lake which had brought them all together, a two-mile stretch of water separated from the sea by a narrow bar of sand. On a day like this, when the sun was high and there was barely a trace of wind, it looked serene and harmless, but anyone who had lived here long enough to be familiar with its history knew to treat it with respect. Unlike many of the legends surrounding Loe Pool, the myth that it took a life every seven years had its basis in fact, and Harry's death was the latest testimony. Archie had yet to hear all the details, but it seemed that Harry had been riding his horse, Shilling, full pelt along the bar when the animal was startled by something and veered wildly into the lake. He had hung on as long as he could, but eventually horse and rider were separated: while Shilling swam to the opposite bank, traumatised but unhurt, Harry was lost in the deepest part of the water, where thick weed and darkness defied all attempts to retrieve his body until it eventually floated to the surface of its own accord. Archie had been saddened by the death of someone he had very much liked – and surprised, as well: he had always regarded Harry as a born horseman. In years to come, strangers would no doubt put such an accident down to the lake's determination to have its way but today, as they were about to bury Harry, it seemed to Archie that the young man's memory demanded more from his friends than superstition.

Several days without rain had left the single-track lane that led to the sea hard and dry underfoot, and Archie – eyes down against the sun – noticed how quickly the dust took the shine off each carefully polished pair of shoes, how it covered the hem of Morwenna's skirt in a stubborn, powdery film, dulling the severity of the black. When he reached the thick stretch of woodland that draped the lake on two sides, he was glad of the shade. The woods were carpeted with bluebells in a profusion which seemed almost indecent, particularly today, but the estate was unusually quiet and the only noise came from the steady rhythm of the cart wheels. Even the rooks, which normally made such a cacophony in the trees overhead, were silent, and Archie was reminded of a story his father had told him as they roamed these woods together, an ancient belief that when the birds abandoned their rookery it was a sign that bereavement lay ahead. After that, every time he had taken the path round the lake, he had slowed his step when approaching that particular section, dreading the silence which might signal some disruption to an idyllic childhood; many years later, when his father was ill, he found himself avoiding that stretch of woodland altogether.

He had always marvelled at how close you could get to the sea on this path without being aware of its existence. Today, the transformation from stillness to the sea's relentless sound and motion was as sudden and miraculous as ever and, when the party left the cushioning of the trees behind, the noise of the waves reached them so abruptly that it could easily have been a sound effect cued by their appearance. Here, at last, was the church. There were surely few more dramatic settings for worship than the precarious position held by this otherwise modest building, now sited less than fifty yards from the cliff edge and looking out to the Lizard in the east and Land's End to the west. Founded well over a millennium ago by a Breton missionary, the existing church belonged to the fifteenth century, but its three low-roofed chapels were made more striking by the presence of a detached bell tower, older than the rest of the building and – according to legend – built on the site of an ancient hermit's cell. It was known as the church of storms, a name which tended to add a somewhat Old Testament feel to the services held there. At high tide, in bad weather, when the waves threatened to engulf the whole building and claim it as their own, it did not require much of a performance from the pulpit to convince those inside of their mortality.

He had quite forgotten it was Sunday until he saw a few people leaving the church by the north side, dressed in their best clothes and with a relaxed, carefree air that could not have been more different from the mood of the party about to enter via the other door. Anyone from outside Cornwall might have found it strange that the dead should be buried on the Sabbath, but here it was common practice, Sunday being the only day that fishermen were back from the sea and able to pay their last respects to friends and colleagues. Funerals were fitted in pragmatically around the other services and, as the two congregations mingled briefly at the gate, Archie noticed that sympathy was mixed with embarrassment in the faces of those whose church business was concluded for the day, almost as if they felt the need to apologise for being excused from grief. Dealing as often as he did with death, he knew what that conflict of emotions felt like, and he would not have blamed anyone for adding a silent amen to those that had already been said inside.

After exchanging one surplice for another, the vicar of St Winwaloe's emerged from the south porch, ready to lead the coffin into the church. Jasper Motley would not have been anyone's first choice for the link between sorrow and hope which most people look for in a minister presiding over a funeral. In fact, he seemed utterly devoid of qualities that would enable him to deliver any of the Church's teachings; humility and compassion, joy and sorrow, were entirely absent from his heart and had no place in his sermons. The fact that Jasper was his uncle could not persuade Archie to feel anything other than contempt for him. It was a sentiment which had been instilled in him from an early age. His mother had been the only girl in a family of three; her elder brother – William – she adored, and they had remained close until her death; the middle child, Jasper, had always been the odd one out in an otherwise happy family, resentful of the bond between his brother and sister and even less forgiving of parents who had been too selfish to bear him first. The only time that Archie had ever heard his mother express hatred for anyone was when she spoke of Jasper, and she did so with a spite and a bitterness which was completely out of character; he didn't doubt that her feelings were justified, but he had never really understood the depth of her resentment.

As the six men prepared to lift the coffin from the cart, Archie noticed how much older his uncle seemed to have grown in recent months. 'I am the resurrection and the life, saith the Lord,' he began, his once strident voice now cracked and weakened with age. 'He that believeth in Me, though he were dead, yet shall he live: and whosoever liveth and believeth in Me shall never die.' No chance for Harry, then, Archie thought drily; he had never been known for his Christian living. Like many men who had been raised on the land and who believed in their own mastery of it, Harry Pinching had worked hard, played hard and thought himself invincible. His arrogance had seemed harmless, but it would exact a high price – not from the dead man, whose troubles were over, but from those who had been left behind to carry on. What would Morwenna and Loveday do now? Archie wondered. Their grief was just the beginning.

Clean-living Harry might not have been, but popular he most certainly was. The small church was packed with mourners – people who had worked alongside him, fishermen he had shared a drink with, and young women who had fancied their chances with his charm and good looks. Harry was an estate worker like his father before him, but his warmth and affability had ensured him a welcome in the village that usually kept itself quite separate from Loe, and he had managed to bridge the gap between land and sea in a way that was rare. That his death should touch a whole community was perhaps no surprise, but Archie sensed Morwenna falter as she entered the church and he guessed that she had been taken aback by the size of the crowd and the strength of feeling for her brother. He heard someone encourage her gently to move on, and the procession passed down the central aisle towards the chancel. As they reached the altar, Christopher Snipe – a boy of sixteen or seventeen and the youngest of the bearers – missed his footing on the top step and the coffin dipped perilously at the back, shooting one of Harry's riding boots on to the floor. Archie steadied the weight while Christopher recovered himself, and the body was delivered on to the bier without further mishap, but the mistake earned the boy a glare of reproach from his father, who clearly believed that someone born into the undertaking trade should have known better. Still frowning, the undertaker returned the boot to the top of the coffin and melted away into the congregation as only those of his profession knew how. Christopher sat down next to his father, flushed and embarrassed.

The other bearers found seats that had been saved for them, and Archie slipped into the front pew next to his cousins and his uncle William. 'Nice catch,' whispered Ronnie, while her elder sister, Lettice, leaned over to give his arm a reassuring squeeze. By now, the Reverend Motley was in full flow from the pulpit, and the words of the thirty-ninth psalm drifted over Archie's head as he glanced round the church. It must have been two years or more since he had last been in here, but he was sure it had not seemed as neglected and depressing back then. Heat made everything look tired, but the shabbiness of the interior was not just down to the wilting flowers. Many of the windows had been boarded against the storms, which gave the building a permanent air of abandonment; even those which remained uncovered were damaged and dirty, and the ledges were covered with sand which a probing wind had blown through cracks in the glass. Constant exposure to the weather had removed several slates from the roof, and a bucket – incongruously placed at the back of the altar, amid more familiar receptacles of worship – testified to the need for repair. The wood of the pews was dull and unnourished, and even the service books were faded and torn. It seemed that

Jasper's constant whining was justified: the church *did* require more money, although Archie couldn't help thinking that the vicar's appeals for generosity might be better heeded if he and his wife moderated their own standard of living and led more by example.

The lesson was over at last, and Nathaniel Shoebridge, curate of St Winwaloe's, stood to give the eulogy. Shoebridge was due to take over the living of the parish when Jasper Motley retired at the end of the year; judging by the state of the church, that was something of a poisoned chalice, but Archie had heard good reports of the young man's dedication, and his appointment was generally looked on as a welcome change to the current regime. As one of Harry's oldest friends, and part of a family which had farmed on the Loe estate for generations, there was no disputing Nathaniel's right to carry the coffin, although the friendship between the two men had apparently cooled of late. Archie wondered if they had settled their differences before the accident, and watched with interest as the curate walked nervously up to the lectern.

For Shoebridge, the pulpit was usually as reassuring as a desk to an office worker, but today he felt confined by it; the familiar, hexagonal space seemed somehow narrower, and its polished, heavily carved wood closed in on him like the sides of a coffin, making it difficult to breathe and threatening to stifle his words. Nervously, he glanced up from the lectern and saw a church full of disparate people with disparate memories turned as one towards him. The shyness of his youth came flooding back, and he felt strangely suffocated and exposed at the same time.

His first words were barely audible. 'Like most of us here, I've known Harry for many years,' he said, aware that

13

his audience was relying on him for an eloquent expression of sorrow which they could share in and claim as their own. 'His loss has been difficult for us all to come to terms with.' He paused, trying to control the anxiety in his voice and speak normally, but the speech ahead of him – even though it had been carefully prepared to mask his emotions – seemed an impossible mountain and he wondered how he was ever to get through it. There was some muttering from the back of the church and he pressed on, concentrating on one sentence at a time and trying to blot out the silent presence of the dead man at his side. 'Harry had an important place at the heart of our community,' he said, rushing his words but no longer caring if they were a disappointment. 'He was honest and hard-working, a loving brother to Morwenna and Loveday, and a good friend to many of us.' Even to his own ears, the tribute seemed oddly impersonal, as if he were conducting the funeral of a parishioner he had never met. The adjectives he used were inadequate, second-hand accolades for a man whose vitality had dominated a room, and, rather than making things easier for him, the banality of Nathaniel's respect stuck in his throat. As he faltered at the simplest of phrases, he could see the congregation growing increasingly bewildered at his failure to dispel the stark reality of the coffin and replace it with an image of Harry as he had been in life – warm, generous and fiercely loyal; memorable from the most casual of meetings, and impossible to forget after a lifetime of friendship.

Flicking his pale blond hair back from his eyes, Nathaniel turned gratefully to the book he had brought with him, glad to be able to take refuge in someone else's words and hoping that he might be able to give them the strength and conviction which his own had lacked. He had chosen a passage from

Tennyson to read, a section from *Idylls of the King* which he loved because it brought together everything he valued most: the stories and legends he had grown up with; the sense of community that drove him on; and the spirituality which now gave him his greatest solace. 'And slowly answer'd Arthur from the barge,' he began tentatively.

'The old order changeth, yielding place to new,
And God fulfils himself in many ways.
Lest one good custom should corrupt the world.'

The familiar lines gave him confidence and, for a second, he dared to hope that he might redeem himself after all, but his optimism was short-lived: he made the mistake of looking away from the page, long enough to see that Morwenna was staring up at him from the front row – accusing, disappointed, unforgiving. He continued hurriedly,

'Comfort thyself; what comfort is in me?
I have lived my life, and that which I have done
May He within himself make pure! but thou,
If thou shouldst never see my face again,
Pray for my soul. More things are wrought by prayer
Than this world dreams of.'

At last, it was over. Nathaniel left the pulpit quickly, making no effort to hide his relief. He glanced apologetically at Morwenna and Loveday as he walked back to his seat, acknowledging that they – and Harry – had deserved better from him.

Loveday giggled and slipped from the church, breaking the silence that followed the concluding prayers, and Archie noted how intently Christopher Snipe watched her leave. The girl's laughter was unsettling in such close proximity to death, and the mourners – embarrassed and unsure of how to react – looked at each other across the aisle or smiled awkwardly at Morwenna. The tension that had begun with Nathaniel's eulogy was infectious, and everyone seemed thankful to follow the coffin outside, knowing that the end of the service was in sight.

Small-leaved Cornish elms clustered round the churchyard, revealing flickering glimpses of the sea beyond. The funeral party followed the line of trees round to the rear of the church, where a pile of freshly dug earth marked a new burial place. Loveday was already at the graveside. As they drew near, Archie heard a gasp from one or two of the mourners and had to hide his own surprise when he saw that Harry's grave was lined throughout with bluebells and primroses, woven carefully into moss and netting to create a living wall of colour where only darkness and soil should have been. The gesture was obviously Loveday's last gift to an elder brother who, since their parents' untimely death, had been the most important person in her world; it was an act of love, and it should have been touching – beautiful, almost – but Archie could only think of how many hours the girl must have spent in the grave to do it. Its aesthetic impact could not dispel the image in his mind of a child's hands working obsessively so close to the dead. A brief look round was enough to tell him that he was not the only one to be disturbed by it, and it was left to Morwenna to embrace her young sister and acknowledge her pride.

As the mourners gathered by the grave, Archie noticed several of them glance instinctively towards their own dead in different parts of the churchyard, remembering other funerals and other losses. Christopher and his father threaded strips of webbing efficiently under the coffin, ready to lower it gently into the grave. 'Forasmuch as it hath pleased Almighty God of His great mercy to take unto Himself the soul of our dear brother here departed,' Jasper Motley continued half-heartedly, 'we therefore commit his body to the ground; earth to earth, ashes to ashes, dust to dust; in sure and certain hope of the resurrection to eternal life, through our Lord Jesus Christ.' Archie wondered how many of the people gathered here actually took any comfort from those familiar words. For him, there was a much greater resonance in the sound of a handful of earth hitting the coffin of a man who would never see thirty.

With heads bowed for the final prayer, Archie looked at his watch and realised that Josephine's train was due to arrive in less than an hour. Because he was expected at the wake, Ronnie had volunteered to collect her from Penzance station and, if she left now, she would be almost on time. As the mourners dispersed, he caught his cousin's eye through the crowd and signalled to her to get a move on.

'Do you have time to come back to the cottage?' Archie had not seen Morwenna come up behind him, and the urgency of her voice took him by surprise.

'Of course,' he said. He leant forward to kiss her and offer what futile words of comfort he could find, but she brushed them quickly aside and turned away from approaching well-wishers so that only Archie could hear her. 'Good, because there's something I need to say to you in private – something I could never tell anyone else.' With no further explanation, she took Loveday's hand and led her firmly away from their brother's grave.

Chapter Two

Josephine Tey sat on a pile of suitcases and waited for her lift, perfectly happy to bask in the sun and do nothing. The broad promenade by Penzance station offered glorious views along many miles of coastline, and she gazed contentedly across at the hills which stretched westwards towards Land's End, then back across the broad sweep of Mount's Bay to the Lizard. Even on a Sunday, the traffic of boxes filled with flowers moved relentlessly from the boats to the railway station, connecting the flower gardens of the Scilly Isles with the markets of England's capital in time for the start of a new week, and turning Penzance into a suburb of Covent Garden. The atmosphere was welcoming and relaxed, and she felt instantly at home. If this was what life in Cornwall was like, she could easily get used to it.

She was sorry not to have travelled down by car with Archie as intended, but his enforced change of plan had left her no time to alter her own arrangements and, in any case, she had no wish to hover in the wings of a stranger's funeral – first visits to other people's houses were difficult enough, no matter how close the friendships. So she had kept her luncheon appointment with her London publisher, stayed overnight at her club in Cavendish Square and caught the 10.30 Limited from Paddington, feeling for once like a proper holidaymaker. The sound of Land's End had a distant, far-away feel which appealed to her fascination for foreign travel, and she had thoroughly enjoyed the journey: it was no hardship to look out over a constantly changing landscape at one of the most beautiful times of year, and the occasional flash of a naval uniform in the corridors had been a pleasant distraction. All in all, she was thoroughly satisfied with the Cornish Riviera Express; it was hardly surprising that the county was no longer a remote, unapproachable land but a Londoner's playground – and a popular one, too, if the number of smart couples and robust families on board her train was anything to go by.

Ronnie made her presence felt as soon as she came into view, hooting irreverently all the way along the street before bringing the Austin to an inch-perfect halt in front of Josephine. She jumped out and rushed round to the passenger side, and Josephine noticed some bewildered onlookers trying to reconcile the black of her funeral clothes with the joyful expression on her face. 'I'm sorry I haven't had time to change,' Ronnie said as she hugged her friend, 'but I was under strict instructions from my dear cousin not to keep you waiting.'

'You don't need to apologise for wearing mourning, only for looking gorgeous in it.' Josephine ran her eyes admiringly over Ronnie's outfit. 'You and Lettice ought to start a new sideline in widows' weeds. I can see the advertisements now – "Grief with Grace". It might even make your fortune.'

'You look pretty damned good yourself for someone who's just got off at the end of the line,' Ronnie said, throwing the cases into the back of the car. 'Most people start to wilt at Exeter.'

'Oh, I don't know – there's a certain attraction in getting as far away as you can.' Josephine smiled. 'I think it might suit me.'

Ronnie raised an eyebrow, knowing how impatient Josephine was with her home town, which simultaneously claimed her as a famous daughter and resented her success. 'Has Inverness been as welcoming as usual, then?'

'A little *too* welcoming if you must know. Every time the papers review one of my plays or even mention my name, I find myself running furtively from the shops to the bus stop, desperately trying to dodge another stream of invitations. If the various societies and committees had their way, I'd be too busy embracing my clan ever to write another word.' She gave an exaggerated shudder as Ronnie slipped the car into gear and moved off. 'Actually, I made the mistake of accepting one last month,' she continued. 'My old school was putting on an adaptation of *Richard of Bordeaux* in honour of – I quote – "the most illustrious foot to step out of Inverness for two hundred years" – and they asked me to introduce it. I telephoned to find out if they wanted the rest of me or just the foot and, if the latter, was it left or right, and ended up agreeing out of sheer devilment.'

They reached a junction, and Ronnie tried to pull herself together. 'Wait a minute while I concentrate on this bit,' she said. 'If I don't go the right way here, we'll end up in Newlyn and I don't see what either of us has done to deserve that.'

Josephine smiled, amused by a sudden image of her glamorous, city-minded friend against a backdrop of steam trawlers and fishermen. 'That's the trouble with you West End types – you can't face a fish until it's on the grill at the Savoy. You should be ashamed to call yourself Cornish.'

'Oh, it's not the fish I object to, it's the artists. It used to be a charming little place. Now you can't move for easels clogging up the street and people in smocks trying to capture the

"Newlyn style", whatever that is. It's a proper little industry – two hundred canvases shipped up to Burlington House every year, and you should see what's left here for the tourists. No, give me a mackerel any day – they might stink, but at least they serve a purpose.'

Pleased to see that being on home territory seemed to have little effect on Ronnie's outspokenness, Josephine let her concentrate on the roads and took the opportunity to get a better sense of Penzance. They passed along a residential street lined with unelaborate stone houses, the ordinariness of which was compensated for by unexpectedly luxuriant displays in the gardens. Rhododendrons and fuchsias flourished in corners and doorways, and more exotic planting was evident in spiky green leaves which peeped out from the terraced rear courtyards. 'All this reminds me of the continent,' she said to Ronnie, surprised at how very un-English everything seemed.

'It's practically Cannes, dear – well, compared to where you're going to be staying it is. I should warn you – there's plenty of peace and beauty on the Loe estate, but not much night-life.'

'I don't want to disappoint you, but it's the peace I'm here for. I haven't been able to concentrate on anything much lately, and I really must get down to some work. I'm hoping that a few long walks and a bit of sea air will do the trick.'

'Lettice said you're doing another crime novel.'

'That's the plan. Having to give evidence in a murder trial rather dampened my enthusiasm for real-life drama, so I thought I'd go back to pure fiction for a bit.' The words were lightly said, but she knew that Ronnie would not be fooled. Last year, during the run of Josephine's most successful play, *Richard of Bordeaux*, the violent death of a young fan had

22

affected Josephine deeply, and all that had happened subsequently still haunted her. There had been moments during the last few months when, had it not been for her friendship with Archie and his cousins, she might have given in completely to the feelings of guilt and sorrow which had hounded her since Elspeth's murder. The trial, and the necessity of having to confront people for whom she felt such strong and differing emotions, had been one of the worst experiences of her whole life; at the end of it, the person responsible for so much grief had been brought to justice, but she had been surprised to discover how little consolation that gave her and that, in turn, led her to question everything she thought she believed in. It was unlike her not to be able to find refuge from sadness in her work, but theatre – for the moment at least – was too closely connected with a sense of loss for her to find any joy or purpose in it.

'My heart's just not in it right now,' she admitted, more seriously this time, 'and there's no point in doing anything if you're going to be lacklustre about it. The publishers have been baying for another shocker ever since *The Man in the Queue*, and with *Queen of Scots* not being quite the success that everyone hoped for, it seemed a good time to give in to them.'

'Well, you know Lettice and I are helping out with the local drama group this week and amateur theatricals always bring out a murderous streak in us, so just ask if you're stuck for a plot line.' They were on the open road by now, although Ronnie was still driving so slowly that Josephine half-wondered if there was something wrong with the car; caution behind the wheel was something she would have expected more from Lettice than her sister. 'I do hope you're going to come out and support the Winwaloe Players on Tuesday night.' She laughed as she saw the expression on Josephine's face. 'They're giving their *Jackdaw of Rheims*.'

'Isn't that a poem?'

'Not by the time they've finished with it. Actually, they're really rather good, and the theatre alone is worth the trip.'

'So I hear. Archie said it was right on the edge of a cliff and absolutely breathtaking. Whose idea was that?'

'A woman called Rowena Cade. She's barking mad, of course – well, you have to be to carve a theatre out of a rock, don't you – but in the best possible way. She started it about three years ago, and we got roped into helping with the costumes for the show that our lot put on there. We've done it ever since – it's really rather magical as long as the weather holds.' Ronnie reached behind her and took a flask and a bag of shortbread from the back seat.

'Do I detect the Snipe at work?' Josephine asked. Having often stayed with the Motleys in St Martin's Lane, she was familiar with their formidable cook, who had travelled with the sisters when they made the permanent move from Cornwall to London just after the war, and who also kept house for Archie. Much to everyone's surprise, the change had suited Dora Snipe and she took instantly to city life, returning only for the occasional holiday and to ensure that standards had not dropped in her absence.

'You certainly do. She's taken control of her old kitchen with a vengeance, and she found time in between the wake bakes to make you these.'

'Good God, does she do funerals as well?'

'Oh yes. In fact, it's a bit of a family business. The undertaker – Jago – is her brother-in-law.'

Josephine took out a biscuit and ate it thoughtfully. 'What

did happen to her husband, by the way? I don't think I ever knew.'

'No one does. She came to us thirty-odd years ago, and she was on her own by then. She never talks about her marriage, and the only thing anyone seems to know is that it ended when it was still very new.'

'But she was widowed?'

Ronnie shrugged. 'Would you be brave enough to pry? The one thing I can say with any certainty is that she'll have got a good deal on the burial if he *did* die.'

Intrigued, Josephine poured some tea from the flask, grateful now for Ronnie's sedate pace. 'How's Archie?' she asked. 'I can think of better starts to a holiday than carrying a coffin.'

'Bearing up, if you'll excuse the pun. Lettice and I always dread any big occasion taking place while we're at home – weddings, funerals, christenings, they're all the same. Everyone's got such a history, you see – they've lived and worked together on that estate for generations, and that makes for very strong alliances, and even stronger grudges. It's like being part of some sort of brotherhood, I suppose – if you imagined something midway between Camelot and Dennis Wheatley, you'd have it about right.' They both laughed. 'Most of the time, it's all perfectly normal. The estate's big enough for everyone to have his role, and there's something rather fine about the way they all work together to keep it going. But when we're gathered together under one roof, it all gets a bit tense and incestuous.'

'Not unlike the theatre, then,' Josephine said wryly. 'It must be home from home for you.'

'I'd never thought of it like that, but now you mention it,

there are some similarities. I have to say, though, it was a very strange do today, even by our standards. The young lad, Christopher – the Snipe's nephew, in fact – he nearly dropped the coffin; the curate bungled the eulogy; and, to cap it all, when we came out of the church desperate to get the man safely in the ground, his little sister had tarted the grave up to look like a florist's showpiece. We rounded the corner and there she was – grinning over six feet of bluebells. All very Lady of Shalott. I could have died, but I'm eternally grateful to you for saving me from the wake. It can only have got worse.'

Josephine pictured the scene with a shudder. She had a hatred of funerals, and in particular of flowers on graves. 'If anything happens to me, I don't want a petal in sight,' she said. 'But are you seriously telling me that someone let a child decorate the inside of a grave?'

'Loveday's not exactly a child. I suppose she's about fourteen, but she's always been precocious and her outlook on the world can be a little – well, fanciful. To be honest with you,' Ronnie added confidingly, 'I don't think she's quite right in the head, but nobody would ever say that. They just accept her for what she is. The parents are both dead, but there's another sister – Harry's twin – and the three of them were devoted to each other. I dread to think how this has affected them.'

'What happened to Harry, anyway? Archie said there was an accident, but he didn't have time to tell me much.'

'Well, Harry's always been one of those daredevil types, but this time his luck ran out. The stupid boy rode his horse into the lake and drowned.'

'What happened to the horse?'

'He swam safely to the other bank. Trust you to think of that first.'

'Well, I've always thought the phrase "daredevil type" was another way of saying "irresponsible bastard", Josephine said tartly, 'so my sympathies are firmly with the horse. Don't you think it's a little selfish to get yourself killed like that?'

'I know what you mean, but don't say it out loud when we get there – you'll be lynched. Everyone loved Harry, and they certainly won't have a word spoken against him now he's dead.'

'Let's ask the older sister in three months' time shall we?' retorted Josephine scornfully. 'I don't think I could ever forgive someone who left me so unnecessarily, no matter how much I loved them – and I'm financially independent. From what you say, she's got a tough time ahead.'

'Pa will look after her – he always has. And Jago – he and his wife were good friends with the parents, and he'll do what he can for Morwenna.' They turned off the main road and followed a narrow lane which ran closer to the sea. Ferns of every description lined the roadside, and the hedgerows were filled with campion and bluebells – as beautiful in their natural setting as they had been sinister a few moments before. 'Pa won't tell you this himself, but he saved Loveday's life when she was a little girl,' Ronnie explained. 'There was a fire at their cottage one night a few years back – a spark must have caught in the thatch and it went up like a beacon. Pa saw it across the park and got there as soon as he could with a couple of men from the stables. He found Loveday crouching by the stairs while another man dragged Harry unconscious from his room, but it was too late for the parents – they both died in their beds.'

'Good God – that's awful.'

'I know. It makes you wonder what the family did in a former life, doesn't it?'

'Where was the other sister?'

'Morwenna? She was away from home, thank God. She'd started to work at the Union over in Helston by then. It's a sort of poorhouse-cum-refuge, and she was on a night shift. As you can imagine, she's had her share of shocks in life, and she's still a way off thirty. So you're right, I suppose – Harry's recklessness *was* selfish.'

'Things could have been so much worse if it hadn't been for your father, though.'

'Yes, although he always shakes it off. He didn't even tell Lettice and me that he was the one who'd saved them – we found out from the Snipe, who found out from her brother-in-law. He's always taken his responsibilities to that estate and everyone on it very personally – although I think diving into burning buildings is carrying things too far. He won't be told, though. He's paid for Harry's funeral, of course, and he'll find a way to ensure that Loveday and Morwenna are all right without making them feel like charity cases.'

'It must be a nightmare overseeing something that size,' said Josephine, thinking of all the once grand estates that she read about which had fallen on hard times in recent years, 'especially since the war. And I can't imagine anything worse than having all those livelihoods dependent upon you.'

'It *is* difficult,' Ronnie admitted. 'God knows how many people live and work on the estate, and I don't even want to think about what's going to happen when Pa's gone. I can't see that Lettice and I have inherited sufficient stoicism and dedication to carry on what he does, and Archie certainly wouldn't want it. Touch wood, though, he's got more energy than people half his age, and he works twice as hard.'

'And that you *have* inherited from him. I'm looking forward to meeting your father – I want to see what else I can trace back to him.'

'I think you'll find there's quite a bit of him in each of us. And a lot of my mother, too, of course. We've been lucky with both of them.'

Not for the first time, Josephine reflected on the degree to which life had blessed the Motley sisters with exactly the right balance of comfort, eccentricity and tragedy for them to flourish in the theatrical world they had chosen to make their living from. She knew that their mother, Veronique, had died when they were still young, grief-stricken by the death of her eldest child, Teddy, who had gone down with his ship before the war was six months old, but she had often heard them speak of her and knew how much they had been influenced by her creativity and flouting of convention. She remembered Lettice once telling her that their mother had brought them up to believe they could do anything, and it was that which had given them the confidence to take on the unwritten laws of the West End, and change them for the better. 'Has your father never been tempted to marry again?' she asked.

'Good grief, no,' Ronnie said. 'He's not been short of admirers, but I honestly think he's still too in love with my mother even to notice when someone's setting her cap at him.' She smiled sadly. 'It's a refreshing change from all the bravado people come out with about getting back in the saddle and moving on with your life. Lettice and I do worry about him, but there's something rather noble about a grief that lasts for life, isn't there?' Josephine nodded, and wondered what it would take to make her want to share her life so wholeheartedly with someone. 'Anyway, Pa's other woman is the Loe estate,' Ronnie continued, 'and she's very demanding.'

29

The road they were on had parted from the sea, and they drove down into a small village, skirting a pretty, sheltered inner harbour before climbing again into open countryside. 'How does Archie fit into life down here?' Josephine asked. 'He's always been a bit vague about it whenever I've asked him.'

'To be entirely honest, I'm not sure he knows himself how he fits in,' Ronnie replied, 'or if he does at all. You know that the Loe estate used to be in his father's family, don't you?'

Josephine shook her head, intrigued. 'I thought his only connection with it was by marriage, through his mother.'

'No, he only missed being Lord of the Manor by two or three generations. Our great-great-grandfathers were best friends out in the Indies together. The Penroses had the land and the Motleys had the money, so they came to a very sensible arrangement: Penrose transferred the estate and all responsibility for the upkeep of it to his friend, in exchange for a house and living on the estate in perpetuity. Everyone got what they wanted and the estate's future was secured. It's all worked out very nicely, even down to a uniting of the clans when Archie's mother – Pa's younger sister – married a Penrose.'

Josephine was quiet for a moment, trying to get the family tree straight in her mind while Ronnie went on. 'So, in answer to your question, Archie fits in rather uncomfortably – he's not the boss, but he's not one of the workers either. And of course a Cambridge education and a job at the Yard haven't helped bridge the gap. The law down here is very much a subjective thing, and something to be worked out privately.'

As the lane bent sharply round to the left, Ronnie took a right turn through some wooden gates, on to a private road shrouded in rhododendrons and variegated laurels. 'Here we are, although I hope you're not expecting the grand country house,' she said. 'I'm afraid it's a rather haphazard affair, and the Penroses were very shrewd to get rid of it; the estate just eats money, and it's the house that's suffered – things get patched and mended in order of urgency, and the Forth Bridge doesn't come into it. There's always some sort of panic on. Don't worry, though,' she added reassuringly, 'it *is* beautiful, and you'll get the peace you need. Archie's moved back in with us for a bit so that you can have the Lodge – it'll be quieter for you to work in, and you can come up to the chaos whenever you feel like a bit of light relief.'

Josephine was about to thank her but, as they rounded another bend and emerged from the trees, the first glimpse of Loe Pool stopped her short. She had lived all her life just a few miles from Loch Ness and the magic of light on water held no novelty for her, but the Loe had a stillness and beauty all of its own. The combination of ornamental parkland in the foreground and a patchwork of fields to the rear gave the scene in front of her an intimate domesticity which could not have been more different from the ostentatious drama of the Monadhliath mountains, but which was no less magnificent. And at the centre of it all, flanked by rich, green woodland, was the lake itself – quiet, smoky-black at the edges where the sun could not reach, and drawing each disparate corner of the landscape effortlessly into one perfect whole.

Delighted, she turned to Ronnie and was moved to see that her cynical, world-weary friend had not become immune to its charms.

'Come on, I'll drop you at the Lodge for a wash and brush-up,' Ronnie said. 'Wander over for dinner when you're ready.'

Chapter Three

Nathaniel Shoebridge leant against the back door of the cottage that Harry had shared with his sisters, clutching a mug of cheap whisky and hoping that the solid stone walls might restore some of the strength which had deserted him the moment he stepped up to the lectern. He didn't often drink, and the liquid burnt a harsh, sour path to the pit of his stomach, but he needed something to dull the memory of the service and the humiliation of standing in front of his own congregation without a single word of comfort to offer them. He had only been in the pulpit for a few minutes, but it had been long enough to remind him of how things used to be and he doubted that the confidence he had worked so hard to find would be quick to return.

His shyness had dogged him for years, clouding most of his childhood with a horror of being noticed that amounted almost to a phobia. He loved learning, but dreaded going to school in case he was singled out to answer a question or read in class, and the pretty, white washed laundry cottage that William Motley had converted into a schoolroom for the estate's youngest children came to represent all that he feared most; just the sight of its slate roof through the trees was enough to send his stomach into spasms, and it made no difference that he was bright or that his classmates were friendly and his teacher kind. His education continued to be a wretched experience until, on Empire Day 1920, almost a year after he had transferred to the small secondary school in the village, everything changed. The teacher, Morveth Wearne, must have been in her fifties even then, but she had an intelligent, gentle manner that created its own discipline and the children were instantly at ease with her, Nathaniel included. As unorthodox in her lessons as in other areas of her life, Morveth had decided to follow the usual flag-waving and patriotic singing with a school play, and – in what Nathaniel later recognised as her own comment on colonialism – had chosen *The Tempest*. He had dreaded that day for weeks, knowing that there were not enough pupils in the class for him to avoid taking a part, and had even feigned illness to get out of it. Fortunately, his parents weren't fooled; if they had been, he would have missed out on the most important day of his life. In his first encounter with Shakespeare, he found something that seemed more real to him than fear. So engrossed was he in the magic of the play and the beauty of the language that he lost all self-consciousness and, by the time he was called upon to speak Ferdinand's opening lines, the words were the only thing that mattered.

After the play, and while the euphoria was still with him, Nathaniel had gone up to Morveth and asked nervously if she might give him something else to read. She looked at him for a long time, as if sensing how important this was to him, then smiled and took an old brown book with faded gold lettering from the back of the drawer in her desk. That was fifteen years ago, almost to the day, but he could still remember the faint smell of leather and the way the prayer book opened at particular passages that Morveth must have read over and over again. He had rushed through his tea that night, scarcely able to wait until he was alone in his room and able to take his time over turning its pages. Some of the words were difficult and strange at first, but the prose – which the Reverend Motley's hurried, half-hearted delivery never brought to life in church – slowly began to speak to him through its rhythms, and he was fascinated by the markers of a man's life which the different sections traced. From that day on, he read the book when he went to bed each night and it came to symbolise a magic even greater than Shakespeare; this, too, was theatre, but it was theatre for every day, written not just for actors but for ordinary people like him and his family and, as he grew older, he empathised with all the emotions it portrayed – anger and confusion as well as love and praise. He was drawn so strongly to these simple phrases, spoken for hundreds of years – phrases that offered a connection to the past as strong as the landscape he had grown up with – that he knew instantly what he wanted to do with his life, no matter how difficult it proved. He kept the leather-bound volume with Morveth's blessing, and it was still the prayer book he used in church; he was forever grateful for the way in which its contents had shown him how to deal with the world and his place in it.

The murmur of voices inside the cottage was growing steadily louder now as more people arrived for the wake and drink loosened the tongues of those who had been there for some time. He knew he should go back in, but another few minutes of air might clear his head and give him the confidence to face everyone again. What would his life have been like, he wondered, if he had never been shown an alternative path to the one that was expected of him? Easier, certainly, especially in those early days. His parents had always assumed that he would work on the farm like his brothers; when he finally plucked up the courage to talk to them about his future, they greeted his intention to enter the Church with a mixture of consternation and pain. Nathaniel understood their concerns – the present incumbent of St Winwaloe's was hardly well placed to defend the institution against accusations of corruption and greed, and people of his class were not obvious candidates for ordination – but he was intelligent and dedicated, and he stubbornly stood his ground. Gradually, with patience and a conviction which astonished them all, he brought his family round to the idea. Each time he returned home from his hard-earned college training, happier and more settled than ever, they softened a little, and were won over completely when they realised that his commitment was to the estate and not to the souls of strangers, that – rather than alienate him from them – the Church would bind him to his community more tightly than putting a spade in his hand ever could.

On a day like today, though, such certainties seemed to belong to another life. First alive, and now dead, Harry Pinching had managed to undermine everything that Nathaniel had ever been sure of. They had been friends for as long as he could remember, drawn to each other's company by a shared love of the Loe estate and by contrasting but complementary personalities. The bond was strong and undemanding, and had fitted easily into each of their lives until one morning, just a few months earlier, when they were out riding together, racing along the sand at Loe Bar as they often did in fine weather. Nathaniel was a good horseman, one of the few people on the estate who could match Harry stride for stride. On this occasion, he had gone one better, reaching the line of rocks which acted as a finishing post a good ten seconds in front. As his friend caught up with him – his eyes bright with the exhilaration of speed and competition, his smile generous in defeat – Nathaniel was astonished to realise that what he felt for him – what he had always felt for Harry – was love. It was a moment of conviction as powerful and overwhelming as when he had first opened the prayer book, but so utterly at odds with it that he had been unable to do anything other than turn his horse and ride quickly for home, flustered and convinced that his shame was written all over his face.

Harry had known, he was sure of it, and could not resist using the power it gave him. For the first time, Nathaniel noticed a self-consciousness about his friend's easy sexuality; perhaps it was his imagination, but Harry seemed to go out of his way to slap him on the back or shake his hand, until the briefest of touches was enough to send a jolt of desire right through him. Bewildered by his own feelings, Nathaniel found it impossible to read Harry's. He was unwilling to believe that Harry would taunt him maliciously, but the thought that his love might be reciprocated was too dangerous even to contemplate. Eventually, unable to stand it any longer, he had simply kept away. When his family asked what had happened, he blamed his own commitment to the Church for the estrangement; the unjustified slur on Harry's loyalty seemed a small act of betrayal in comparison with the truth.

If Nathaniel had not suspected – albeit reluctantly – that his own vulnerability had laid bare a spiteful streak in Harry, he would have dismissed outright the revelation that had come his way two or three days before the accident – a revelation which had left him wrestling with lust and guilt, love and disgust. At first, he had turned to denial as the best antidote to them but, once the suspicion was there, he could never quite convince himself that Harry was innocent of the charge laid against him. Perhaps Harry's death was the best possible outcome – for everyone. Certainly, his own first reaction to news of the accident had been relief, and he had seen God's hand in a situation which was beyond human intervention. But if that was the case, why did it feel so wrong, and so painful? Was that his punishment for feelings which should never have been acknowledged? Despite the words of comfort that he delivered so sincerely to others, he realised now that it was only possible to make your peace with the dead if you had reconciled your differences with the living.

He took another swig of the whisky, hoping that the sour taste in his mouth might temporarily overshadow the bitterness in his head.

'Don't think that will help.' Morwenna could barely keep her fury in check, and the contempt in her voice hurt him far more than any physical blow could have done. 'How could you let him down like that? You were supposed to be his friend.' Nathaniel turned to look at her and, for a moment, it was as though Harry were standing in front of him. How alike they were if you looked closely, he thought, although anger – which had always brought a sulkiness to Harry's mouth, detracting from the strength of his face – seemed to enhance his sister's beauty, alleviating the exhaustion which made her look a decade older than her twenty-six years. He could see why so many people were attracted to her. How much easier life would be if only he could have been one of them.

'I know you're upset about the funeral,' he began, 'but you can't expect me to stand in church and lie now that I know the truth. I'm sorry if I let *you* down, but I can't pretend that my feelings for Harry are straightforward.' That was an understatement, but he had no intention of letting Morwenna see how much he had loved her brother, or how deeply he was grieving for the loss of everything he had believed Harry to be. 'I couldn't find the words you wanted to hear,' he added, knowing he was doing no better now, 'and I wouldn't have trusted myself to speak them anyway.'

'It's a shame you haven't always been so tongue-tied,' Morwenna said bitterly. 'Why did you have to say anything, Nathaniel? Couldn't you just pretend you hadn't heard and carry on as normal? Isn't that what they teach in your Christian schools – how to turn the other cheek?' She looked away from him, and he could see what an effort she was making to prevent her anger from dissolving into tears. 'I thought you were different, but you stand up there like all the rest of them, armed with your self-righteousness and your phrase-book of forgiveness, and when you have the perfect opportunity to practise what you preach, you don't have the strength even to *try* to understand. Well, let *me* give *you* a lesson in absolution – there is *no* atonement for what you've started. Harry's dead, and it's too late to make amends.'

Nathaniel's head was heavy with heat and whisky, and his temper got the better of him. 'So ignorance is best, is it?' He was shouting now, and the change in him took Morwenna by surprise. 'You'd rather I let him get away with it than shatter your fantasy of a perfect brother? There's a big difference between turning the other cheek and blindly refusing to see – and Harry went too far for either.' He softened a little, trying to put himself in Morwenna's shoes; if he was guilty about his estrangement from Harry, how must she feel? The memory of those final, angry words she had exchanged with her brother would be almost too much to bear. 'Look, I told you what

I'd heard because I thought you'd want to know. You can't blame yourself for the accident or anything that happened before it.'

She rounded on him suddenly and, for a moment, he honestly thought she was going to strike him. 'I don't blame myself for Harry's death,' she replied, her face just inches from his. 'I blame you. And according to your precious textbook of right and wrong, the way he died was as great a sin as anything he did in life.'

Archie took a cup of tea out to the garden and waited for Morwenna to seek him out. She had been continuously surrounded by people since the funeral party arrived back at Loe Cottage, and he hadn't even tried to speak to her: what she wanted to say to him could clearly not be said in public. In any case, the silence during the long walk back from the church had been uncomfortable rather than respectful and he was glad of a moment or two on his own, free from the tensions that had seeped into a community which he remembered as harmonious and good-natured. A lot seemed to have changed here in just a few months – but then he only ever came home fleetingly these days, so perhaps it had been different for some time and he had simply never noticed. More than ever, he looked forward to seeing Josephine; things might have been difficult between them, but at least the awkwardness was familiar; the drama that he sensed here made him feel like an understudy who had learnt the lines for the wrong play.

As brief as his visits were, though, he was sure he would have noticed how shabby and neglected the cottage had become if it had been that way when he was last here. The flowerbeds which Mary and Sam Pinching had taken such a pride in, and

which Morwenna always tended meticulously as a tribute to her parents, were now overgrown and full of weeds; terracotta pots remained empty and covered in the dark-green moss of a damp winter, and the trailing honeysuckle which covered the south-facing gable end seemed to have given up hope of anyone noticing that its trellis had come loose from the wall and was crushing the branches into the ground with its weight. The house – which his uncle and some of the men from the estate had restored after the fire – had fared no better. Stubborn orange rust marks circled the hinges of doors and windows, weeds grew out of the thatch, and the paintwork looked tired and dirty. Loe Cottage seemed to Archie to share the family's grief, although he couldn't help feeling that to get to this state the deterioration must have begun some time before Harry's death. He had always admired the strength with which the twins had kept the family together after their parents' death, but lately they must have let things go. Why, he wondered? Some lines from Tennyson came into his head – one of those merciless evocations of sadness and isolation that the poet was so good at. This was hardly a moated grange but the dreariness was the same, and Morwenna certainly looked every bit as weary as the Mariana of the poem's title – weary, and tired of life.

Archie had no idea what she needed to talk to him about so confidentially, but it would take more than kind words and sympathy to alleviate the depth of misery he sensed in her. He finished his tea and decided to go inside: on such a hot day, he and Morwenna might stand more chance of finding some peace and quiet there. In the front parlour, where all the food for the wake had been laid out on borrowed trestle tables, he found yet another crowd of people but Morwenna was not

41

among them. He tried to push his way further into the room, but his path was blocked by two of his fellow bearers. The elder man, Joseph Caplin, was obviously drunk – although as far as Archie could remember, he had not been truly sober since the break-up of his family – and it was the younger of the two who spoke first.

'Well, if it isn't the famous Inspector,' he said sarcastically. 'We *are* honoured, although I'd have put money on the fact that you'd come sniffing round Morwenna again the minute she was on her own.' Archie ignored the bait. Simon Jacks – or 'Kestrel' as the gamekeeper was usually known – had always hated him and his friendship with Morwenna was top of a long list of reasons. Jacks had always wanted her and, just after the fire, when he thought Morwenna was vulnerable, he had pursued her so relentlessly that she had begged Harry to make him back off. Usually, Jacks took his resentment out on the woman he eventually married, but today he seemed happy to share it with Archie. 'She's got friends here, you know, and she certainly doesn't need you, so do us all a favour and fuck off back to London.'

Jacks's wife – a tired-looking woman with thin, mousy hair and no light in her eyes – opened her mouth to say something but Jacks silenced her with a look. For her sake, Archie tried not to let his diminishing patience get the better of him. He turned his back on the insult, and noticed with relief that Lettice and her father were over by the food, talking to Mrs Snipe. Before he could join them, though, a child's voice cut through the room with a lightness more appropriate to a birthday party than a wake.

'Don't forget to leave some food for Harry.'

Everyone turned to look at Loveday with the same mixture

of embarrassment and horror that had greeted her laughter in church. In the stillness that followed, Archie could hear the ticking of the clock from the hall and the insistent tapping of a fly against the window. In the end, it was Mrs Snipe who broke the silence. 'Don't you worry, my love, there's plenty to go round,' she said breezily, as if the girl had said nothing out of place. 'Why don't you come through to the pantry with me and I'll show you what we've got in there.'

She led the girl away and the sound of voices built gradually again. Lettice grimaced at Archie from the other side of the table. 'I know actresses who'd kill for an exit line like that,' she called, picking up a bread roll smothered with jam and cream. 'Isn't it nice to be back?'

He laughed, glad to share a moment of normality, but the respite was short-lived. Joseph Caplin had climbed unsteadily on to a chair and was striking an empty whisky bottle with a knife to get the room's attention. What was it about the British that made them insist on this excruciating moment at any wedding or funeral, Archie wondered, trying to remember if he had ever been to one which did not reduce somebody's past or future to a drunken display of emotion.

'Ladies and gentlemen,' Caplin slurred, not quite sober enough to focus on anyone in particular. 'I'd like you to raise your glasses – to the death of Harry Pinching.'

'To Harry Pinching.' A number of voices spoke up loudly around the room, as if volume could compensate for Caplin's drunken slip of the tongue. The farmer got down from his chair, smiling to himself and apparently oblivious of what he had said. Wondering how much of a mistake it had actually been, Archie left them to their drink and went through to the kitchen, glad that Harry's sisters had at least been spared the awkwardness of the moment. He opened the back door just in time to catch the end of an angry exchange between Morwenna and the young curate. Surprised, and aware that he had walked in on a private conversation, he hesitated. Morwenna had her back to him but Nathaniel saw him instantly and disappeared quickly round the side of the cottage, though not before Archie had noticed how pale he was.

Morwenna turned to face him and, as she showed no sign of embarrassment, Archie decided against pretending not to have heard. 'What's Nathaniel done to make you so angry with him?' he asked gently. 'Is it because he and Harry had fallen out?'

'God, how quickly word gets round – even as far as London,' Morwenna said sharply, then seemed to regret her sarcasm. 'I'm sorry – you didn't deserve that, but it's been a long day and I'm sick to death of sympathy, particularly the sort that comes tied to a dog collar.' She paused for a moment and pushed her hair back from her eyes. 'No, it's nothing to do with that – boys will be boys, won't they? It's just that Nathaniel and I have different ideas of comfort, and I don't want him to keep passing his on to Loveday. I've spent the last few weeks preparing her for the idea that she's never going to see her brother again, and he wrecks it all by filling her head full of nonsense about the resurrection and eternal life. It's a lot to ask of a normal fourteen-year-old to understand the difference between a pretty fable that makes adults feel better and a literal promise that someone's immortal, but Loveday's *not* a normal fourteen-year-old. You know how it is – she lives in a world of her own, and half the time I've no idea what goes on in her head. She idolised Harry, and it won't take much to make her believe he was invincible. That's just not fair – on either of us. It's me that has to deliver the cold, hard truth and pick up the pieces afterwards, and I've got my own grief to deal with.'

Archie understood the resentment that certainties about life and death could create in someone whose whole sense of purpose had just been destroyed – he had felt it often enough himself – but there had been more to the exchange between Morwenna and Nathaniel, even in the brief snatch that he had heard. 'Sin is a big word to use, though – is that what you wanted to talk to me about?' he asked and, when she nodded, added: 'Let's go somewhere a bit more private.'

They walked away from the house, down to the edge of the garden where a narrow lane separated them from trees that marked the northern boundary of the Loe estate, still in sight of the cottage but far enough away to be able to talk freely. The soft afternoon light filtered through new leaves on to a sweep of bluebells which seemed to drift like smoke through the woods, and Archie wondered if Morwenna, like him, was thinking of the last time they had sat together in this very spot. It was more than eight years ago now, not long after her parents had died, but the time of year was the same and then, too, she had been racked with grief and in despair about her future. They were already good friends – some people guessed there was more between them, but he was still fighting his feelings for Josephine and Morwenna, who was never short of suitors, treated him more like an older brother – and she had asked him to go with her to salvage what was left of her life from the burnt-out shell of the cottage. Afterwards, he had sat outside with her, holding her as she cried and waiting until she felt ready to leave. He remembered looking down through the bluebell woods: the view had been much as it was today, except for two dead magpies which the gamekeeper of the time had strung up by the neck on the fence – a deterrent to other vermin and, it seemed, a potent denial of the rhyme which he had learnt by heart as a boy. The birds moved gently in the breeze, and the green and violet sheen of their feathers mirrored the flowers that covered the ground, but the lifelessness in their eyes mocked any promise of summer. The image had stayed with him, allied to Morwenna – a pairing of beauty and death which made each the more powerfully felt, and which now seemed more poignant than ever.

'Just like old times,' Morwenna said, as if reading his thoughts, but her attempt at lightness was not very convincing. 'I seem to make a habit of running to you whenever there's trouble, but I really didn't know who else I could talk to at the moment.'

'Twice in eight years is hardly a habit.'

'No, I suppose not.' She sat down on an old tree trunk and invited him to do the same. 'I thought I could carry this on my own, but it's been eating away at me since Harry died. Somehow it's easier to talk to you because you're not here all the time – and I know I can trust you not to pass judgement.' Archie wondered again about the sin that Morwenna had thrown back at Nathaniel, but he said nothing and let her continue. 'You see, I don't think his death was an accident,' she said quietly.

It was the last thing that Archie had expected to hear. 'Are you saying that someone killed him?' he asked, careful to keep the disbelief out of his voice.

'What?' Morwenna looked horrified. 'No – God, no, nothing like that.' She gave him a look that seemed to doubt, after all, the wisdom of confiding in a policeman, then explained what she had meant. 'I think he took his own life – it's the only thing that makes any sense.'

This time, Archie thought before speaking. The idea that Harry Pinching would kill himself seemed to him so unlikely that he had not even considered it as a possibility, and he chided himself for betraying years of training by subconsciously subscribing to the idea that there was a suicide 'type'. 'What makes you think he'd do that?' he asked. 'Harry always struck me as remarkably positive about life, even after your parents died.'

'Yes, he was strong *then* and I don't know how Loveday or I would have got through that without him, and it's not that anything's changed – it's more the *way* he died. He was far too good a rider to drown like that. Even if he couldn't keep Shilling out of the water, he'd have known that his best chance of survival was to hang on and get them both to the other bank. He loved that horse and they trusted each other – I've never seen such a bond between a man and an animal. There's no way he'd simply let go.'

'Perhaps not, if he could help it – but the Loe's a law unto itself. You don't need me to tell you how dangerous it is. We've both been here long enough to know that the stories about it live on for a reason – I can think of at least five people who've died in the lake or off the Bar in the last thirty years.'

Morwenna looked at him defiantly for a moment. 'Tell me honestly, Archie – what was your instant reaction when you heard about the accident?'

He couldn't deny his surprise at the news of Harry's death – surprise and, if he thought about it carefully, a touch of disbelief which he had put down to his natural tendency to over-analyse. But suicide? There was the sorry state of the cottage, of course: he had assumed that it was Morwenna who was at her wits' end but perhaps that was simply grief and worry – perhaps it was her brother who had given up on life? Somehow, though, it still didn't seem to fit with the Harry he had known. 'I admit I was surprised,' he said, 'but it's a big leap from that to suicide.' He looked back towards the house, and noticed that Jago Snipe and Morveth Wearne had come out on to the lawn and were looking over to where he sat with Morwenna. 'You and Loveday meant the world to Harry,' he continued. 'Look at how hard he worked when your parents died, how readily he accepted responsibility for the family and the future.' How he had grown up at last was what Archie really wanted to say, but there was no point in antagonising Morwenna by criticising her brother in any way. 'Do you really think he'd have left you to manage like this if he had any choice in the matter?'

The pain in Morwenna's eyes told Archie how many hours she had lain awake trying to answer that question for herself. 'I don't know any more,' she said. 'I hope not, but I'm too tired to be sure of anything at the moment.'

'Have you talked to anyone else about this?'

'No, although I think Morveth suspects. She sees right through me – always has. I nearly told Nathaniel just now – I was so angry after that pathetic speech he made that I would-n't have been able to stop myself if you hadn't turned up when you did.' Judging by the look of horror on Nathaniel's face, Archie thought, the curate had already guessed what Morwenna was about to spell out to him, but he decided to keep that suspicion to himself for now. 'I can't tell anyone else because I don't want people to think badly of Harry,' she explained. 'I can be as angry as I like with him – he's my brother – but I can't bear the thought of everyone else talking

48

about him and judging him, or saying something that Loveday will overhear. There's such a stigma to suicide.'

'Surely not these days. People are more sympathetic now – they do at least try to understand, even if the law takes a dim view.'

'Do they?' She looked at him wryly. 'Have you forgotten how your uncle Jasper refused to give Arthur Pascoe the full service because he died while he was drunk? If the Reverend Motley got the slightest whiff of suicide, we'd have been burying Harry at a crossroads halfway between here and Helston.'

'Surely Nathaniel's different, though?'

'In some ways, perhaps, but even he doesn't understand the despair that people feel sometimes – people who have no faith, I mean. How could he? I don't think he's had a moment of doubt in his entire life.'

That might have been true until recently, Archie thought, but just now Nathaniel looked as though his whole world had been shaken. More convinced than ever that Morwenna was holding something back, he tried again. 'Did Nathaniel say or do something to make Harry take his own life?' Just for a moment, he thought he saw fear flicker across her face, and she seemed to wrestle with her conscience, trying to decide whether or not to say more.

'Loveday's looking for you, Morwenna. She shouldn't be left on her own for long – not today.'

Morveth had come up to them so softly that neither Archie nor Morwenna had seen her arrive. How much had she heard, he wondered? In any case, the moment for confidences was lost, and they stood up. Morwenna smiled apologetically at him, but seemed relieved to go in search of her sister, and he was left alone with Morveth.

'We don't see you down here often enough, Archie,' she said warmly, reaching up to give him a hug.

Archie smiled, genuinely pleased to see her, even if he would have chosen a different moment. He had known Morveth all his life, first as his parents' closest friend and then as the person to whom he had turned in his own moments of crisis. She was one of the few people who played a full part in the life of the Loe estate – bringing in its babies, teaching its children, laying out its dead – yet who managed to keep her distance from it, living alone in a small, thatched cottage on the outskirts of the village. When Archie had come home to Cornwall after the war, still grieving for the loss of his closest friend and believing Jack's death to be entirely his fault, he had gone to that cottage to heal. The feeling of peace which he found in those afternoon visits was hard to describe and, for someone who had trained in science and whose career relied on logic and analysis, hard to understand, but Morveth's wisdom – her ability to make good, for want of a better phrase – was one of the very few things in life which he had never questioned.

'How are you?' she asked.

'I'm well,' he said, marvelling at how little she had changed in all those years, 'but I wish we hadn't had to meet here like this.'

Morveth watched Morwenna as she walked back towards the house. 'You'll have noticed quite a change in her, I expect?' she said, and Archie nodded. 'It was the waiting that nearly killed her. It nearly killed us all, to tell you the truth – watching the two of them by the water's edge every day, pale as death themselves and praying he'd be found. Loveday thought it was some sort of game, I think – best that she didn't understand, perhaps – but Morwenna had to be half dragged away each night. First thing the next morning, though, she'd be back. She couldn't rest until they'd got his body. The lake played a cruel trick in keeping him for so long.'

Not for the first time, Archie thought about the darkness that was masked by the beauty of Cornwall. He busied himself with violence on a daily basis in London, but the close proximity to death in which people lived their lives here still had a way of unsettling him. 'Why do you think Harry let go of the reins, Morveth?' he asked.

She looked at him for a long time before speaking. 'Don't search for things that aren't there, Archie,' she said at last. 'It will only bring unhappiness.'

Archie had searched often enough to acknowledge privately how right she was, but he was reluctant to let the subject drop so easily. 'Unhappiness for whom?' he asked urgently, aware that Jago Snipe was on his way over to join them.

'For people you care about,' she said, then added more quietly, 'perhaps even for you.'

There was no time to press her any further. He nodded at the undertaker, whose greeting – or so Archie fancied – was uncharacteristically suspicious, and they talked for a few minutes about the weather before Christopher Snipe excused them both from the effort of finding something else to say.

'Dad, I need to talk to you,' he said, and his earnestness made him look even younger than he was.

'Not now, Christopher – I'm talking to Mr Penrose.'

Archie was surprised at the response. His conversation with the undertaker was hardly too important to be interrupted, and he knew how close father and son were; their relationship had been Jago's only solace after his wife died in childbirth.

The boy seemed reluctant to be dismissed so easily. 'But it's urgent,' he said.

'Even so, this isn't the time or the place,' Jago snapped. 'You've already done enough for one day.'

The boy blushed and walked away. Feeling sorry for him, Archie said: 'Loveday must be glad to have Christopher around at a time like this.'

'What makes you say that?' the undertaker asked sharply.

'Nothing, really, except I noticed that he was kind to her at the funeral. With everything that's happened, having a friend near her own age must help.'

'They're not friends, particularly, and being kind is what we do. If Christopher spent any time with her today, he was just doing his job.'

Archie apologised without really understanding what he had said to cause such offence. Feeling more like an outsider than ever, he excused himself to go and find Lettice and her father.

Jago and Morveth watched him walk back up the lawn. 'Did she tell him anything, do you think?' Jago asked.

'I don't know. He asked about the accident, but then he would, wouldn't he? That's only natural. I'll find out what he knows, though. Leave it to me.'

'Don't get sucked in, Morveth,' Jago warned. 'I know you were close to the family and Penrose is a good man, but he's not one of us any more. If it comes to loyalties, I know which side he'll be on. Just be careful.'

'One of us?' The scorn in Morveth's voice was out of character and took Jago by surprise. 'Don't be so naive. Harry was one of us, and look how he behaved. He went too far, but if we'd thought more carefully about what we were doing, he'd still be alive and none of this would have happened.'

'It has, though,' Jago said, regaining his composure and,

with it, his authority. 'Now we just need to make sure that we keep it to ourselves.'

Christopher hung around outside the cottage, trying to find the courage to talk to his father again and waiting for a moment when he might get him on his own. It was vital that he got to speak to him soon, before some do-gooder like Shoebridge found out what was going on and tried to interfere. It had to be Christopher who broke the news. He had sat by the church for a long time after the funeral, wondering what words he should use and watching Loveday, who had slipped back to the graveside while everyone else drifted off to the wake. She was beautiful, even there. Her white-blonde hair fell forward over her face as she looked down into the grave, taking some of the flowers from the netting around the side and dropping them gently on to her brother's coffin. Intent on her task, she hadn't noticed him at first, but a smile lit her face when she glanced up and saw him and, in that second, he was overwhelmed with relief that Harry was dead and buried. He wouldn't have stood a chance with Loveday otherwise; the undertaker's son would never have been good enough for Harry Pinching's little sister. He remembered the time he had seen Harry coming out of the Commercial Inn with a bunch of his friends; buoyed up by beer and bravado, he had taunted Christopher and told him to keep away from Loveday, saying that his hands were only fit to play with the dead. It had made him so angry, and he smiled to himself now to think that his tormentor was suddenly a lot less free with his mouth.

Christopher had grown up in a house that lived with death and had never known anything else, so he found people like Harry – who covered their fear with mockery or superstition –

difficult to understand. When he talked to girls in the village, he knew that they always had half a mind on what he did for a living; he might as well have worn his mourning suit all the time because it hovered around the edges of even the most inconsequential conversations. Loveday was different, though. She could see beyond the black. The first time they were together – properly together – she had sensed his hesitation and gently kissed his fingers one by one, letting him know that she didn't mind, telling him without words that he should be proud of his work, that the dead deserved to be cared for as tenderly as the living.

It was always assumed that he would help his father run the business when he was old enough, and he had been happy with that – happy, and a little nervous at first. There was a lot to learn, but he enjoyed the camaraderie of working alongside his father and the satisfaction of doing a job which really mattered. Only once had he been truly afraid, and that was early on, when he had just turned thirteen. It was winter, the evening before a funeral, and he and his father had gone to a farmhouse half a mile or so out of the village on the Penzance road to make the final preparations. They were given a warm welcome – Jago Snipe knew everyone and was well respected in the community – and the dead man's widow, glad of the company, had insisted on making tea. As she busied herself with the kettle, his father handed him a screwdriver and nodded towards the door to the stairs. 'You start to screw him down, lad,' he whispered, 'I'll be up in a bit.' Christopher took the screwdriver, desperate not to let his father down, and made his way upstairs, looking more confident than he felt. His courage deserted him at the third stair from the top and he sank down onto the step, staring straight ahead at the room where the coffin lay, wanting to go on but reluctant to leave behind the comforting sound of voices from the kitchen. He sat there for half an hour or more, until he could barely make out the door in the darkness, and all he could think of was the first dead body he had ever seen, carried easily over Jago's strong shoulders, pale hands tapping the backs of his legs as he walked. When his father came up to look for him, he realised immediately that he had asked too much of his son and gave him an apologetic hug. They went in together to shut the light out on the corpse for the final time, but the incident made such a strong impression on Christopher that he could still remember every detail of that room – the Bible under the dead man's chin, the spectacles and pipe placed carefully under the coffin lining, the clock stopped at five minutes past three.

After that, his father was more careful about what he asked Christopher to do, ever mindful that he was still a young boy. Even now, he was not allowed to help with bodies which came in from the sea or after violent deaths – his father said there would be plenty of time for him to witness that sort of sadness when he was older, and always sent him on some sort of convenient errand when such a job was on. He was grateful for his father's consideration, and knew how much he was loved, but today, thinking about what he had to do after the funeral, he was back on that third stair from the top – uncertain of what to say, scared of letting his father down, and wanting more than anything to run away. This time, he couldn't count on reassurance and a hug – not when his father heard about Loveday, and certainly not if he ever found out that Harry Pinching's death was Christopher's fault.

Chapter Four

The sun sank lower over the trees, taking with it all the blue from the lake and transforming the surface of the water into a metallic palette of silvers and blacks. A heron took off from the tangled mass of shrubs on the opposite bank, its slate-grey plumage in perfect keeping with the rest of the landscape and, from her window at the Lodge, Josephine watched its languid progress across the water, enjoying the familiar, rhythmic beat of its wings until it reached the other side of the lake and disappeared into the impenetrable shadow of the trees. In the distance, a delicate curl of smoke from one of the farm cottages was the only indication of human activity. Except for the occasional drumming of a woodpecker from the trees at the back of the house, all was quiet and still.

The estate lodge was a handsome building of pale-grey stone, dating back, Josephine guessed, to the mid-nineteenth century and conceived in Victorian Tudor style. There was a small, sheltered garden at the side – well stocked with foxgloves, rose bushes and gnarled old apple trees – and she found it hard to imagine a more idyllic location. She had yet to see the main house, of course, but it seemed to her that in exchanging the worries of the estate for this peaceful retreat, the Penrose family had got the more desirable end of the bargain. She tried to imagine Archie here, but found it hard to separate him from their familiar London circles. The demands of Scotland Yard and the glamour of a West End first night were worlds apart, but he seemed equally at home in either and moved between them with an effortlessness which she admired, and occasionally envied; perhaps there was another, more rooted side to him which she was still to discover. He had always spoken lovingly of his parents, but never in much detail, although it may well have been her own tendency to compartmentalise areas of her life that discouraged Archie from sharing everything about himself. Certainly, looking around now at the images of a family home, stamped deeper with every generation, she realised how little she knew of his background, despite their long friendship.

She could scarcely believe that she had known Archie for twenty years: so much had happened since that first meeting, a year into the war, when her lover, Jack, had invited his closest friend – a fellow medical student from Cambridge – home to Inverness for the month. The three of them had spent much of that summer together, walking barefoot for miles over the soft, yielding moss of the flats by the loch, then climbing heathery slopes which recent burning had left too rough to cross unshod. As time went on, she had come to value Archie's humour and sense of adventure as highly as Jack did; he, in turn, fell immediately in love with Scotland and – she knew, although it had never been spoken aloud – with her. They shared a passion for history and romance – in later years, it would be Archie who reawakened her fascination with theatre – and, while tramping over the white sands at Nairn or collapsing, exhausted, on the flat top of Tomnahurich, dark with cedar and with legend, they would entertain Jack for hours with richly inventive tales of Scotland's heroes, both real and imaginary. For all of them, the month had been tinged with sadness: when it ended, both Jack and Archie were off to war, swapping the heroics of the past for supposed glories of their own. Jack's death at the Somme just a few months later had created an awkwardness between Josephine and Archie from which they were only just recovering, and she looked forward to seeing him now, free of the strain that had hung over them for so long.

On the table in the kitchen, as if to echo her optimism, she found a box of Miel chocolates with a Bond Street stamp, a bottle of Burgundy, and a note from Archie propped up against a jug of bluebells. She read it and smiled: making herself at home wouldn't be difficult, although the combination of beauty and indulgence boded ill for her work ethic. She had written her first mystery novel in a fortnight to meet an impossible deadline, but that was six years ago and the effort had nearly killed her, sitting up until three every morning and falling half dead into bed. She had vowed never to do it again. This book was bound to take longer, but if she could leave Cornwall with a satisfactory plot and a few thousand words, the hardest part would be over. Personally, she felt she had too logical a mind to write a real shocker, but the last novel had sold well enough to make her publisher eager for another, and she enjoyed the demands of a medium which was as disciplined as any sonnet. In any case, it would be nice to see Inspector Alan Grant again, she thought, selecting a chocolate from the box. She had grown rather fond of him in the fortnight they had spent together, not least because she had borrowed heavily from Archie to create him, and it was about time he had another murder to get his teeth into; an unbeaten case record was hardly an achievement if she only gave him an outing every decade.

In the meantime, there was dinner in a strange house to get through. The first night of any social visit was always an ordeal for her, no matter how much she liked her hosts and, even though the Motleys were easy company, the prospect of meeting their father brought out a shyness of which no amount of fame could cure her. Resisting a second chocolate, she went upstairs to change and was dismayed to find that the two suitcases which she had packed for every occasion now seemed to contain nothing remotely appropriate. Nerves made her impossible to please, and outfit after outfit was removed from its tissue paper and flung into the wardrobe with a contemptuous shake of the head. How formal would dinner be, she wondered, hesitating over a pale gold satin evening dress; then she remembered Ronnie's casual instructions and picked up something less showy instead. In the end, annoyed with herself for making such an issue of it, she settled for a compromise, put on a blue silk trouser suit, which she hoped would impress the girls with its daring, and left the house before she could change her mind and her clothes yet again.

The heat of the day had subsided, and a slight edge to the air reminded Josephine that summer was still in its infancy. She crossed the narrow gravel driveway which ran past the Lodge and walked down to the water's edge, where a small wooden boathouse reminded her that there was good fishing to be had in the Loe if she found time. Once again, a nagging little voice with a definite Highland twang whispered the word 'deadline' in her ear, but she chose to ignore it; a rowing boat in the middle of the lake would make a very satisfactory study for the preliminary plotting, she decided in her own defence, and if she came home with a couple of trout for supper, no one could accuse her of idleness. From where she now stood, she could see that an odd sort of vessel was moored at the front of the boathouse. It was more a barge than a boat, about the length of a punt but slightly wider, with a flat bottom and a raised platform rather like a bier at its centre. It seemed half decorated for something: green ribbons hung from the stern, trailing down into the water. On the floor in the middle of the craft, tucked under the platform, were some candles and what looked like a pile of garlands, presumably waiting to be draped around the edge of the barge. She couldn't begin to imagine what sort of occasion demanded such efforts, but Ronnie's opinion of the decor was bound to be worth hearing.

She set off for Loe House, leaving the lake behind for a moment and skirting marshes and parkland before joining the main driveway through the estate. As she followed the road around to the left and towards a tiny bridge, she saw Archie in the distance, on his way over to meet her, and realised to her surprise that she was a little nervous of seeing him, too. It was over a year since they had spent any amount of time together – and that had been in the middle of a murder inquiry which affected them both deeply and which had led to recriminations on either side as harsh as they were honest. His recent letters had been warm and friendly, but the next couple of weeks would show to what extent the air really had been cleared between them. He waved when he saw her, and she waited on the bridge, glad of the chance to spend a few minutes alone with him before meeting the others. Dressed casually in a blazer and flannels, and already tanned from the early sun, he looked more relaxed than she had seen him since that first Highland summer, before the war made him disillusioned enough with life to give up on medicine and choose instead a career which demanded a less idealistic view of human nature.

There was no sign of cynicism now, though, as he lifted her off the ground, smiling broadly. 'You look wonderful,' he said, 'and I'm glad to see you made it here in one piece. I had no doubts about the train, but your escort from Penzance worried me a little – she's been known to take three days to find her way back to the house from there. Have you settled in all right?'

'Yes, it's lovely,' Josephine said, giving him a hug. 'But the flowers on the table were enough – you didn't have to decorate a whole boat.'

Archie laughed. 'So you've seen the ferry to Avalon already?'

She looked bewildered. 'To where?'

'Avalon – or at least our version of it.' They sat down on the edge of the bridge for a moment, looking back towards the lake. 'Did I tell you that lots of the towns and villages down here still celebrate their own feast week?' Josephine nodded. 'Well, ours is this week – the play at the Minack is part of it, but there's also a cricket match on the Bar, a fair down on the beach, and various processions and blessings. The boat by the Lodge is for the final night. You see, the Loe was where Excalibur was thrown when Arthur died.'

She raised a doubtful eyebrow. 'Oh yes – the Loe and a thousand other lakes. Don't forget – I live next door to the Loch Ness Monster. You're talking to an expert in legends for the gullible.'

'Kings and oversized eels are hardly the same thing,' he said, feigning offence. 'And anyway, none of those other lakes has Tennyson on its side. It's all in "The Passing of Arthur" – an old chapel near a dark stretch of land, with the ocean on one side and a great water on the other.'

'Oh well, that's different,' said Josephine with good-natured sarcasm. 'If it's that specific, it must be true.'

'Quite,' said Archie, laughing. 'So every year we cast a sword into the Loe from the bank outside the Lodge, and send Arthur – otherwise known as a chap from the village – on his last journey across the lake to the sea, accompanied by three lamenting queens.'

'Let me guess – otherwise known as three girls from the local Co-operative stores,' she said wryly. 'What happens when they get to the other side – sorry, when they get to Avalon?'

'They have a glass of cider and a sausage sandwich – made by the Snipe if she's here – and that's it for another year.'

Josephine was torn between amusement and scepticism. 'Is it all as peculiar as it sounds?'

'Surprisingly, no. It's actually quite spectacular – they put candles round the edge of the boat, and if it's a clear night with the moonlight shining on the water, it looks beautiful. The lamenting can get a bit out of hand, though,' he admitted. 'It depends what the Co-operative has to offer. But you'll see for yourself on Thursday – it all goes on just below your window.'

'It's still going ahead, then? Even after the death here?'

'Apparently so. William offered to call it off this year because he was afraid it might be in poor taste, but Harry's sisters insisted on having it. It's probably a good thing – the feast week tends to bring the whole community together, and from all the bickering I saw today we could do with a bit of that right now.'

Won over by his enthusiasm, Josephine said: 'The Lodge is stunning, but you didn't have to move out for me. You don't get much time here, and I could have fallen in with the girls.'

'You wouldn't have had any peace, though, and I know you need to work. Anyway, the Lodge is special and I wanted you to have a chance to spend some time there. I don't mind – I quite fancy a couple of weeks in the big house, seeing how the other half lives.'

'Playing at Lord of the Manor? I didn't know you were really in line for it.'

'Ronnie told you that? Thank God the family had the sense to bow out gracefully. I could never see myself taking this lot on. William's dedication to it is extraordinary, but I don't know where he finds the patience. I used to think the challenge of my job was dealing fairly with so many different people and trying to keep the peace in a community, but believe me – a day in Tottenham Court Road has nothing on this place. I wouldn't last five minutes here before the temptation to bang their heads together got too much for me.'

'Oh, I don't know,' Josephine said, thinking again how at ease Archie looked. 'You seem quite at home to me.' She touched his forehead playfully. 'It's a long time since that hasn't been knitted together in a frown. I might have to rethink my prejudice against aristocratic detectives.'

'I wouldn't bother. There are more than enough of those already.' He stood up, and they walked on towards the house. 'By the way, Bill sends you his regards.' Archie's sergeant at the Yard was an avid reader of crime novels in general, and a big fan of Josephine's books in particular. 'Between you and me, I think he's hoping for another appearance in this new one.'

'I'll see what I can do,' she promised, 'although I can't say I'm feeling very diligent at the moment, and somewhere as beautiful as this is hardly likely to put me in the mood for murder.'

'Don't you believe it.' He told her briefly about the funeral, Morwenna's fears, and the tensions at the wake afterwards.

'What a terrible suspicion for his sister to have to live with,'

Josephine said. 'I can understand why she's angry. Do *you* think there's more to it than an accident?'

'I don't honestly see how there could be, but there's no doubt that certain people are closing ranks about something. It'll be interesting to see if William's got anything to say about Harry's death, although obviously I can't talk about suicide. You know how indiscreet Ronnie and Lettice can be, and Morwenna wouldn't thank me for spreading that round the estate. It'd be me they'd have to fish out of the lake next.'

They rounded another bend in the drive, and Josephine saw Loe House in its entirety – an embattled seventeenth-century mansion, with two slightly projecting wings and many features which had clearly been added at various points over the two hundred years that followed. She could see why Ronnie had warned her not to expect anything too grand: constructed of a self-effacing pale stone and topped with a grey slate roof, the building seemed to crouch into the parkland and its obvious restorations gave it a rather patched-together appearance; nevertheless, taken with the landscape on either side, there was something quite noble about the house in front of her. A long garden wall stretched out from both wings, topped to the right with a line of dark yew trees and forming a pair of linked enclosures on the left-hand side, one of which was filled with apple trees in blossom so thick that snow seemed to have settled on the leaves. Just past the kitchen garden, where the driveway joined a track leading round the lake to the sea, there were some ramshackle farm buildings and an immaculately kept stable block, built in a U-shape and crowned with a clock turret. It was just after seven, but a couple of men were still working in the yard, taking advantage of the pleasant evening and, as she watched them go leisurely about their tasks,

Josephine found it hard to imagine the kind of friction here that Archie had just described. To her, Loe House seemed to be that rare sort of place which encouraged the illusion that certain corners of England might never again be touched by conflict, the sort of place where a personal life undisturbed by politics might still be possible – and for that, she blessed it.

'It *is* beautiful, isn't it?' he said, pleased at how captivated Josephine seemed by her surroundings. 'It does me good to see it through your eyes for the first time – I tend to forget how special it is, particularly after a day like today. Let's go in – the Snipe has pulled out all the stops in honour of your arrival, so I hope you're hungry.'

Josephine nodded, noticing that there were three more cars in the driveway, parked next to Archie's and the Austin in which Ronnie had collected her from the station. 'Is anyone else coming for dinner?' she asked casually, waving to Lettice, who was waiting in the doorway.

'Good God, no,' he said, knowing how she felt about parties. 'William isn't the type to stand on ceremony – he just has a passion for motor cars. And apart from being proud of Lettice and Ronnie, he's not particularly interested in theatre, he won't have read your novels, and he has no appetite whatsoever for the London crime scene. We might even have a nice evening.'

Kestrel Jacks stood under a sycamore tree at the edge of the small clearing, smoking a cigarette and watching as the bird beat out the last minutes of its life in the trap that he had set for it. Jackdaws were less of a threat than magpies or crows, but they were still a menace in the nesting season, hunting eggs in all the likely places, and the more he could wipe out the better.

It was his father who had taught him to build this particular ambush – a wire cage with an opening at the top which formed the mouth to a funnel; a pheasant's egg, placed carefully on the grass below, was enough to seal the fate of any unsuspecting predator: as soon as a bird went down to get the egg, it lost all sense of direction and was powerless to find the narrow end of the cone which was its only hope of escape. Now, Jacks watched his latest victim panic and batter itself against the sides of the cage as it became increasingly disorientated, catching its feathers on the wire and emitting a sharp, almost doglike cry. The kind thing to do would be to wring its neck, but he waited a moment, enjoying the fact that the bird's characteristic jauntiness had been so easily defeated. As it tired, he opened the door and walked over to where it was flapping pathetically on the floor. He picked it up by one of its wings and it lay still in his hands, seeming to know that he held its life in the balance. In that second, the bird reminded him of his wife and he turned and swung it hard against the fence, putting it out of its misery sooner than he had meant to. Annoyed with himself, he placed a new pheasant egg on the ground and shut the cage door securely behind him.

Jacks walked through the wood with the dead bird in his hand. When he got to the fence, he wound a piece of string around its neck and hung it on the fence next to the others, far enough away from the trap to ensure that the carcasses did not deter other birds from showing the same, fatal greed. As he looked up from his work, he saw Penrose in the distance, walking towards Loe House with a woman he didn't recognise. He watched as they went inside, and followed their progress from room to room through the open curtains, feeling the anger well up inside him again as he remembered the wake.

Why Morwenna let that bastard get so close to her, he couldn't imagine. When he had seen them alone together earlier, he had wanted to smash his fist into Penrose's face and beat him to a pulp, just as he had wanted to hurt Harry Pinching all those years ago when Pinching warned him to keep away from his sister. But now, as then, he needed to play a cleverer game. He was accustomed to waiting and watching, protecting what needed protecting and destroying anything that threatened it, and he would have Morwenna, one way or another. Penrose – like that opportunist bird, the jackdaw – should look around carefully before assuming that the prize was his.

There were nine birds on the fence now, he noted with satisfaction. He was good at his job, and people would do well to remember that.

'Is it me, or is this trout even tastier than usual?' asked Ronnie with a devilish twinkle in her eye. 'Must be something we put in the water.'

Lettice's fork clattered to her plate as she realised what her sister was hinting at. 'If you must say whatever comes into your head, could you at least do it before it's too late?' she asked sharply, looking ruefully at the head and bones which were all that remained of her fish course.

'Just think what those eyes might have seen,' Ronnie continued, warming to her theme. 'We should have let Archie interrogate the poor thing before handing it over to the Snipe.'

More than used to sparring with his cousin, Archie flashed the smile he reserved for her across the table and decided to drop the subject of Harry's death. His casual efforts to find out if any rumours were circling around the estate had only earned him jibes from Ronnie about bringing the Yard with him in a suitcase, and when Josephine – in an effort to help – had asked William to describe the accident, his uncle's reply told him nothing new. A straightforward question about suicide would, no doubt, wipe the smirk off Ronnie's face very quickly and have them speculating for the rest of the night, but he couldn't betray Morwenna's confidence like that, so it was best to leave it and try again another time.

Josephine – who was far more interested in the people round the table than she was in the mythical Harry – was much better placed to satisfy her curiosity. She liked William Motley instantly – a reaction rare for her – and responded easily to his warmth and humour. He was, she guessed, in his early sixties, which was younger than she had expected, and he had an attractive, infectious vitality about him which had been passed down to his older daughter. Lettice was generally the more like him of the two – there was something continental about Ronnie's beauty which she must have inherited from her mother – but William seemed to have Ronnie's mischief as well as Lettice's kindness, and Josephine could easily understand why many people would try their luck with him – and why it would take something very special to succeed.

'Of course, what *was* remarkable was the way they found Harry's body,' he said now, refilling Josephine's glass with the last drop of an excellent Chablis. 'Did Morveth tell you about that, Archie?'

Archie shook his head, interested. 'No. She just said that Morwenna was in a terrible state because of the waiting.'

'Yes, that's true, so Morveth took things into her own hands. She asked to borrow one of the boats from the Lodge and made Jago row her out to the middle of the lake early one morning with some of Harry's clothes.'

'Why? In case he was cold?' quipped Ronnie, pouring herself a generous glass of red in preparation for the next course.

Josephine couldn't help laughing, but thought she knew what William was getting at. 'To find out where the body sank?' she asked.

'Exactly – you've heard of that before?'

'Once, when I was a child. A holidaymaker went missing near the loch one summer, and his wife was convinced he'd drowned. Everybody else assumed he'd left her – we're not a nation inclined towards the benefit of the doubt – but she insisted she could find him. Apparently, there's an ancient belief that you can find drowned bodies by casting some of the dead person's clothes on to the stretch of water where they died. The clothes are supposed to float on the spot where the body went down.'

'Gosh – did it work?' Lettice asked, fascinated.

'Well, they found the man's body about half a mile out from the shore at Foyers, so I suppose in a way it did. I couldn't swear to you that any strange powers were involved, though. Personally, I think she did him in – but perhaps that's just the Scot in me talking.'

'And you say you haven't got a criminal mind?' Archie said, amused. 'How old were you when this Loch Ness murder went undetected?'

'About six,' she admitted, 'but I didn't say I hadn't got a criminal mind; I said I was too logical to be another Edgar Wallace. Readers seem to expect characters in fiction to do the most preposterous things, and I'm happy to oblige, but if I wanted to commit a real murder, I genuinely think I'd be very good at it.'

Archie held up his hands in defeat. 'Just make sure you are,' he laughed, 'because I don't want to have to arrest you. Bill would never forgive me.'

'Perhaps Morveth bumped Harry off, then?' Ronnie suggested helpfully.

'That would certainly be the Scottish way of looking at things,' Josephine said, 'and I might bear it in mind for the book. If it's good enough for Mr Wallace . . .'

They chatted inconsequentially for a while as a pretty young girl from the village came in to clear the plates away. 'Mrs Snipe says I'm to apologise for the state of the lamb,' she said earnestly, 'but apparently things aren't quite up to scratch in the kitchen. Half the stuff she expected to find is missing, she says, so I'm to tell you she's done her best but she can't perform miracles. She says she don't know what sort of house we run here, and it wasn't like that in her day. Honestly, sir, I've never heard of most of the things she was grumbling about – I think the city must have gone to her head.'

'Don't worry, Sheila,' William said with a conspiratorial wink. 'Things will be back to normal soon, and I'm sure the lamb will be perfect. Just tell her I'm sorry and that we all appreciate her efforts.'

Sheila smiled, winked back, and left to deliver her message. Lettice watched with relief as the trout bones were removed from the room, but the door had barely closed before Archie returned to the lake. 'You're not honestly telling me that Morveth conjured Harry's body up with a pair of trousers are you?' he asked William incredulously.

'I wouldn't have put it quite like that, but there's no denying that the body came to the surface soon afterwards. Not quite where Morveth laid the clothes, but not far off. Jago spotted it later that day, under those low-hanging branches along the western side by Bar Walk plantation.'

'But that's a coincidence, surely?'

'I know what you mean – I suppose I'm sceptical about it, too, but there's a part of me that *is* inclined to give Morveth the benefit of the doubt.' He smiled at Josephine. 'The English part, probably. Don't ask me why, Archie, but you know how people round here trust her and believe in her – you included, if I remember rightly.'

'I believe she's a good person, yes. I'll even go as far as to say that I believe she has the wisdom and the power to heal in ways that aren't open to doctors and ordinary medicine. But I can't stretch to magic tricks – not even from Morveth.'

'What's the difference? In the sense that finding Harry's body brought comfort to Morwenna, don't you think that what she did – if she did it – *was* a kind of healing? Your mother . . .' He hesitated for a second, and Josephine got the impression that he had changed his mind about the rest of the sentence. 'Your mother always said that Morveth could work miracles,' he finished more gently. 'Don't be too dismissive.'

Archie seemed to relent a little. 'You're right,' he said to William. 'Where Morveth's concerned, I'm happy to accept more things than any self-respecting policeman should. I just think that in this case there's a more rational explanation. The body must have got caught in the weeds on the bed of the lake. The longer it was down there, the more it'll have been eaten away at by fish and God knows what. It'll have floated to the surface quite naturally sooner or later.'

'For goodness' sake, Archie, not during dinner,' Lettice pleaded, and even Ronnie lost her colour for a moment.

'All right, I'm sorry – but just one more thing. You say that

Kestrel Jacks was the only person who actually saw the accident?'

William nodded. 'That's right. It was early morning, and he was coming back by Lower Pentire at the time. We've had some trouble with gypsies out that way, and he'd been over to check the pheasants.'

'And did he see what startled the horse?'

'No. He wasn't watching them, particularly. He saw Harry riding along parallel with the bank, and the next time he looked up, Shilling had changed direction completely and was heading towards the lake.'

'How is Shilling now?' Josephine asked.

'Better, but still not himself. It's a terrible shame – he's a magnificent animal. I've had him brought to our stables for the time being – it didn't seem fair on Morwenna to have him at Loe Cottage as a constant reminder of the accident. You must go and see him when you're passing – him and the others. The girls told me how fond of horses you are, and you'd be most welcome to take one out any time you like.'

'Was there anyone else about that morning?' Archie asked, keen to return to the accident. From Jacks's account, it seemed that Harry *could* have guided the horse towards the Loe himself.

'No. It was still early,' William said. 'But Lettice is right – this is all too gloomy for the first night of a holiday. We should change the subject. Archie – have you told Josephine about our Minack performance?'

'From one funeral to another,' Ronnie muttered under her breath.

'I just hope they've sorted out some of the problems we had with the theatre last year,' Lettice added, helping Josephine and herself to generous portions. 'I was speaking to Hephzibah the other day, and she's told Rowena straight – she's not performing there again until they make the stage a little safer.'

'What went wrong?' Josephine asked, intrigued. 'You never mentioned it.'

'They were doing the *Dream*,' Ronnie explained, 'and Rowena decided to put it to music. The dancing fairies kept falling over the forest of Athens, and they kicked up so much dust that the front three rows were either blinded or choked or both.'

'But how was that Hephzibah's fault?'

'I'm coming to that. We can forgive her the dust – although she's never been light on her feet – but it didn't stop there. The audience sits on a very steep slope, and a woman was on her way back to her seat during the sandstorm. She couldn't see where she was going, missed her footing on one of the steps and started to roll perilously towards the cliff edge, picking up speed as she went.'

'It was so very nearly heroic,' Lettice added. 'Hephzibah was on stage at the time and saw what was happening, and she ran over . . .'

'Thundered over,' corrected Ronnie.

'All right – thundered over to the woman and fielded her into a gorse bush.'

'It sounds like she saved a life,' Josephine said. 'Surely that *is* heroic?'

'Hardly,' countered Ronnie. 'There was a perfectly good pillar that would have saved her quite gently. Hephzibah broke the woman's hip.'

'She *was* quite elderly,' Lettice admitted, as the rest of the table dissolved into laughter, 'and her family threatened to sue

Rowena. She was lucky not to have the whole place closed down. As it was, they had to cancel the rest of the run. Now, they won't even acknowledge the *Dream* of '34 at all.'

'You'd better be careful, Archie,' said William, wiping his eyes while Sheila cleared away the main course. 'Keep away from the edge of the stage, and watch out for any unexpected entrances from the audience.'

'What's this?' Josephine looked questioningly at Archie, who blushed slightly.

'Hasn't he told you?' Ronnie jumped in wickedly. 'He's starring in *The Jackdaw of Rheims* this week.'

'Really? I didn't know you were *in* it.'

'I'm afraid it's my fault,' William admitted. 'We were one short because of poor Harry, and everyone else was either involved already or too busy on the estate, so I volunteered Archie and we've swapped a couple of parts round – Archie's going to narrate, which leaves Nathaniel – our young curate – free to be the Jackdaw.' He topped up his nephew's glass by way of apology. 'I knew you wouldn't mind.'

'You mean you knew I could hardly refuse,' said Archie drily. 'Just don't expect me to do it every year.' He pointed his fork at Ronnie. 'And if you even think of trying anything amusing while I'm on stage, I'll make sure you pay for it afterwards.'

Ronnie held up her hands in a passable impression of innocence and William smiled at Josephine, who was beginning to understand how he had run the estate so successfully for all these years. If Sheila was anything to go by, his staff obviously loved him and she had very little doubt that, in spite of his protestations, Archie would now be persuaded to take part in any Loe estate venture that took place while he was south of the Tamar.

'They might have chosen something with a bit more potential for costumes,' Lettice grumbled through a mouthful of lemon tart. 'There's nothing very challenging about a monk's habit and a few old feathers.'

'Don't knock it, dear. If it means we have more time for sunbathing, then bring on the cowls – that's what I say. And we'll have to get you measured up after dinner,' she said to Archie, smiling sweetly. 'We need to make sure that Nathaniel's old costume will fit you.'

'I expect it's a busman's holiday for you, Josephine,' William said, 'but if you'd like to go, you'd be more than welcome to come with me. No obligation, though – see how you feel.'

'I wouldn't miss it now I know about the casting,' she said, surprised to find that she meant it, 'and it'll be a joy to go to a play and have absolutely no responsibility for anything that happens.'

'Splendid. I'll ask the Snipe to do us a picnic.' He jumped up from the table. 'Now, shall we try some of those strong waters you brought down from Scotland with you? We'll have coffee in the library, Sheila. You don't mind somewhere a bit less formal, do you?' he asked Josephine, while the other three excused themselves briefly. 'The sitting room's in better nick, but it's nowhere near as comfortable. We only use it to get rid of people we didn't want to invite in the first place.'

The library was a large, beautiful room, and Josephine could easily see why William would choose to spend most of his time there. The once fine plasterwork on the ceiling needed some attention, and the enormous chocolate-coloured carpet – covered in shells, palm fronds and garlands of flowers – was worn right through to the floor in places, but there was nothing tired about the browns and golds that shone out from the bookshelves, giving the room a warm, autumnal feel that was belied only by several vases of bright pink tulips. William pulled some well-used armchairs up to the fire, and threw another couple of logs into the grate. 'It was supposed to be Cerberus guarding the gates of Hades,' he said, pointing towards an animal's face which had been cast into the black iron of the fire surround, 'but my wife had it modelled on her favourite dog of the time – a spaniel without an ounce of aggression in him – so the overall effect is rather tamer than I'd hoped for. Still – that's probably no bad thing. Make yourself at home and I'll get us some drinks.'

While he busied himself with opening the whisky, Josephine walked over to the bay window. The dark-green shutters were still folded back against the wall, and she could just make out the edge of the lake in the darkness.

'Do you take anything with it?' William waved a generous inch of Dalwhinnie at her.

'Just a drop of water,' she said. He nodded approvingly and brought three glasses over to the window, leaving brandies by the fire for Ronnie and Lettice. 'It's nice to have you with us,' he said, raising his glass to her, 'but I'm sorry that your first day was clouded with a death. It's not what anyone needs on a holiday, and I gather from the girls that last year was difficult for you.'

'I certainly wouldn't want another one like it,' she said, touched by his concern. 'People still tell me what a memorable play *Richard* was, and I suppose I should be pleased, but my memories are so different from theirs that I'd really rather forget the whole thing ever happened. In fact, I wish it *hadn't* happened – no matter how much satisfaction it's given me or anybody else.'

'Yes, it's hard to be proud of something when it's bound up with sadness,' William said, 'and I suppose you're utterly sick of people telling you those deaths weren't your fault.' She nodded, glad not to have to repeat a conversation which she had had many times in the last year. 'You know that the girls had a brother who was killed in the war? Well, I spent a lot of time in London after Teddy's death – threw myself into the war effort because I couldn't get over the guilt of having encouraged him to join the navy in the first place.'

'What did you do?'

'I was in with the Room 40 lot – cryptography, you know? We did the Zimmermann telegram, among other things.'

'A lot of people say that turned the war.'

'Yes, and that's my point. People expect me to be proud of my involvement with it, but all I know is that while I was engrossed in that, my wife was here alone, dying of grief for our son. I'll never forgive myself for that, no matter what I achieved elsewhere and how many lives it saved, and of course I'd change it if I could – doing something for the greater good has never been much of a consolation for her loss. Personal sorrow – it's a very selfish thing, isn't it?'

'Yes, but there's nothing wrong with that. I sometimes think that's the danger of our age, you know – we've become far too abstract about the things that matter, particularly death. We read the newspapers and shake our heads at the numbers, but we've lost sight of the horror of it – the horror and the permanence.' She took a sip of her whisky and thought for a moment. 'I remember during the last war – and I don't suppose the one they're threatening now will be any different – it got to the point where we were almost embarrassed to be angry about our own dead. Perhaps it was a British thing – we instinctively look for someone worse off, don't we? – but with everyone suffering so much, it was as if we were being selfish to focus on a personal grief rather than a collective one. That always seemed to me to be a betrayal of the people we'd lost. Surely they deserved to be mourned – no, not just mourned, remembered – for who they were rather than why they died? So I don't blame you for being selfish or for valuing one person more than thousands – if we all did that, we probably wouldn't be in this mess.'

'No, I don't think we would. I stayed away from the estate for a long time after Veronique died, but you can't run away forever and I think coming back helped in a funny sort of way.'

'I can understand that – you can see the lives you're responsible for. Sheila's happiness matters as much as the League of Nations. Personally, I think that's as big an achievement as your war work. From what Ronnie told me in the car, you have something very special here – and not just because it's beautiful.'

'Yes, you're right,' he said. 'It does heal, I suppose . . .'

'Up to a point?'

He smiled. 'Yes. Up to a point.'

Sheila arrived with a tray of coffee, and Archie and the girls soon followed. An old black Labrador trailed behind them and made straight for the hearth, and Josephine was amused to see how quickly William went over to move one of the chairs back so that the dog could stretch out in front of the fire. She handed Archie his whisky. 'All measured up?'

'Yes, although a steady stream of this throughout the week might not go amiss.'

'It can be arranged. There's another bottle back at the Lodge. I've got something for the Snipe, too – do you think now would be a safe time to give it to her? I'd like to say hello.'

'I don't suppose it's a basket of everything she's missing

from the kitchen, is it?' William asked. 'That would make Sheila's life a little easier.'

'No, it's a bottle of sherry – but it might have the same effect.'

'Excellent idea, although if I'd known your luggage was largely drinkable, I'd have been more careful with it,' Ronnie said. 'Take it through now and put her in a better mood for the morning. There's no point in ringing for her – she had the housekeeper's grating blocked up when she first got here so that the bells wouldn't disturb her.'

'Yes, there was never any doubt as to who was in charge,' William agreed, and pointed Josephine in the direction of the kitchen.

In spite of Mrs Snipe's reservations, the servants' quarters seemed to be tidy and well ordered. The kitchen was not especially large – about twenty feet by twenty – but the ceilings were high and every inch of space had been put to good use. Sturdy wooden pegs were everywhere, set along the beams to hold pots and pans, as well as a few provisions – onions, garlic, a large flitch of bacon – which were presumably needed close at hand for regular use. How little must have changed here over the years, Josephine thought; she might easily be looking at an Edwardian or even a Victorian kitchen. Fascinated by the scale of some of the implements – in one corner, there was a slice of tree trunk bound with iron hoops to make a fine chopping surface; in another, a massive mortar stood mounted in a heavy wooden stand, with the long handle of its pestle held in a high wall bracket above – she realised that the Snipe must have a physical strength to match her spirit, and her opinion of the Motleys' cook – which was already high – went up a notch or two. In the grate, a big black kettle hung on an iron bracket over the coals, but the fire was beginning to die down and the chairs on either side of the hearth remained empty. Sheila was still there, scrubbing down the large oak table ready for the next morning, but there was no sign of Mrs Snipe.

'She's through there,' the girl said, nodding to one of three doors that opened off the kitchen. 'Popped through to her sitting room, then told me to put the kettle on. I thought we were having tea, but she's told me to go when I've finished this.' She looked at the sherry in Josephine's hands. 'You go through – I'm sure she won't mind being interrupted for that.'

Feeling a little like the proverbial fly, Josephine did as she was told. She wasn't surprised to see that the Snipe's personal domain – at the end of a short corridor from the kitchen and well placed to overlook other areas of work – was a spacious, comfortable sitting room, plainly furnished but lacking nothing, and rivalling William's library for faded but cheerful warmth. There was a jolly wall-to-wall carpet, matched with pleasant chintz curtains which had probably hung higher up the house in their younger days, and a pile or two of cushions made the old chairs look loved and inviting. The room was lined on two sides with well-stocked linen and china closets and, on another, with a mending table and desk which stood side by side. On top of the desk, grouped affectionately in the middle, there was a small collection of photographs of the Motley family which Josephine would have loved to explore – had she not realised immediately that she was intruding. At the round central table, where tea cups had been pushed to one side to make room for a large pan of water, Mrs Snipe was bending over another woman, gently bathing her face.

It was the other woman who noticed her first. She jumped up from her chair, nearly knocking the pan over as she did so, and turned quickly away from Josephine – but not quickly enough to hide her injuries. Her left eye was so badly swollen that she couldn't open it, and a cut to her lip had covered her jaw and collar with blood. Startled, the Snipe looked up.

'Miss Tey,' she said, horrified, and Josephine realised it was the first time she had ever seen the cook at a disadvantage. 'I didn't see you there. Is there something I can get for you?'

Surely they weren't going to pretend that nothing was wrong, Josephine thought. That was ridiculous. 'Has there been an accident?' she asked. 'That cut looks like it might need stitches. Do you want me to call a doctor?'

'No, please don't.' Panic-stricken, the stranger found her voice and took a couple of steps forward. She was about forty, Josephine guessed, although her fear might have made her appear older than she was. 'I don't need a doctor, really I don't,' she insisted, and there was a pleading, pathetic note in her voice which was dreadful to hear. She tried to pull her long, mousy hair forward over her face, as if covering up her bruised and battered features would convince them that she was not really hurt. 'Just let me sit here for a moment and I'll be fine.'

Her face betrayed her words, but Mrs Snipe was quick to regain her composure. She led the woman back to her chair and handed her the soaked cloth for her eye. 'It's all right, my love, we'll get you sorted just fine on our own. Stay here while I have a word with Miss Tey outside.'

Josephine found herself ushered back to the kitchen, still holding the increasingly absurd bottle of sherry. She put it down on Sheila's freshly scrubbed table. The girl had now left for the evening, and the room was calm and peaceful.

'I know you mean well but I can handle this,' Mrs Snipe said firmly. 'Getting a doctor in would only complicate things.'

'But that woman's obviously been badly beaten, and somebody needs to do something about it. Who is she, anyway?'

'Beth Jacks, the gamekeeper's wife.'

'Then shouldn't someone fetch her husband and let him know what's happened?' Josephine's naivety was reflected back at her in the look on Mrs Snipe's face. 'You mean *he* did it to her?' she asked, shocked. 'Then you can't possibly keep it quiet – it's assault and she needs to be protected from him. I'm going to fetch Archie – he can tell whoever's in charge down here.'

She turned to leave, but Mrs Snipe caught her arm. 'Down here, no one's in charge of what goes on behind closed doors between a man and his wife – just like anywhere else in the country. What do you think will happen if you get the police in? At best, someone will go round to have a word with Jacks and be palmed off with a load of lies and men's talk, and the minute he's gone, Jacks will knock Beth from here to next week, probably half kill her, and everything'll go back to normal.'

'What about William, then? He wouldn't allow this to go on if he knew. Can't he sort it out without the police?'

'Oh, he'd certainly try. First whiff of any violence and Mr Motley would have Jacks off this estate faster than he could skin a rabbit. The trouble is, Jacks would force her to go with him, so she'd be destitute as well as beaten. Look, don't think I don't agree with you,' she said, more softly this time. 'I can't tell you how many times I've wanted to pick up a knife and sort him out myself for her, but it wouldn't do no good. I've seen it before with another woman from the village, and it only gets worse if you fight back. At least here she's got friends to keep an eye on her.'

'But you're not here most of the time.' Josephine sat down at the kitchen table, still unsure of what to do for the best. 'What happens then?'

'She's always got Morveth,' Mrs Snipe said. Josephine recognised the name of the woman whom Archie and William had spoken so highly of, but she couldn't help feeling that it would take more than a bit of white magic to sort this one out. 'Beth went there first tonight, but Morveth was out for some reason, so she came here instead. There's a few of us she can turn to. Please don't say anything, Miss Tey – not even to the girls or Mr Archie. You don't understand what you're dealing with.'

The words echoed those that Archie had repeated to her earlier when he was talking about Morveth and the funeral, and reluctantly she acknowledged defeat. She *was* an outsider here, although it was more the logic of Mrs Snipe's reasoning that convinced her to keep quiet, at least for tonight.

'This is for you,' she said, pushing the bottle across the table. 'You may want to share it, though.'

The night air was anything but springlike by the time Archie walked Josephine back to the Lodge, but the beauty of the moon over the lake more than made up for the chill that partnered the clear skies. They paused at the end of the drive, transfixed by the silver light playing on the water, but – as magical as it was – Josephine's mind was on other things.

'Are you all right?' Archie asked. 'You've been a bit quiet since dinner.'

'I'm fine,' she said, taking his arm. 'It's just the journey catching up with me. It was a lovely evening, though, and William's marvellous.'

'He is, isn't he? I knew you'd like him. In all the years . . .'

A gunshot rang out through the woods, muffling Archie's words and startling Josephine. 'What was that?' she asked, looking anxiously towards the trees.

'Don't worry – it's only the gamekeeper, and it sounds closer than it is. That'll be one fox less after the pheasants – unless one of those gypsies William mentioned has run out of luck.'

He was joking, but the thought of Kestrel Jacks with a gun didn't exactly reassure Josephine. Before she could ask him anything about the gamekeeper, she noticed a young woman coming towards them along the path from the direction of the Lodge. 'Gets busy, doesn't it?' she said wryly to Archie.

'That's Morwenna,' he said. 'What on earth's she doing wandering the woods at night?'

'She's probably just glad of the peace and quiet. From what you tell me, I imagine she's had enough of company for one day.'

Certainly, Morwenna showed no inclination to engage for long. 'I'm sorry to hear about your brother,' Josephine said when Archie had introduced them. Morwenna shot an accusing glance at him and, realising her mistake, Josephine tried to rectify it. 'William told me about the accident,' she said quickly. 'It must have been a terrible shock.'

'Yes, yes,' she said dismissively, but seemed to soften towards Archie. 'I've been looking for Loveday,' she explained, glancing at him and ignoring Josephine completely. 'She went for a walk after the wake. You haven't seen her anywhere, have you?'

'No, I'm afraid not. Have you tried Morveth's?'

'Not yet, but I'll go there now. I just thought I'd drop in at the Lodge in case she'd gone to say hello to you. She likes to see you when you're home.' It might have been her imagination, but Josephine thought she detected a slight emphasis on the last word. 'We both do,' Morwenna continued, and Josephine could only admire her for delivering such a loaded sentiment without a hint of coyness. She wondered if she should walk on and leave them to it, but Archie showed no sign of awkwardness.

'I'm sorry we were interrupted earlier,' he said, 'but I'll come and see you at the cottage. We can talk properly there.'

'Thanks, Archie,' she said, genuinely grateful. 'I'll see you then.'

'All right – unless you need any help looking for Loveday?'

'No – she'll turn up. You know what she's like – she runs wild everywhere at this time of year. I wouldn't normally go out looking, but it's been a long day and she's over-excited, and the wake carried on at the Commercial Inn – God knows what state some of them are in by now.'

'There'll be a few wavering footsteps along the cliff path tonight, then.'

She smiled. 'Exactly, so I don't want her getting into any trouble.'

'Look, are you sure you don't want me to come with you?'

'Yes, I'm sure. You're probably right about her being with Morveth – and I'd rather be on my own for a bit.'

She was gone before Archie could argue. 'Beautiful but difficult?' Josephine guessed when they were out of earshot. 'I'm sorry – I didn't mean to drop you in it, but there was no reason for her to assume you'd told me anything I shouldn't know.'

'It's not your fault. She's so on edge at the moment that anything you said would have been jumped on. And the difficult does tend to outweigh the beautiful.'

'Even so, I imagine there'd be plenty of people willing to overlook that. Has she always been on her own?'

'As far as I know. Her parents died when Loveday was still

very young, though, and she's brought her sister up. A lot of men round here might be happy to overlook difficult, but being saddled with a child as well is very different.'

'She obviously thinks a lot of you,' Josephine said, but Archie looked uncomfortable and she didn't press the point. When they arrived back at the Lodge, she led the way round to the back door, shining her torch ahead of them and fumbling for her key. Suddenly she let out a cry and dropped the torch. The beam of light went out as soon as it hit the ground, leaving them in complete darkness.

'What is it?' Archie asked anxiously.

'There's something on the doorstep,' Josephine said. 'I thought I saw blood.'

'Stand back a minute.' Archie fumbled around on the floor to find the torch, and shook it back into life. Placing himself between Josephine and the door, he shone the light on the step. 'It's all right,' he said with relief. 'I suppose you could call it a present.' He held up a rabbit. 'I don't know if you've come across our cat yet, but she obviously wanted to welcome you with something.'

Josephine laughed, a little embarrassed to have made a fuss. 'Is she black with white paws and very talkative?'

'That's her. She divides her attentions – and her appetite – impeccably between here and the house, so we call her Motley Penrose.'

'Then we have met. She was sitting on the window sill when Ronnie dropped me off. She likes ham.'

'If you're on those terms already, this is probably a thank you. Don't tell the Snipe, though – she accuses us of spoiling her, but she's far worse than anyone else when she thinks no one's looking.'

Dora Snipe had more on her mind at the moment, Josephine thought, as Archie disposed of the rabbit in the bushes. She wondered again if she should say something to him now, in spite of her promise. 'Shall I open that whisky?' she asked, putting the light on in the kitchen and going over to fill the kettle.

'It's tempting,' he said, washing the blood from the step with a glass of water, 'but not tonight. You need a good night's sleep and I wouldn't mind one myself. We'll have a couple tomorrow to toast our victory at the cricket match.'

'Are you that confident?'

'Not really. To be honest, the Loe House team is a bit of a motley selection, in more ways than one – but then the estate can't be any less united than it was today. Sleep well – I'll see you in the morning.'

He kissed her goodnight and she watched from the door until the beam of light from his torch disappeared, vaguely aware of something she had meant to say to him but unable to put her finger on what it was. It was only later, as she lay in bed thinking about Kestrel Jacks and his wife, that she realised what had been hovering at the back of her mind: Loveday couldn't possibly be at Morveth's, because Morveth had not been at home. So where was she? She fell asleep, still trying to decide if she should telephone Archie or not.

Chapter Five

Loveday sat for a long time on the Bar, midway between the lake and the sea, waiting for the tide to turn and the waves to get smaller. Now, satisfied that the sea was at its lowest point, she crept into the church through the side entrance. The moon shone through the open door, throwing its magical light on to the painted screen that stood just inside the porch. Harry had told her once that it came from an old ship, a galleon which had been wrecked on the beach a long time ago. He had shown her where the ship sailed from on a map, but she couldn't ever remember the name and he'd had to keep reminding her. The aged wood was covered with exotic painted figures – men with dark faces and funny eyes – and they looked even stranger now in the moonlight. He had said that there really were people like that in the world if you went far enough away, but she hadn't believed him and so he had promised to take her travelling one day and show her. She closed the door behind her and the faces disappeared. She was glad they were gone. Without Harry there, they frightened her.

The church was quiet and dark inside, and she could barely hear the sound of the sea. It was a completely different place from earlier in the day, when so many people had come to see Harry. She walked up the middle aisle to the front and sat in the first pew, bowing her head solemnly. That was what you were supposed to do when you sat down in a church – she knew that, because she had watched other people do it. It was how she had found Nathaniel earlier this evening, sitting quietly in the pew with his face hidden. Now, she waited for what she thought was the right length of time, thinking how old and peculiar the church smelt, then lifted her head. As her eyes got used to the darkness, she could just make out the familiar figure on the cross. He looked so sad, she always thought. She remembered how Nathaniel had explained it all to her one day – the man was sad because people in the world did bad things and because of that he'd had to die. That didn't seem fair, but Nathaniel had said it was all right because he came back, stronger and better than before. Thanks to the man on the cross, he said, it was the same for everyone. People never died if there was someone left to care for them. Love brought them back.

She liked Nathaniel. He was kind and gentle, and talked to her about things which didn't seem to interest other people. And he never seemed to mind how many questions she had, or tried to shut her up with silly answers. He had asked her that same day what made her sad, and she told him about the night her parents died in the fire. *They* hadn't come back, she said, but Nathaniel explained that just because she couldn't see them, it didn't mean they weren't there; they were still looking out for her, he said, and always would be. He'd asked what she remembered, and she told him. When she'd finished, she noticed that Nathaniel looked a little bit like the man on the cross, because he was crying. He asked her if she'd told anybody else the story and she explained that she hadn't because no one ever wanted to talk about the fire in front of her, not even Morwenna. But she liked the idea of her parents looking over her shoulder. Since then, she had hoped more than ever to see them; she kept turning round suddenly to see if she could catch them out, but so far they had been too quick for her.

As she got up from the pew, she heard a noise from the door at the back of the church. Not wanting to be caught, she hurried to the side wall where some tiny steps led up to a rood loft, barely big enough for her to squeeze into. It was just like the hide-and-seek games she played with Harry. Excited, she tried not to laugh or do anything to give herself away. She peeked out through the gap in the stone, putting her face close enough to the opening to make out a large figure coming down the aisle. It must be the vicar – no one else she knew was that round and stout – and she was horrified to see that he was heading straight for her. If he found her here at night, she'd be in terrible trouble. She held her breath, but at the last minute the vicar turned right into the small room at the side which he and Nathaniel sometimes used to get changed in, and where she knew they kept the valuable things. He stayed in there for several minutes, and she heard the chink of coins against metal. Then he muttered something – something which sounded like a word Morwenna often used and always scolded Loveday for repeating – and left the church as quickly as he had entered it.

All was silent again. Loveday waited a few seconds, then left her hiding place and went over to the north chapel to set about her task. In the darkness, she didn't see the bucket by the altar and walked straight into it. Water spilt on to the floor, and she did her best to mop it up with the sleeve of her jumper, but it was the noise that worried her. She paused again to make sure that the vicar wasn't on his way back in, then took one of the candles from the altar and lit it with the matches she'd

91

brought. Just in case it let her down, she lit a second candle and left it burning in its pillar to guide her back to safety. Now that she could see properly, it was easy to find what she was looking for – a wooden trapdoor, just to the right of the altar table, with a metal hook in one corner. The door covered some steps down to a passage under the church. Harry had shown it to her, but warned her not to come here without him because it might be dangerous: it led to a sort of cellar under the bell tower, and then down again to the sea. Sometimes – at high tide – the water filled the lower part of the passage completely. The first time he brought her here, they had stood in the cellar and listened as the sea crept gradually towards them. She had said it sounded like the hiss of snakes and Harry had laughed, but not unkindly – Harry was never unkind.

After that, she had pestered him to bring her here as often as possible and he had agreed – on the condition that she promised never to come alone, and that they never went further down. No one else seemed to know that you could get right to the sea – Harry said that people used the passage regularly in the olden days, had even lived in the cave which it led to – but nobody bothered with it now. She loved the idea of sharing something so exciting with her brother. One day, she announced proudly to Morwenna that she and Harry had a secret, but Morwenna had been furious; she had tried everything to make Loveday tell her what it was, had even started following her for a while to see what she and Harry were doing, but Loveday knew every hiding place there was on the estate and her sister could never keep up with her. After that, though, she hadn't boasted to anyone else, not even Christopher – and anyway, she and Christopher had a secret of their own.

As she set out down the passage, she felt a little guilty about breaking her promise to Harry. Still, she would only go as far as the room under the bell tower and she wouldn't stay long – just long enough to leave the parcel of food that Mrs Snipe had let her take from the pantry. After her conversation with Nathaniel, Loveday had thought long and hard about where Harry would go first when he came back, and this seemed to her to be the obvious place. The tunnel widened out into a small room, about ten feet wide in each direction; she held up her candle, hardly daring to look, but was disappointed to see that the space was empty. In her heart, she had hoped that Harry might be here already, smiling at her and holding up his hands the way he always did when she found him out in a game of hide and seek. The candle sputtered for a second and some wax dripped down on to her hand, burning her fingers and forcing her to let go of the precious light. The flame went out and, as she stood there in the darkness, peeling the hardened wax from her skin, she had a sudden moment of doubt. What if Nathaniel was wrong? When she'd told Christopher that love brought people back, he'd told her not to be silly – that wasn't how it happened and Harry would never come back. She'd stood her ground and Christopher had apologised for calling her silly, but now, all alone, she was less sure. After all, Christopher worked with the dead and surely knew more about them than Nathaniel – perhaps he was right after all? The idea of Harry being gone for ever was too much to bear, and she shook it off obstinately. All she had to do, she thought, remembering Nathaniel's words, was to have faith and she would be sure to see her brother again one day. She must be brave, and keep looking.

The candle had not rolled far and she didn't have to grope

around on the floor for long to find it. She picked it up gratefully, then felt her way back along the passage and climbed the stone steps to the church, where the second flame was still burning brightly on its pillar. As soon as the trapdoor was closed, she relit the candle she had dropped, blew the other one carefully out, and made her way down the aisle and back to the entrance. She left the church, shutting the door softly behind her, and followed the path round to the graveyard. The path was sunk quite low into the ground, and the gravestones stood up tall on either side like soldiers. When she got to the place where Harry had gone, she looked sadly down at the mound of earth. All her work had been covered up, and the flowers that lay on top of the soil were nowhere near as pretty as the ones she had picked for her brother. She wished he could have seen how nice the bluebells looked, but she would make sure to tell him. For now, she would leave him her candle. She placed it, still alight, next to the flowers and was pleased to see that the grave looked instantly more cheerful.

It was time to go home. She'd been out too long, and Morwenna would be looking for her. She turned and headed towards the cliff path, noticing suddenly how cold it was and deciding to take the shortest route through the woods to the cottage. When she reached the edge of the trees, she turned back for one last look at Harry's grave, and was astonished to see Christopher standing on the spot she had just left, staring down at the candle which the breeze had already blown out. He had his back to her, but there was no mistaking his silhouette, clearly outlined in the moonlight. What was he doing, she wondered? As she watched, he turned and walked back behind the church, following the path which would bring him round to the lych gate. She retraced her steps to meet him, pleased that they could walk back together but, when she got to the gate, there was no sign of him. She waited a couple of minutes, then went further into the churchyard to look for him, peering behind the gravestones, even trying the church itself, but Christopher was nowhere to be seen. Puzzled, and annoyed with him for giving her the slip, Loveday set off for home.

It was already long after midnight when Morwenna began to clear away the mess left behind in her cottage after the wake. She had refused all offers of help: the women meant well, but she just wanted everybody out of her house and out of her head, no matter how many hours it took her to wash the endless dirty cups and get rid of the smell of stale drink which hung around the downstairs rooms. Sighing heavily, she began to gather together the empty bottles and leftover food; her weariness made things look worse than they were, she was sure, but it felt as though the rituals associated with Harry's death – even down to the chaos left behind by his friends – would never end.

Certainly, there was plenty here for her to do while she waited up for Loveday. In the end, she had given up trying to find her sister: she might be anywhere on the estate, and she would no doubt come home when she was ready. Taking responsibility for raising a young child had not come easily to Morwenna and even now, after eight years, the protectiveness and sense of duty which she thought she ought to feel still eluded her. It was hard to be a second-hand parent. Unlike her mother, Morwenna hadn't planned Loveday or longed for her, and it was hardly surprising that she felt no maternal instincts towards her whatsoever – the emotions which came with motherhood could not be handed down through the family like old jewellery or precious bits of furniture. It had been easier when there were two of them – at least in the early days, before Harry became someone she did not recognise – and she missed her brother's reassurance, his strength. She had no idea how she would cope financially without him, and she would rather die than go to the Union again, but she had Loveday to consider as well as herself. Things might have been different if she'd only been braver when she had had the chance to make changes: people often told her that there were opportunities outside the estate for someone as bright as she was, but she had clung to the life she knew, terrified of trying anything unfamiliar on her own. Looking back, though, she knew that nothing could have been as unfamiliar as this grief – this vast landscape of sorrow, emptiness and guilt, in which there were no signposts, and no rules on how to behave. If she weren't so numb, she might be amused by the irony of it all: the first thing she had ever had to do without Harry was mourn him.

Overcome now by weariness, she abandoned the cleaning to the morning and sat down at the kitchen table, thinking back over the events of the day. She was surprised at how pleased she had been to see Archie, although she half regretted talking to him so openly. Still, at least it had stopped her from going too far with Nathaniel: the violence that she had felt well up inside as she watched him in the pulpit had frightened her, and it was only now that she began to analyse why his eulogy had made her feel the way she did. She was concerned about the curate's influence on Loveday – that much was true, but there was more to it than that. Put simply, she was jealous of his faith: Harry's death had made her crave the certainty of which she had been so scornful, the certainty which Nathaniel carried with him every day, and she did not want to be teased by the hope of immortality and reunion if she could not believe it in her heart.

And anyway, was that really what she wanted? To see Harry in another life when she could never forgive him for what he had done to her in this one? How could he treat her like that, then leave her to pick up the pieces? That wasn't reassurance and strength; it was cowardice – despicable cowardice – and the injustice of it was that she was the one left to atone for it as best she could in the blank, meaningless days that lay ahead, when Harry's death would continue to hang over her like a silent, angry accusation.

She could bear it no longer. Hardly caring that it was Loveday's favourite picture of her brother, Morwenna tore the photograph of Harry from the wall and ripped it from its frame. She walked over to where the fire burned low in the grate and placed one corner deep into the coals, watching as the flames made easy work of his smiling face – and wishing that everything else could be wiped out as easily.

Chapter Six

The indigo tide stole ever further across the sand like a stain of spreading dye, and campion tinted the cliff-top in every direction. Josephine was glad of the holiday mood which had driven her early from her bed and out along the coastal path for her first glimpse of the sea. She was not an early riser by nature, but one evening at Loe House had shown her that she would be wise to snatch some peace and quiet at the beginning of each day if she was to get any work done at all. The Motleys' hospitality was infectious, and she was intrigued by the estate traditions which were to be played out over the coming week – above all, she wanted to spend some time with Archie away from the professional demands that dominated their time together in London. If sleep had to be sacrificed, then so be it.

It was a glorious morning, and it seemed to belong entirely to her and to the flock of young herring gulls who swung overhead, testing their broad, muddy-brown wings and repeating a strident, laughing note as if they sensed that their first long winter had finally come to an end. It was the essence of the coast as surely as the pipes were the essence of the Highlands, and it would, she guessed, arouse the same feelings in the heart of someone born to the sea as a few notes of 'The Flowers of the Forest' could stir in her. The gulls' dissonant song followed her along the cliff path, past the church and away from the estate. When she came to a spot which offered a particularly good view of the long beach stretching back towards the Lizard, Josephine left the path and made her way down a gentle slope of springy turf to the cliff edge, where a group of flat, grey boulders created exactly the working space she was looking for. Apart from a solitary figure heading towards her from the direction of the village, there wasn't a soul in sight. If she couldn't find peace and inspiration here, it was time to look for another job altogether.

The figure on the path – a small, dark man with heavy black boots and a paper tucked under his arm – waved jovially as he passed her, and went on his way, whistling tunelessly. Josephine sat down on the smallest of the three rocks and took a notebook and pen from her bag, enjoying the ritual and the sense of possibility that these early stages offered before the inevitable frustrations had a chance to take hold. She looked at her watch and made a start, intrigued to see where the first few words would take her. 'It was a little after seven on a summer morning,' she wrote, 'and . . .' She cast round for a name. Archie? No, too obvious, and he'd only be embarrassed. William, then – that would do. '. . . and William Potticary was taking his accustomed way over the short down grass of the cliff-top.' The words seemed to run into each other on the page, and she reached impatiently into her bag again to look for the reading glasses which she had recently accepted as a necessary evil. They felt strange and uncomfortable, and she hated the way she looked in them, but she had to admit that the wretched things made life easier. 'Beyond his elbow, two hundred feet below,' she continued, and glanced up from the paper to consider the image. As she looked at the sea, her attention was caught by a shape on the sand down to her left, where the beach cut between two rocks. Glad of any excuse to remove her glasses, she peered more closely at the object and saw that it was a young girl in a green dress, lying on her back with her arms stretched out behind her. The tide was on its way in, and an occasional wave came far enough up the beach to wet her feet. Josephine watched for a moment, hoping that the girl would sit up and move out of reach of the water, but she lay there motionless, allowing the sea to wash over her bare legs and threaten the rest of her body, and Josephine knew instantly that she was dead.

Battling with urgency and hopelessness, Josephine flung her notebook down and ran back to the coastal path. The cliff-top church, which offered the closest safe access to the beach, was about a hundred yards away and she reached it in good time, but then had to double back via the sand, which was much harder going. There was no doubt in her mind that the girl was Loveday, and her concerns of the night before came back now to haunt her. Why hadn't she telephoned Archie before she went to sleep? No young girl should be allowed to wander about near the sea in the middle of the night, let alone one who had so recently suffered a devastating bereavement and who, in Ronnie's words, 'wasn't quite right in the head'. What were they all thinking of? What a terrible way to go – alone in the cold, black water, just like her brother.

She rounded the rock, no longer able to keep up more than a jog, and saw with relief that she was at least in time to stop the body being washed back out to sea. As she approached the girl, she noticed that her hair and upper body were completely dry but, in her panic, the significance of this did not register – until, as she stretched out her hand, Loveday sat up quickly and looked at her.

Josephine screamed and stepped backwards. 'Jesus Christ –

I thought you were . . .' She stopped in mid-sentence, trying to maintain some sort of tact in spite of her shock.

'No, I'm not dead – I'm just pretending,' said Loveday, with a matter-of-factness that defied any pretensions to sensitivity. 'I'm sorry if I frightened you.'

Still breathing hard, Josephine said: 'Don't worry about that. I'm glad you're all right – but why would you want to pretend something like that?'

'I wanted to know how my brother feels,' she said earnestly. 'Everyone keeps saying he's at peace and nothing can hurt you when you're dead, and I just wanted to make sure they were telling the truth.' There was such a powerful combination of logic and impossibility in the reasoning that Josephine did not even begin to argue. 'It's a nice idea,' Loveday continued, standing up and brushing the sand off her skirt. 'Just being quiet, with no one shouting or crying. I think I'd like that a lot.'

The remark was made without any sense of self-pity, but it told Josephine more about Loveday's short life than half an hour of conversation could have done. 'Do people often shout at you?' she asked.

'Not *at* me, but they shout at each other all the time, and that's worse. You're the lady staying with Mr Motley, aren't you?'

'Yes – how did you know?'

'Because you've got a funny accent. My sister said you come from somewhere strange.'

Josephine could not help but laugh at this innocent betrayal of a passing insult. Clearly Morwenna was no more enamoured of her than she was of Morwenna. 'Your sister's absolutely right,' she said. 'Scotland is a very strange place indeed.' She held out her hand and Loveday shook it solemnly. 'I'm Josephine and you must be Loveday. Shall we go and sit somewhere safe while the tide comes in? I've left my things up on the cliff, so I must go and get them.' Loveday said nothing, but followed her back up the beach. 'I met your sister last night,' Josephine said. 'She was out near the Lodge looking for you. That's why I was so worried when I saw you this morning. You *have* been home, haven't you? Morwenna does know you're all right?'

'Yes, but she was tired so I didn't get into too much trouble. Anyway, I only went to the church to see Harry.' It took Josephine a second or two to realise that Loveday meant Harry's grave. She remembered what Ronnie had told her about the bluebells, and tried not to show how unsettling she found the girl's preoccupation with her dead brother. 'Christopher was in the graveyard, too,' Loveday added. 'But he didn't see me.'

'Who's Christopher?' asked Josephine, who was beginning to think that everybody on the estate must have been roaming around outside last night. Were beds and firesides out of fashion in Cornwall?

'He's my friend, but he and Harry don't get on. They had a fight and Christopher got really angry because Harry told him to leave me alone. I think he must have gone to the grave to say sorry.'

'Why didn't Harry like Christopher?'

'I don't know. Perhaps he thought I'd tell Christopher all our secrets, but I'd never do that.'

'Did you and Harry have lots of secrets?

Loveday's face lit up with a smile. 'Loads. He knows everything. Some of them are better than others, of course, but I'd

103

never tell anyone, not even Christopher. I promised Harry, and he'd be sad if I broke my promise. What about you? Do you have a secret with someone?'

'People my age are full of secrets,' Josephine said, 'but they're not as much fun when you're older. They're usually things you'd rather forget about, and you certainly wouldn't want anyone else to know about them. It's not like when you're young and you can share something with one special person.'

'Oh, I've got secrets with other people, too,' Loveday explained proudly. 'Christopher's shown me things that I mustn't tell Harry or Morwenna about, and Morwenna tells me that I mustn't talk about the family to anyone else. It gets complicated, doesn't it, trying to remember who knows what? Sometimes it's easier not to say anything at all, just to be sure you don't make a mistake.'

Loveday had a knack for expressing the complications of life in very simple terms, Josephine thought, and the sense she spoke was a long way from Ronnie's assessment of her. It sounded as though she'd had to deal with grown-up pressures from a very young age, but she still articulated them as a child, with a directness which was alien to adult ears; she hadn't yet learned the tricks of evasion and pretence that most people adopted, but that certainly didn't make her odd or stupid – and it could prove invaluable if there really was a mystery surrounding Harry's death. 'When I was your age, the fun was trying to guess other people's secrets,' Josephine said. 'Do you ever do that? I bet you're good at finding things out.'

The girl smiled again. 'Morveth always says I'm clever,' she said. 'She says I see more than other people because they're all too busy to notice. We play a game sometimes – I tell her

things I've seen, and if I find them out before she does, she gives me a book.'

How very enterprising of Morveth, Josephine thought, reluctant to call it exploitation when she was doing exactly the same thing herself. A girl with the face of an angel and a reputation for being fanciful would be the perfect informant. 'And what sort of things have you found out?' she asked, hoping that Loveday would not swear her to secrecy as well. She wanted to be able to tell Archie anything that the girl told her, but she could not betray her confidence with a clear conscience.

Loveday thought for a moment, and obviously decided to trust her. 'I know that Mrs Jacks hides money from her husband,' she said. 'I've seen where she keeps it, buried in the garden, and she only ever goes there when she knows he's out in the woods somewhere.' With a bit of luck, the woman would be saving to leave, Josephine thought; perhaps she should ask Loveday to add something to the pot on her behalf. 'Mr Caplin steals pheasants from the pens and sells them to the gypsies in Helston,' Loveday continued, 'and – you won't say anything about this one, will you?' Josephine's heart sank, but she shook her head. 'Good. Well, Mr Motley isn't as happy as he pretends to be. He always cries when he comes to the churchyard with the flowers for his wife.'

The last revelation came as no surprise to Josephine: even without Ronnie's comments in the car, she would have recognised in William that part-absent quality which was obvious in people who carried their grief with them, even in happier times. It had been there in her own father ever since her mother's death twelve years earlier. Her promise to Loveday was safe, but she still had not touched on anything that could relate to Harry's death. She decided to try a more direct

approach. 'When my sisters and I were all living at home, we hated it if one of us had a secret that the others couldn't guess.' 'We're the same,' Loveday agreed, as Josephine had hoped she would. 'I used to be so jealous of Harry and Morwenna when I was little. They were always telling me that I was too young to play with them, and it didn't seem fair that there were two of them and only one of me. I wanted a twin, too. But then they fell out, so Harry tells me his secrets instead. That makes Morwenna really angry.'

She could hardly blame Loveday for the note of satisfaction in her voice: it was difficult to be one of three children, and allegiances could be cruel and short-lived. 'When did they fall out?'

'They stopped hanging around together so much before my parents died, but I don't remember them arguing as much as they have done lately. They've been shouting all the time – well, whenever I was in bed and they thought I couldn't hear them. In the end, Morwenna used to lock herself in her room so that Harry couldn't get in to talk to her.'

What had happened to sour things between the twins so badly, Josephine wondered? Siblings grew apart all the time, but there was obviously more to this than a straightforward change of heart. Had Morwenna been afraid of Harry for some reason? 'What were they shouting about?' she asked.

'I don't know – I always put my head under the pillow when it started. People die when they've been shouting, and it frightens me.'

'Loveday, what do you mean?' Josephine asked gently. 'Who else has died?'

'My parents. They shouted a lot before the fire.'

'At each other?'

'Yes, and at Morwenna and Harry and me, and even at Morveth when she came round to see us. It was horrible when they died, but at least the shouting stopped for a while. Then it started all over again, and Harry died.'

Loveday was upset now, and Josephine was reluctant to push her any further. 'Has the shouting stopped again?' she asked.

'Yes, most of the time, although Morwenna's always watching me as if I'm about to do something bad. Sometimes she's really nice to me and we're friends, and the next minute she acts as though she hates having to look after me at all.'

Josephine found this easier to understand than the rift between the twins. The plight of the oldest daughter was something that she and Morwenna *did* have in common, and she knew what it felt like to want to be free of someone, no matter how much you loved them. In her case, the responsibility was for her father. They got along well, and these days it suited her to be able to spend long periods of time at home writing, especially as she had the money to make sure that someone else kept an eye on him whenever she was away, but she had always resented the assumption that it would be she who gave up her first career to return to Inverness. Like Morwenna, she had been just a young woman when – still grieving for her mother and with a very bad grace – she had gone back home to Scotland to run the household, so she sympathised with the other woman's situation: the difference in age between Morwenna and Loveday meant that a central part of the older sister's life would have to be sacrificed, and those glorious years of freedom between childhood and marriage would never be hers. 'Sisters are funny creatures,' she said to Loveday. 'I bet Morwenna's as angry with herself as she is with you, so try not to take it personally and don't be too hard on her. She's got a lot to think about.'

They were back on the cliff-top now, and Josephine gathered up her things. Loveday looked intently at her notebook. 'What are you writing?' she asked.

Josephine glanced down at the depressing ratio of ink to paper. 'It's a mystery story,' she said, 'but as you can see, I haven't got very far with it yet.'

'What's it about?'

'Good question. I don't really know yet, but I dare say there'll be secrets in it.'

'Have you written many books?'

'One mystery and two other novels, but I've done some plays as well.'

'My brother was supposed to be in a play tomorrow, but now Nathaniel's going to be him instead.'

'Are you going to see it?'

'Yes, Morwenna's promised to take me. It'll be nice to see Nathaniel, but I'm not supposed to talk to him any more.'

'Why not?'

'Morwenna says he's a bad influence because he makes up stories and fills my head with things that aren't true.' She thought for a moment and looked again at the notebook. 'Does that mean you're a bad influence as well?'

'Oh, I should think so,' said Josephine, laughing as they started to walk back towards the estate. 'But don't worry – I doubt that anything too terrible will happen to you.'

'It's not fair, really, because Morwenna makes things up. She told everyone that she was at home on the morning of Harry's accident, but that was a lie.' Josephine tried not to look too interested and let Loveday go on. 'I went out the night before because they were shouting again, and I fell asleep in the stables. When I woke up, it was just starting to get light and I ran home thinking I'd be in terrible trouble, but there was nobody there. Morwenna didn't come in until later. She looked in on me and I pretended to be asleep, but I could see she'd been crying. She told people she was in bed all night, so that was a story, wasn't it? It's not as interesting as Nathaniel's stories, but it's still made up.'

'I'm sure she had her reasons,' Josephine said, although she hardly liked to imagine what they could be. Why would Morwenna lie, when she could have easily said that she was worried about Harry and went to look for him? What was she doing that she didn't want anybody to know about? Was she protecting someone or could it be that *she* wanted her brother dead? She thought again about the locked door and, for some reason, the image of Beth Jacks's bruised and beaten face came back to her. Morwenna had told Loveday not to talk about the family, as if there were some source of shame that she didn't want people to know. Perhaps Harry was violent towards her. Had Morwenna suffered for years and finally snapped? She was trying to think of a harmless way to ask Loveday if her brother ever hit her sister, when the girl tugged at her sleeve and pulled her off the main path and through the lych gate to the church.

'Thank goodness I remembered,' she said. 'I borrowed a candle from the altar last night for Harry, and I've got to put it back before the fat man notices it's missing.'

'The fat man?'

'The vicar – Mr Motley's brother. They're not at all alike.'

'I'll wait here for you,' said Josephine, who had no desire to start rescuing stolen goods from graves at this hour or any other.

'No, don't be silly. Come and look at the flowers.'

Reluctantly, Josephine followed. She had been brought up to despise the conventions of mourning, in a family which preferred to keep its grief private and understated, and she certainly had no wish to intrude upon anyone else's. She knew it was an attitude which people found hard to understand – when her mother died, her father's discreet instructions in the newspaper that there were to be no flowers, no cards and no mourners outside the family had been viewed at best as selfish, at worst as cold and unfeeling – but she could not help how she felt. The only time she had ever wavered and had a sense of that need to shout goodbye in public was when Jack had been killed in the war and buried under French soil along with thousands of others. Perversely, the fact that his body was forever lost to her made her crave the physicality of a funeral – the tears and the black and the sound of earth on wood. Back then, she would willingly have ordered the flowers, sung the hymns and wept with strangers, but it was not to be, and she had never since felt the need to mourn in that way.

Nothing that she saw on Harry's grave changed her mind. She admired the flowers for Loveday's sake, and praised the workmanship that had gone into the carving of the horseshoe, but was glad when the girl picked up the ivory pillar candle and headed back towards the church. It was cold and dreary inside, and the waves streaming past on either side as the tide came in gave the building an unnerving, claustrophobic feel which was entirely at odds with the expansive beauty of the day outside. Josephine stood by the old rood screen, staring into the Moorish faces of the apostles, and waited while Loveday set about her task, talking all the time as she did so.

'I'd have been in such bad trouble if I'd forgotten to do this,' she called back over her shoulder. 'The vicar's so mean about buying things for the church, but that's only because he wants to spend the money on himself. Nathaniel says that he's no better than a common thief.'

Nathaniel would do well to learn some discretion, Josephine thought. He should keep his jackdaw-like chatter for the play if he wanted to make his way in the Church. Once again, she felt a reluctant sympathy for Morwenna and her efforts to look after her sister.

'Everybody knows he's got his fingers in the collection,' continued Loveday, undaunted by Josephine's lack of encouragement. 'I told Morveth that, but it didn't get me a book. But Nathaniel says there's something more serious going on, as well. He's trying to find out what it is.'

At last the candle was positioned to Loveday's satisfaction, and she came back down the aisle. Josephine turned to follow her out, but a movement in the vestry caught her eye. The door was ajar, and she could see a figure – obviously the fat man – standing quietly in the shadows, listening intently. Loveday's words had rung bright and clear through the empty church, and it would have been impossible for him to miss anything of what she had said. Josephine put a protective arm round the girl's shoulders and ushered her quickly from the church. It seemed that Nathaniel would be learning his lesson sooner rather than later, and she certainly wouldn't want to be in his shoes when the Reverend Motley caught up with him.

Morveth Wearne slowed her pace, as she did instinctively each time she approached Helston's poorhouse. The Union stood imposingly at one end of the main street – hardly a matter of civic pride, but still managing to dominate the buildings nearby. Part home for the elderly, part hospital, part refuge for the lost, its stigma loomed as large in the local psyche as the physical structure did over the townscape, and the solidity of its dark, forbidding walls seemed to mock the more fragile cottages and shops which stood around it. Morveth crossed Meneage Street and knocked at the gatehouse, returning a cheerful greeting from the owner of Poltroon's Garage as she waited to be admitted. She was a familiar figure in this part of town: her mother had taken a job at the Union shortly after it was built, and Morveth had been coming here for as long as she could remember, reading to the elderly, teaching the younger children as best she could, and – when extra help was needed – assisting at births and in the laying out of the dead. She was one of the few who could come and go at the Union as they pleased, and for that she never ceased to be grateful.

She heard bolts being drawn back on the other side of the gate and a well-known face appeared in the gap, smiling when he saw who it was. Isaac – no one knew any other name for him – had arrived at the Union more than twenty years ago and, in all that time, Morveth had never seen him look any different from the way he did now – cheerful, proud of the duties with which he was entrusted, and dressed in a collarless shirt and waistcoat, trousers which were too big for him and tied at the waist with a piece of cord, and an old tweed jacket. Everyone assumed he was a vagrant but his past was a mystery; the only sure thing was that Isaac was one of the rare people whom this managed and ordered life seemed to suit, and God only knew what that said about his previous existence. He greeted her with a small bunch of bluebells, and, before moving on, she spent several minutes admiring the circular flowerbeds and close-cut lawns which he kept immaculate throughout the year. As she went through the inner archway into the main grounds, passing a toy pram on the cobbles which formed a small playing area for the matron's young daughter, she could not help but contrast this deceptive scene of happy domesticity with the reputation that the Union had outside its four walls: the luck which brought people here took many forms, but the misery was universal; it was the last resort, a shameful confirmation that you had nothing and no one left – in this world, at least.

A young nurse, dressed in a pale-blue serge dress and starched white cap, met her at the door to the main building. 'I've been looking out for you,' she said. 'Thank you for coming so quickly.'

Morveth brushed her gratitude aside. 'I promised Jane I'd do the last for her when the time came, and she knew she could rely on that. If it brought her some peace, then I'm glad.' They walked in silence up two flights of granite steps and along a narrow, gloomy corridor, with wards leading off it. Through each break in the lime-washed walls, Morveth caught a glimpse of what passed for life in the Union: in some rooms, the elderly were lying in bed, too feeble to move; in others, children crawled across the floor and found what amusement they could in each other's company. Metal gratings ran along either side of the walkway, allowing her to see the pattern replicated on the floors below. It was a necessary precaution – only a handful of staff oversaw the welfare of nearly three hundred people, many of them physically weak or mentally fragile – but it added to the feeling of incarceration. Everywhere was spotlessly clean, but Morveth could never decide if that was reassuring or simply another rebuke to the messiness of the lives inside; certainly, the building had no empathy with the untidy, tainted circumstances which brought people continually to its door.

The Union's mortuary was at the back, tucked away from the main public areas, and the nurse showed her into the familiar room where the body of Jane Swithers was waiting for her. 'She wanted these with her,' the woman said, handing Morveth a small box. 'Make sure that Mr Snipe takes them when he comes to collect her, will you?' She left quickly, closing the door softly behind her, and Morveth put her bag down on the floor. She removed her hat, and walked quietly over to the slab.

Jane Swithers could only have been in her early forties, but she was old before her time and even death had not been able to return any sort of youthful lack of care to a face transformed by misery and pain. Her skin was pale, almost translucent, and the sunken cheeks and pronounced line of her jaw testified to the self-neglect of recent years, when neither the anxiety of friends nor the more managed concern of an institution could make her care whether she lived or died. Sadly Morveth remembered how many times the young Jane had come to her for advice, and wished now that she had offered something more tangible than words which always went unheeded.

A bowl of water, some soap and a towel stood ready on the bench which ran the length of one wall. She brought them over to the middle of the room and rolled her sleeves back, glad to feel the warmth of the water on her hands. Gently, she unbuttoned the well-worn nightdress and began to wash the body, tenderly lifting Jane's breasts and trying not to be shocked by how visible her ribs were beneath the fragile skin. Morveth was used to people looking to her for guidance and she had always given it willingly, confident of her own judgement, but now, past the threshold of her three score years and ten, she was growing weary and beginning to doubt the wisdom which others took for granted in her. Perhaps it was the shock of Harry's accident and the memories of that terrible fire which it reawakened, but it seemed to her now that she had sometimes been too ready to manage other people's lives. Her own past was comparatively free of emotional complications: she had never felt the need to marry or have children but, in preferring to remain detached, perhaps she had been blind to the internal conflicts that most people experienced, and had overestimated the ability of good common sense to wage war against the power of love and hate.

Her intentions had always been good – that was true enough, but how must she appear to an outsider? Just a do-gooder, with no life of her own, meddling in other people's relationships to compensate for her own solitariness. Remembering what she'd said to Archie yesterday about inter-ference leading to unhappiness, she was brave enough to face the unintentional hypocrisy of her words: how easily wisdom could lead to vanity and a foolish belief in your own infallibil-ity. She crossed Jane's thin arms over her chest, then went to her bag again and removed a stretch of bandage, but paused with it in her hand, forgetting her task for a moment as she thought back to the night before Harry had ridden his horse into the Loe. He had come to her in despair and the advice she offered was meant to protect those he loved, but it had only served to bring more sadness to the family. It had seemed the only way out at the time, but was that really true? The look on Harry's face came back to her as she washed Jane's legs and wound the bandage around the toes to keep her feet together. How could she ever have believed that his death would bring comfort to anyone? Morwenna was inconsolable, and Morveth's heart was full of dread when she considered Loveday's future.

She picked up a comb and began to tidy Jane's auburn hair, which felt dry and brittle between her fingers. There was a big difference between strength and a need to be in control, she thought, as she arranged the collar of the nightdress to hide a stain on the material, and her situation – which was increasingly the latter – was beginning to get out of hand; one decision was forcing another, and she was losing sight of the kindness that had motivated her behaviour in the beginning. Just look at the way she had behaved towards Archie, whom she had loved since he was a boy. He was her best friend's son and she had promised his mother to look out for him, and here she was treating him like a stranger, keeping him at arm's length from his own community and playing people off against each other to protect their secrets and mask her own involvement in their lives. Sadly, Morveth took one last, long look at Jane's face and stroked her cheek gently before tearing off four small pieces of cotton wool to plug her ears and nostrils. She wound another stretch of bandage around her head and tied it securely under the chin, then took two pennies out of her own pocket and placed one reverently on each eye. This final part of the ritual had always struck her as particularly poignant, but today it seemed more relevant than ever, and carried a silent accusation: if only she had kept her eyes closed and her mouth shut all these years, might she and those around her know the meaning of true peace?

She looked in the box that the nurse had given her and found the pathetic remnants of a life which had come to an end long ago: a photograph of Jane as she had once been; a tiny bunch of dried primroses, washed-out and fragile; an old pair of spectacles; and a well-thumbed prayer book, similar to the one Morveth used to have before she gave it to Nathaniel. The reminder of the young curate was unwelcome here, where she was feeling so vulnerable; his well-intentioned involvement in the lives of their community was so much like her own, and, judging by what Morwenna had said, he was set on making the same mistakes. Unlike Morveth, though, Nathaniel had youth on his side and all the optimism which that entailed; he still thought he could help everyone, and that made him dangerous. With a heavy sigh, she remembered the panic in Morwenna's eyes when she realised what Nathaniel had found out and naively repeated, and she knew that something would have to be done about it. Would this burden of responsibility that she had brought upon herself never end?

By the time she heard the undertaker's van draw up below the window, Morveth had fulfilled her promise to Jane and was nearly ready to go. That, at least, was a relief; she hated seeing Jago here in this building, where the memory of another secret hung so tangibly in the air between them. His debt to her could never really be repaid, but it meant that he would always do as she asked, even if, in his heart, he knew it to be wrong. She wrapped Jane's fingers lovingly around the prayer book and placed the primroses and Isaac's bluebells on her chest, surprised at how insignificant the fresher flowers suddenly looked next to those that had been picked so many years before. Then Morveth left the room, bowed by a grief which she would have found impossible to put into words.

Chapter Seven

'How he expects these poor people to fight Satan on an empty stomach, I'll never know,' said Lettice, tossing the book aside in disgust. 'Apparently, eating weakens your resistance to the devil. If that's true, I welcome him with open arms at least four times a day. I hope your book's going to be a little more believable, darling.'

Josephine looked at the cover and was amused to see that Lettice was reading the new Dennis Wheatley. 'I didn't have you down as a follower of the occult,' she said, leaning back and closing her eyes again. The May sun was a shadow of its August self, but it was glorious to feel the promise of summer on her face.

'I'm not usually,' Lettice admitted, 'but I found this in the Snipe's room and, after what Pa said last night about Morveth and her conjuring trick, I thought I ought to give it a try. I'd hate to think I was missing something on my own doorstep and I thought Dennis might tell me what to look out for. I'm not impressed so far, but I'll keep going until we get to the Devil's Mass.'

'Where exactly did all that business with Harry happen?' Josephine asked, sitting up and looking back towards the lake.

'The body or the accident?'

'Both.'

Lettice refilled their glasses with lemonade. 'Well, you can't see the place where the body came in from here – it's just round that bend. But this is where he went in.' She pointed to the nearest shore of the Loe, where it bordered the beach. 'It looks harmless enough, but it shelves so steeply that you're soon out of your depth.'

'And the horse? Where did he swim to?'

'Right across to the far bank. You see the track that runs back across the fields, just before the trees start on that side?' Josephine nodded. 'That's where Shilling came out. He was in a shocking state – absolutely terrified.'

Josephine looked across Loe Bar, a short band of sand and shingle – no more than a few hundred feet wide – which separated the lake from the sea. It was an extraordinary experience to be able to take in these very different stretches of water in a single view. She was at once enchanted by the unique, detached beauty of the place and fascinated by its violent past; hundreds of people must have died at sea along this stretch of coast, their bodies buried without ceremony where they came ashore, and their souls scorned by the church which stood at the head of the Bar, its stones looking smugly out towards the unmarked graves from the safety of their own sanctified earth.

The beach now was a very different spot from the one she'd been in a few hours ago – the one which was deserted except for what she thought was the body of a young girl. The cricket match – Loe House versus the rest of the estate – was due to get underway shortly, and people had been arriving for the last half-hour or so, dressed in varying shades of white, warming up as if they meant business and seemingly undeterred by the erratic nature of the pitch. The sound of a motorbike drifted across from the track, and shortly afterwards she saw Archie walk leisurely across the sand to where William was gathering his team together. Nearby, the Snipe was spreading crisp, clean linen over a couple of trestle tables and organising her band of cricket wives, who obeyed her instructions with a military deference. Obviously they would have to do without the smell of freshly cut grass and the tap of boot studs on a wooden pavilion floor, but everything else she expected from an English cricket match was in place. The only note that jarred slightly was walking across the sand towards her: Ronnie's exquisite wide-brimmed straw hat would have been more in keeping at Henley or Ascot.

'Those tables have come down here from the wake with indecent haste,' Ronnie said, looking over her sunglasses. 'I hope they've scrubbed them well.'

Josephine laughed. 'They don't actually use them for the body, so I think you'll be all right.'

'You didn't see some of the people at the funeral,' Ronnie retorted.

Lettice glanced across to where the Snipe was unwrapping plate after plate of sandwiches and cakes. 'I think I'll risk it,' she said, and got up from her deckchair. 'Looks like Pa's won the toss, so I'd better go and pad up. Wish me luck.'

'I didn't know she was playing,' Josephine said, impressed, as Lettice walked away.

Ronnie sat down in the vacant deckchair. 'They don't call her the Slogger for nothing, you know.'

'She must be solid if she's opening.'

'Oh God, don't tell me you actually understand the bloody game,' Ronnie groaned. 'I was sure I'd have an ally in someone from the land of brown heath and shaggy wood.'

'And I thought cricket would be right up your street. There's something very elegant about all those men in white.'

'Nonsense, dear. Cricket whites have exactly the same effect on a man's looks as alcohol has on his mood – they just emphasise what's there already, for better or worse.'

As Archie walked over to say hello, Josephine decided that it was certainly the former in his case, but Ronnie seemed unimpressed by her cousin. 'I have to say, your daywear has been a little monochrome so far this visit,' she said to him. 'Perhaps tomorrow you might be tempted to strike out into a daring shade of grey?'

'We can't all be Ivor Novello,' Archie said good-naturedly, lightly throwing a cricket ball into her lap and helping himself to a cigarette from the case which Ronnie had brought with her.

'Isn't it time you got started?' she asked, lighting it for him. 'You take all day about it as it is.'

'We can't start yet – we've only got one umpire and the other team's a man short. Jago and Christopher haven't turned up.'

'Good, then I've got time to see the Snipe about some drinks. Come and get me if I'm not back in time for the beginning.'

'For a non-believer, you seem very keen not to miss anything,' Josephine said.

'I've got no choice, dear – I'm supposed to be scoring. But you can help me as you're such an expert.' She strolled off, and Archie sat down on the sand to put his pads on.

'Are you in at number three?'

'Four, but it's best to be prepared. Our number two's very unpredictable and Lettice will either stay there all day or be caught behind in the first over.'

'Is that gamekeeper here?' Josephine asked.

'Jacks? Yes, he's their wicket-keeper.' He pointed to a tall, broad-chested man with curly black hair and a moustache. 'Why?'

'I always like to put a face to a gun.' She watched Jacks practising with one of his team-mates. He was younger than she had expected, and had an effortless strength about him. She could only imagine what it must be like to be on the receiving end of a blow from one of those fists, and she wondered again what she should do about the secret she had unwittingly walked in on.

'Here's our missing umpire,' Archie said, as a white-haired man hurried down the slope, holding his hand up in apology. 'Looks like he's on his own, though.'

They heard William call across the sand to the late arrival. 'Where's Christopher?'

'Your guess is as good as mine,' the other man shouted back impatiently. 'He hasn't slept in his bed, and there's no sign of him this morning. I would have been here earlier, but I'm having to do everything without him and I've only just got back from the Union.'

'Don't worry – you're here now.'

'I won't be able to stay for the whole match, though,' Jago called, struggling into a white coat. 'Mrs Trevelyan's not got long and I can't stand round here all day. Her grandson's coming to fetch me when I'm needed.'

'Christopher's his son?' Josephine asked as the umpire walked out to the middle of the rough and ready pitch.

'Yes. He was the one I told you about who nearly dropped the coffin.'

'He was in the churchyard late last night, near Harry's grave.'

Archie looked at her in surprise. 'How do you know that?'

'Loveday told me.' As Lettice walked out to the crease – or the closest approximation that the Bar could manage – she told Archie what had happened earlier that morning. 'I was just glad to see she was all right,' she said, looking around for Ronnie. There was no sign of her, so Josephine picked up the scorebook. 'It worried me to think of her wandering round late at night so soon after her brother's death.'

'Yes, although it's not unusual for Loveday to be on her own,' Archie said, and Josephine wondered if he realised quite how alone the girl felt. 'I saw Morwenna on the way here, and she said she'd got back all right.'

'What was their relationship like? Harry and Morwenna, I mean.'

Archie considered for a moment. 'They were always close as children,' he said, 'in that exclusive way that twins often are. It was a very carefree sort of thing, as far as I can remember, even as they grew up. Neither of them was particularly responsible – but then I was that bit older, and the next generation did seem carefree coming out of the war. It was hard for people my age not to resent that, I suppose. It all changed when their parents died, though. They had to grow up suddenly and pull together, so it was a different kind of relationship – but still close.'

There was a triumphant cry from the pitch, and several of the fielding side ran up to the bowler to slap him on the back. The batsman's middle stump lay dejectedly on its side, and he walked away from the wicket looking furious with himself. 'Would it surprise you if it was different behind closed doors?' Josephine asked as another man walked out to the middle to join Lettice. She told Archie what Loveday had said about the arguments between the twins. 'I wondered what would make

124

Morwenna lock herself in her room,' she said, 'and the only thing I could think of was that she was afraid of him. If that's true, you've got another candidate for wanting him dead.'

'You think Morwenna had something to do with Harry's accident? That's ridiculous.'

'Is it?' she asked, slightly irritated by the dismissal. 'Loveday says Morwenna lied about being at home when he went into the water, and sending you off on a suicide trail is a marvellous smokescreen.'

'You didn't see her,' Archie insisted. 'She's devastated. The idea that Harry committed suicide is tearing her apart. You're way off there.'

'All right, all right – I'm only telling you what I thought.'

'Anyway, you can't necessarily trust what Loveday says,' Archie continued, less abruptly but still a little defensive.

'So everybody says, but she seemed to talk a lot of sense to me.' They both applauded as Lettice executed a surprisingly elegant square cut for four from the last ball of the over, and Josephine decided to change the subject. 'Anyway, discovering Loveday has given me an idea,' she said while the fielders were swapping ends. 'I've got a body on the beach, so I suppose that's a start. I'll worry about who she is tomorrow.' The bowler charged in, seemingly spurred on by his team-mate's success, and there was a dull thud as the ball hit the new batsman's pads. 'That looked pretty plumb to me – I think you're in.' Her verdict was confirmed by Jago's raised finger, and Archie got up. 'Good luck,' she said, and he smiled, the tension between them disappearing as suddenly as it had arrived.

As he walked out to the wicket, Archie had to admit to himself that his reaction to Josephine's hypothesis had

125

surprised him as much as it had her; he was usually more objective. He chose middle and off, and made his mark on the sand.

'Don't make yourself too comfortable, Penrose,' Jacks said behind him. 'You won't be there long.' There was a chuckle from the slips, offered in a good competitive spirit and without a hint of the malice that lay behind the wicket-keeper's remark. Well, thought Archie, if he wanted a fight he could have one. The first two balls were short, and he brushed them easily away towards cover for a couple of runs apiece. Comfortably back in his own crease, he smiled at Jacks. 'It's a shame Harry's not here today,' he said, aware that few things would needle Jacks more than the thought of his old enemy. 'He was always the star of your team.'

'We've started well enough,' Jacks said. 'We don't need him.'

The next delivery veered wildly to the leg side. Jacks dived to his left, but the ball went wide of his gloves and sped to the makeshift boundary for four byes. 'Are you sure about that?' Archie asked as the wicket-keeper picked himself up and scowled. Someone went chasing after the ball, and the estate captain drew back the two slips to create a more defensive field. 'I gather you saw the accident?' Archie said, taking advantage of the fact that everyone else was now out of earshot. Jacks ignored him, but Archie had no intention of giving up that easily. 'I bet your heart leapt,' he goaded, 'and I don't suppose you tried too hard to save Harry.'

'He was past saving, so don't start coming the policeman round here. No one in his right mind would go into the Loe, and I'm certainly not playing the hero for that little shit.'

The ball was returned to the bowler, who, as Archie had suspected he would, tried to make up for the loose delivery by concentrating on a good-length ball. He played a defensive stroke, straight back down the pitch. 'You must have thought all your dreams had come true at once with Harry out the way. It couldn't have worked out better if you'd forced him in there yourself.'

'It wasn't me doing the forcing that morning. You need to look elsewhere for that.'

'You mean there was someone else there?' Archie could have kicked himself for the eagerness in his voice, but he managed to stop short of asking if it was Morwenna. He'd have to sound less desperate for information if he wanted to get anything else out of Jacks, who was clearly enjoying having the upper hand for a while.

'There might have been,' the wicket-keeper said, and crouched down ready for the next delivery.

Archie played the next ball effortlessly off his pads, edging it down to long leg, and was furious when Lettice pushed for a third run which took him away from the strike and from Jacks. Stranded at the other end, he opened his mouth to tell Jago about Christopher, but the umpire told him to be quiet before he could utter a word. 'It's cricket, Archie, not the bar at the Commercial. There's been enough chat from you down the other end.'

Never mind: this was the last ball of the over, and Jacks would be back with him as long as Lettice didn't try too hard to keep the strike. The bowler ran in purposefully, but Slogger had her eye in by now and hit the ball easily away on the off side. It went straight to the man at extra cover and there was no real hope of a single, but Lettice had a habit of being undone by her own optimism and never learned from past mistakes. 'No!' Archie shouted, but she was on her way down the pitch and he had no choice but to run as well. He had started far too late to stand any chance at all: the ball was already coming in from the fielder and, although he dived recklessly for the crease, his bat held out in front of him, he was unlucky with the quality of the throw. Jacks swept the bails off easily, and Archie found himself face down in the dirt.

There were cheers from the crowd and the estate team circled round the jubilant fielder – all but Jacks, who bent down low and spoke quietly to Archie. 'You might want to ask young Christopher Snipe what he was doing out by the lake that morning,' he said. 'He's got a throwing arm almost as good as Roland here, and he put it to good use that day.' His face was so close that Archie could see the spittle at the corners of his mouth, but his pride – or what was left of it – kept him from moving away. 'Christopher doesn't know it, but I saw him waiting for Harry in the bushes with a rock in his hand. I suppose I could have stopped him, but I don't like to interfere in other people's business. It's live and let live down here, except in Harry's case of course, so I let him throw the rock at Harry's horse and I watched as it bolted.' He stood and looked down at Archie. 'If you must know, I was cheering all the way, but I'd like to see you arrest me for that.'

Archie got up and looked at Jago, but he was talking to the other umpire. Jacks, too, had gone off to celebrate with his team-mates, so he walked back to where Josephine was sitting, thinking about what he had heard. Eager to share it with her, he cut short her commiserations on his run-out.

'Do you believe him?' she asked when he had finished.

'I don't know. It might explain why Christopher's suddenly gone missing. Perhaps he *did* know he was seen after all, and thought it was only a matter of time before Jacks mentioned it.

I have to say, it sounds more likely to me than Morwenna taking revenge on a violent brother.'

Anything would sound preferable to that, Josephine thought, but she said nothing. A small boy suddenly appeared from the direction of the church, and ran over to where William was sitting with his increasingly dejected batting side. She and Archie watched as he listened to the boy, then exchanged places with Jago, who hurried back off towards the village. 'I suppose that means curtains for Mrs Trevelyan,' Archie said drily. 'It's reassuring to know that not even cricket can stand in the way of a good send-off.'

'Didn't you tell me that Jacks was in love with Morwenna?' Josephine asked thoughtfully.

'Obsessed by her would be more like it, but what's that got to do with anything?' She just looked at him and raised an eyebrow. 'You're not suggesting that he'd make up something like that to protect her? Surely it's much more likely that Christopher has panicked and run off?'

'Wouldn't he have done that a lot sooner if he was going to?' Josephine knew she was playing devil's advocate, but Archie's stubborn resistance only made her more determined to argue her case.

'Maybe.' He thought about it. 'If it is true, though, I wonder why he'd do it? What could Christopher have against Harry?'

Reluctant as she was to give up her theory, Josephine came clean with Archie and told him what Loveday had said about the fight and Christopher's resentment of it. To his credit, he managed not to look smug. 'That's interesting,' he said. 'I think I'll give Jago a bit of time, then I'll see if he can shed any light on what these secrets might be.'

*

The cricket match was well underway when Jasper Motley made his way slowly down the narrow path which led from the rectory to St Winwaloe's, but he had no desire to take any part in it. If his brother wanted to convince himself that he was running a peaceful estate where everyone lived in perfect harmony with one another, then so be it, but it would take more than a game of cricket and a handful of festive days to make the pretence a reality: it was human nature to hurt and dominate, and that was as true here, in a place of beauty, as it was in the bleakest of city slums. A pretty backdrop was nothing more than that – and he had his own charade to maintain before he concerned himself with William's fantasies.

It was another warm day, and the sweat was already running down his back by the time he had walked the short distance to the churchyard. He stopped just inside the gate, running his finger round the inside of his collar and regretting the excesses of his lunch, and looked out over the yew hedge to the stretch of sand below. There was, he feared, more to the discomfort he felt than indigestion: it was pointless to pretend that what he had overheard in the church that morning had not unsettled him, but the important thing was to keep calm and decide what to do about it. He heard Loveday's singsong voice again in his head, and turned instinctively to look at the pile of fresh earth that marked her brother's grave. The girl was a halfwit; you only had to look at her behaviour yesterday to realise that, and, if he had his way, she'd be taken straight to the Union now that Harry was dead – along with that cold bitch of a sister, who seemed completely unable to control her. William would never countenance such a thing, though; apart from anything else, it would be tantamount to an admission of failure on his part. But something would have to be done now that Loveday had started to spout her nonsense to strangers – someone might take her seriously. As it was, he was sure that the dark-haired woman had caught him listening from the vestry; he wondered who she was and what she was doing on the estate.

The path to the south porch took Motley past his own family plot, and he paused briefly by the grave where his sister, Elizabeth, was buried with her husband; next to them, a simple stone stood over the final resting place of William's young wife. Both graves were, as always, marked with flowers, and the understated bluebells – the flower of constancy, he remembered bitterly – opened the door to that familiar twinning of jealousy and spite which accompanied any reminder of his childhood. His earliest memories were of exclusion and resentment: despite being born between his brother and sister, he had never been able to insert himself into their affections or, failing that, to undermine the bond they had with each other. His parents had always been scrupulously egalitarian in their love, but that simply made Jasper despise them for being too dishonest to admit that he was cared for less than the others, and, in any case, no amount of fairness could compensate for the injustice of being born in second place. As he grew up, he learned to reward himself with petty retaliations – usually against his sister – to show how little he needed their approval or any wholehearted acceptance into the precious family ring. If he could not be part of something, it seemed reasonable to him to sully or destroy it – and, before he knew it, that childish logic had become the private religion upon which Jasper built his adult existence.

He turned away from his buried resentments and went back inside the church, where he sat down heavily in the vestry. The slightest exertion left him short of breath these days, and years of immoderate behaviour were finally catching up with him. Is that what it had come to, he wondered, looking around at the tricks of his godly trade. Would a little breathlessness and a modest annuity be all that he had to show for his life? He laughed to himself as he remembered the look on his parents' face when he had announced his intention to go into the Church; they knew as well as he did that he had no calling for it, but he stuck to his decision, realising that it would offer him certain privileges and comforts which it would have been harder to come by any other way. It was a position of power, although he never fooled himself that his teachings could influence anyone: the vast majority of local people went to chapel rather than church, and it wasn't difficult to please a minority who were already convinced of their status. At first, he tried to fake a sincere piety but he soon realised that the effort was more than his flock required; they were creatures of habit, as undemanding in their worship as he was lethargic in his preaching, and he felt no connection with his community. He knew that and so did they, and it would have been hard to say who cared about it less. In the early days, the Church had at least afforded him certain sensual pleasures: the music and intoxicating smell of incense; the chink of coins on a collection plate; the placing of a communion wafer on an eager young woman's tongue. Now, any sensual pleasures he took were as worn and as dirty as the ageing altar cloth.

Which brought him back to the problem of Loveday Pinching and his curate. He had always despised Nathaniel for his faith and his obvious popularity but, after what he had heard earlier, his hatred intensified as any emotion does when mixed suddenly with fear. Determined not to panic, he tried to judge what he could get away with – personally and professionally. His wife would turn a blind eye to most things as long as her standard of living was not affected, and family ties would no doubt outweigh any rumours of pilfering and hypocrisy as far as William was concerned, but the slightest whiff of a more serious scandal would leave his brother no choice but to act, even if it was not a criminal matter, and that was something he absolutely refused to risk. How much did the curate really know, he wondered, and what could be done to ensure that it could never be used against him? He could combat the threat of shame with shame, of course: satisfying his needs in secret was second nature to him after all these years, but no man – if he was honest – was any different, and he had heard Nathaniel asking his God for forgiveness at the altar one day when he thought he was alone – but forgiveness for what? He had no idea what sin Nathaniel was guilty of, let alone any proof, and he doubted that it was serious enough to serve his purpose. As he looked around the vestry, trying not to give in to the anxiety that gnawed away at him, his eye fell on a brown monk's habit which hung next to Nathaniel's surplice and altar robes. He knew it was only the costume for a play, but its insistence on chastity spoke to him as accusingly as if the curate had been present to deliver the reprimand in person, and anxiety turned quickly to anger. Why, after all this time, should he be made to feel guilty by a weak and ignorant boy? And why here, in his own church, where even God had never been able to touch his conscience?

Jago Snipe's workshop was in the village, in a narrow lane which ran between the backs of two rows of houses and rose sharply at the far end. The workshop was on the left-hand side of the street, just where the hill was at its steepest, and

Penrose – feeling the climb in his calf muscles – sympathised with those who had to carry anything other than themselves up the slope. The two-storey building was set back slightly from the road, and the sound of sawing came from the ground floor, making it clear where Jago was to be found. Penrose walked across the yard towards a set of double doors, whose paintwork – which was chipped and rather shabby – claimed the colour of brick but not the endurance. The right-hand door was open, and a solid chain and padlock hung redundant from its handle. Penrose could see Jago inside, bent low over a piece of wood and dressed in a pair of bib-and-brace overalls, pulled hurriedly on over the shirt he had worn for the cricket match. The undertaker was intent on his work, and only looked up when Penrose knocked.

'Archie,' he said, sounding surprised and a little suspicious. 'What are you doing here?'

'I wanted to talk to you about Christopher, but we can make it another time if you're too busy.'

Jago glanced over at another man who was busy polishing the lid of a coffin towards the rear of the workshop. 'Take a break, Jim,' he said, 'You're making a first-class job of that, and we've got a bit of time yet.' Jim looked curiously at Penrose, but gladly exchanged his cloth for a packet of tobacco and nodded as he went out into the yard. Jago beckoned Penrose inside. 'Whatever it is you've got to say, you'll have to do it while I'm working. Mrs Trevelyan won't bury herself.'

'That's fine,' Penrose said. 'I won't keep you long.' He stepped into the narrow, low-ceilinged workshop and looked around. The building was out of the sun and very little daylight made it over the threshold, so a row of hurricane lamps provided the light to work by. Two benches, each about four feet wide, ran end to end, punctuated by heavy wooden vices and decked with large piles of shavings. There was a stack of oak by the door, and a larger pile of elm – more suitable for most people's pockets, Penrose guessed. The wood, which probably came from the Loe estate, was laid flat with strips in between to allow the air to circulate and season the timber, and the smell of it filled the room, reminding Penrose of a walk through the woods after rain. Several different groups of tools were displayed here and there, sharp and immaculately kept, and Archie was touched to see a set which looked much newer than the rest. He could imagine the pride with which Jago had handed them over to his son, looking forward to the years of working together and, eventually, to the time when he could let the business go altogether, confident that it was in safe hands – the hands that he had trained himself.

He watched as Jago resumed sawing through the elm, carefully judging how far he could go to ensure that the wood could be safely bent to form the coffin sides, and opened the conversation as casually as he could. 'No sign of Christopher yet, then?'

There was a sharp crack, and Jago swore loudly as the wood snapped in his hands. 'Christ, I haven't done that since I was twenty,' he said angrily, looking at the saw as if he could blame it for his carelessness.

Penrose waited while Jago selected another piece of wood, and heard the squeak of the vice as it was clamped viciously in place on the bench. 'Is there anything I can do to help?' he asked.

'You can help by finding my son, not standing round here like a bloody apprentice,' Jago growled, then softened a little. 'If you really want to make yourself useful, you can check that pitch isn't about to boil over. We don't need a fire on top of everything else.'

The outburst surprised Penrose, who had not realised that Jago was anything other than irritated by his son's sudden disappearance. He walked down to the far end of the workshop, past the nearly completed coffin that Jim was making such a good job of, and another two which were half made, presumably for sudden emergencies. The pitch crock – a large iron bucket with a spout and handle – stood right at the back on a primus burner, and was filled with a dark bubbling liquid, the consistency of toffee, which was used to line the coffins. The effect of the whole thing would not have been out of place in *Macbeth*. The heat coming off the stove was no doubt welcome in the winter months, but Penrose found it oppressive in May and was pleased to turn the flame down slightly. He noticed a couple of refectory benches and a group of wooden bowls over in a corner. 'Are those for the play?' he asked, nodding towards the items, whose period feel was out of place next to the more timeless objects that usually came out of the workshop.

'Yes, Christopher made them,' Jago said. 'We're doing the scenery together tomorrow night – at least, we were supposed to be before he went missing.' Archie was about to say something but Jago held up his hand to stop him. He put his ear close to the wood, listening for the slightest crick, but this time the line was cut to his satisfaction. 'It's quite a job, getting anything into that theatre, and not something for one person to do on his own.'

'You're close, aren't you? You work well together.'

'You have to in this job. No point in being at odds with someone. There's a lot of sadness, and you need to keep each

136

other going – otherwise you're no good to the people who really need support. Those who've just lost someone, I mean.'

Penrose came over to where Jago was working and stopped by a table piled high with cardboard boxes marked INGLE-PARSONS OF BIRMINGHAM. The top box was open, and he could see that it contained sets of coffin linings – stretches of ruched white silk, skilfully made and elaborately decorated, some with purple rosettes and others with white. If you could forget what they were used for, they were actually quite beautiful, but he had had enough of coffins lately and turned his back on them. 'Why are you so concerned?' he asked. 'Christopher hasn't even been gone for twenty-four hours yet, and he's sixteen. Lots of boys his age stay out all night occasionally.'

'Not Christopher. He wouldn't do that without telling me and, even if he did, he'd turn up for work the next morning. This is not the sort of job where you can come and go as you like, and he's got a sense of responsibility.'

In spite of his weariness with funerals, Penrose found himself fascinated by the speed with which Jago worked. It was second nature to the undertaker after all these years, but the level of craftsmanship was extraordinary, and Penrose had to remind himself that he was here for a reason. 'Does your concern have anything to do with Harry's death?'

Jago stopped working for the first time and looked at him sharply. 'What do you mean?'

'Oh come on, Jago. We've always been friends, haven't we? When my mother died so quickly after my father, it was you who got me through it – you and William and Morveth. You made it clear that I was part of this place even though my parents were gone, but you didn't exactly give me a warm welcome yesterday, did you? You treated me like a stranger, and that was because I was asking questions about Harry.'

'I didn't want to upset Morwenna,' Jago said. 'She's had enough to put up with, and Harry's death is best forgotten.' He turned back to the wood and took a pencil and rule out of his top pocket, then made a carefully measured mark on each side of the coffin.

'You of all people should know the dead aren't so easily left alone,' Penrose said. 'Give Morwenna a bit more credit than that.' He watched as Jago drilled into the marks on the wood, and tried another approach. 'I had a word with Kestrel Jacks at the cricket match.'

'So I noticed. Since when have you two been best friends?'

Ignoring the remark, Penrose said: 'He says he saw Christopher out by the lake on the morning that Harry died.' Jago swept the shavings into his hand and put them on the pile. He took a small brown-paper parcel from a box behind him and unwrapped a brass handle ready to test the hole for size, but he said nothing. 'In fact,' Penrose continued, 'Jacks said that Christopher threw something at Shilling to frighten him, and that made the horse bolt.'

Jago looked up, and his shock was obviously genuine. 'Are you saying Christopher killed Harry?' he asked.

'I'm not saying anything. I'm just trying to piece together what really happened – for Morwenna's sake, more than anything. She thinks Harry killed himself.' He expected another look of surprise, but Jago merely nodded. 'You knew that?'

'Morveth said as much.' The undertaker was silent for a moment, and Penrose gave him time to think. 'He was desperate to tell me something at the funeral, you know – well, you were there. But I was cross with him about that slip at the altar, and it had been such a bloody awful day, so I just sent him away. If only I'd listened.'

If only indeed, thought Penrose. Apart from anything else, Christopher might have been able to tell them if anyone else was around that morning. 'Was that the last time you saw him?' he asked gently, and Jago nodded again. 'Is it likely that Christopher could have done something like that?'

'Yes,' the undertaker said at last. 'Yes, I suppose it is.'

'Why?'

Jago took a piece of sandpaper and began to smooth down blemishes that were invisible to Penrose, but the undertaker was nothing if not a perfectionist. 'It's because of Loveday.'

'Loveday?' Penrose asked, then remembered Jago's sensitivity to his innocent remark the day before.

'Yes. She was always hanging around here, and we thought nothing of it at first.' Thinking nothing of a fourteen-year-old hanging round coffins seemed a strange reaction to Penrose, but he reminded himself that the reaction to death down here was very different from up country. 'Then Christopher started getting keen on her, and there was obviously more to it than friendship. One day, I caught them in here alone and I had to lay the law down to him myself, tell him that it wasn't right what he was doing – not with that girl, anyway. Harry found out about it, too, and I doubt that his words of warning will have been as gentle as mine were. I don't know what he said to the boy, but Christopher hated him after that.'

'Why did you object so strongly to Christopher seeing Loveday?'

'She's far too young, and anyway, she's been ... well, she's damaged. You know that as well as I do. Boys of his age – they're easily tempted, and I didn't want him to take advantage of her and land himself in a mess.'

'Loveday says she saw Christopher in the churchyard last night,' Penrose said.

'In the churchyard? What the devil would he be doing in the churchyard? Did she take him there?'

'No, he didn't see her apparently, but she said he was near Harry's grave.'

'And then what?'

'I don't know. She came home because she thought she was going to get into trouble with Morwenna for staying out late.'

Jago rubbed his hands over his eyes. 'Christ, this is even worse than I thought. Anything could have happened to him.'

'Not necessarily,' Penrose said. 'I don't think for a minute that Christopher ever intended to kill Harry, but if he was feeling guilty, and if he'd plucked up the courage to tell you but didn't have the chance, it would be understandable if he simply decided to take the easy way out and run off rather than face people. He'll probably come back of his own accord but, if not, there are ways of finding him and reassuring him. He's not facing the gallows, for God's sake – it sounds like a childish act of spite, and anyone would take that into account.'

'He's not a child, though, is he? Not in the law's eyes. And what if he hasn't run off? What if someone knows what he did and blames him for Harry's death? They might have hurt him.'

Jim came back in, clearing his throat tactfully, but Jago was caught up in his own fears and seemed oblivious to anything else. Penrose moved sideways to allow the assistant to take one of the lining sets out of its box. He washed his hands at a small sink near the stove and then, back at his bench, carefully removed the protective tissue paper and unfolded the silk.

There was a small pillow made of the same material, and he filled it with some of the wood shavings from the pile before arranging the rest of the silk inside the coffin, cleverly putting in nails to create a quilted look. There was something very moving about his unhurried attention to detail, Penrose thought, and the quiet satisfaction he took from the work. He remembered William telling him that Jago had once caught one of his assistants cutting back on the coffin materials for a tramp who was found dead on the beach, and had sacked him on the spot; the coffin would be lined even if there was no one to view the body, and he refused to work with anyone who differentiated between the dead. He was one of the most honourable men that Penrose had ever met – the sort of man it was a privilege to know – and he felt deeply for him now, at the same time as being infuriated by the fact that he was obviously holding something back.

He took Jago's arm and moved him out into the yard, where the afternoon sunlight took them both by surprise. Looking away down the street, the undertaker said: 'Please find him, Archie. I can't lose him – not now, not after all these years.'

It was a strange way of phrasing it, Penrose thought, but he was touched by the request. Jago was cast in the role of prop by the whole community, and it did not come easily to him to ask for help. 'I'm not official here, Jago,' he said. 'If it turns out that Christopher needs more than a bit of friendly advice, I'd be treading on toes to give it.'

'But you know the estate, and the people know you – they'll talk to you.' He attempted a smile. 'If you can get Jacks to open his mouth, you can do anything.' Perhaps he'd opened his mouth a little too readily, Penrose thought, remembering what Josephine had suggested and regretting being so prickly with her about Morwenna; in his heart, he wouldn't trust a word Jacks said. 'You're a fair man, Archie,' Jago added. 'If Christopher's done something wrong, he'll have to be punished, but he's a good lad really. I just want to know he's all right.'

Penrose gave in. 'I can't promise anything, but I'll see what I can do.' They turned back towards the workshop. 'William told me you found Harry's body when it came ashore,' he added.

Instantly, the defences came up again. 'What of it?' Jago said, stopping by the doors.

'Nothing in particular. I was just interested in what Morveth did out on the lake.'

'It was probably a coincidence, but at least it gave the girls some comfort. It's not knowing that breaks people.'

'Was Christopher with you at the time?'

'No, thank God. The body wasn't a pretty sight after being in the water all that time.'

'But surely he helped you afterwards?'

'No, he didn't, but there's nothing to read into that. I don't let him near any drowning.'

'You weren't protecting him for any other reason?'

'Like what? I didn't need any other reason. Do you think a sixteen-year-old should be exposed to that sort of misery? My father broke me into this business gently. He didn't let me near a drowning until I was a man, and I fully intend to offer Christopher the same courtesy. Even so, I can still remember the first time I had to put a drowned man on a stretcher – the smell of it, the touch of his skin, or what was left of it.'

Penrose acknowledged to himself that it was the same in his own job. As a young detective constable, he'd been lucky enough to work for a boss who had carefully judged when he was ready to face the more unpleasant crime scenes, and the sergeant had managed to protect him without making him feel patronised or useless. 'I'm sorry,' he said.

'It's all right. You and I both remember a time when kids had to grow up too quickly – you were one of them. But war's one thing – let's not destroy the innocence of a peacetime generation earlier than we have to. I know you think I'm over-reacting, but can't a father be worried about his son? What if someone's taken him to punish me?'

Penrose was taken aback. 'Punish you? What have you done to make enemies?'

Jago seemed to have no answer to that, and was saved from having to find an explanation by the sound of footsteps coming up the lane. A boy of about ten appeared, panting hard and flushed pink by the sun. 'Mum sent me to say you can come whenever you like, Mr Snipe,' he said. 'Miss Wearne's finished now, and the parlour's ready.'

'All right, lad, well done. We won't be much longer.' He turned to go back inside, already removing his overalls. 'I've got to go,' he said to Penrose, but Penrose was not so easily dismissed. 'Look, Jago,' he said, catching hold of his sleeve. 'I *will* do my best to find Christopher, but you have to be straight with me. Is there anything else I should know about Harry's death?'

Jago looked straight at Archie, but his eyes were unreadable. 'There's nothing else to know,' he said firmly. 'Please – just find my son.'

Chapter Eight

The music drifted across the Bar as the fair got underway, replacing the deceptive serenity of the cricket match with a Celtic brand of merrymaking that seemed much less alien to the Cornish sand. It was not yet dark, but a bonfire had already been lit in the centre of the beach, and it threw its warmth and energy out to a growing band of dancers. They cheered as the musicians – a young trio of concertina, fiddle and tin whistle – struck up another round of jigs and reels, gathering speed as they went and seemingly oblivious to anything other than the next tune. Behind them, where the shingle met a rough stretch of grass, a row of colourful makeshift stalls had been set up with an almost magical efficiency, and stood facing the sea from a safe distance. Some of the vendors were peddling cheap and cheerful trinkets, but most offered food which was no less appealing to the eye: jars of sweets stood in rows of silver and scarlet and green, interspersed with slabs of toffee and long, pink sticks of peppermint rock; clean, white cloths were spread with tiny plates of limpets, mussels, shrimps and other tasty delicacies at a penny a time; and freshly baked breads, mixed with the distinctive deep yellow of saffron, threatened to spill out from their baskets as they were carried amongst the revellers. The whole beach buzzed with the excitement of a high-spirited crowd determined to make the most of a weekday holiday, and to forget about work the following morning.

Joseph Caplin drained the cider from his glass and watched Loveday as she moved through the fair. She stopped near the band, entranced by a marionette which kept time with the music, and her upturned face and long blonde hair reminded him – as it always did – of his own young daughter, or how she might have been had she lived beyond those four short years. Joseph had grown up determined to be different from the unhappy man his father had been, always so dissatisfied with the gruelling monotony of life on the farm, and capable of communicating only through work or through sex. Unlike his parents, he had married for love and, when his wife left him for another man just days after bearing their second child, he remembered the resentment which had constantly eaten away at his father and fought against it in his own life, even though he had much more to be bitter about. Forced to cope on his own with a young daughter and a baby, he had vowed still to be the father he had always wanted to be even if he could no longer be the husband, and he worked harder than ever, comforted by the fact that his days moved along familiar paths, worn as deep into the fabric of the community as the ruts in the tracks between the fields.

William Motley had been good to him, and had found him some help with the children and the house. He remembered every inch of that cottage as it was in those days – back when he was proud of it, back when he still had a reason to care if the blue slate slabs on the kitchen floor were clean or the tiny windows in the rooms upstairs were so rotten with rain that they no longer fitted well enough to keep the draught out. He remembered how glorious the small parlour had looked in the days leading up to Christmas, warm from the glow of the fire, the sideboard already piled with dates and nuts and holly from their own garden. He sold his father's watch for the presents and went into Penzance for something more special than the shops in Helston could offer. When he returned, clutching his daughter's new blue jumper to his chest, he remembered thinking that he wouldn't have swapped places with anyone in the world. She had been so thrilled to find the parcel under the tree and had plagued him to let her open it early; eventually, three days before Christmas, he allowed her to unwrap it and it was hard to say who was more excited when she tried it on and strutted round the cottage in it. It would be filthy by Christmas morning, no doubt, but what did that matter compared to her joy now? That night, he was so tired that he dozed in front of the fire, his daughter on his lap. While he slept, she slipped from his arms and climbed onto a chair to admire herself again in the mirror over the fireplace. As she leaned forward towards the looking glass, a flame caught the bottom of her skirt, and he was awoken by her screams. Disoriented, and praying to be still asleep and the victim of a hideous nightmare, Joseph put the fire out, covering her small body with his own, but she was already too severely burned. She died in hospital two days later, and was buried before the new year. His wife had not come to the funeral.

The beach was more crowded now, and it seemed to him that the whole of the estate had come out to enjoy itself. He watched as couples and young families walked around the fair, relaxed and happy to be together, and he was suddenly overwhelmed with sorrow that he would never see either of his children in love and married. He had given his baby up after the accident, before they could come and force him to do it. He knew that he wasn't capable of looking after a child, but didn't want to give anyone else the satisfaction of making his decision for him, so he walked to the Union the day after his daughter's funeral and handed the baby over at the gate, trying not to notice the pity in the woman's eyes. He went straight across the road to the nearest bar and drank as much as he could pay for, determined to prove to himself that he was unfit to be a father, and to resist the temptation to run back to those gates and say it had all been a mistake. It was a Friday, and the bar was packed with people by six o'clock. A group of young fishermen had been there, surrounded as usual by women. As he watched them, Joseph felt his father's resentment coming back to him like an unwanted legacy. If his wife hadn't left him, if there weren't men like that in the world, handsome young men to whom words and charm came easily, his life would have followed that well-worn path, uneventful but content. He had hated them then, and he hated them still for turning him into the man he had never wanted to be.

Voices were raised in song around the bonfire now, rowdy but good-natured, and it reminded him of a different life. It was the same comfortable sound that accompanied his going to sleep on Friday and Saturday nights, when the men from the estate passed his house singing on their way home from a night out in Helston after a hard-working week. Some held the notes as steadily as they held their drink, others were worse for wear and broke the melody, but the voices and laughter sounded sweet in the road outside, mingling with his drowsiness and the warmth of his wife's body next to him, with the security of four walls and the promise of a life to come. He closed his eyes, weakened by this persistent nostalgia for memories that were not truthfully his. When he opened them again, he saw Loveday looking at him curiously and her very presence seemed to taunt him. Fire had not been able to tear her family apart. What made them so much stronger than him? He threw his glass down on to the sand and turned towards the coastal path that led to the village. He needed something stronger than cider. It was harder these days to forget.

The soft sea wind stirred the leaves of the ancient oaks and sycamores as Josephine and Archie wandered back through the woods to Loe House. 'There's something about a fair,' she said, stopping to admire a pair of swans as they flew low over the evening lake. 'All those miserable months I spent in Nottingham were worth it just for that one week when the Goose Fair arrived.'

Archie smiled at her. 'I'm not sure we can compete with that, but I'm glad you had a good time.'

'Don't put yourself down – you've got the sea on your side.' They rounded a bend in the track, and the Lodge came into view on the opposite side of the water, grey and solitary in the waking starlight. 'And the company's better, of course,' she added, taking his arm, 'even if it is a bit quiet. I hope you're not still smarting over that run-out.'

'Don't even mention it,' he said through gritted teeth. 'Sometimes I wonder which side Lettice is on – she took nearly as many of our wickets as they did.'

'Yes, but you can't knock a hundred and three not out. And I don't think the name "Slogger" really does her justice – there was a lot of finesse in some of those boundaries. Anyway, you certainly wouldn't have won without her.'

'No, you're right, as much as I hate to admit it. But that's not why I'm quiet. To be honest, I was just enjoying the peace – it's been a strange couple of days, and I think I might have got caught up in things which are really none of my business.' He told her about his conversation with Jago, and the promise he had made to look into Christopher's disappearance.

'That doesn't sound like much of a holiday to me.'

'I know, but what can I do? They're my friends.'

'And you feel guilty for never being here, so you think this might make up for it.'

'Something like that. Next time we want some time together by the sea, remind me to book a weekend in Brighton.' She raised an eyebrow. 'Sorry, you've got your reputation to think of. What would the good people of Inverness say if they opened their *Tatler* over breakfast and saw you letting your hair down on the pier with Scotland Yard?'

'I think they'd be sorely disappointed. It's nowhere near as exotic as some of the things they imagine I get up to.' They reached a fork in the road, and took the path that led past the stable block and through the walled gardens to Loe House. 'So what *are* you going to do about Christopher?' she asked.

'Well, I can't do much tomorrow because of this wretched play but, if he hasn't shown up by Wednesday, I'll have a word with the local station here and ask around a bit on the estate, then put a call in to Bill just in case he's gone further afield. Apart from that, I don't really see what I *can* do. You might have another word with Loveday for me, though – she's the last person to have seen him as far as we know.'

'Of course, but if you don't mind, I'll leave her sister to you.'

'It's a deal.' The gentle, contented sound of a horse came from the stable block and Archie saw Josephine glance towards the door. 'Go and have a look if you like,' he said. 'The world and his wife's at the fair, and there'll be nobody around at this time of night. You'll love it – William's as discerning about his horses as he is about his cars, and I know you're dying to see Shilling.'

'All right. I won't be long, though.'

'Take your time. I'll go and see what the Snipe's got for supper.'

The stable block was built of handsome grey stone and took up three sides of a large courtyard, with the fourth open to the ornamental parkland beyond. Horseshoes hung over the arched door, and inside there was a soft light from four hurricane lamps which were nailed to a beam. It was a scene of extraordinary peace, and the only noise came from the horse nearest to her, who – wary of a stranger but interested nonetheless – offered a low-pitched nicker as she entered. She was on her way over to return the greeting when one of the estate workers emerged from a stall further down with a sack of oats in his hand.

'Oh, I'm sorry,' she said, startled. 'I didn't mean to interrupt, but I didn't think there was anybody here. I'm staying at the Lodge and I can never walk past a stable.'

The man grinned at her. 'No reason why you should have to, Miss – they're friendly enough, and you're not interrupting. Come and say hello to them. I wasn't expecting to see anyone either – most people are down at the fair.'

'You weren't tempted, then?' she asked, walking over to the nearest box.

'No, not this year,' he said, and carried on measuring out the feed. 'I usually go, but I've got to hold on to my money at the moment.'

'Saving for anything special?'

Most of the blush was lost as he turned back to the stalls, but she could still see enough of his shyness to warm to him instantly. 'Yes, if she'll have me. I want to take her somewhere nice, so I chose the short straw and let the other lads go off to the fair.' He stroked the neck of the horse nearest to him. 'It's not that short, though, if you ask me – they're a fine lot, these creatures.'

They were indeed, Josephine thought. She looked down the line at the horses; some of them were working animals and others very fine hunters, but they all shared the brightness and vitality that came only from good, knowledgeable care. Their names were over their boxes – Gilbert, Sorrel, Violet, Diamond and Boxer – and five very different faces looked back at her, curious and attentive, with ears which were seldom still.

'They're in grand condition,' she said admiringly.

'Oh yes – Mr Motley doesn't stint on his horses.' He watched as Josephine held her hand out to the dark-grey Percheron, making no attempt to pat or slap him but gently touching his mane, emulating the nibbling action of another horse's mouth. 'You know about horses, then?' he asked, impressed.

'A bit,' she said, as Gilbert twisted his head round and returned the compliment so vigorously that she wondered if the sleeve of her coat would ever look the same again. She glanced round at the other horses and noticed a magnificent grey hunter at the far end of the stables, set slightly apart with no name above its stall. 'Is that Shilling?' she asked, and the man nodded. Josephine looked for a long time at the animal she had heard so much about, and couldn't remember when she had last seen anything as beautiful.

'He's something else, isn't he?' he said, and there was a note of awe in his voice which she had heard before from people who spent their lives with horses. 'Worth a bit more than his name implies. That used to be the standing joke.' He walked slowly over to the horse, but stopped when Shilling began to flare his nostrils nervously.

'He must have been very disturbed by what happened,' Josephine said.

'Yes, he was, and I suppose he's bound to be a bit suspicious of people after what he's been through. He hates water, you know – even rain – so it's not hard to imagine how he must have felt in that lake.' He held his hand out to the horse, who continued to flick his tail from side to side. 'I'm sorry you had to go through that, my boy,' he said softly, and turned back to Josephine. 'I thought they were pushing their luck to use him for the funeral, but he seemed to get through it all right so he must be getting a bit of his old confidence back.'

Another horse nudged his arm, as if to remind him of his duty, and he obliged with a generous helping of oats. 'All right, Violet – how could anybody forget you?' he said fondly, as the old face nuzzled him eagerly.

Josephine looked over Violet's gate and saw the C mark branded on a back which was hollow with age. 'Is she a war horse?' she asked.

'Yes. She's the only one we've got left now, but there were several here at one time. Mr Motley went over to bring as many back as he could – anything to stop them being sold off to French butchers. I remember one in particular, a chestnut called Timber. She'd lost an eye in the Dardanelles, but she was sound as a bell otherwise and God, was she a beauty. When you gave her her head, it was like riding fire.'

What a powerful image, Josephine thought. She watched as Violet ate contentedly. The hair around her muzzle was mostly grey, but her eyes were half-closed in delight and it was hard to believe that she had ever been shipped off to a world which was as unfamiliar and horrifying to her as it had been to her human counterparts. 'At least she found a good home in the end,' she said.

'And it's no more than she deserves after what she's been through. It must have been terrible for them – flogged through the mud by city men who hadn't a clue about horses.'

Josephine had to agree. She remembered one letter that Jack had sent her just before he was killed. He'd described finding a mule in the middle of the road with both of its forelegs shot away. The poor brute was battling with the mud, writhing and tossing its head, and trying desperately to get to feet which were no longer there. Jack had stopped to put it out of its misery with a bullet and, in so doing, had probably risked his own life and those of his companions – but there were no complaints. It was a long time before the image stopped visiting her in her dreams, and it had never lost its horror. 'Sometimes it's too easy to justify the cost,' she said, stroking Violet. He said nothing, and she wondered if he was quietly thanking fate for the handful of years which had kept his generation from that conflict, or imagining when his turn would come. They stood in silence for a while, both of them taking pleasure from the horses' obvious happiness. 'I'd better go,' she said at last, 'but I'll drop in on them again if that's all right?'

'No problem,' he said, and turned back to his work. 'If it's not me, just tell whoever's here that you're at the house and they'll let you stay as long as you like.'

Josephine took a last, admiring look at Shilling, and went to find Archie and supper. The elegant line of a formal laurel hedge, dotted with tall, exotic-looking palms, led her on towards the house but she paused at the edge of the kitchen gardens for a moment, enjoying the silence of the evening and the illusion that the crumbling, red-brick walls could somehow protect these ordered, domestic areas from the unhappiness that trespassed on the rest of the estate. She was a guest here and the problems were not hers; nevertheless, she welcomed a peace which seemed as precious and as fragile as the flowers grown in the nearby hothouses. She walked on after a few minutes, through an old arched gate, and was pleased to see that Archie had left some lights on to show her the way. The back door opened straight on to the dairy, where black and white marble slabs on the floor and a series of broad slate shelves along the length of the walls made for a chilly, unwelcoming room that she was glad to leave behind. A short corridor with larders on either side led to the kitchen, and she was drawn towards the cheerful sound of voices. She stood unnoticed at the door for a second, watching as Archie wrestled a large ham out of the oven under the Snipe's careful supervision; Ronnie was perched on a wooden tinderbox by the hearth, entertaining her father with a long and salacious story about Gertrude Lawrence, while Lettice chipped in and picked idly at the dishes laid out on the kitchen table. Brief as the scene was, it gave Josephine a marvellous sense of how it must have been in that kitchen while the girls were growing up, and the insight into this small, private world – a carefree haven from the responsibilities that lay outside – both warmed and saddened her; whether the sadness was because she sensed that this haven was now under threat, or whether it was a more selfish longing for something similar in her own life, she chose not to analyse.

William was the first to notice her. 'Ah, Josephine – lovely to see you,' he said, getting up to welcome her with a kiss. 'Did you manage to find Shilling?'

'Yes, and he's magnificent,' she said. 'There's no doubt about that, but he's obviously finding it difficult to choose between proud and haunted at the moment – not unlike someone else who's grieving for Harry, I suppose.' She looked at Archie, who nodded in agreement. 'They're all beautiful in their own way, though – and I'm afraid I already have to confess a particular soft spot for Violet.' William looked pleased, and she guessed that her preference reflected his own. 'The estate must have lost a lot of horses to the war – it's nice to see that you got some back.'

'Oh, it was terrible,' William said. 'We had to beg the ministry to leave us something to breed from. The money was welcome, if I'm honest, but I'd rather have managed without it – it was heartbreaking to lose so many of them, especially when I knew damned well what I was losing them to.' He thought for a moment, and Josephine imagined the horrific scenes that must have greeted him in France when he went to fetch those poor, bewildered animals. 'They say that seven thousand horses were killed in a single day at one stage,' he added quietly. 'Just blown to bits, and I suppose they were the lucky ones. You wouldn't wish what the rest of them went through on your worst enemy. Lots of them starved slowly to death, you know – the men used to have to punch hole after hole in the girth just to keep the saddles on. Poor creatures – it was never their mess.'

'You could say that about the men, too.' Josephine spoke softly, hoping that Archie was too busy with the Snipe to overhear; he was already preoccupied, and this was not the time to give him reason to dwell on ghosts from his own terrible war. 'Very few of the people responsible for the mess actually had to deal with it.'

'Yes, but at least the men knew why they were there. You can't expect a horse to understand why he has to leave somewhere as beautiful as this.' Ronnie and Lettice had begun to carry the food through to the library, and William rinsed his cup at the sink, ready to help. 'Still, we got a fair few back,' he said, 'and they've had as good a life as we could give them ever since – no one could stop us doing that.' He smiled, and Josephine caught a glimpse of the determination which he had passed on to his daughters. It was an attractive quality.

'You're lucky with your stable hands, anyway,' she said. 'The horses are very well looked after.'

'Harry's a hard act to follow, but everyone's pulling his weight,' he agreed. 'When things settle down a bit, we'll look for someone permanent but, in the meantime, the lads are all doing their share. They're a credit to the estate.' Josephine didn't embarrass William by suggesting that the credit was largely his, and held the kitchen door open for him and the ham. 'Thanks, Dora,' he called over his shoulder.

'Yes, thanks,' Archie said, embarrassing the cook with a kiss. 'You've done us proud as usual. Can you manage that tray, Josephine?'

She nodded, but lingered behind in the kitchen until he was out of sight. 'I saw Beth Jacks was at the cricket match,' she said with an attempt at nonchalance. 'How is she?'

'Not too bad, Miss, thank you.'

'You mentioned another woman last night, Mrs Snipe – someone else from the village who was in the same situation. Did you mean Morwenna?'

'Morwenna Pinching? Why would you think that?' She looked hard at Josephine, then went over to the door and closed it quietly. When she sat down at the table, she seemed unable to meet Josephine's eye. 'I was very young when I got married, Miss Tey,' she said, and Josephine realised with horror what she was about to say. How could she have been so insensitive? 'My husband – well, it turned out he was a weak sort of man, but he made up for that with his fists. At first, it was only when he was drunk. He'd come home late every Friday night, and anything I said would start him off. Then he acquired what you might call a taste for it.' Her hands – red and rough with years of work – played restlessly with a loose piece of cotton on her apron, and Josephine could only begin to imagine how difficult it was for this proud, reserved woman to make such a confession. Once again, she cursed herself for prying into things which did not concern her, and wondered what on earth she could do to make this less excruciating for both of them. 'It was much worse when he was sober,' Dora Snipe continued. 'It took him longer to tire of it.'

'I'm sorry,' Josephine said quietly. 'For what you've been through, and for arguing with you last night. You're right – it's none of my business. It was stupid and naive of me to interfere.'

'You meant well, Miss Tey – and don't think I don't agree with some of the things you said. But it's difficult for anyone who hasn't been through it to understand. Of course women shouldn't put up with that – but somehow we all do. You get used to the bruises, but not the humiliation – and it's the humiliation that keeps you quiet. Men understand that.'

'What happened to your husband?' Josephine asked gently, trying not to look sorry for her: the one thing for which she would not be forgiven here was pity.

'He disappeared,' she said, and then, noticing Josephine's expression, 'but there's no mystery about it – I know what happened, or most of it, at least. Charlie – that's him – used to be clever enough not to touch my face, but one day he forgot himself and Jago saw me before I could get rid of the bruise. I denied it, but he knew his own brother. He was so angry, and that frightened me more than Charlie ever had, I think – seeing how upset he was. He swore he was going to teach him a lesson, and he must have done because I never saw Charlie again. He came to fetch his things from our cottage one day when I was out, and that was that.' She shook her head at the memory of it. 'You'd think Jago would have stuck with his own family, wouldn't you, but he didn't; he chose to drive his own flesh and blood out of the village rather than ignore what he knew was wrong. I obviously married the wrong brother, didn't I?' She attempted a laugh. 'Jago told everyone that Charlie had gone up country to look for work. Nobody believed him but they all pretended to, like people do when they'd rather not know the truth. It's never been spoken of since.'

'Does William . . .'

'Oh no, Miss,' the Snipe said before Josephine could finish. 'Nor Archie and the girls. It all happened before I came to them, and I haven't looked back since – never needed to. They're my family now. I'd be grateful . . .'

It was Josephine's turn to interrupt. 'Of course,' she said.

'I suppose you're wondering if anyone will do the same for Beth?' Mrs Snipe asked, and Josephine nodded. 'I doubt it. Jacks is very different from my Charlie – there's nothing weak about him, and there's not many that'd take him on, let alone win. And Jago's far too old now to be throwing his weight about.' Josephine remembered how fit and strong the undertaker had seemed when he arrived at the cricket match earlier, and privately questioned Mrs Snipe's judgement on that point, although she had no doubt that it would take something more personal than sympathy for Beth Jacks to make him act again as he had all those years ago. 'Now you go through, while there's still some food left,' the Snipe said, getting up brightly as if nothing more serious than supper had been spoken of. 'And don't worry about Morwenna – Jacks is a brute, but she's the one person he wouldn't hurt.'

That wasn't what Josephine had meant, of course, but she smiled and took her cue to leave. She walked slowly across to the library, deep in thought. Had it ever occurred to Mrs Snipe that her brother-in-law might have done something more serious to Charlie than scare him, she wondered, or did she simply choose to ignore the possibility? And was Jago capable of frightening Harry to death – literally frightening him to death – if he had threatened Christopher or hurt Morwenna, of whom Jago was by all accounts so fond? Somehow, after what she had just heard, Josephine thought that he might be.

Kestrel Jacks took his gun and crept as quietly as possible through the line of fir trees. Normally, he wouldn't have stood a chance at this hour but the moon was on his side, shining down on the old, sunken rabbit earth which lay just ahead of him. He made sure he was within shot of it, and settled down to wait, feeling lucky. After ten minutes or so, he saw a movement in the grass to his left and fired instantly into the middle of a family of stoats. One broke off to the left, and he killed it with his second barrel, but the rest disappeared back underground. He cut a long elder stick with the knife that had been his father's, and knelt down, holding the gun fully cocked in his left hand. The stick rattled in the earth as far down as he could reach, and another desperate creature bolted from the hole, only to be cut down at once. Satisfied, Jacks stood up and walked over to the spot where he had made his first shot. It was better than he expected. Five stoats – one adult and four big youngsters – lay still on the ground, making a total of six dead with three shots. Not a bad night's work, he thought, as he headed for home.

His satisfaction faded as he walked back through the woods to his cottage, where his wife would be waiting. He could hardly bear to be at home these days, so deeply did she disgust him. The more she tried to fade into the background, the more he noticed her; the more submissive she became, the greater was his need to dominate; and the more she tried to be what he wanted, the more he wanted her to be someone else. He should never have married her – he knew that now – but he had needed a wife, and thought that someone as insignificant as Beth Porter would keep herself out of his way. He had reckoned without her gratitude, though: she was older than him, and had long since given up hope of leading anything other than a single life, and he discovered too late that her expectations of happiness were all the stronger for having been so long out of reach. At first he simply ignored her, but the contrast between her feeble devotion and Morwenna's arrogant disdain gnawed away at him, seeming to mock everything he did until he could bear it no longer. The first time he hit Beth, the rage had come upon him with such intensity that he had no control over what he was doing, and it was almost as if the violence belonged to someone else; gradually, he learned how to make it his own, and he now managed his domestic life with the same cold efficiency that he applied to his work.

Jacks opened the back gate and walked up the long, narrow garden to the house. There was a light on in the kitchen and, through the window, he could see his wife pouring some water from the kettle into the sink, turning her face away from the rising steam. She turned round quickly when she heard him at the door, and her expression surprised him; he was used to fear, but this was more like guilt. He saw her glance involuntarily towards the small, square table in the centre of the room, and the look on her face was immediately explained. She opened her mouth to speak, but seemed to realise that lies were pointless; she had not had time to wash away all evidence of her visitor, and he knew what the two cups meant, placed one on either side of the familiar Bible. How dare she invite someone into their home and talk about their marriage behind his back? He didn't have to try too hard to guess the identity of the caller, either: he had seen pity in the curate's eyes whenever he looked at Beth in church, but he never dreamed that Shoebridge would be stupid enough to try to do something about it. The anger came back, as sudden and uncontrollable as it had been in those early days, and his wife seemed to recognise the difference. The terror in her eyes only enraged him more.

He was across the room before she could move, and grabbed her hair with one hand and her jaw with the other. The deep cut on her lip, which had not had a chance to heal, opened again with his touch, and he smelt the sharp, metallic scent of blood as he put his face close to hers. 'Confessing on my behalf, were you?' he asked, and pulled her away from the sink, kicking her legs from under her so that she fell backwards on to the floor. He knelt above her and she started to fumble with his belt, hoping to divert this new violence by re-enacting past humiliations, but he pushed her hands away in disgust. Reaching across to the table, he tore some pages from the Bible and shoved them hard into her mouth. As she choked on the paper, struggling to breathe, he turned her over and pressed her face into the cold, rough flagstones. If he didn't have to look at her, he could almost believe that she was Morwenna.

Chapter Nine

Archie turned the Norton away from the main road, taking a narrow, winding lane which followed the soft undulations of the countryside and enjoying a freedom which he could never find in London. His home county might be famed for its seas, but it was these quiet, inland gems that he most loved her for: the peace of the lake; the rolling hills which formed a backdrop to the village, with Breage Church resting gently on the horizon; the sunrise across the fields on the way to Camborne – all these were ordinary miracles of which he could never tire. He pulled in to a farm gate for a moment and looked out over countryside which was a hundred shades of green, from darkest gorse to pale, sunlit grass. Cornish granite hedges criss-crossed his view, dividing the landscape into small, irregular sections and giving cows and sheep much-needed protection from the wind. To his right, a flock of lapwings rose as one from a ploughed field and he watched as their slow, flapping wing-beats took them leisurely further inland. For work and for pleasure, he had visited some of the finest rural areas that England had to offer, but nothing resonated more intensely with him than scenes such as this – partly, no doubt, because he was born here, but partly because the unrelenting drama of the sea made this mild-tempered, forgiving countryside all the more precious.

He kicked the motorbike into life again and moved off, through the village of St Buryan and steeply down into

St Levan, then past the headquarters of the Eastern Telegraph Company and on towards the coast. The Minack Theatre – named after the enormous rock on which it sat – lay just a few miles short of Land's End and a few feet above the Atlantic, enjoying all the excitement and danger that such a location offered. Archie parked at the makeshift entrance near Minack House and made his way down the steep slope of a cliff. Almost immediately, he had his first glimpse of the white, shell-strewn sands of Porthcurno to the east and, with a few minutes to spare before his two o'clock rehearsal, he paused again to savour the view. The bay was a brilliant blue in the afternoon sunlight, with the majestic cliffs of Porthgwarra and Nanjivey stretching out to the west. As dramatic as the scenery was, though, this wild and lonely cliff was the last place in the world where anyone would expect to find a man-made stage. It must have taken extraordinary imagination and vision even to conceive of the idea, he thought, let alone to make it happen, but Rowena Cade had decided that come hell or high water – and both usually did, at least once a summer – she would have a theatre in her back garden.

As he continued down the cliff, and Miss Cade's vision became his, he thought again how surprisingly natural the whole thing seemed once you got used to the idea. The stage was a beautiful stretch of greensward, bordered on either side by granite outcrops which formed natural wings, and, along the cliff edge, by recently constructed balustrades and walls with a solid stone throne on a dais as centrepiece. The natural curve of the slope had been carefully tiered and turfed to provide the seating, giving the audience a perfect view of the play of the moment as well as uninterrupted sightlines across some of the finest cliff scenery in Cornwall.

'Archie! Over here.' He looked to his right and acknowledged Lettice's wave. She and Ronnie were both on their knees on the grass, in apparent supplication to the robed figure who stood above them on a stool. It was impossible for him to tell who it was because of the heavy cowl that draped the monk's face, but it amused him to see his cousins in any sort of pious position, and he couldn't resist making the most of it.

'I thought the rest of the world knelt to you as far as theatre was concerned,' he said mischievously. 'Surely you're not losing your touch?'

Ronnie, her mouth full of pins, was unable to offer any of her usual tart retorts, but Lettice smiled good-naturedly. 'Actually, you're not as far off as you may think,' she said. 'We could do with a bit of divine assistance, as it happens, and I'm never too proud to beg.'

'I think it's called praying, dear, when God's at the other end of the call,' Ronnie said as she placed the last of the pins in the hem of the habit. 'Although I've never been too sure of the difference.' She patted the monk's thigh in a less than sacred fashion. 'There you go, Brother – all done. Take that off again and we'll get it sewn up for you. It's not the place to trip over your skirt.'

The monk removed its hood and Archie was surprised to see that the brother in question was a woman – the costume had made it impossible to tell. He recognised her vaguely as one of the young farmers' wives from the estate, and she smiled at him shyly before slipping behind one of the rocks to change.

He sat down on the grass next to Lettice and Ronnie and lifted his face to the sun. 'I'm not looking forward to getting into one of those,' he said. 'Don't monks have a summer wardrobe?'

'You don't have a wardrobe at all at the moment,' said Lettice, unscrewing the top of a thermos flask and pouring three cups of strong-looking tea. 'That's what I meant about divine assistance – we haven't got a costume for you.'

'I thought you said Nathaniel's would fit with a few minor adjustments?'

'It would have done – you're only slightly broader than him – but he can't find it anywhere. Says he's sure he left it in the vestry after the fitting but now it's nowhere to be seen. It must have been put into the laundry by mistake.'

'But he's a curate, for God's sake,' Archie said, bewildered. 'Surely you're not telling me that he can't lay his hands on a cassock?'

'Oh, Archie – don't be silly,' said Lettice, a little impatiently. 'You can't just wear any old thing – it's got to fit in with the scheme of the play.'

'Quite right,' Ronnie said, tongue in cheek. 'Just think of what the critics would say – not to mention the *Anglican's Weekly*.' She received a glare of reproach from her sister, and added: 'Lettice has a point, though. You're the narrator and you're on stage all the time, holding the thing together, so you've got to look the part.'

'And we've still got time to run you something up from scratch if we get on with it now,' Lettice said, reminding Archie of the spirit which had taken his cousins to the top of a very slippery profession. 'When Janet's hem is done, everyone else will be sorted. You'll have to do the dress rehearsal in your own clothes, but come up to Minack House when it's finished and we'll have something for you. Rowena's put her work room at our disposal.'

As the girls went off up the cliff, laden with everything they needed to perform the impossible, Archie finished his tea and watched the bustle of activity on stage. Jago Snipe had arrived now and was setting about the unenviable task of unloading scenery from his van at the top of the cliff. He watched as the undertaker carried the simple refectory benches which Archie had seen in his workshop down the narrow path to the stage, putting them in place one by one under Morveth's direction. He was a strong man, more than used to lifting heavy wood, and he made the shifting of the scenery look easy, but there was a poignancy to his solitary task – a task which he seemed to be pursuing with a fierce concentration, as if it could take his mind off the fact that his son was supposed to be helping him. Where *was* Christopher, Archie wondered? He had been sincere in his reassurances to Jago the day before: a lot of missing-person cases had come his way in the course of his career and, while some of them had ended in tragedy, many had concluded with nothing more serious than an embarrassed son or daughter returning home, hungry and contrite. From what Archie had seen of him, Christopher was not the sort of boy who had either the courage or the selfishness to stay away for long, but he had been brought up to respect life and death and, if Jacks was to be believed, Archie wasn't surprised that guilt over his part in the last morning of Harry's life – as childish and out of character as it had been – would sit heavily on his conscience.

A steady trail of people made its way down the cliff, indicating that the bus laid on by Poltroon's, the local garage, to transport villagers and estate workers to and from the Minack had completed its first journey. The early arrivals were those involved in the production, either as cast or crew, and Archie was surprised to see that Joseph Caplin and Kestrel

Jacks – neither of whom he would have had down as aspiring entertainers – were among the crowd. Clearly William's powers of persuasion were not confined to family, he thought wryly as he got up to join everyone.

'You can have half an hour to settle in, and then I want you all back here in your costumes ready to start,' Morveth was saying, and he was amused to note that she had not lost her touch: most of the villagers – himself included – had been taught by Morveth Wearne at one stage or another, and they filed off now as dutifully as they had ten, twenty or thirty years ago in the playground.

'This brings back a few memories,' he said, and she smiled warmly at him.

'As far as I remember, drama was never your favourite subject, so it's nice of you to help us out now.'

The 'us' wasn't intentional, he knew, but the idea that he was an outsider doing a favour struck him all the more forcefully for the casual way in which it had been expressed, and he was irrationally irritated by it. 'It's the least I can do while I'm at home,' he said, unable to avoid placing a slight emphasis on the final word, 'and some would say I've chosen drama for a profession.'

Morveth did not flinch at the rebuke, and seemed amused rather than embarrassed by his offence. 'Then come home more often, Archie,' she said, with that quiet way of defusing any antagonism which had served her so well in teaching. 'Hasn't anyone told you that resting is part of the job?'

Suddenly, he felt like a petulant ten-year-old, inclined to unreasonable tantrums, and could only smile in defeat. 'I'll bear it in mind,' he said, 'but only if you don't put me through this again. What do you want me to do?'

'Well, I gather your costume's still to come, so you've got some time while the others get changed. Why don't you make sure you're familiar with the stage? You'll be standing there,' she continued, pointing to a circle of grass, stage right, which stood about a foot higher than the rest of the performance area, forming a natural platform, 'and you won't be going backstage like the others, so you don't need to worry about all the entrances and exits, but I promised Miss Cade faithfully that everyone would know what was safe and what wasn't. After last year . . .' She tailed off, knowing that the story was legendary enough for her not to have to repeat it. 'If there's any time left, have a look through the script – but don't worry too much. We'll have long enough to run through it carefully.'

Morveth disappeared to make sure that everyone had found their costumes, and Archie walked over to the rear of the stage. He was familiar with the Minack, having been to the productions which his cousins had taken part in, and he knew what to expect when he looked over the balustrade, but the sudden drop to the rocks below still made his heart stop. About eight feet beneath him, there was a narrow path – accessed by two sets of steps – which ran behind the stage area and which the actors used for most of their entrances and exits. Beyond that path, and with only a fragile-looking wire fence in between, the ground simply fell away into nothingness. He leaned further over and looked down into the zawn, a rift in the cliffs which – at high tide, as it was now – was filled with an angry, churning sea. No wonder the balustrade and pillars had been added, he thought; the stage must be eighty or ninety feet above the rocks, and an actor making a wrong move or getting carried away with his performance faced a perilous fall. Apart from anything else, it wasn't good for the nerves of an audience to spend the entire performance in fear of an unscripted accident. As he watched, thinking how easy it was to become mesmerised by the motion of the waves, a woman of about forty with a shock of untidy brown hair – already dressed as a pilgrim for one of the crowd scenes – descended the steps to his right and walked quickly along the backstage path, apparently oblivious to the steep drop at her feet. She stopped immediately below him, where a recess directly under the balustrade offered actors a welcome spot of shelter to await their cues, and took out half a dozen lanterns, which she placed at regular intervals along the edge of the path.

'Billy,' she called back over her shoulder to a middle-aged man in a flat cap, whose tanned, muscled arms wouldn't have looked out of place on someone ten years younger, 'I've put the lanterns in place. Check they're working when you have a minute, will you?'

'Right-o, Miss Cade,' the man said, and set about his task immediately.

Archie watched as the pilgrim went back up the cliff, stopping occasionally to pick up a bit of litter or a stray stone and shadowed by a pair of King Charles spaniels. What an extraordinary woman Rowena Cade was, he thought – he looked forward to meeting her later. Now, he still had a few minutes to spare, so he decided to climb up into one of the granite outcrops that formed the wings and see what the view was like from there. He hadn't got far before he realised that someone else had had the same idea. Nathaniel was sitting with his back against an enormous boulder, out of sight of anyone on stage or in the auditorium, holding the jackdaw costume which should have been Harry's and which he was now due to wear. Unaware that anyone was watching, the young curate lifted the black silk cowl to his lips and held it there. It was a moment of absolute tenderness, and it told Archie more about Nathaniel's feelings for Harry than words could ever have done. He realised that he was intruding, but knew also that to turn and leave without being noticed would be difficult. Before he could resolve his dilemma, Nathaniel glanced up and saw him.

'I'm sorry – I didn't mean to disturb you,' Archie said, noticing how tired the curate looked. 'I'll go back down and leave you on your own.' Nathaniel's face was pale against the dark material and, although he appeared startled at first, he seemed to relax a little when he saw that it was Archie who had discovered his hiding place.

'No, don't,' he said, with a nervous half-smile. 'I mean, you don't have to go if you don't want to. I was just trying to keep out of the way for as long as possible.' He held up the costume. 'Quite frankly, I'm dreading this and I don't know why I ever agreed to go through with it after everything that's happened. For two pins, I'd make a run for it.'

'You and me both,' Archie said. 'The trouble is, compared with the wrath of Morveth, going through with it is the lesser of two evils.' Nathaniel smiled again, and this time the nervousness was gone. He had a very attractive face, Archie noticed – open and sensitive, with intelligent sea-blue eyes and a small furrow in his brow which made him look thoughtful rather than sullen. It was the face of a born cleric, he thought, although judging by what he had just witnessed, Nathaniel's choice of career could hardly have been without conflict.

'I can barely bring myself to put his costume on,' the young man admitted as Archie sat down beside him. 'Not because I'm superstitious – it just doesn't seem possible that he's dead. We grew up together on the estate, and he's the first person I've lost who's always been there. Does that make sense?'

'Yes, of course,' Archie said. He offered Nathaniel a cigarette, and lit one for himself. 'For me, it was my father. My closest friend was killed in the war, and that's something I don't think I'll ever get over, but we'd only known each other since the first year of university. My father – well, that was something else altogether, and you're right – it's a very different sort of grief; not necessarily harder or easier, but definitely different.' He thought for a moment, allowing himself a rare glimpse into the dark days that had followed his father's death. 'When someone you love dies, you're always changed; when you've never known life without them, everything you've ever been sure of is suddenly snatched away.'

'Perhaps it's because it's the first thing that makes you aware of your own mortality,' Nathaniel said.

Archie was silent. No one who'd spent time in the trenches had to wait for a parent or a lifelong friend to die to know that his own time would come sooner or later. Nathaniel had missed that realisation by a few years, but, if Archie's doubts that any lessons had been learned proved justified, the curate would come to understand the paranoia of war all too soon. 'Harry's death must have been difficult for you for lots of reasons,' he said gently.

Nathaniel looked at him sharply, but seemed to realise immediately that there was no point in lying to Archie and, more importantly, no need to try. 'Yes, not least because in some ways it made things easier,' he said. 'Believe me, no one was more shocked than I was when I realised how much I loved Harry – and not just as a friend or a brother. Nothing was the same after that. '

It occurred to Archie that, despite his reputation as a bit of a ladies' man, Harry had never – to his knowledge, at least – had any serious relationship with a woman, and it was rare in this sort of community for a man not to have settled down by his mid-twenties. 'Did he feel the same way about you?' he asked.

'I doubt it, but I don't know,' Nathaniel said. 'I could never have said anything to him. It probably would have disgusted him – and if not, if he *did* have those feelings, that would have been worse in a way: it would have made life impossible.'

'Because of your job?'

'My job, yes, and my family – it took a long time to persuade them that this was right for me.' He stubbed his cigarette out on the rock, and refused another. 'In a way, I asked them for a bigger act of faith than anything I've ever been tested with – until now, that is. And once they were sure it made me happy, they did everything they could to support me. Can you imagine what sort of sacrifices that involved? They're not wealthy people – they work hard, and they get by; they didn't bargain for a son to put through college, but they haven't wavered once. That's real love – how could I ever throw it back at them?'

'Isn't that the point, though? They *do* love you, they're proud of you, and your happiness comes first. They might understand.'

Nathaniel shook his head. 'Of course they wouldn't. I don't, so how can I expect them to? Oh, I don't mean they'd turn me away like a criminal – but they'd think it was their fault, that if they'd done something differently, I'd have turned out all right. And they have never, *ever* done anything wrong – this is my guilt, not theirs. That's another reason why I couldn't tell Harry – I could never have trusted him to keep quiet about it. Can you imagine the shame of it if anyone found out? If I went to prison, for goodness' sake?' He changed his mind about the cigarette, and reached for the packet. 'And I have got a job to do here,' he said earnestly. 'A job that I believe in. I belong here – and everyone on the estate seems to know that. It's not just my parents – the whole community's welcomed me into that church. They want a change after all the greed and hypocrisy that Motley's got away with for so long. They want – they deserve – something real.' Nathaniel realised instantly what he had said, and looked mortified. 'I'm so sorry – I forgot he was family.'

'I wish I could,' said Archie, who was not in the least bothered by the lack of regard in which his uncle was held. 'There's no need to apologise. You know what they say – you can choose your friends . . .'

'Anyway, I can't let them down,' Nathaniel continued, still embarrassed by his *faux pas*. 'The people here trust me, I think, and religion should be about the specific, not the abstract. You have to look after those close to you – your family, your community – and that means having some integrity, not behaving differently when they're not looking.'

The curate's passion and sincerity impressed Archie, who had expected his questions to be deflected with the standard scriptural rationalisations, but he was keen to get back to the subject of Harry, and Nathaniel seemed to sense his impatience. 'Sorry,' he said again, 'you didn't ask for a lesson in pastoral care – but that's why I didn't say anything to Harry about how I felt. That, and the fear of losing him as a friend.'

'You lost him anyway.' It sounded harsh, but, if he were ever to get to the bottom of Harry's death, Archie needed to understand his rift with Nathaniel. 'You were estranged when he died, weren't you?'

'Yes, but that was my fault, not his. I couldn't be around him – it just wasn't right. And he . . . well, he started behaving differently towards me.'

'So he *did* know how you felt?' asked Archie again, surprised.

Nathaniel hesitated for a moment. 'Neither of us ever mentioned it,' he reiterated, 'but I think he must have suspected. He kept . . . well, goading me in a way.'

'As if he wanted you to say something?'

'Perhaps. Or perhaps it just amused him.'

If it was the latter, Archie thought, Harry must have had an exceptionally cruel streak. No wonder the curate had made such a mess of the eulogy: it was never easy to face up to flaws in people you wanted to idolise, and he already felt ashamed of his love for Harry; if Harry had proved himself unworthy of it, Nathaniel's pain – his sense of betrayal – would have been so much worse.

'I just wanted him to go away, you know,' Nathaniel admitted. 'It seems selfish now, but I even prayed for it. Not like this, though,' he added, fighting back tears. 'I never wanted it to happen like this.'

'Did Morwenna know what was going on between you?' Archie asked, and Nathaniel shook his head. 'So the other day, after the funeral, when she said she blamed you for Harry's death – what do you think she meant?'

Nathaniel answered Archie's question with one of his own. 'Did she say he killed himself?'

'Yes, but she couldn't – or wouldn't – tell me why. Do you know?'

It seemed a long time before Nathaniel answered. 'If Morwenna's right,' he said eventually, 'and I hope to God she

177

isn't – but if Harry did commit suicide, it'll be because of something I found out about him. Something I couldn't keep to myself.' Archie waited, knowing he had no authority to press Nathaniel but hoping that the curate would want to talk. 'It was Loveday who told me,' he continued. 'She didn't know what she was saying, of course, but it was about the night of the fire – the night their parents died.'

This was not at all what Archie had expected, but he nodded encouragingly at Nathaniel to go on. 'She told me that she went back downstairs that night, after her parents had gone to bed. She often used to sneak down, apparently. She liked to hide under the table in the sitting room, snuggled up to their dog, and watch the fire die down in the grate. After a while, she heard Harry come downstairs and go into the kitchen. She was worried at first, because the kitchen was under her parents' room and she didn't want Harry to get into trouble – they'd been arguing recently, she said, and there'd been a lot of shouting, although they'd tried to hide it from her. She crept to the door and watched her brother moving about in the kitchen.' He paused, not for dramatic effect but as if he found it hard to believe what he was saying. Archie, who had a horrible idea of what was about to come, realised he was holding his breath. 'She saw Harry take a piece of paper – a letter of some sort – and set light to it in the kitchen fire. He watched it burn for a few seconds, then walked across the room, still holding it. She couldn't see what happened after that because the door was half closed, but he came out soon afterwards and shut the door behind him. She said he was crying when he went back upstairs.'

'So Loveday said that Harry started the fire deliberately, then went back upstairs to die with his parents and his little sister?' Archie's tone was incredulous. 'Did you believe her?'

'I believe that she saw what she says she saw. She didn't draw any conclusions from it – Loveday doesn't analyse things, and she doesn't make connections between events – things just are what they are. People are either good or bad, and she doesn't see any of those grey areas that make life so complicated for the rest of us. But she doesn't lie, either, and she doesn't exaggerate. So yes, I did believe her, and I reacted in exactly the same way as you.'

'Has she never told anyone else all this?'

'Apparently not. She said that no one ever wanted to talk about the fire in front of her – and that's certainly true. I've seen people go quiet the minute she appears. If anyone had taken the trouble to ask, I dare say she'd have told them – but they didn't. Everyone assumed it was a tragic accident, and even Loveday doesn't understand what she saw.'

'But you told Morwenna.'

'Not straight away. I confronted Harry first – I suppose I hoped he'd explain it somehow, and convince me that Loveday had got it wrong.'

'But he didn't?'

'No. He didn't admit it, but he didn't bother denying it either. He just stared at me while I talked – while I shouted – and I don't think I've ever seen anyone look so sad. In the end, he simply turned and walked away. That was the last time I saw him. I had to tell Morwenna after that – I was worried about what he might do to Loveday.'

Archie tried – and failed – to reconcile the Harry Pinching he knew with someone who could harm his parents, let alone his little sister. 'How did Morwenna react?'

'She was hysterical,' Nathaniel said. 'I honestly thought she'd gone out of her mind with shock. First, she screamed at me that it was a pack of lies, then she cursed me for opening old wounds when it could do no good for anyone.'

'Implying that she knew already?'

Nathaniel shrugged, almost dismissively, and Archie could see how much he wished he could simply brush this conflict of loyalties aside. 'I don't know if she knew or simply suspected. She tried to persuade me not to tell anyone else, but I couldn't do it – it didn't seem right to keep quiet about something like that if it was true. She threw me out of the house after that.'

'When was this?'

'A few days before the accident.'

'And *have* you told anyone else?'

'No – not until now. It didn't seem right to betray Harry either.'

'The other day, when Morwenna confronted you – I saw the look on your face when you realised what she meant. The idea of suicide was a shock to you, wasn't it, even with what you knew about the fire?'

'Yes, it was,' he said emphatically, and Archie was sure he was telling the truth.

'So you accepted that Harry's death was an accident?'

'I suppose I thought he might have brought it on himself,' Nathaniel admitted, 'but not in the way Morwenna meant. He'd been drinking heavily lately, and getting into a bit of bother here and there. He took up with Joseph Caplin not so long back, and the two of them were hardly ever without a glass in their hand. I used to wonder how Harry managed to stay on his horse – he was in no fit state to ride anywhere. When I heard what had happened, I assumed he'd pushed his luck too far.'

Why hadn't Morwenna mentioned Harry's drinking, Archie

wondered? He could understand her being loyal to her dead brother's memory, but did she really prefer to believe that he had taken his own life? And if she was so outraged at Nathaniel's raking up the past, why risk it becoming public by mentioning the subject of suicide to a policeman? She must have known he'd ask questions – or had he been in London too long? Was her confidence simply that of a friend unburdening herself to someone she thought she could trust? Reconciling her love for her brother with a sense of justice for her parents must seem an impossible task to face alone – no wonder she'd needed to talk. 'What sort of bother did Harry get into?' he asked.

'Oh, the usual stuff – brawling, gambling, and I heard that he'd run up a few debts. He was barred from the Commercial for a while for getting into a fight with some visitors from up country, and he'd fallen out badly with Jago because of something he'd said to Christopher.'

'That's all a bit out of character, isn't it?' Archie said, frustrated that he seemed to have got only half a story from Jago, too.

'For the Harry we thought we knew or for the man who burned his parents to death in their beds?' It was a good point, to which Archie had no answer. 'It would have been at one time,' Nathaniel continued, 'but he'd changed so much. He was always a bit reckless, but he had a gentle side to him, a caring side – and he loved being with people. Lately, it was almost as if he was trying to alienate everyone who was close to him. Perhaps that was what his behaviour with me was about – he knew I'd keep away rather than confront him. The only time I ever saw a glimpse of the old Harry was when he was with Loveday – she seemed to be the only person he could trust. I know I panicked when I found out about the fire, but he was always the sort of big brother that any kid would want.'

Archie remembered Josephine's suggestion, and how quickly he had dismissed it. Suddenly, he was less sure. 'Did Harry ever hurt Morwenna?' he asked.

'You mean physically? Not to my knowledge.' He thought for a moment, then added: 'I'm sure he didn't – well, as sure as I can be. That's the trouble with finding out a secret about someone, isn't it? You start to doubt everything else about them. I know the change in him hurt her, though. Sometimes I'd catch her looking at him as though she couldn't understand why he was behaving like that, like he'd betrayed her in some way and she didn't know how to reach him any more. She told Morveth that they'd argued on the night he died – she was very hard on herself about that, apparently, and there was nothing Morveth could say to comfort her.'

'And what about you?' Archie asked, conscious of how alone Nathaniel must feel. 'Who do you have for comfort?'

He took a small, leather-bound book from the top pocket of his shirt, a battered old volume which Archie recognised as the Book of Common Prayer. 'I've always had this,' he said, trying to smile. 'It doesn't do a bad job – at least it didn't. You know, since I first picked this book up, I've never been afraid of anything; now, after Harry's death, I sleep with a lamp burning every night. Actually, that's a lie – after what Morwenna said the other day, I hardly sleep at all. All I want to do is forget him, wipe him out of my mind – but he haunts me. I keep thinking about him going into that lake all alone – those waters are so cold, so dark. What sort of despair must he have been in if he really did think that was easier than living? I can't get that out of my head. I've always thought of a loved one's presence after

182

death as some sort of consolation for their loss, an affirmation that it doesn't all just end when we die. But this isn't any comfort – this is hell, and he's beside me all the time, inviting me in.'

Archie heard a noise behind him and looked up. 'So this is where my two leading men have got to,' Morveth said. She spoke lightly but her face was anxious, and Archie wondered how much she had heard. 'I'm sorry,' he said, standing up in front of Nathaniel to give the young man time to pull himself together. 'We've had a touch of stage fright and we thought if we hid here long enough, you might let us off the hook altogether.'

'You'll have to try harder than that, my lad – nothing gets past me. I need my jackdaw to practise his take-off.'

'His what?'

'She means the jump off the balustrade into thin air,' Nathaniel explained, trying to emulate Archie's easy banter. 'Don't worry,' he continued as he saw the look of horror on Archie's face. 'All I have to do is drop down on to the backstage path, but it looks spectacular from where the audience is. It's the highlight of the play, and there'll be someone there to make sure I don't overshoot. We wouldn't do it if it wasn't safe. After last year . . .' He grinned, and handed his costume to Archie. 'Look after this a minute. I'll try it a few times in normal clothes first.'

Nathaniel followed Morveth down on to the stage, leaving Archie holding the habit that Harry should have worn. As he looked down at the black silk, he thought about the strange hold that the dead had over the living: they had buried Harry on Sunday, but he had been by far the most powerful presence of this visit so far. What would have made him set that fire all those years ago? Archie wondered. What was so terrible that he would kill *and* die for it? More to the point, he thought self-ishly, what was *he* supposed to do about it? Was Nathaniel's motive for telling him just the lightening of a heavy burden or a plea for more tangible help? Even if Loveday were telling the truth, and Harry was a killer, he couldn't see what good it would do to open up the case now – perhaps that was what Morveth had meant when she warned him to leave things alone – but it wasn't in his nature to turn a blind eye. So what was he supposed to be – policeman or friend?

Whatever it was, it certainly wasn't an actor, he thought resentfully as he walked down from the wings and took his place on the platform which Morveth had pointed out. The stage felt suddenly claustrophobic to him, and far too close to the audience for comfort. As he looked up at the steep grass slope, imagining what it would be like later when it was full of people, he wished more than ever that he had never agreed to take part in *The Jackdaw of Rheims*.

Chapter Ten

William parked the Lanchester next to Ronnie's Austin, and he and Josephine gathered up the picnic things between them and walked over the brow of the hill towards the sea. The view of the headland stretched out for miles before her, and she could see people making their way in twos and threes to the Minack, following coastal paths or taking shortcuts across fields, laughing and chatting and, for the most part, laden with hampers and warm clothes in preparation for the evening. A table – covered carefully in pristine white linen and giving the air of a vicarage tea party – stood on the lawn in front of the big house, and served as a box office. After a good-natured skirmish in the queue, William reluctantly conceded the right to buy the tickets and the two of them joined a trail of people making their way down a steep, narrow path lined with furze bushes. As the crowd zig-zagged to left and right, eventually striking off in different directions to stake a claim on a patch of turf or find a more sheltered position against one of the rocks, Josephine could not help but think that this was the strangest entrance to a theatre she had ever encountered – but she was by no means the only person to stop in wonder and pleasure at her first sight of the stage itself, crisp and clear in the evening sunlight.

She spread the rug out on the ground about halfway up the auditorium and allowed William to wrestle with the deckchairs, aware of the peculiarity in the male psyche that insisted on mastering anything to do with the outdoors. It was a little after six, and there was still an hour and a half to go before the Minack's equivalent of curtain-up – sundown, she supposed – but already the open spaces were filled with eager theatre-goers and, every now and then, the sound of a popped cork underlined their hopes for the performance ahead. She recognised a few members of the audience: Morwenna was there with Loveday, who waved excitedly from the back of the seating area when she saw Josephine; the unmistakeable bulk of Jasper Motley sat with his back to her in the front row; and several of the spectators from the cricket match had turned out again to support their friends and family – but she was impressed to see that the crowd was largely made up of people who seemed to have no vested interest in the play except a passion for theatre. Looking over their heads and out to sea, she noticed how different this section of coast was from the stretch which bordered the Loe estate; here, on a headland devoid of harbours or any other human footprint, the serrated line of cliffs had a frowning, wave-beaten grandeur which seemed cold and immovable – hostile, even. As the waves frilled around the jagged bases of the rocks, which clawed their way towards the horizon like skeletal fingers, the landscape seemed far more in touch with an ancient, unfathomable past, and Josephine could easily understand how myth and legend still held the balance of power here.

'It's quite something, isn't it?' William said, following the direction of her gaze. 'Coming here always reminds me of something my father said about Cornwall: it's the best place God ever made – when He finishes it.'

Josephine laughed and sat down on one of the deckchairs. It

was true though, she thought, looking out to sea again; the rocks did have an unfinished look about them, as if someone had laid the foundations for a project and then had to abandon it in a hurry. 'I imagine it takes on a different character altogether when the weather's in a less forgiving mood,' she said, waving to Lettice and Ronnie, who had just emerged hand in hand from the backstage area, looking a little shaky. Lettice appeared to have her eyes shut, and Ronnie's signal made it clear that a drink would be in order.

'Lettice is terrible with heights,' William explained, lining up the champagne glasses as his daughters made their way up the slope. 'The dressing area here always makes her dizzy.'

'Remind me never to go back there again,' Lettice confirmed, sitting down heavily and asking a lot from her deck-chair. 'If they want alterations doing, they can come out here for them.' She leaned over to cut herself a generous slice of pork pie. 'That wire fence wouldn't save anyone from an accident – I'm beginning to agree with Hephzibah.'

'Although don't you find it interesting that Rowena didn't see fit to tell her about the new walls behind the stage?' Ronnie asked, pointing vaguely towards the offending stonework with a stick of celery. 'If I were being cynical – which of course I never am – I'd say that was a deliberate omission.'

'Is Archie all right?' Josephine asked, peeling a hard-boiled egg and smothering it with salt. 'I expect he'll be glad to get it over with.'

'He's a bit quiet,' Lettice admitted, 'but we think that's just fear. He refused anything to eat or drink in favour of a few minutes alone with his script. He sends his love, though,' she added, taking a jar of pickles from the hamper.

'I must confess, I feel a bit guilty for strong-arming him into doing it at all,' William said. 'But I didn't see what else we could do.'

Ronnie picked up the champagne that William had poured for Archie and divided its contents between Josephine's glass and her own. 'I wouldn't worry about it, Pa – a bit of community spirit won't hurt him,' she said, with all the benevolence of someone who was rarely required to indulge in it herself. 'It'll make a nice change from all that paperwork.'

'Will anyone mind if I pop backstage and wish him luck?' Josephine asked.

'No, dear, of course not – but for God's sake watch your step. I'm not climbing down after you in these heels.'

Josephine picked up her glass and followed a circuitous path through the rugs and hampers to get to the performance area. A sign marked 'Players Only' indicated the backstage quarters. She made her way carefully round the rock, and was surprised to walk in on what felt like a cast of thousands. It was a strange and wonderful spectacle. The actors were clad in a Motley array of holy vestments and, although her knowledge of religious orders didn't stretch to a confirmation of the costumes' authenticity, she had no doubt of how effective the colours would be on stage: just to her left, a dark-haired man – clothed all in white – stood patiently waiting for the play to begin, holding a brown velvet cushion and a bright red mitre with flamboyant tassels; by contrast, his neighbour wore an extravagant red outfit which draped to the floor in lavish folds and was finished off by a triangular hat in a matching shade of scarlet. The majority of the Winwaloe Players formed an army of monks, largely indistinguishable from each other in their rough, brown habits and hoods; they were gathered round a crate of ale which William had sent backstage to wish everyone luck, nervously stubbing out cigarette ends with their sandalled feet, while six angelic choirboys, dressed in white, received last-minute instructions from over-anxious parents whose pride had got the better of their composure. Faced with so many characters, she tried to remember what *The Jackdaw of Rheims* was about: the Ingoldsby Legends had been a favourite of one of her teachers at school, and she vaguely recalled that this particular poem told the story of a jackdaw who stole a cardinal's ring, had a curse put on him, then repented and subsequently became a saint. It was a bit thin on plot, she thought, although she was hardly in a position to criticise – one dead blonde didn't make a crime novel. Visually, though, it was bound to be fabulous, but she would have expected nothing less from Ronnie and Lettice.

There was very little room to move in the crowded backstage area, but she eventually found Archie sitting on an upturned bucket behind the props table. He had his head down, although he appeared to be lost in thought rather than studying his script, and she was taken aback a little at how fine he looked. He, too, wore a white habit but his was made of satin rather than wool. It was offset by a black cowl which covered his shoulders and was tied at the neck by a beautiful silver cord that matched the inner lining of his hood. The familiarity of a twenty-year friendship had taught Josephine to take Archie's good looks for granted, but the costume lent him an austerity and remoteness which were absent in his everyday clothes, and she looked at him now with an admiration that had little to do with piety – although she was honest enough with herself to admit that it was precisely the forbidden element in his clothing which attracted her.

'Here,' she said, holding out her glass, 'Dutch courage.' He

looked up, delighted to see her, and accepted her offer gratefully. 'I hate to say it, but holy orders suit you. You'll steal the
show in that costume – I hope those cousins of yours haven't
been guilty of favouritism.'

'You know, they made this from scratch in two hours flat –
and you're right, it is rather grander than the original. It's not
something I'd ever admit to their faces, but they're remarkably
clever.'

'Have you only just realised that?' She waited while he
turned another bucket upside down and brushed the dust off
it, then sat down next to him, grimacing as Kestrel Jacks
walked past, looking as sullen as ever. 'If you want my opinion,'
she said archly, glancing back to the playing area, 'he'd be a
grand candidate for testing the strength of that wire behind
the stage. There aren't many people I'd wish a nasty accident
on, but I'd happily wave to him on his way down.'

Archie smiled, unaware that her comment had more to it
than an automatic sharing of his own dislike. 'Nice of you to be
so partisan,' he said, then lowered his voice and added more
seriously: 'I had a chat with Nathaniel earlier.'

'The curate?'

'Yes – he and Harry were friends. This isn't the time or place,
but I'd like to hear what you think.'

'Sounds interesting.'

'It is. At least two nightcaps' worth, I'd say.' He shuffled his
bucket forward a little to allow Jago Snipe to step past. The
undertaker was carrying a hand bell and had exchanged his
customary dark suit for one of the brown habits, but the lightening of tone had no effect on his demeanour, which seemed
particularly dour as he headed towards the stage. Josephine
watched him with interest. Rounding the rock, he bumped

into Joseph Caplin coming the other way; Caplin looked unsteady on his feet and was already the worse for drink, and the collision sent him reeling perilously close to the cliff edge. In his panic, he clutched at Jago's costume and only the undertaker's strength and bulk saved them both from going over. There was a gasp of relief from a few of the actors, and Josephine watched as Jago shook the other man off in disgust. Impatiently, he pulled his hood over his head and continued out to the auditorium to ring the bell.

'That's five minutes to go,' Archie said, draining the glass. 'You'd better get back to your seat and pour yourself a drop of this. Go up that way,' he added, pointing to a narrow set of steps which led up one side of the auditorium, out of view of the audience. 'You don't want to make an appearance on stage now or they'll think we've started early.'

'I don't think this outfit is quite old enough to qualify as period dress,' she said in mock indignation. 'Where do the steps come out?'

'Up at the back of the seating area. There's a set the other side, as well – it's designed so that an actor can exit one side and make his entrance at the other without the audience noticing, but you have to be fit to do it. Getting round in time is one thing, but having enough breath left to speak your lines is something else altogether.'

She picked up the glass and gave him a kiss. 'Good luck. You can have my critique later over a large malt.'

'I can't wait, but I need a favour first.'

'Of course – what is it?'

'I'll introduce you to Morveth when the play's over, and no matter how terrible it is, or how long an evening you feel you've had, would you congratulate her? She's put such a lot

191

into it and a word of praise will really mean something if it comes from you. '

'You know me,' she said, smiling mischievously. 'Sincerity is my middle name.'

'That's what worries me,' he called after her. 'And don't take your eyes off the action – you wouldn't want to miss the moment when our jackdaw takes flight.'

Intrigued, Josephine set off back to her seat. As she paused to catch her breath at the back of the auditorium, mourning the days of her early twenties when she taught physical education and would have thought nothing of such a steep climb, she noticed that the blanket which Morwenna and Loveday had put down was empty, except for a hamper and a dog-eared copy of Tennyson's poetry. It would be just like Loveday to run off now and steal the show, she thought, and, although she didn't particularly like Morwenna, she sympathised with her for having to spend so much of her life worrying about where her sister was. She could still remember how terrified she'd been every time she was left in charge of her own little sister – and Moire was an angel, so God knows what sort of responsibility Loveday must be.

In deference to the drop in temperature, the chink of glasses on the air had been replaced by the unscrewing of thermos flasks, and William welcomed her back with hot coffee and pastries. 'Everything all right back there?' he asked, unscrewing a silver hip flask and passing it over.

'Fine, in a chaotic sort of way, and the costumes are wonderful,' she said to Lettice and Ronnie, settling back in her seat to enjoy the performance. 'I've just seen Archie in a whole new light – very ascetic.'

As twilight fell, and a flock of jackdaws flew noisily home to roost in the cliffs, oblivious to the story about to be played out in their honour, the shadows lengthened on the rocks and stage area. Moths, and a bat or two, fluttered past the lanterns which were dotted about the stage and, with the auditorium shrouded in dusk, the magnificent backdrop came into its own. Josephine didn't envy any playwright the task of inventing lines which would compete with such splendour for the audience's attention, but how Shakespeare would have loved this setting, she thought, watching as a small fishing boat followed its familiar course back to Newlyn, pulled on as if by a magnet. The moon seemed determined to play its part in the performance, effortlessly providing a light more intense and somehow more illusory than any lighting designer could devise, and she could only imagine how wonderful *The Tempest* must have been when it was played here. The goodwill of the elements seemed to underline the transient nature of the performance and intensify the anticipation amongst the audience, and their excitement was infectious. Josephine had seen many of the finest productions that London had to offer, in theatres peopled by stars of today and ghosts of past triumphs, and she had herself been the centre of attention at many of them – but tonight, caught up in the scent of the sea and the magic of the evening, she could not imagine a grander scene.

The call of a trumpet heralded the beginning of the play, and Archie had the unenviable task of appearing first on stage. Carrying a large, leather-bound book which looked like one of those hefty family Bibles found in every well-to-do Victorian household, he walked out to the circular patch of grass at the edge of the stage, where a church lectern awaited him. There had been no dimming of the auditorium lights, of course, no raising of a curtain – but even without the customary signals to an audience, he had their attention from the start. The outside world carried calmly on but, without the artificial trappings of a theatre building, there was a greater bond between the stage and the auditorium, as if by sharing the same sky the audience became part of the unfolding story. Archie spoke a little hesitantly at first, but soon shook off his nerves. The sound of the waves against the rocks below punctuated each line, giving a natural rhythm to the rather contrived words of the poem. It seemed to Josephine that the sea brought out a west-country softness to Archie's voice that she had never noticed before, and she soon found herself enclosed in the world of the play. Suddenly the greensward was teeming with people, all making imaginative use of the theatre's many entrances and exits and bringing Archie's words vividly to life: monks walked purposefully across the forestage, carrying jugs of water and platters of bread for the large refectory table; bishop, prior and abbot filled in behind, leaning on the balustrade and pointing out to sea or towards the back of the auditorium; and the cardinal sat at the centre of it all, resplendent in red and issuing orders from the imposing granite throne which might have been created specially for this production, so well did it suit the setting. In fact, it was an excellent choice of play all round: the Minack stage lacked depth but it was broad and gave the impression of a spacious abbey hall, an image which was further strengthened by the stone pillars and floor around the throne; the performance itself relied on energy rather than on scenes of great intimacy which would have been ruined if the weather had been less kind; and, despite Lettice's misgivings, the simplicity of the costumes worked beautifully with the timelessness of the setting. Relieved that she wouldn't have to lie to fulfil her promise to Archie, Josephine asked William to point Morveth out to her, but there was no sign of her in the auditorium. It was always the same for directors, Josephine thought: you put in all the work, then were too busy on the night even to see the play, let alone enjoy it.

The ensemble effort delighted the audience, but the applause for Nathaniel's performance as the eponymous jackdaw was particularly warm – partly, no doubt, because everyone sympathised with the circumstances which had brought about his change of role, but also because he managed to draw every ounce of humour and pathos from the thinly sketched part. For a while, he sat perched on the arm of the throne, dressed in a starkly beautiful black silk habit and a deep ash-grey hood which hid his blond hair and made his expression impossible to read. The only thing that marked him out as a bird was a subtle row of feathering down each sleeve, a restraint which – to Josephine's relief – kept the production on the right side of farce; in fact, it gave the ecclesiastical thief a human air and added a satirical depth to the play that she doubted the original poem could claim.

Considering that they were both playing roles given to them at the last minute, Archie and Nathaniel soon developed a good rapport. Archie knew exactly when to pause in his narration to give his lead the space to improvise, and the spectators chuckled in delight as the jackdaw moved in and out of the monks, leaning over their shoulders to pick scraps of food and silver from the table and throwing his treasures out into the auditorium or over the balustrade to the sea. His antics escalated as the play went on and, at the words 'The Devil must be in that little jackdaw,' he set out to prove the point. At the rear of the stage, next to the cardinal's chair, was a mock altar, full of silver plate and other gifts which the various orders had brought to ingratiate themselves with the Archbishop of Rheims. In a single bound, Nathaniel was among the riches, and unhooked a red velvet bag which draped sacrilegiously from the arm of a cross. He opened it and ran the contents through his fingers, allowing the audience to see the wealth of gold and silver coins inside, then he moved to the front of the stage and walked slowly along the first row of spectators. Josephine could tell from Archie's uncertainty that he was as much in the dark as the rest of them about this particular scene, and she watched with interest as Nathaniel stopped in front of Jasper Motley, held the bag up high and allowed the coins to fall in a steady stream on to the vicar's lap, where they glinted in the lantern light, as eloquent an accusation of greed as anything that could have been conveyed by words. The inference was obvious, even to those who had no knowledge of the rumours of corruption that circled the estate, and every-one's attention was drawn from the stage to the front row as they waited to see what Motley's reaction would be. It seemed to take him a moment to register the insult. When he did, he rose awkwardly to his feet, sending the money rolling back across the stage, and struck Nathaniel hard across the face with the back of his hand. As the audience looked on, stunned into silence, Archie and a couple of the monks moved forward to prevent the fight that was threatening, but there was no need for intervention. Motley turned and strode angrily up the steps without once looking back.

'I don't think that was in the script,' Ronnie muttered.

'No, there was far too much substance in it,' agreed Josephine. 'I think our young curate fancies himself as

Hamlet's Player King, except it's obviously the conscience of the Church he's after.' She looked on while the vicar paused briefly at the top of the cliff, leaning heavily on a rock and struggling to get his breath; as the path took him out of sight, she noticed that Morwenna's rug was still empty. It was a shame that Loveday was missing the performance she had so looked forward to, not to mention the added drama, but perhaps the effort of watching someone else in the role their brother should have taken had been too much for them both. One thing was certain, though – it was a more eventful piece with Nathaniel in the title role, and she looked forward to hearing what Archie had to say later.

Taking his cue from the jackdaw, who seemed remarkably undaunted by the incident, Archie carried on admirably with his narration. The six choirboys appeared next, clearly responding to a good shove from the wings; one carried a bowl of water and another held some soap, and the cardinal went through the ritual of washing his hands and removing his ring, which he placed conveniently in reach of the devil-ridden jackdaw. While no one but the audience was looking, the bird swooped down on the band of gold and took it off to the side of the stage, where he perched on a boulder and watched the chaos that broke out below when the theft was discovered. The monks ran to left and right, turning their pockets out and declaring their innocence to an enraged cardinal, while the servants and choirboys fell to their knees and scoured the floor for the missing ring. As the cardinal called for his bell, book and candle, ready to curse the thief, Nathaniel bounded across the stage and leapt quickly on to the balustrade. The audience gasped, but laughed in relief as he found his balance and stood there for a moment, holding the ring up in triumph. Then he turned his back to them, and the laughter took on a nervous edge as the jackdaw seemed to hover on the brink of disaster: after the last departure from the script, they no longer trusted that everything taking place on stage was solely for their entertainment. Josephine knew that what she was about to see was an illusion, but the power of the image – a black silhouette, framed by burning torches fixed to the stonework at the back of the stage – was so great that she could not help but feel a stab of apprehension. Nathaniel might be acting, but she could only imagine what was going through the young man's mind as he stood on the very threshold that his friend had crossed just a matter of weeks before – the threshold of life and death – and she was suddenly relieved that Morwenna and Loveday were not here to witness the re-enactment of that choice. The audience had gone completely silent now, and the only noise came from the sea below. She counted three cycles of waves breaking and receding before Nathaniel raised his arms, ready to take flight or embrace his fate. Then the jackdaw stepped forward, out into oblivion.

Archie paused in his reading to give the trick time to play with the audience's imagination, and looked down to his left to make sure that Nathaniel was safe. About half the backstage path was visible to him from where he was standing and, in the lantern light, he could just see a monk's arm reaching out from the small recess under the stage to steady the actor as he hit the ground – but there was no need: Nathaniel had practised the jump fifty times or more during the afternoon, and he landed effortlessly on the narrow path, apparently oblivious to the danger that lay just a few inches in front of him. He crouched there for a moment to make sure of his balance, then looked back over his shoulder towards the stage and gave a jubilant thumbs-up sign. The hood had fallen back from his face and, in the light from the lanterns which lined the backstage path, it was obvious that his smile was a genuine one. For the moment, his troubles were forgotten in the exhilaration of performance.

Archie glanced back towards the audience to gauge their reaction, and he was not disappointed. The murmur of conversation and appreciative laughter which had under-scored the lightness of the play so far was now entirely absent, and there was a tension in the faces still fixed on the empty balustrade that not even the awkwardness of the conflict between curate and rector had created. Nobody seemed sure of what they had just seen, and those closest to Archie looked to him for guidance; when they noticed the faint smile on his lips, a ripple of relieved applause began in the front row and soon spread through the whole auditorium. One or two people – William and Josephine amongst them, he noticed – stood to show their appreciation, and he waited for everyone to settle down again before continuing to read from the poem. While the cast played out his words, he looked backstage again and was surprised to see that Nathaniel hadn't moved from the spot: he was due back on stage any second, and should have walked over to the wings to wait for his cue. One of the lanterns had gone out, but the moonlight was strong enough for Archie to see that the smile which had so recently trans-formed the curate's face seemed to have been extinguished along with the light.

Distracted, he stumbled over the next line and lost his place on the page. It took him a few seconds to find the right section, and the actors paused awkwardly while he tried to catch up with them. When he spoke again, the words were rushed and indistinct; the rhythm and the timing that he had worked so hard to perfect were, he knew, entirely lost, but he was more concerned now with what was going on behind the scenes. He looked again at Nathaniel, and immediately abandoned any thought of continuing with the play. The curate was staring straight ahead towards the recess under the stage. As Archie watched, the arm that had been there before to steady him reached out again, but this time it was not to ensure Nathaniel's safety. Nathaniel took two steps backwards, and the figure hidden from view moved out a little further from its hiding place, far enough for Archie to make out a brown hood in the light of the remaining lantern. Behind him, he was aware that the audience had begun to fidget. One or two of the actors were walking over to see what he was looking at, but everything happened so quickly that even Archie doubted what he was seeing. Nathaniel moved back as far as he could, but found himself trapped against the wire fence. There was nowhere else for him to go, no way of escape from whoever was threatening him. Archie began to run, calling out as he went, but the curate had his hands pressed over his ears as though he were trying to blot out some insidious, demonic song that only he could hear, and the words of warning drifted uselessly out to sea.

Even as he made for the perilous steps which would take him down to the backstage path, Archie knew that he would not reach Nathaniel in time. Inevitably, the fence started to give under the strain. Desperately, the curate looked up, but the moment for rescue was long gone. Before Archie had a chance to set foot on the top step, the wire snapped completely and Nathaniel fell backwards, his hands clutching frantically at empty air.

The bulk of the cliff hid his dreadful descent, but Archie's mind played tricks on him, convincing him that he could see Nathaniel's body plummeting downwards, his arms outstretched and his black costume billowing out behind him. The image stayed with him, lurid and sensational, like the suicide engravings so popular in cheap Victorian street literature, where fallen women chose death off Westminster Bridge rather than face the misery of their everyday lives. But there was no choice involved here, and Archie tried to rid himself of that haunting mental picture and concentrate instead on the person responsible for it. He was halfway down the steps by now, but the path was suddenly plunged into darkness as the hooded figure kicked the two remaining lanterns over the edge after his victim. Disoriented, Archie clung to the rock for a second, trying to get his balance on the steps. Without the comforting flicker of the storm lamps, the power of the landscape and the immensity of the sea were overwhelming. He called out for more lights and continued down carefully, a step at a time, but he knew pursuit was hopeless; already, he could hear footsteps receding along the path, footsteps more familiar with the layout of the Minack than he was, or driven to desperation by an urgent need to escape. The whole incident had lasted barely fifteen seconds, but it was long enough to take him to a different world: the colour and artifice of the play were long gone, and he was left alone with the solid darkness of the cliffs, with the certainty that somewhere far beneath him, where fringes of white foam played around the Minack rock, lay Nathaniel's broken body.

Chapter Eleven

It was Rowena Cade who met Archie at the top of the steps with two storm lanterns. She peered past him down to the backstage path and the look of horror on her face told him that she could see the broken fence, but he was grateful that she also seemed to sense the importance of remaining calm; it was going to be virtually impossible to control such a large crowd, and the main thing was to avoid alarming them for as long as possible to allow him to take charge of the situation. The cast on stage were looking at each other in bewilderment, and other actors drifted out gradually from the dressing area or various hiding places behind the rocks where they had been awaiting their next cue. As they each removed their cowls and became individuals again, Penrose realised the futility of searching for Nathaniel's assailant: the Minack's layout was such that he or she could easily have taken the steps around the auditorium and left the theatre without being seen by anyone, or, in the confusion of the comings and goings on stage, it would even have been possible for someone to blend into a group of identically dressed actors without drawing particular attention. The hooded figure he had seen could be standing just a few feet away or could be long gone; either way, the priority now was to locate Nathaniel.

There was a murmur of conversation among the audience, and some people had got to their feet to try to see what was happening. Penrose held up his hand for silence and asked everyone to stay where they were for the time being, and there was a note of authority in his voice that made them reluctant to question his instructions – all except William, who strode anxiously over to see if he could help. Penrose took him and Miss Cade to one side and spoke quickly and firmly. 'Nathaniel's gone over into the zawn,' he said, choosing his words carefully. 'How much time do we have before the tide comes in?'

'Not long,' she replied. 'An hour or two before full tide, but the water will already be high up the rocks.'

'Then we can't wait for help. I need ropes and as much light as you can find. Will you sort that out for me, and bring everything down by the side steps? And the police need to be called immediately – make sure to tell them I need full back-up, with forensics and a photographer.'

She nodded and hurried off up the slope towards Minack House. 'You're not going down there, surely, Archie?' William asked.

'I don't have a choice. If he's fallen all the way down, we're already too late. Let's just hope he's on one of the rocks higher up – we won't know until we can get some light down there.'

'Do you think he's still alive, then?'

Archie remembered how he had felt earlier when he looked down into the zawn. Even the highest level of rocks was sixty or seventy feet down, and only a miracle would save a man's life after such a fall. 'No, I'm afraid I don't,' he said, 'but we can't let his body be washed out to sea if there's anything we can do to stop it.'

William looked down into the blackness, his face full of sorrow. 'Then at least let me get some of the men here to help. It would be madness to go down alone.'

The last thing Archie felt like doing was entrusting his safety to a man in a brown habit, but William was right – he did need someone to anchor the rope, and his uncle would not be strong enough on his own. 'All right – fetch Jago. Make sure he comes on his own, though – the last thing we want is a crowd tramping all over the cliff, and come back as quickly as you can.'

Left alone for a moment, Archie took one of the storm lanterns and went along the path to the recess, but whoever had been waiting there had left no trace of his or her existence behind. When he got back to the steps, Rowena Cade and the man called Billy were already on their way down, laden with ropes, torches, climbing gloves and a heavy tarpaulin which could be used as a stretcher if necessary. 'I don't want to tell you your job, Inspector,' she said as she set everything down on the floor in front of him, 'but I have been down there a few times myself, and the best route is over that grass slope on the right, then down the rope on to the first level of rock. From there, if you're careful, you can climb all the way round the zawn. Do you want me to lead the way?'

He refused the offer, but was grateful for the advice. Removing the silk habit which covered his more conventional clothes, he selected the sturdiest-looking rope and waited impatiently for William to return. When he appeared at the top of the steps, Archie was horrified to see that he was accompanied not by Jago but by Kestrel Jacks and a young man he didn't recognise. 'Jago's nowhere to be found, I'm afraid,' William called, 'but luckily I bumped into Jacks coming down from the auditorium. And this is Angus Trew. He's a constable over in Penzance, and he happened to be in the audience. He's been keeping the peace out there – everyone's getting a bit restless.'

'Just wondered if there was anything else I could do to help, Sir,' the policeman said.

'Sounds like you've already been doing the most important thing, Constable,' Penrose said. 'Thank you for that.' He thought for a second: there was little to be gained from keeping the audience here, and the process of recovering Nathaniel's body would be a whole lot easier and more dignified without a crowd of people watching. 'Perhaps you and Miss Cade could clear the auditorium for me. Explain as briefly as you can that there's been an accident, and take names and addresses as people leave just in case we need to contact them later. Try to keep everyone as calm as you can. Gather the cast together in one place – the stage is probably best – and keep them there until I come and find you. We'll need to speak to everyone who was involved in the play before they leave tonight.' He was impressed to see that the significance of his instructions was not lost on Trew, but the constable did not waste time by asking questions. 'I know you can't be everywhere at once,' Penrose added, 'but I don't want anyone down on the backstage path so all the steps will have to be watched. William will introduce you to my cousins and a friend of mine who are in the audience – they'll help out if necessary.'

Trew turned to go, but William caught his arm. 'Just one thing, Archie,' he said. 'Nathaniel's parents – they're in the audience, and obviously they're worried. I haven't said anything to them yet, but they need to be told something before Angus makes his announcement.'

Damn, thought Penrose – of course they were here; it should have been a proud evening for their son, and he reproached himself bitterly for not thinking of them before. 'Will you take them to one side and break the news to them first?' he asked William, desperately sorry that they had already had to wait so long. 'Tell them we're doing everything we can to find Nathaniel, but try not to give them false hope. I'll come and talk to them as soon as I know how things are.'

He was less grateful to William for his choice of climbing companion, but there was no time to argue, nor to read anything into Jago's absence. He handed a torch to Jacks, trying to ignore his smirk, and took the more powerful light for himself. 'Where would you like to go over, Inspector?' the gamekeeper asked insolently. Penrose said nothing, but led the way along the outcrop of rock to the point which Rowena Cade had identified as the safest from which to start his descent. About fifteen feet of rough grass and gorse stretched out before him, sloping down sharply and culminating in nothingness. He walked as far as he could and looked to his left, using the position of the balustrade to calculate where Nathaniel had gone over the edge; from this angle, he was able to see the rocks immediately below the backstage path and, with the help of the moonlight, could just make out a dark shape on a flat piece of stone six feet or so above the encroaching tide.

Jacks joined him, although the silent presence by his side was anything but a comfort. The gamekeeper tied the rope firmly round his waist, smiling again as Penrose checked the knots, and threw the other end over the side of the cliff. He stood at a safe distance from the edge, looking defiant, and Penrose hesitated, wondering if he should, after all, ask for more help. There was no question that Jacks had the strength to act as anchor – if he chose to, but William's casual words were significant; where had the gamekeeper been if he was coming down from the auditorium? If he had pushed the curate over, then made his escape up the side steps to rejoin the play from the other direction, how easy it would be now to untie those knots and make it look like another terrible accident. Fleetingly, Penrose questioned the wisdom of his decision to keep the truth of Nathaniel's fall to himself until someone in authority from the local police arrived; if anything happened to him, no one would ever know that the curate's death was murder. Standing now on lower ground, he felt the sea against his face and, as fine a mist as it was, it weighed heavily on his conscience. There was no option but to trust Jacks: he had not yet allowed himself to analyse his own reaction to Nathaniel's sudden death, but the young man's confusion and vulnerability had moved him deeply during their conversation, and he felt an obligation to ensure that his body, at least, had the refuge which his mind had been unable to find.

Giving Jacks only the briefest of glances, Penrose tucked the torch into his belt, grasped the rope firmly and eased himself backwards over the edge of the cliff. It took all the self-discipline he had to put his misgivings about Jacks to one side and take his time over the descent; the temptation to hurry was almost irresistible, but he lowered himself down methodically, hand over hand, and – although he would not have won any marks for elegance – he soon reached the layer of rock that Rowena Cade had described. From there, he took the safest-looking route back into the heart of the gully, noting with relief that it would be at least another twenty minutes before the tide was far enough in to affect the level he was on.

As he approached the flat rock where Nathaniel lay, he realised that – in spite of his sober words to William – he had been subconsciously nurturing the hope that the fall might not have been fatal, and that Nathaniel might have been one of the miraculous few who escaped unscathed from the severest of accidents. The unnatural arrangement of his body made the idea laughable even before the light from the torch reached his face. The curate lay on his back, and his shattered corpse seemed to reflect the emotional fragility which had marked his last few weeks of life. The folds of his costume hid his legs, but his arms were twisted at an impossible angle to his body, like a doll which had fallen foul of a particularly spiteful child, and Penrose could only imagine the extent of his internal injuries. His blond hair was matted with blood, thick and viscous and dark; blood also pooled out from beneath his skull, soaking into the grey lining of his hood and following the contours of the rock, running down towards the sea as if to beat the tide at its own game. Nathaniel's face was tilted slightly away from Penrose but his eyes stared up at the cliff, still fixed on the horror that had brought him to this, looking upwards not to heaven but to hell. The prayer book which he always kept with him lay a little to the right of his body, next to one of the lanterns which the killer had kicked over; it had obviously been dislodged from his pocket by the impact of the fall, and Penrose found its distance poignant: even the curate's most trusted solace had abandoned him in the end. In fact, standing alone with the body, so close to the elemental power of the sea, Penrose found it hard not to resort to an age-old language of good and evil, to look for the imprint of the devil himself in Nathaniel's eyes.

There was no doubt that death had been instant, but how long must those final seconds have seemed when he realised that his fate was unavoidable? Had he used them to contemplate his killer, or to find some sort of peace from the anguish which had dogged him since Harry's death? Penrose mocked his own wishful thinking. He had seen Nathaniel's face and there was no way that his last emotion had been anything other than terror, a continuation of the living hell that he had spoken of. Why? What had he done except fall in love with the wrong person, and battle with his own ideas of right and wrong? Penrose knew that the sorrow he felt at Nathaniel's death was due in part to the pain and confusion which any investigation would create amongst those who loved him. Secrets were spilled by any sudden fatality: a letter or diary, left out in the morning because someone took it for granted that they would return later to keep it safe, could lay a life open to a thousand different stories, and murder was by far the harshest interpreter. He hoped desperately that the darker parts of Nathaniel's heart could be kept from his parents, but he knew that was unrealistic; if he were in charge of this investigation, he would feel obliged to discuss Nathaniel's feelings for Harry and his parents would be left mourning a stranger, at a loss to know who their son really was and with no opportunity to find out. Nathaniel had experienced that sense of betrayal when Harry died; now, the people whom he had been so anxious to protect were about to find out exactly how that felt.

Josephine slipped the Lanchester into gear, removed the handbrake and allowed the car to roll gently down the slope towards the cliff edge. More light was needed in the stage area, and those with cars had been asked to bring them as close to the scene as possible, with their headlamps turned full on; William was understandably busy with Nathaniel's parents, and she had been glad of something to do, however small, to take her mind off the fact that Archie was still out on the cliff-side, alone with Kestrel Jacks. She left the engine running, made sure the car was safe and went back down to see if there was any news.

The audience had gone now, efficiently ushered from the auditorium by Rowena Cade and a young man whom Josephine guessed was an off-duty policeman. Everyone else had gathered together on the stage, as if solidarity could somehow soften the tragedy of the evening's events, and she noticed that Lettice and Ronnie were doing their best to offer some sort of solace with hot tea and brandy, brought down on vast silver trays from Minack House. Most people were still in their costumes and there was a surreal quality to the scene, but nothing would surprise her any more tonight; like everyone, she had been utterly bewildered by the sudden change of mood signalled first by Archie's distraction, and then by his obvious alarm; when news of an accident filtered back to the audience, the incident – coming so soon after the tension of Jasper Motley's exit and the drama of Nathaniel's leap into thin air – seemed to bear as little relation to the real world as the tale of a devilish jackdaw and a stolen ring.

It took a lot to subdue Ronnie and Lettice, but they met her at the bottom of the steps looking as shocked and bewildered as everyone. 'Any news?' Josephine asked, and Lettice shook her head.

'No, absolutely nothing. I don't suppose we can hold out any hope that he's still alive. What a dreadful, dreadful thing to happen. I can hardly believe it.'

'Selfishly, it's Pa I'm worried about,' Ronnie said. 'He was very fond of Nathaniel, and this will really hit him hard coming so soon after Harry's death. I don't know why we worried about Hephzibah – tonight makes her look like a lucky charm.'

Lettice was first to ask the obvious question. 'I wonder what on earth went wrong?' she said. 'It can't have been the jump

211

from the balustrade because Archie didn't panic straight away, so how could Nathaniel have fallen?'

'You don't suppose he threw himself off deliberately, do you?' Josephine asked. As the sisters looked at her in astonishment, she realised how out of the blue the suggestion must have sounded when they were oblivious to the suspicions surrounding Harry's death.

'What makes you say that?' Lettice asked, and Ronnie looked at her inquisitively.

'Oh, I don't know. It just seems strange that he should fall from the path when he managed the jump so easily. And you never know what's in people's minds, do you?' she added rather weakly.

'This crime business is going to your head,' Lettice chided her. 'You're spending too much time with unlikely scenarios.'

Ronnie, however, was more persistent. 'Do you know something we don't?' she asked.

'Only that I won't come to Lettice if I want a glowing review of my plots,' Josephine said evasively. 'Look – that constable's coming over. I wonder if they've found him?' But the only announcement was that the police were just a few minutes away now, and someone would be along to talk to everyone as soon as possible.

'Oh, I thought that was some definite news,' said Lettice, disappointed.

'Even so, I find that young man's presence *very* reassuring,' said Ronnie with a flash of her old charm. She smiled at the constable as he passed, and he nodded and blushed.

'Don't be ridiculous,' said Lettice. 'He must be at least fifteen years younger than you.'

'Perhaps, dear, but look after the nights and the years will take care of themselves. I might just go and see if he needs some sugar in his tea.'

Josephine watched her go. 'You have to admire her spirit, I suppose,' she said, 'and he *is* very good-looking. He reminds me a bit of Archie when he first joined the police.' She glanced across to the back of the stage, where the steps led down to the cliff. 'I wish we could see how he's getting on.'

'He won't do anything stupid,' Lettice said, squeezing her hand. 'I'm going to pass these last few drinks round and go back up for more. Come and fetch me if anything happens.'

'All right, but let me give those out,' Josephine said. 'I can't just sit here.'

She took the three glasses from Lettice's tray and gave two of them to a couple standing near her, then carried the third over to the balustrade, where an elderly woman stood clutching a rug round her shoulders and looking anxiously out to sea. 'This might warm you a little,' Josephine said, holding out the drink.

The woman turned to her, and startled Josephine by putting the glass straight down on the stone ledge and taking her hand instead, clasping it affectionately as if they knew each other well. 'You're Archie's friend from London, aren't you?' she said, and Josephine – who was getting used to being at a disadvantage whenever she met anyone for the first time in Cornwall – smiled and nodded. 'I saw you with him backstage before the play. I'm Morveth Wearne.'

So this was the woman she had heard so much about. 'I was looking forward to congratulating you tonight,' she said. 'I'm sorry that something so wonderful has ended in tragedy.'

Morveth brushed over the compliment as if the play had never existed. 'What happened exactly?' she asked anxiously. 'I know Nathaniel's fallen, but has Archie said anything else to you?'

'No, I haven't had a chance to talk to him yet, and he's the only person who could have seen how it happened. No one else seems to know for sure what went on. William's with Nathaniel's parents, but it hardly seems possible that there'll be anything other than the worst news for them.'

'He was barely more than a boy,' she said softly, more to herself than to Josephine. 'I taught him, you know, him and all the other children on the estate – Harry and Morwenna, Simon Jacks, and Archie, of course.' She smiled sadly. 'I still can't look at them without remembering what they were like as children, and they haven't really changed, not any of them – not deep down, where it matters.'

'What was Nathaniel like?'

'Clever, but shy and terribly earnest. He came from a loving family, but he seemed lost at times and desperate to find a place for himself in the world. He thought about that at a much earlier age than most of us do.'

'And did he find it in the Church?'

'He found it in the scriptures, which isn't always the same thing. His faith was remarkable. It was the words he loved, and he knew his prayer book off by heart – in the truest sense of that phrase, though, not as an exercise in learning. He always found a way of making it mean something to people, no matter who they were or where they came from.'

'That's a rare talent to have.'

'God-given, some might say. Perhaps it made him a little naive – there's a limit to how much faith can help people at times, and he didn't always see that. Sometimes he tried too hard when it would have been wiser to let go, but that's hardly a crime.' It was an interesting choice of words, Josephine thought, looking down into the blackness. There was a pinprick of light over to the right, stationary as though someone had put a torch down on the ground and left it there, but she could see no sign of Archie, and her unease was growing as time went on. She found Morveth's presence faintly unsettling, too; it was as if their conversation had a number of layers and only the most superficial was obvious to her. 'There's something not right here,' Morveth said eventually. 'I can sense it.'

'What do you mean?' asked Josephine.

'Nathaniel seemed troubled of late. He wouldn't talk about it, and I suppose it's arrogant of me to think that I could have helped if he had. But I wish he'd come to me, and now it's too late.' She turned back to Josephine, and the anxiety in her eyes was infectious. 'Whatever happened here tonight, I don't believe it was an accident. It's too much of a coincidence, coming so soon after Harry.'

It seemed to Josephine that the time to keep silent out of loyalty to Archie's confidences was long gone, and this cloud of secrecy was beginning to irritate her. In any case, she had no doubt that Morveth would see right through any pretence that Archie had not discussed people on the estate with her. 'Do you mean it was suicide or murder?' she asked bluntly, and then, exasperated by Morveth's reluctance to continue the conversation she had started: 'Look, if you know something about Harry's death *or* Nathaniel's, you must tell Archie, even if it affects someone he cares for. Does it have something to do with Morwenna? Or Kestrel Jacks? Or your vicar?'

The older woman looked genuinely startled. 'Why should it have anything to do with them?'

'Well, Morwenna's taken against Nathaniel for some reason,

I doubt there's a woman on the estate who doesn't know what Beth Jacks goes through behind closed doors, and I can hardly believe that Jasper Motley is particularly well disposed to his curate after that little stunt with the coins. And that's just what *I* know about after two days here.'

'What are you talking about? What stunt?'

'During the play – didn't you see it?'

'No. I had to go back to the bus for something.'

Morveth listened quietly while Josephine described the improvised scene which had taken place in her absence. 'You've no idea what that man is capable of,' she said at last.

'The obvious inference is that he's defrauding the Church of funds, but Loveday told me that much. She also said that Nathaniel had found out about something more serious. Perhaps that's earned him more than he bargained for – more than a book off your shelf, at least.'

Morveth looked at Josephine with a growing respect. 'You've met Loveday, then? What do you think of her?'

'I like her very much. She says what she means, and so far she's the only person I've met here who does anything of the sort.'

Her honesty seemed to defuse the tension and drew a reluctant smile from Morveth. 'I don't know a better way of finding out what someone's really like than through their reaction to Loveday,' she said. 'Most dismiss her instantly; some feel sorry for her; only a handful are wise enough to listen to her.' She held out her hand again, and Josephine sensed a fresh start between them. 'I can see why Archie trusts you,' Morveth continued, 'and I'll ask something from you, if I may. The past is dead and buried now. Don't let Archie unsettle it if there's anything you can do to stop him.'

Was Harry the past, Josephine wondered, or was Morveth speaking metaphorically? She didn't seem the type to deal in clichés. 'Archie's a policeman,' she said, more gently this time because the request had been a plea rather than a threat. 'I can't stop him doing his job if that's what it comes to, and I wouldn't try.'

'He's a policeman in London, yes, and a good one I've no doubt. Here, he's vulnerable because he cares too much. He could so easily lose himself again, just like he did when his parents died – like he did when he came back from the war. You and I both know how close to despair he's come in the past, and how distant he can be.'

Josephine was disconcerted by how much Morveth obviously knew about her shared past with Archie, but she, for her part, knew that his commitment to the truth was more than a professional obligation. 'If you're telling me that Archie is the last person to ask for help when he really needs it, then I couldn't agree with you more, and I'll always support him if he'll let me – but I can't ask him to turn his back on something that matters to him, particularly when I don't even understand what it is I'm asking.'

'Not even if there are things he's better off not knowing?'

'You see? That's exactly what I mean. If you stopped talking in these ridiculous riddles for a moment, I might have a better idea of what I'm supposed to help you protect Archie from. What sort of things is he better off not knowing?'

Morveth turned to her, and it occurred to Josephine that she had rarely seen a face with more strength in it. 'Archie's mother, Lizzie, was my closest friend,' the older woman said quietly. 'In the days leading up to her wedding, I could see something was bothering her, and we took a boat out on the lake to talk. It took her a while to tell me, but she was worrying about whether or not to tell her new husband that her brother, Jasper, had taken advantage of her.'

'The vicar?' asked Josephine, shocked.

Morveth laughed bitterly. 'Yes, the Reverend Motley. It began when she was ten and he was thirteen, and continued on and off for three years. By that time, getting pregnant frightened her more than he did, so she had the courage to defy him and lock her bedroom door at night so that he couldn't come and go as he pleased.'

Her words echoed Loveday's description of Morwenna's behaviour with Harry, and Josephine was more convinced than ever that she had been right about the violence in their relationship, but it was Archie's family which concerned her more at the moment. 'Did William know?' she asked.

'No. She didn't tell anyone while it was happening because Jasper had convinced her that it was her fault for leading him on, and that she would be the one to be punished if they were caught. And afterwards, when her parents had died and William inherited, she couldn't tell him because she knew he'd force Jasper to leave and she was afraid of the scandal. Shame is a powerful emotion, isn't it? Much more powerful than love or even jealousy. She told her husband, James, though, and her marriage was the stronger for it, but it was her worst fear that her son would find out. She never wanted him to think of his mother as frightened and ashamed, you see. It was obvious to everyone that she despised her brother, because she rarely set foot inside that church from the day he was ordained, and she left him a pinch of salt in her will. No one really knew why she hated him so much, though, except Archie's father, and he was a good man – wise enough to see that loving Lizzie was much more important than punishing Jasper.'

'Do you think that's what Nathaniel knew?'

'I doubt it. I don't see how he could have found out. There are only two people left alive who do know; one of them certainly won't want it talked about, and I've only ever told you. But that's what I mean – it's all very well to say truth must out, but it's not always best; sometimes the braver thing is to keep silent. There's a darkness in most households if you look hard enough; you just have to do the best you can with the knowledge you have.'

Josephine doubted that Morveth would trust her with any knowledge of the Pinching family, but she needed to ask the question. Before she could think of the best way to phrase it, however, there was a murmur of relief from the stage as the powerful headlights of two police cars and an ambulance appeared at the top of the slope. Morveth walked over to stand with Nathaniel's parents while William greeted the officers, and the opportunity, for now, was gone.

Penrose waited with Nathaniel's body while the police made their way across the rocks. The senior officer introduced himself and Penrose gave a succinct account of what had happened, then left the team to its work and retraced his footsteps wearily round to the outcrop, where a more secure method of access had now been put in place.

William and Rowena Cade were standing on the backstage path with a distinguished-looking man who was familiar to Penrose but whose name he did not know. 'This is Chief Constable Stephens, Inspector,' explained Miss Cade. 'He's always been a great friend to the Minack and to me, and I wanted him to know what had happened straight away.' And to find out what it means for your theatre, Penrose added mentally, but he could not blame Rowena Cade for her concern; the Minack was her vision and, by all accounts she had created it virtually single-handed and spent a considerable amount of her own money on it. In her position, his priorities would have been exactly the same.

'Penrose – good to meet you at last, but I wish it had been under happier circumstances. Terrible thing to happen. Rowena tells me you've had everything under control, though. Thank God you were here.'

Right at this moment, Penrose could hardly agree but he didn't argue. Instead, he took the chief constable tactfully to one side and explained again what he had seen from the stage. 'I'm afraid there's no doubt that it's murder, Sir,' he said. 'I'll obviously give your investigating officer a full statement as soon as he's ready,' he added diplomatically, knowing that county forces were loath to call in Scotland Yard, even when a major crime occurred in their area. 'And it goes without saying that if there's any help London can give, you only need to ask.'

'What do you mean?' Stephens asked. 'You'll take it on, surely? I can call the Yard and clear it with them tonight. Who's your superior officer?'

'Superintendent Goodman, Sir, but don't you want your own force to investigate?'

'The best man's a local one, you mean? Well, there's something to be said for that, I suppose, but you *are* local, Penrose, and I've heard excellent things about you. What's more, you're the only witness and it's not often the police have the advantage of seeing the crime as well as investigating it. We're not too arrogant to accept help, particularly when it's the best we can get, and I'd be happy to think that my boys can learn from you. There'll be no arguments from anybody, believe me, and all the resources you'll need will be yours. You will do it?'

Penrose hesitated, knowing that he was effectively being asked to tear apart some of the lives he cared about most, and resenting the reduction of the process to an exercise in model policing. 'There might be a conflict of interest, Sir,' he said. 'It involves my uncle's estate, after all.'

'Nonsense. You've proved yourself to be above all that. If that's your only objection, we'll have the body taken to Minack House in the first instance and I'll notify the coroner.' Penrose nodded his agreement, realising that he really had no choice.

Chapter Twelve

Wednesday was the first morning since her arrival that Josephine had not awoken to sunlight on the lake, but more than the weather had changed overnight. When William telephoned early to make sure she was all right, he was understandably in sombre mood and even his daughters were uncharacteristically lethargic about their plans for the day. Josephine refused the half-hearted offer of a run into Penzance for some shopping and settled down at the desk in the sitting room's large bay window, full of good intentions to do something about the woeful lack of progress she had made with her book – but it was not to be: the bland, grey cloud which hung motionless over the water – mocking any celebrations promised by the half-decorated boat   seemed to recognise the futility of a glorious morning after such a senseless waste of life the night before, and she felt much the same. Every sentence she wrote was contrived and artificial, and her mind refused to engage with William Potticary's progress along an imaginary cliff-top; instead, she kept mulling over her conversation with Morveth and the uncomfortable knowledge with which it had left her. She had no idea what, if anything, to say to Archie, but at least while he was busy with Nathaniel's death she would have plenty of time to think about it.

She looked around the room, knowing that it was much as it had been when Archie's parents were at the Lodge and intrigued to see what it might tell her about them. Like William's library, it was spacious and comfortable, and had clearly been designed for living in rather than effect. A warm Brussels carpet ran the length of the floor, rich in reds and blues, but otherwise the space was divided in character: the area in which she was sitting had two tall windows, one looking out over the lake and the other along a private road that led to Helston, and its pale-green walls and drapes gave it a light, airy feel and an affinity to summer; the half which contained the fireplace was lined with dark oak bookshelves, possibly made from the wood on the estate, and would make a cosy retreat on a winter's afternoon. She walked over to look at the books, smiling as she noticed that both the fireside chairs and the footstool had been frayed at the edges by Motley Penrose. The shelves held an eclectic selection of fiction and non-fiction, and there was a predominance of volumes on natural history, botany and gardening. Someone was fond of the Victorians, and there was a complete set of Trollope which must, she thought, have belonged to Archie's father – she couldn't see Lizzie Penrose having a taste for chronicles of clerical life. All the books were fine editions, but that had not stopped them being read and loved, none more so than a collection of battered children's books which sat next to a shelf of novels and plays that Archie had added in adult life. She recognised his tastes and was amused to see that her own books – particularly *The Man in the Queue* – looked a little out of place alongside Waugh, Forster and Bowen, but were just as dog-eared; at least she hadn't had to suffer the indignity of finding them pristine and unread.

Her eye fell on a volume of Tennyson's poetry and she took it down, remembering the empty blanket and the book that

Morwenna and Loveday had left behind last night. Where had they gone? she wondered, turning to 'The Passing of Arthur' and looking for the reference which Archie had mentioned. Before she could read much, she heard a car draw up outside and went back to the window. Archie got out, looking tired and worried, and Josephine found it hard to believe that he even owned cricket whites, let alone had worn them just the day before yesterday.

'I'm sorry not to have spoken to you properly last night,' he said as she met him at the back door, 'but there was no chance of getting away.'

'Don't be silly. I knew I wouldn't see you as soon as William told us what had happened.'

'I don't know what I'd have done without him last night,' Archie said, giving her a hug. 'He was wonderful with Nathaniel's parents.'

'Yes – he's going over to see them again today.'

'That's good.'

'What a dreadful way to lose a son.' She looked at the suit and the frown, and gave Archie a resigned smile. 'You've obviously accepted the case. Maybe we should have gone for that weekend in Brighton after all?'

'It's certainly not the holiday I had planned,' he agreed. 'A nightcap with the chief constable doesn't have quite the same appeal, somehow.'

'I bet his single malt isn't a patch on mine, either. It's a bit early for that now, but I could manage bacon and eggs. Have you time?'

Archie looked at his watch. 'Just about. I've got to call the Yard, but I can do that from here. After last night, it's vital that we find out what's happened to Christopher Snipe and

Bill can help with that up there – he's got all the resources at his fingertips.' He left Josephine in the kitchen and went through to the hall to let his sergeant know what was happening. As he was waiting to be put through, he had time to notice things he occasionally took for granted, and found a comfort in their familiarity which he did not often experience. He had always admired the painting that hung over the stairs, an oil by Stanhope Forbes which his father had bought for his mother shortly before the war. The picture showed a team of horses pulling a quarry cart through the Cornish landscape, and he loved it as much for the slash in the bottom right-hand corner of the canvas as for the quality of the brushwork. It was one of several works of art damaged by suffragettes in order to draw attention to their cause, and had met with a particularly militant umbrella while on display at the Royal Academy. The tear, and the spirit which it represented, was what made his father buy it in the first place, and his mother had resolutely refused to have the canvas repaired. Archie remembered how united they had always seemed. He was trying not to think too deeply about the consequences of this investigation on his relationship with the estate but – amid the doubts and suspicions that now surrounded some of his oldest friends – he knew that he desperately needed to find something in his past of which he could be confident, and the uncomplicated strength of his parents' marriage took on a new resonance.

'Can't let you out of my sight for a minute, Sir, can I?' Bill Fallowfield's voice cut in on his thoughts, as cheerful and reassuring as ever. 'I did try to tell you that theatre in the open air was a daft idea, but you wouldn't listen.'

Archie laughed. 'News travels fast, Sergeant – have you

also heard that I'm forfeiting my holiday as penance for not listening to you?'

'They did mention something of the sort. A bit selfish of you, Sir, if you don't mind me saying. A fortnight with Inspector Rogers in charge is more than enough for anyone, so I'd appreciate it if you could get everything cleared up down there as soon as possible – for my sake, if nothing else.'

'I'll do my best, Bill, but I could do with a bit of help. We've got a missing person down here – could be in the frame for the killing, could be a victim himself, or could simply have disappeared up country to get away from a bit of trouble. Could you put a note in the *Gazette* for me and see if anything turns up?'

'Must be something in the air down there,' Fallowfield said after Penrose had given him the details. 'That's the third disappearance we've had word of in a month – a lighthouse keeper from Penzance, a clerk in Cornwall on holiday and now an undertaker's son. Are you sure you don't want me to throw a few things in a bag and come down to sort them out for you? I'd go a long way for a sniff of the sea and some of Mrs Snipe's cooking.'

'You'd be very welcome,' Archie said, wondering if Bill knew how much he meant it, 'but I'd better give the local boys a chance.' His sergeant made a noise that indicated quite clearly what he thought of the Cornish force, but he dutifully read back the details that were to go into the police newspaper. They talked for a bit about various cases that were ongoing, then Archie rang off and went back to the kitchen, where a cup of strong, black coffee was waiting for him.

'You look like you need that,' said Josephine. 'Scrambled or fried?'

'Is that a question about my breakfast or a comment on my state of mind?' he asked drily. 'I don't mind – which do you do best?'

'Scrambled. You won't taste better outside of Scotland.'

'Then scrambled it is. Bill sends his regards, by the way, and asks what chapter you're on.'

She grimaced as she broke the eggs into a bowl. 'I suppose that's the only advantage of your holiday going up in smoke – think of it as doing some sort of service to crime fiction. It's a drastic way of forcing me to work, though. Have you had *any* sleep?'

'Yes, but only a bit – perhaps that's why this all seems so surreal.' He sipped his coffee appreciatively. 'You know, I can hardly believe that Nathaniel's dead. One minute, we're sitting on the rocks in the sun talking about Harry, and the next he's falling over the cliff dressed as a jackdaw. And God knows what happened in between.'

'You said the conversation was interesting.'

'It was. I'd never really talked to him before, although I'd heard lots of good things about him from William – and I can see why now.'

'You liked him, then?'

'Yes, very much. He seemed to take his role so seriously,' he explained, echoing Morveth's description of Nathaniel as a boy, 'and his dedication to the estate and the people on it was extraordinary. He was honest, too – or at least that's how he came across in the brief time we spent together.' He got up from the table and cut the loaf of bread into thick slices. 'Perhaps he just needed a stranger to talk to – there was certainly a lot on his mind. He admitted to being in love with Harry.'

Josephine stopped beating the eggs and looked at him. 'A vicar in a small village? He certainly wasn't after an easy life, was he? How terrible for him – having to keep all that anxiety and grief to himself. Is that what you were going to tell me last night?'

'Not just that.' He repeated what Nathaniel had told him about the fire at the Pinchings' cottage.

'So Harry set the fire, with his parents and little sister in the house asleep – or so he thought – and went back upstairs to die as well?' Josephine was incredulous. 'Poor Loveday, walking around with all that stuff in her head and no one to help her through it.'

'And poor Nathaniel – having to carry it alone and reconcile it with his feelings for Harry.'

'Do you think he *was* the only one who knew?'

'I've no idea – that's one of the things I've got to try to find out today. You can imagine how much I'm looking forward to running the scenario past Morwenna.'

'She was away from home on the night of the fire, wasn't she?' Josephine said, remembering what Ronnie had told her on the journey from Penzance.

'Yes – she was working at the poorhouse in Helston.' He watched as she put a mountain of butter in a saucepan to melt. 'Why? You're not reading anything into that, are you?'

'No, not really. It's just that she doesn't strike me as the philanthropic type.'

'Based on the two minutes you've spent with her?' he asked, but the sarcasm was tame, with no hint of the defensiveness that had touched their earlier conversations about Morwenna. 'You may well be right, but it was a job, not an act of generosity. There aren't that many career options here, you know.'

'I suppose you've got to look at that as a serious motive for Nathaniel's murder,' Josephine continued thoughtfully. 'Protecting Harry's reputation, I mean.'

'Yes, although I'm inclined now to think that Harry's death was suspicious, too.'

'Why more so than before?'

'Well, if I hadn't seen someone force Nathaniel over the edge, I'd have been convinced that he either slipped or – after the conversation I'd just had with him – threw himself off. The circumstances are different, but the deaths could be interpreted in the same way by an outsider – an accident seems the most obvious explanation, suicide's a possibility, but murder seems unlikely. The sightlines are marginal on that stage – if I'd been standing a foot or two forward or to my right, I wouldn't have seen a thing – in the same way that no one saw the actual moment that Harry went into the water. Apart from Christopher, perhaps – and he's vanished.'

'It's very risky to rely on where you might choose to stand, though,' Josephine argued, turning the bacon in the pan. 'It's either audacious or desperate, and it backfired completely. And surely there are easier ways of killing Harry and making it look like suicide than a riding accident? Horses are so unpredictable, and you say he was a good rider – it would be very hard to be sure of the outcome.'

'All right, all right,' he said, holding his hands up. 'I admit that, as patterns go, it's tenuous to say the least. I suppose I'm just trying to justify my instincts. Even though I know for a fact how many people have drowned in the Loe Pool – strong swimmers as well as idiots – I was surprised when I heard about Harry's accident, and downright disbelieving when Morwenna mentioned suicide – and I haven't changed my mind on either count. Harry did seem to have upset a few people of late.'

'But what Loveday said about the fire shows that he *was* capable of taking his own life.'

'I know, and I'm probably being too blinkered, but I simply don't believe it.'

'It seems unlikely that the same person would kill Harry *and* kill to protect him, though.'

'Exactly. That just doesn't make sense. So either I'm wrong altogether about Harry's death, or there are two murders and two murderers, or the fire and Harry's reputation had nothing to do with Nathaniel's killing.'

'What if Nathaniel had something to do with Harry's death? I'm assuming his love was unrequited?'

Archie nodded. 'As far as I know, yes.'

'Perhaps he just couldn't take it any more. Maybe Harry tried to blackmail him or threatened to expose his homosexuality. It would be the end of Nathaniel's life here if that happened, and the scandal would be terrible. That's a powerful motive for murder, and if someone found out, perhaps they took it upon themselves to avenge Harry's death. An eye for an eye, and all that.'

They sat down to eat, and Archie considered Josephine's suggestion. 'I really can't see Nathaniel as a killer,' he said. 'His reaction to Harry's death was genuine, I'm sure, and anyway – if someone found out that Nathaniel had killed Harry, surely they'd just go to the police.'

'Yes, of course,' said Josephine wryly. 'I was forgetting how law-abiding you all seem down here. I don't suppose for a moment that anyone would take the law into their own hands.'

He laughed. 'How quickly you've settled in.'

'I haven't asked you what you actually saw last night,' Josephine said. 'How did it happen?'

Archie went through the whole incident, from the moment he suspected something was wrong to his finding of Nathaniel's body. 'And I don't need to tell you how many suspects there are. Most of the cast were wearing brown habits and, if that weren't bad enough, an identical one – Nathaniel's original costume – went missing from the vestry a few days ago. The only people we can really rule out are the audience and the handful of actors with more individual costumes.' He rubbed his hands wearily over his eyes. 'If only I'd reacted more quickly. I doubt I could have saved Nathaniel, but I might at least have caught his killer.'

'That's ridiculous,' she said bluntly. 'Even from where we were sitting, everything happened so quickly, so God knows what it must have been like for you.'

'What do *you* remember about the evening? Any comings and goings I should know about?'

'Well, Morwenna and Loveday were there early on, but they'd disappeared by the time the play started – I didn't see them again, but they left their things behind. Morveth picked them up, I think. You know that the vicar stormed out, and his wife went after him as soon as the play was stopped. I noticed Kestrel Jacks in the audience around then, as well – he was standing at the back until William fetched him.'

'That doesn't rule him out – he could have gone up the actors' steps like you did to get to the back of the theatre.'

'Yes, and the same goes for the undertaker. I didn't see him leave, but he came back down from the cliff-top quite a while later. The audience had gone by then, and the rest of us were gathered on the stage. He seemed flustered about something – other than the accident, I mean.'

'Yes. He says his van was stolen last night.'

'You sound like you don't believe him,' she said cautiously, at a loss to know how she could question Jago's capacity for violence without betraying the Snipe's confidence.

'To be honest, Josephine, I'm not sure what I believe,' Archie said, his frustration getting the better of him. 'You were spot-on just now – everyone's a law unto themselves, and they've been palming me off with half-stories and veiled threats ever since I got here. I thought Jago was as straight as they come – but he's the worst of the lot. He asks me to help him find Christopher, but he won't tell me anything that might allow me to do that – he just mutters some obscure reference to his being punished by Christopher's disappearance. What's that all about, for Christ's sake?'

'You mean Christopher's punishing his father by staying away?'

'No – the implication was definitely that someone might hurt Christopher to get back at him, but I couldn't get anything more out of him.'

'Did Jago have any reason to want Nathaniel out of the way?'

'Not to my knowledge, but what does that prove? So no, I don't know whether to believe Jago about the van – it could have been taken by the killer, or it could be that he knows exactly what happened to it and just won't tell me. Perhaps he suspects Christopher of having something to do with Nathaniel's death and stealing the van to get away quickly. Or perhaps he had a reason to get rid of it himself.'

Josephine could easily understand how Archie felt. Absolute

ignorance was one thing but there was nothing worse than being taunted with something that was never fully revealed. His anger mirrored her own irritation with Morveth last night, and it made her even more uneasy about carrying so many secrets which had not been shared with him. Could it really be that he had no idea what his mother had suffered? 'Tell me about your uncle,' she said, trying to sound casual about it. 'He must be in the frame after that impromptu scene.'

'Jasper? He's greedy, hypocritical and thoroughly vile – and despite all that, completely unsuited to a career in the Church.' Josephine laughed, and wondered if Archie got the scepticism which she had often heard him express from his mother. 'There are rumours that he has his hand in the church till – they've been going around for as long as I can remember – but no one's ever proved it. Needless to say, there was a collective sigh of relief when he announced his retirement, and I think William's more relieved than most, but even that's not straightforward now.'

'But nothing else?'

'Not that I know of. Why do you ask?'

'Because of something Loveday said. She told me about the pilfering – that's old news, as you said, and not at all interesting, apparently – but she also said that Nathaniel had discovered a more serious misdemeanour and was trying to find out more about it.'

'So she doesn't know what Nathaniel was talking about?'

'No – but the vicar overheard her telling me all about it. We were in the church at the time, and I caught a glimpse of him in the vestry.' She remembered the shadowy figure at the door, and how intently he had been listening to Loveday's innocent chatter. 'My God, I should have told you that before. I knew it was stupid of Nathaniel to talk so carelessly, but I didn't think it would get him killed.'

'Calm down – I'm sure that's not the reason. Jasper's a despicable human being, but I don't think he's a killer. Apart from anything else, the person who ran away from that cliff was a damned sight fitter than my uncle. And I know you like Loveday, but people don't often take her very seriously, and her comments won't have been as significant to Jasper as you thought they were.'

'I think you're underestimating Loveday, you know. Morveth and I talked for a while last night when you'd gone down to look for Nathaniel's body, and she certainly takes her seriously.'

'Does Morveth know what Nathaniel had discovered about Jasper?'

'No,' Josephine said but, on reflection, she realised that Morveth had not actually said that she didn't know – just that she didn't think it was anything to do with Lizzie Penrose.

'All right. I'll drop in on Jasper later if it'll put your mind at rest.' Josephine doubted that any conversation between Archie and his uncle would put her mind at rest, but she let it pass without comment. 'Where was Morveth, by the way?' Archie asked. 'Did you see her during the play?'

'I hadn't met her before,' she reminded him, 'but William looked for her at one point and couldn't see her. I know she wasn't around to see the incident with Jasper, though, because she told me she'd had to go back to the bus for something.'

'For an ensemble piece, there were precious few people around when it mattered,' he said.

She laughed. 'Morveth seemed anxious afterwards, though – more so than everyone else. She implied it wasn't a straight-forward accident right from the start.'

'That's interesting. I know she has a habit of getting to the truth before the rest of us, but even so . . . And I can't be sure, but I think she overheard at least some of my conversation with Nathaniel.'

Josephine realised that they hadn't really talked about Morwenna yet. She was reluctant to mention her name after Archie's sensitivity during their earlier conversations, but she needed to convince him to explore the nature of Morwenna's relationship with her brother. She considered how best to raise the subject without being too specific: now wasn't the time to reveal Morveth's confidence to Archie – wittingly or unwittingly – but she wasn't entirely convinced by Morveth's argument that ignorance was best. There was a horrible irony in being the last to know something about your own family. She would never forget going home to Inverness for Christmas one year and being the only one who didn't know that her mother had just been diagnosed with cancer. An air of forced jollity hung over all the usual rituals and traditions; she noticed, but could not explain it, and later, when Christmas was over and the news was broken, she felt isolated and humiliated. She had never entirely forgiven her family for not telling her straight away, no matter how well intentioned the decision had been, and she knew that Archie would feel the same. For now, though, he had enough to worry about. 'Morwenna had fallen out with Nathaniel, hadn't she?' she said warily. 'Loveday wasn't allowed to speak to him any more.'

'No. Morwenna told me it was because he'd been confusing Loveday by talking about eternal life and making it difficult for her to accept Harry's death. That made perfect sense to me at the time – it's a big responsibility to have to manage your little sister's grief as well as deal with your own – but obviously there was more to it than that. Nathaniel said he'd faced them both with Loveday's revelation about the fire, and she blamed him for Harry's death.'

'You don't think it was suicide, though.'

'No. Do you still really think Morwenna killed Harry?'

'Well, she *had* just discovered that he killed her parents,' Josephine pointed out. 'And perhaps she wanted Nathaniel out of the way to make sure the family's reputation wasn't completely destroyed.' Archie didn't dismiss this as she had feared he might, and she took advantage of his silence. 'Or perhaps there are other family secrets that we don't know about.'

'Go on.'

'Look, I know you weren't convinced the other day when I suggested that Morwenna might have been afraid of Harry, but something Morveth said last night made me even more sure that there's some truth in that.' She bent down to give some bacon to Motley Penrose, who had appeared at the door just in time to excuse her from looking at Archie while she spoke to him. 'She was talking about a woman on the estate who had been ill-treated by someone close to her, and she said that the woman had to lock herself in her room to get away. That's word for word what Loveday said Morwenna used to do when she and Harry were arguing.' She paused, but still he said nothing. 'You find that impossible to believe, don't you?'

'Perhaps I just don't want to believe it,' he said honestly, 'but it's possible, I suppose. He was the man of the house after his parents died, and he'd have had virtually free rein to do anything and get away with it.'

'It would explain why Harry and Nathaniel had to go, and perhaps Christopher, too. He was close to Loveday, and

Morwenna must have worried about what was said between them.'

'We don't know that anything's happened to Christopher,' Archie said cautiously. 'I'm not dismissing it, but to kill three people is a very extreme reaction.'

'Don't underestimate the shame of it,' said Josephine gently. 'Talk to her about it. It might have absolutely nothing to do with these killings, but she might still appreciate a sympathetic ear from a man she can trust. And she does trust you – that's obvious.'

'I'm beginning to think you care about this as much as I do.'

She smiled. 'I can't stop thinking about Loveday,' she admitted. 'That conversation we had really affected me, and I can see why Nathaniel was troubled by what she told him. It's so obvious that she's caught up in a relationship which she simply doesn't understand. There's something intense and dark about it – about the family in general.'

'Who was Morveth talking about?' he asked.

It was the question she had been dreading, and she knew one secret would have to be sacrificed to answer it. 'I promised the Snipe I wouldn't tell you this,' she said, trying to convince herself that it was a sin of omission rather than a lie, 'but in light of what's happened, you ought to know because it shows he can be violent. When I went down to the kitchen the other night, the Snipe was with Beth Jacks, bathing her face. She'd been beaten up by her husband, and I gather it happens regularly.'

'You've found out a lot in forty-eight hours,' he said, impressed.

'You don't have to be here long to realise that the men think they run things, while the women unite and get on with their lives in their own way.'

Archie nodded. 'That's true, and I don't know why I'm shocked about Jacks – he's a brute at the best of times – but I am. I'm beginning to feel more out of touch with my own home than ever.'

Josephine looked at him with concern. 'This is going to be hard for you, isn't it? Should you have agreed to take it on?'

'I'm involved whether I like it or not,' he said. 'It sounds stupid, but, if nothing else, I feel as though I owe it to my parents. They loved this place – it was so much a part of who they were, and if the heart of it has to be torn apart, then it should at least be done by someone who cares. Protecting it – if I can protect it at all from whatever's going on here – feels like doing something for them.' The tenderness in his voice when he spoke of his parents made Josephine all the more convinced that now was not the time to make him any more vulnerable to his emotions. 'I suppose all I'm saying is that it's personal,' he added, 'and I don't know yet if that's a good thing or a bad. But either way, it's time I made a move.' He got up, looking a little embarrassed, and walked over to the dresser, where she had left the volume of Tennyson. 'Brushing up on your Arthurian legends?' he asked, picking it up.

'I thought I'd better. I'm embarrassingly vague on anything between Shakespeare and Kipling, and I'm ashamed to say that Tennyson has passed me by completely.' She watched as he turned the pages, and couldn't help feeling that he needed the peace and quiet of the Lodge rather more than she did at the moment. 'Are you sure you won't stay here instead of at the house?' she asked. 'It must be chaos over there and we can easily swap. Or you could offer me police protection,' she added as he started to protest. 'I wouldn't mind some company with what's going on at the moment.'

'That is utter rubbish, Josephine, and you know it,' he said, laughing. 'You're perfectly happy on your own – irritatingly so, in fact.'

'Okay, I admit I've made more convincing excuses – but it's not as if there isn't plenty of room for us both.' She raised an eyebrow. 'And think of how much it would give the girls to talk about. Seriously, though – I really do think you'd be better off here at the moment. You need familiarity and time to think, and – much as I love them – you won't get that with Lettice and Ronnie breathing down your neck for every detail of the case.'

'What about your work?'

'Now *you're* talking rubbish. If it's anything like your cases in London, you won't be here enough to disturb me. In fact, it's probably the only way I'll get to see you at all.'

'All right – as long as you're sure your reputation can stand it?' She nodded. 'I really must go,' he said again. 'I think I'll start with Morwenna – it can only get easier after that. I'll see you later, then.'

'Yes, but there is one condition,' she said as she walked him to his car. 'I get to tell Ronnie that we're moving in together.'

Chapter Thirteen

Penrose knocked at the door of Loe Cottage and waited, but there was no answer. Just as he was raising his hand to try again, he heard footsteps inside and the heavy curtain which had been drawn across the entrance was pulled roughly back. Even through the glass, Archie could see that Morwenna looked exhausted; there was no colour in her face, and the dark rings around her eyes which had shocked him at the funeral were even more pronounced now. He had expected her to be surprised to see him but, if she was, she showed no sign of it. 'Archie,' she said, with a trace of impatience, 'I thought it was only a matter of time before you'd show up. I hear the play didn't exactly go off as planned.'

'You know about Nathaniel's death?'

'Yes. Morveth came over early this morning. She had to bring some things back that I left at the Minack, and she told me then. I suppose you're here to find out why I left in such a hurry.'

'Amongst other things, yes. Can I come in?'

'All right, but you'll have to be quiet. Loveday's not well, and I don't want her disturbed.'

She stood aside to let him through into the kitchen. 'Sit down. I'll make some tea.' He took a seat, and looked with interest at the picnic rug and familiar copy of Tennyson's poetry which had been left on the table – presumably the items which Morveth had returned during her early-morning visit. Inside, the cottage showed no sign of the neglect which had puzzled him in the garden on Sunday: the blue slate slabs of the kitchen floor had been swept clean and the furniture was scrubbed and tidy; all that was left of the wake was a pair of empty whisky bottles on the floor in the corner.

'I'm sorry to hear about Loveday,' he said, conscious of how formal and strained his words sounded. His relationship with Morwenna had always been relaxed and straightforward; even their brief exchange at the funeral – although dominated by her anxieties – had felt natural and warm, but today he was uncomfortable around her, knowing that he was about to stretch the limits of their friendship. 'What's the matter with her?'

'Stomach cramps,' she said, bringing the pot over to the table. 'Girls' problems, in other words. They came on suddenly last night and she was in agony. I had to get her home, and Jago had been obliging enough to leave his keys in the ignition, so I borrowed his van.'

At least that was one search which could be called off, he thought. 'Where's the van now?'

'Morveth took it back with my apologies,' she said, and pushed a cup across the table towards him. 'So you can arrest me for theft, if you like, but not for murder. There have been times recently when I could happily have killed Nathaniel, but I didn't.'

He was inclined to believe her, but had no intention of leaving the matter there. 'So how do you feel about the fact that someone else has?'

'It's another thing that will hurt Loveday when she comes to understand it properly, and I'm sorry about that, but I've used up all my grief lately. I don't have any left for Nathaniel, as callous as that might sound. He has a community to mourn him, and a God to save him. He doesn't need me.'

Archie realised that he was going to get very little out of Morwenna if she continued in this mood. He had years of experience in breaking down the barriers that people put up against his questioning, but he sensed that this was different: Morwenna wasn't being evasive; she was simply past caring, about herself or anyone else, and it was almost impossible to get someone in that state of mind to co-operate. There seemed little point in being anything other than direct with her. 'It seems to me that Nathaniel knew a lot about this estate,' he said, 'and he wasn't particularly wise about who he shared his information with. Was he right to think that Harry deliberately started the fire that killed your parents?'

She looked at him, and he was ashamed of the satisfaction he took from having managed to surprise her. 'How should *I* know?' she said, recovering quickly. 'I wasn't here.'

'No, but you've had eight years to think about it. Surely you don't expect me to believe you didn't confront Harry after what Nathaniel said to you, even if that was the first time you suspected anything other than an accident?' Her defiance was irritating him, and he saw no reason to hide his impatience. 'Harry's dead, Morwenna – I can't hurt him, and neither can you. But other people *are* going to get hurt if someone doesn't start telling the truth. This estate will be torn apart by lies and secrets, and I'm not just talking about reputations and loyalties. Nathaniel was murdered. Right now, while we're sitting here drinking tea, his parents are at the mortuary viewing a body that has been smashed to pieces. His God *didn't* save him, and neither will He save the next person who opens their mouth at the wrong time. And there *will* be more killings, I promise you, because none of you are as careful as you should be with your secrets and your threats – it might be you, it might be me, it might even be Loveday, but someone else will die if I don't get some help.'

'That's quite a speech, Archie,' she said flippantly, but he could see that she was unsettled. 'How do you know that the fire had anything to do with Nathaniel's death?'

'I don't,' he said frankly, 'but I've got to start somewhere. Would you rather I went upstairs and got the truth from Loveday? I'm happy to do that, and I'm sure she'd give it to me.'

'All right,' she said, and then, more to herself, 'what harm can it do now, anyway? Nathaniel was right – Harry did start the fire, and he did it deliberately. I didn't know at the time, but he told me afterwards. Neither of us knew that Loveday had seen anything, but Nathaniel was only confirming what I knew already and thought I could leave in the past.'

'Did Harry threaten to hurt you if you told anyone about it?'

'He didn't need to threaten me. I wouldn't have betrayed him.'

'Not even for killing your parents and – for all he knew – Loveday as well? It's hardly betrayal. He must have forced you to keep quiet somehow.' She stayed silent and, convinced now that Josephine was right, Archie searched for the best way to ask the question. 'If he was violent towards you, it's understandable that you should be too frightened to say anything. Anyone in your position would have done the same.'

'What?' She looked at him in confusion, then seemed to realise what he was getting at. To his astonishment, she started

244

to laugh, but it was a hollow sound, close to hysteria, and it filled him with an unaccountable sadness. 'You've got it so wrong, Archie,' she said eventually. 'Is that really how you see me? As another Beth Jacks? I loved Harry.'

'Of course you did, he was your brother.'

'Oh, what's the use any more? It's all falling apart. I didn't love him as a brother, Archie. We were lovers, and we had been for years. That's why I would never have said anything. My loyalty has always been to him, not to my parents, and it will always be to his memory, not to theirs.'

Suddenly it all fell into place – the secrecy, the shame, as Josephine had put it; that was the darkness at the heart of this family. How odd that she should be so close to the truth, and yet so far away. Archie could only imagine the strain of keeping such a secret, and the way in which it must have influenced all of Harry and Morwenna's relationships – their every meeting with another person, in fact. The split between the mask and the reality must have been unbearable for Morwenna since Harry's death; she must have longed for someone to listen without judgement – or was that simply his own arrogance speaking, his need to do something constructive when he really felt hopelessly inadequate to deal with the strength of Morwenna's emotions? 'When did it start?' he asked gently.

'In the way you mean, when we were twelve. Loveday had just been born, and she was the centre of attention, so you could say we made our own amusement.'

'And in the way I don't mean?'

She smiled, genuinely this time. 'Years before, I suppose. Harry and I were always together – we had no choice. Everyone thought we made a perfect family, but we'd been two separate couples – mum and dad, Harry and me – for as long as I can remember. Our parents never treated us as individuals – it was always "the twins this" or "the twins that". We were told to play together, put to bed together, punished and rewarded together. They rationalised it by saying they were determined never to have a favourite, but that's not how it felt to us – it felt like we had no identity except as a pair. There was nothing intentional about it, no hostility – I don't think they even realised they were doing it, and they'd probably have been horrified if they knew how isolated we felt emotionally. But they were always more interested in each other than in us, and there's a limit to how long you can push and shove for attention.'

Her words reminded Archie of Josephine's concerns for Loveday, and he wondered if Morwenna knew she was behaving in the very same way towards her little sister. 'But they did pay more attention to Loveday,' he said.

'Yes. They'd been trying for another child for years, and my mother had had several miscarriages by that time. When Loveday came along, all the focus was on her and it was as if they suddenly realised how to be parents. They talked to her all the time, and played with her so naturally and spontaneously. We'd have had to be saints not to resent all that individual care – and we certainly weren't saints, either of us. We got so tired of hearing that Loveday was special, and we just retreated into each other even further. It was a dangerous age to do that, of course – we were curious about sex, and our parents weren't about to take us to one side and explain everything, so we decided to find out for ourselves.' She drank her tea, hardly seeming to notice that it was long cold. 'Harry was my reference point for everything,' she continued. 'I don't mean that he forced me to do anything – it was entirely mutual; I just mean that I depended on him, and he on me. One minute we were brother and sister, fighting and playing together, and the next, we'd crossed a line. It all seemed to start so naturally – we had this game where we'd throw stones into the lake or skim them across the sea, and compete for kisses. One thing just led to another.' She looked down, embarrassed, and Archie waited for her to go on. 'I think it was the safety of it all that we loved as much as anything,' she said, and he sensed that she was desperate for him to understand. 'It meant that we didn't have to break out of our cocoon and establish our own identities with anybody else. We'd never had to do that, and I think it terrified both of us. There was an emotional security in what we had, and a safety valve against our feelings for everyone else – by loving each other, we avoided being angry with our parents and jealous of Loveday.'

With no brothers or sisters of his own, Archie had only ever experienced a sibling relationship second-hand, but it did not take much imagination to see that a brother and sister – who already knew each other so intimately – would share an intense private world if they ignored all the taboos.

'I shouldn't describe it in such negative terms,' Morwenna said. 'It was something precious and uniquely ours, and we both took a great deal of pleasure from it. It seemed so innocent, really. I remember thinking that it was just a childish thing, and one day I was sure to grow up and tire of it. I kept expecting the sheer joy of him to wear off, but it never did.'

'Weren't you afraid that someone would find out?'

'Yes and no. We had no other supervision, really, and I suppose there was an element of rebellion in it. If they were going to treat us as one, then we might as well be one – physically and emotionally. We soon discovered that there's a remarkable power in being able to deceive everyone.'

'Even yourselves? You must have known how people would have viewed it if you were discovered.'

'Yes, but we were each other's moral guide – and the one great thing about it was the honesty. It's so rare that you can show your truest self to someone, whether you love it or hate it. How many people have you allowed that close?' He considered, and was ashamed to admit that there was no one. 'It was our integrity to ourselves and to each other that mattered,' she said, 'not rules that someone else had laid down. Sometimes I think Harry felt guilty because of all the old sexual prejudices – he was the boy, and perhaps he'd taken advantage of me in some way and violated my trust, but it was never like that. I worshipped him. I would have done anything for him, and he for me.'

'Hence the fire? Is that why he did it? Did your parents find out?'

'Yes. It was a stupid way to get caught, really, but we thought we were invincible by then.'

'That's love for you.'

'I suppose so. Dad always had to be out of the house early to see to the horses, and he'd take Harry with him to exercise them. Whenever he could, Harry would come back to the cottage after my mother had left for the Union. One day she came back early because she wasn't well, and she caught us in my bed. It was as simple as that. I don't know who was more shocked when she opened the door, her or us. She just stood there with her mouth open for what seemed like an age, and eventually Harry laughed. That did it, of course – it was a nervous reaction more than anything, but I'll never forget the look of disgust on her face, or the things she called us. '

'What did they do about it?'

'Well, all hell broke loose – behind closed doors, of course. My father ignored me entirely as if he just wanted to gloss over my part in it all, but he beat Harry within an inch of his life. I suppose that was the only response he understood. I was so angry. I've never known a rage like the one I felt when I saw what he'd done to Harry – to his son, for God's sake. After that, the shame set in and it was never mentioned again.' She ran her fingers round the rim of her cup, apparently absorbed in her own thoughts. 'How ridiculous that all seems now – we were never given a chance to talk about it or explain how we felt, and neither of them seemed to understand that there might have been a reason for it. Or perhaps they did, and just didn't want to acknowledge that they'd had anything to do with it. Either way, they just closed down and tried to behave as if nothing had happened.'

'What about you and Harry? *Did* you stop?'

'Of course we didn't. It just made us more secretive, and more contemptuous of them. We laughed at how impotent they seemed – when of course it was Harry and me who couldn't control what we were doing. They knew we were carrying on as before, and it didn't take them long to realise that nothing would stop us except physical separation. I was sent to the Union until they could arrange something more permanent, and that's why he started the fire – they were going to send him away. My father had a sister who'd married up country, and they asked her if he could go and live there.' She paused and looked around the kitchen, as if trying to imagine what that night had been like. 'Harry told me he started the fire here, with the letter our aunt wrote to say yes.'

'But why wipe out everyone, himself and Loveday included?' Archie was trying to keep his voice as dispassionate as possible, but it was hard to disguise his anger at the recollection of how William had risked his own life to save Harry and Loveday, and how guilty his uncle had felt for failing to rescue the whole family. 'Everyone except you, that is.'

'Yes, that must have looked suspicious. I suppose it crossed your policeman's mind that I might have started it for some reason?'

'Yes, or that you knew he was going to do it.'

'No, I had no idea, and it wasn't a calculated thing on his part – please believe that. He was in absolute despair – it was a kind of madness, I suppose. I'm not trying to excuse what he did, but he was eighteen and utterly lost. Our relationship was the core of who we were, and the only reality we knew. Without it, there was nothing, and you're absolutely right to say he wanted to wipe everything out; he didn't care because the rest of the world simply didn't exist for him any more. What we had wasn't just one relationship that existed alongside others – it was *the* relationship, something that belonged to the past and the future. Nothing could be allowed to stand in the way of it.'

Archie said nothing, but he thought about what it must have been like in that household before the fire. Love amongst members of a family often turned to hate but rarely to indifference, and he could only begin to imagine the trauma involved when the temptation to possess each other sexually became too much.

'I don't expect you to understand,' Morwenna said, misreading his silence. 'I'm not sure we did.'

'It sounds to me like you have a fairly good understanding.'

She smiled. 'I've had plenty of time to think about it.'

'Did anyone outside the family know?'

'Morveth – they asked her to look after Loveday for a few days to get her out of the house when things were at their worst. And I think my father must have told Jago – they were good friends, and he always went to him for advice.'

'Do you think Loveday had any sense of what was going on?'

'No, she was far too young to understand.'

She wasn't too young now, though, Archie thought, and there was no way that all the complexities of Harry's love for Morwenna would have died with his parents. 'Loveday said you'd argued a lot with Harry recently, and that you even had to lock yourself in your room to keep him away.'

'She told you that?'

He hesitated. 'Not exactly.'

'Ah – she told your friend, then. How useful for you to have a spy in residence.' Archie started to deny that it was like that, but of course – in effect – it was. 'You might as well hear it from me, I suppose,' Morwenna continued. 'Strangely, no one seemed to suspect that the fire was anything other than an accident, but that left Morveth with a dilemma – if Harry was sent away, who would support Loveday and me? You know how it is – breaking a family up is the last resort and the Union gates are always open, so Morveth allowed him to stay on the condition that we behaved ourselves.'

The flippancy of her words would have annoyed Archie if he didn't know her well enough to see through it. 'And you managed to convince her that you could?'

'We did better than that – we did stop, at least the physical side of our relationship. It went against everything in my heart and you've no idea how badly I craved that sort of affection, but it was the only thing to do. We had a responsibility to Loveday, and sometimes I've hated her for it.'

'And Harry accepted that?'

'Yes, because it was only supposed to be temporary. I let him think that we'd begin again when she was grown up, and I suppose it was easier to tell myself that as well. We started pulling together for us, for some sort of mythical happy ending. It's funny – everyone admired Harry for taking the disappointment of missing out on his new life so well. As far as most of them were concerned, he'd given up his future to do his duty, when in reality he didn't have a future that wasn't here with me.'

'But you obviously knew in your heart that things would never work out for you.'

'I didn't love him any less, but things were different after the fire and after what he'd done – different for both of us, I think. We kidded ourselves that we could simply emerge from behind our secret one day and live a normal life, but our relationship was never going to be a permanent sanctuary. You can't be responsible for a death and not be affected by it. The beauty of our love was that it was exclusive – there was no one else in the world but Harry and me. Suddenly that changed. There was Loveday to worry about, and the spectre of my parents hanging over us, and all the guilt that we'd kept at bay for so long was with me all the time. When Loveday was older, he started to talk about us again, and tried to pick up where we left off. Don't think I wasn't tempted – locking my door was as much about keeping myself back as keeping him out – but I couldn't do it. It was tainted, somehow, and I think that deep down he knew that.'

'How did he react?'

'Badly. He drank, he gambled, he took his frustration out on everyone. And he . . . well, he looked elsewhere.'

'That must have hurt.'

'Yes, but it was my choice. I could have brought him back to me at any time, but I didn't.'

'Who did he turn to?'

'No one you know,' she said quickly, and he detected the first lie of their conversation but was reluctant to press her. Was it Nathaniel, he wondered? Had the curate – out of loyalty or out of shame – only told him half the truth?

'Did Nathaniel ever find out that you and Harry were lovers?' he asked.

'No, although he may have guessed in time, I suppose. But, as you said, he wasn't the type to cover up what he knew and I'm sure he would have tackled us about it if he'd known.'

'How did Harry feel when Nathaniel confronted him about the fire?'

'Betrayed. Things had been strained between them for some time, and Harry could never work out why. He said he kept going out of his way to be friendly towards Nathaniel, but all it did was drive him further away. He finally understood what had gone wrong between them when Nathaniel came to see him about the fire, but that only made things worse. Harry thought true friendship was strong enough to withstand anything – you were loyal to him or you weren't, you loved him or you didn't. He wasn't unlike Loveday in that respect. It sounds simplistic to you, I suppose, but he expected Nathaniel to be on his side, to know that he'd have had his reasons and to trust him; the fact that he didn't was unforgivable, but by that time he was mixing in very different company anyway.'

'The argument you had with Harry on the night before he died – was that about renewing your relationship or Nathaniel's knowledge of the fire?'

'Both, I suppose. They were interlinked by then, and there were always new variations on that old theme.' Morwenna closed her eyes briefly, as though wanting to shut out the image of that final night. 'We had a terrible row, and I accused him – amongst other things – of never having truly loved me. I said it in the heat of the moment, but if I'd sat down and thought for hours I couldn't have come up with anything that would have hurt him more. He hit me – just a slap, nothing more, and I deserved it, but it horrified him to realise that he could do such a thing. Anything other than tenderness was alien to him as far as I was concerned. Then he stormed out, and I heard him take Shilling from the stable.'

'And that was the last time you saw him?'

She hesitated. 'No. I saw him once more, not long before he died.'

'Where?'

'At the boathouse by the Lodge.'

'What were *you* doing there?'

'I couldn't take it any more, Archie,' she said, unable to hold back the tears any longer. 'The pain of living with Harry and not being with him, of bringing up Loveday in some sick parody of a happy family. And he'd changed towards me – he'd look at me sometimes as if the hopelessness of it all was my fault, as if I'd wantonly destroyed our happiness. You have no idea how claustrophobic I felt in this house. We couldn't get away from each other. And with everything that Nathaniel had said, it could only be a matter of time before it all came out. I just needed peace – peace for me, without having to bear the responsibility of Loveday and Harry's feelings, and there was only one way I could think of to make it all go away.'

'You were going to take your own life?'

254

'Yes. I left the house shortly after he did, just to get away from these four walls, and I didn't even stop to think about Loveday. I walked by the lake for a long time. You know what it's like at night – there's nothing as quiet, nothing as close to oblivion as that water when it's still. I made my way to the boathouse, knowing that there was no one at the Lodge to see me, and I decided to take the boat out to the middle and put an end to the misery – for all of us. I sat on the landing stage for a long time, watching it get light, thinking about what a mess everything had become and how our parents had died for nothing, and trying not to think about what would happen to Harry when he knew what I'd done.'

'But he found you there?'

'Yes.'

'How was he?'

'He looked terrible. He'd been drinking again and fighting, and his face was cut and bruised, but he was different, somehow – calmer, resigned. I think he guessed immediately what I was going to do, although he didn't say so; he just talked to me – gently, like the old Harry, convincing me to live. He said nothing could ever take away what we had, but he realised that he had to get away from the estate and everything that had happened. We walked back here together, and he told me he would always love me, no matter where he went. I had no idea what he meant to do, and I didn't have the strength to argue with him any more. I thought he was going away, just like he was supposed to all those years ago. I didn't know the selfish bastard was going to ride his horse into the lake.' She broke down completely now, and Archie got up and went round to the other side of the table, unable to do anything but hold her. 'How could he let me down like that? He forced me to go on

255

without any hope of him, looking after Loveday in this living hell. Sometimes, when I think of how he's betrayed me, the hatred sticks in my throat and I can hardly breathe. It should have been him who had to live, but he fooled me, and I'll never forgive him for that.'

If Morwenna really blamed Nathaniel for Harry's suicide – and Archie was now convinced that it *was* suicide – she would have had a powerful motive to kill him, and her grief might easily have driven her to it, but he couldn't help feeling that he was no nearer to understanding Nathaniel's murder and Christopher's disappearance than he had been two hours ago. All the things that had confused him about Morwenna's behaviour in the past, however, were suddenly explained: her defiance and lack of trust, her reluctance to make friends with other women on the estate, even the ease of their own relationship; he had, he realised now, filled the gap that her love for her real brother had left vacant.

After a while, she pulled away from him, in control once more. She started to tidy away the things on the table, and gave an ironic smile when she got to the Tennyson. 'At least we're in good company – Arthur's sister was his downfall, wasn't she?'

'Is that how you see yourself – as Harry's downfall?'

'Of course it is. He killed himself because I wouldn't do the one thing that could have made him want to live. You can be very persuasive, Archie, but even you couldn't convince me that I'm not to blame for his death.' In a story, this would no doubt have had some sort of heroic grandeur to it, but all Archie could see was a very human misery. He watched as Morwenna picked the book up and opened it. 'You gave this to me after my parents died,' she said. 'Do you remember?'

He nodded. 'It was meant to be a comfort, but perhaps it wasn't the most appropriate present I've ever given.'

'You know, all I could think of then was how envious I was of the way that you'd mourned your parents. I wished more than anything that I could have felt a grief as pure as that, as simple. I'm sure it didn't feel simple to you,' she said, as he opened his mouth to disagree, 'but at least there were no secrets and nothing to hide.' She flicked through pages which looked well read. 'It's turned out to be a very valuable present now. Harry died to me twice, you know – as a lover, and then as a brother. I thought I might feel a sense of freedom somehow, but I don't. Perhaps if I read this often enough, I might believe in something, though. You never know.'

It would take more than Tennyson to comfort Morwenna, Archie thought. Death ended a life, but not a relationship, and grief was always worse when so much had been left unresolved. He doubted that there was anything cathartic about what Morwenna was feeling; all she had to define herself by now was her dead brother's ghost. There was a noise from above and Morwenna looked up. 'I must go and see how Loveday is,' she said. 'I suppose the things I said about her sounded terrible to you, didn't they?'

'Not terrible, no. It must be difficult to have to step into a parent's shoes when it's not your choice.'

She seemed grateful for his answer. 'Difficult isn't the word. But I *am* trying to do the best I can for her.'

'And helping her deal with Harry's death must be torture for you. I can see why you didn't thank Nathaniel for confusing the issue.'

'I have no idea how to cope with it,' she admitted. 'What do you tell a fourteen-year-old about death, let alone a death as complicated as this? And because I can't bear to talk about it, it makes it all unreal to her, somehow – he's just gone away, and she can't understand why I've taken his photograph down.'

'They got on well, from what I can remember.'

'Yes, and more so as she got older. He showed her an exciting world of freedom while all I ever did was tell her what she couldn't do. She's lost that now, and I know she blames me in some way. She stays away from home whenever she can, and doesn't ask much of me. I blamed Nathaniel for that, but it's my fault, not his. I *am* sorry he's dead, you know,' she said as Archie stood up, ready to go. 'Do you have any idea who killed him?'

'No, not yet.'

'And you wouldn't tell me if you did.'

'Probably not,' he admitted, 'but – for what it's worth – I will tell you to stay safe. When Loveday's well again, try to keep an eye on her. No one should be wandering around at the moment, and steer clear of Kestrel Jacks.'

'Why? Do you think he had something to do with it?'

'There's no reason to suspect him more than anyone else, but you know how he feels about you and, with Harry gone, he might try and do something about it.'

'It's ironic, isn't it? He beats his wife up and we all turn a blind eye to it, but Harry and I loved each other and that's the sin. Nothing makes sense – not to me, at least.' Put like that, Archie thought, it was not surprising that she should feel so bitter. 'Anyway, I doubt Jacks would want me if he knew Harry had got there first,' she added, walking him to the door. 'I'd be damaged goods as far as he was concerned. It's almost worth telling him just to see the look on his face.'

'You're not serious, are you?' he asked, with an urgency in

his voice. Her words reminded him of what Jago had said about Loveday, and suddenly he feared for Morwenna: there was a fragility about her which her defiance had never entirely masked, and he sensed in her now a lack of concern for her own welfare which bordered almost on self-loathing. It would smoulder in her, he knew, if she did not try to get over what had happened, but how on earth was she supposed to do that? 'If you're worried that I'll make this public, then don't be. You've told me in confidence, and it has nothing to do with the investigation as far as I can see.'

She surprised him by lifting a hand tenderly to his cheek. 'It's nice that you care, Archie,' she said, 'but how can it matter now if someone finds out? I don't feel anything any more. What can hurt me?'

Chapter Fourteen

It had begun to rain softly by the time Penrose arrived back at the Minack and, as the mist drifted in from the sea, drawing the horizon ever closer like a magnet, he saw a very different side to the theatre's character – a side which made Rowena Cade's stoic determination to make a success of the venture even more remarkable. He had arranged to meet Angus Trew here to review the scene before proceeding with the investigation; last night, it had been virtually impossible to do anything except get Nathaniel's body to safety and take the necessary photographs. This morning, while he had no great hopes that the Minack would give up any significant physical evidence, he wanted to fix the area firmly in his mind and make sure that every possibility was covered in the questioning which lay ahead. On the way over, he had called in at the police station in Penzance to see what the camera had managed to capture in its race against the tide, and the stark, black-and-white record of the curate's terrible death helped to focus his mind. Penrose was aware that his attention had, until now, been spread too thin; he had to concentrate on Nathaniel, and stop letting the business with Harry and Morwenna distract him from a murder case. Their grief needed to be laid to rest, in his own mind at least.

Out of courtesy to Rowena Cade, he stopped briefly at Minack House to update her on the police presence on her property, but she was out walking the cliffs so he made his way over the brow of the hill. No time had been wasted today: a thorough search of the scene itself and the nearby cliff paths had begun at first light and was now drawing to a close. Penrose watched, impressed, as a line of men made their way slowly and systematically up the turf slope towards him; everyone involved was, no doubt, aware that this was likely to be a fruitless search but there was no indication of this in their attitude. A single piece of carelessness at this stage could prove to be costly, and Penrose – who had always been used to a trustworthy second in command – thanked his lucky stars for PC Trew. The young constable – who looked altogether different in his uniform – seemed very at home in charge of the proceedings. He had an easy rapport with the older men, Penrose noticed, and it was no small feat to command respect at such an early stage in his career. If he wanted to, there was no doubt that Trew could rise quickly through the ranks, and he smiled as he remembered his sergeant's cynical remarks; even Bill would be hard-pushed to find fault here.

Trew looked up and waved. 'Just finishing up here, Sir,' he called as he came over.

'Anything I should know about?' Penrose asked, without any real optimism.

'Not a great deal,' Trew admitted. 'We've been over the whole theatre now, including the steps at either side and the backstage areas, and we've combed the coastal paths for a mile or so in each direction, but there's nothing of any obvious significance. Miss Cade showed us all the routes down to the sea that she knows of, just in case whoever it was clambered down one of those and got away by boat – but if that's the case, he left no traces.'

Penrose walked over to the edge of the cliff, feeling the

clammy sea wind on his skin, and thought for a moment. 'It's possible, I suppose, but it seems a lot to ask. It's a risky enough crime as it is, without having to climb down cliffs in the dark and fight an incoming tide.' He saw Trew's face fall a little, and remembered that this responsibility was new to the boy. 'We can't rule anything out at this stage, though,' he added. 'Get in touch with the nearby harbourmasters – there's a chance they might have noticed someone bringing a boat in late last night. It's not exactly normal behaviour.'

'The call's already gone in, Sir,' Trew said, pleased.

'Good. I've asked the boys at the station to put a notice in the local paper, asking if anyone gave a stranger a lift last night. Something may come of that. What else have you got here?'

'Very little in terms of forensics, I'm afraid. The weather's been so good lately, and all the paths are bone dry – there's no chance of tracking any escape that way. One exception, though – you know the recess under the stage, where he must have waited?' Penrose nodded, although he wasn't prepared to rule out the possibility that they were looking for a woman. 'Well, the sun doesn't get right in there so it's quite muddy at the back. We've got a clear footprint – left boot, patched with nails that look different from the ones on the sole. It's not much to go on, and there's not even anything to prove it's our man – lots of people went in and out of there during the day, apparently – but I've had photographs and a cast done all the same. You never know.'

'No, you don't. Well done. No sign of a cast-off monk's habit complete with laundry marks by any chance?'

Trew smiled. 'I'm afraid not, Sir. Nor a signed confession placed carefully in that script you were using, but we'll keep looking.'

'Any progress on the audience lists?'

'We've worked through as many as possible, but it's taking a while. Everyone's so shocked to find out that it wasn't an accident and, as soon as murder comes into the frame, they fall into one of two categories: either they're so anxious to oblige that they give you every detail down to what they had in their sandwiches, or so worried about getting mixed up in something that they couldn't swear to anything, even their own name.' He sighed, and Penrose was amused to see how quickly the young constable had acquired a world-weary approach to witnesses. 'There's still a few to go, but it's very obvious that nobody remembers anything odd except that business between the dead man and the vicar.'

'Yes, we'll pay a visit to the rectory later,' Penrose said. 'It's high time I caught up with my uncle.' It was obvious from the startled look on Trew's face that he hadn't made the connection, and Penrose was quick to reassure him. 'Don't worry – there's no love lost between us and it would be my great pleasure to wipe the self-satisfied smirk off his face, but I can't believe that he's capable of killing Nathaniel – physically, I mean, rather than morally. He's just not fit enough to have got away so quickly.'

'It's a tall order for anyone, Sir. I tried it myself earlier, and I'd had it by the time I got to the top.'

'Yes, it's a steep climb. Still, it's the only obvious hostility we've got towards Nathaniel at the moment, so we'd better make that a priority. Clearly there was something going on between them.'

'And no one had better access to the costume that went missing from the vestry, I suppose.'

'Exactly.' Penrose walked back across the stage to the top of the steps, and looked down to the path and cliffs below. Glancing back at the balustrade, he remembered something that Nathaniel had said as he left with Morveth to practise his leap into thin air. 'There was supposed to be someone in position on the path to make sure that Nathaniel had a safe landing when he jumped,' he said. 'Have we any idea who it should have been?'

Trew looked at his notebook. 'A man called Caplin, Sir. Joseph Caplin. Do you know him?'

'Yes, he's a farmer on the estate,' said Penrose, surprised by the response. From what he'd seen of Caplin the night before, he was in no state to steady himself, let alone anyone else. He thought Morveth would have had more sense. 'We'll have to find out why he wasn't there.'

'Are you certain it couldn't have been him, then, Sir?'

Trew's question forced Penrose to analyse his assumption of Caplin's innocence, and he reconsidered. 'Well, I can't immediately think of any reason why he'd want to hurt Nathaniel – but that's true of most people. And I know he was drunk last night – too drunk to do anything in cold blood.'

'Unless he was putting it on, Sir. Alcohol's a great alibi if you do it convincingly enough.'

Penrose looked approvingly at him. 'I like your scepticism, and you're right, of course. We'll add him to the list of calls. Oh – one thing I do have to report. Our missing van's turned up.' He repeated what Morwenna had told him about Loveday's sudden illness. 'There's no reason to think that she's lying,' he added, anticipating Trew's next question, 'but we'll look the van over when we go to see Jago Snipe.' He took one last look around: there was nothing more to be learned here, and he couldn't help feeling that the area which warranted their attention was a few miles back along the coast. 'We'll go there first. Christopher Snipe's disappearance has got to be a priority now, whatever's behind it.'

'Are you looking for him as a suspect or another potential victim, Sir?' Trew asked as they walked back up the hill.

'To be honest, I have absolutely no idea,' Penrose admitted. 'I can't imagine what he'd have against Nathaniel or, if it's the latter, why anyone would want them both dead. There's no immediate link that I can see. Tell me honestly – what sort of resources can we rustle up for a search of the estate?'

'Nothing like enough for an area that size.'

'Then we'll get the locals involved. My uncle William will help with that. We might as well start with the area around the church as it was the last place he was seen. I suppose, out of courtesy, we should let the Reverend Motley know before we go over his graveyard with a fine-tooth comb – that can wait until we see him later. It'll take a while to get the search organised – realistically, we're looking at first light tomorrow.'

'What about the lake itself, Sir?'

Penrose's heart sank, but he knew it was something he had to consider. 'I can't even begin to imagine dragging the Loe,' he said. 'It's just too deep in some places. Legend aside, there's no way we could get the better of it – it's just not practical. Let's hope for now that it won't come to that.'

'There is *one* thing they have in common – the curate and Christopher Snipe, I mean,' Trew added thoughtfully. 'They were both bearers at Pinching's funeral recently, weren't they? Perhaps we should look into their connection with him. I don't want to be melodramatic about it, but I know you were there, too, Sir; if there's a chance that the other bearers are in some kind of danger, perhaps we ought to warn them.'

'It's difficult not to sound melodramatic about the prospect of a psychopath stalking pallbearers,' Penrose said, frustrated once again by the fact that he simply could not shake off the ghost of Harry Pinching. His words were more scathing than he had intended, though, and he tried immediately to soften their impact. 'But it's definitely something we should follow up. Let's go carefully, though – Caplin, Jago and Kestrel Jacks were all here and unaccounted for last night, and one of them could easily be our man. We don't want to show all our cards at once – God knows, there are few enough of them.' He stopped by his car and took the keys from his pocket. 'How did you get here?'

'One of the patrol cars,' Trew said, pointing to a group of vehicles parked by Minack House.

'Get someone else to take it back and come with me now. It's time we got some statements taken, and we'll start with Jago – I want to know everything he can tell us about his son's behaviour lately.' Trew hesitated. 'Is there a problem?'

'Not really, Sir. It's just that I've got my dog with me.'

Penrose laughed. 'Then go and fetch him. There's plenty of room for one more.'

Trew beamed and disappeared, returning a couple of minutes later with what looked like a typically well-trained Airedale terrier. 'This is Treg, Sir,' he said as Penrose knelt down to greet the dog. 'It's short for Tregeagle. Looks good as gold, doesn't he? But if I don't keep him busy, the devil takes him back.' The dog looked adoringly up at his owner and jumped obediently into the back seat as if to disprove such a wicked slur on his character. 'Seriously, though, he's good company. It can be a lonely beat at times, and we fall between two workhouses, so we get a lot of tramps passing through.

They'll try anything, given half a chance – but one bark from him and they think twice about it.'

'They'd be wise to if he's anything like the Airedales I've known,' Penrose said, catching Treg's eye in his rear-view mirror as he turned the car round and headed towards Penzance.

There was no reason to call in at the station again and, in any case, Penrose was keen to get back to the Loe estate. As he drove, he asked Trew about his work and his hopes for the future and, in the young man's answers, he could not help but recognise the enthusiasm and determination that he himself had had for the job when he was twenty-five – and which, he was relieved to say, he still felt, at least most of the time. But if Angus Trew's zeal was similar to his own, their reasons for turning to the force in the first place could not have been more different. It had never been Penrose's first choice, but he remembered as if it were yesterday the anger and bitterness which had accompanied him home from war. By then, the naivety and good intentions with which he had set out on his medical career seemed laughable to him, and made him a figure of ridicule in his own eyes, and he had turned instead to policing – not because he wanted to fight evil, but simply because he knew that there would always be evil to fight. Evil and ignorance and selfishness. Perversely, in this sad realisation, he also found comfort and a reassurance that there was a place for him – as long as he wanted one – in a world which bewildered him with its injustice. He admired, perhaps even envied, Trew's more positive reasoning, though; it reminded him of Nathaniel's passionate belief in his own role amongst the community, at the same time as the cynic in him muttered that such dedication had hardly served the curate well.

Jago Snipe's workshop was deserted, so they carried on through the village and reached the estate in good time. Penrose parked outside Loe House. 'I need to make a quick call, so we'll go inside for a minute,' he said, 'then we'll try Jago at home and you can start to get a feel for this place. Something tells me we'll be spending a bit of time here.'

'I practically lived here as a lad,' Trew said, looking affectionately out over the parkland.

'Really? Are your family nearby then?'

'They've moved out St Ives way now, but I grew up in Helston. There were five of us kids – I'm in the middle – and we used to come here a lot. Dad was away for most of the war, and Mum was pleased to have us out of the way for a bit.' He blushed slightly. 'If I'm honest, Sir, I think we might have had a rabbit or two from you in our time.'

'You and the rest of the village,' Penrose laughed. 'There was no one here to stop you with all the men gone. My uncle was at his wits' end. Still, at least you've come over to the right side now. Did your father make it back in one piece?'

'Yes, we were lucky. He doesn't talk about it much, though – never has. I'll wait here,' he added as Penrose let himself in.

'Don't be silly – come and wait inside. I'll only be a minute.'

Ronnie and Lettice were in the hall, getting ready to go out. 'Archie! This is a nice surprise,' Lettice said, coming over to give him a kiss, and welcoming Trew with a smile. 'We thought we'd pop over and see Rowena – lift her spirits a bit after last night.' She left a decent pause before adding: 'I don't suppose there's any news we could give her to cheer her up? All in the strictest confidence, of course.'

'Of course, but I'm afraid we can't disclose anything yet,' Archie said diplomatically, aware that his cousins could dress up a fact as efficiently as they could a tailor's dummy. 'We've just come from the Minack, actually, so Miss Cade knows all we can tell her at the moment.'

'Oh, that's a shame,' said Lettice, deflated.

'I didn't recognise you in your uniform, Constable.' Ronnie was standing in front of a full-length mirror, adjusting her hat. She glanced up and down at Trew's reflection in the glass. 'I do hope you haven't been hard at it all night. My cousin can be a terrible slave-driver.' She turned round to make a big fuss of Treg and Lettice raised an eyebrow: Ronnie wouldn't normally give a dog a second glance, something which was clearly evident to Treg, who ignored her completely.

'I'm fine, Miss, thank you,' Trew said, embarrassed.

Penrose went through to the library and dialled the Lodge on the private line. 'Sorry to interrupt your work again,' he said when Josephine answered, 'but I wondered if you could do me a favour?'

'Of course,' Josephine said. 'And actually, you've called at a good time. Is chapter four too early for an inquest?'

'No – they hold them as soon as possible.'

'And would Grant go? Even if the body isn't on his patch?'

'I'm assuming it's not a straightforward death, so yes – he's likely to be called in by the chief constable. I know how the poor devil feels, so give him my regards when you see him.'

'I will, but I'm afraid I'm only at the plotting stage, so it'll be a while yet. Now, what can I do for you?' She listened as Archie gave a brief account of his visit to Morwenna. 'Jesus, that poor woman,' she said when he'd finished. 'How very cruel that so much tragedy should come from a love as strong as that. No wonder she's angry. Part of her must hate him for leaving her like that. She's got no life left, has she?'

'Not at the moment, no.'

The implication that Morwenna might, in time, get over Harry's death seemed to Josephine to be wishful thinking, but she said nothing. 'I don't think she'll take kindly to any hand of friendship from me, if that's what you were going to ask. I'm happy to try, but if she thinks you've broken her confidence, it'll destroy her trust in you as well.'

'That wasn't quite what I had in mind,' Archie confessed. 'Morwenna told me that Harry started seeing someone else. She said it was no one I knew, but I think she was lying. I wondered if you might find a way to see Loveday and have a chat with her – see if she knows anything. I'm particularly interested in finding out if Harry was closer to Nathaniel than Nathaniel admitted.'

'I see – nothing too difficult, then. You just want me to find out from a sick and grieving fourteen-year-old if her adored, dead brother started having sex with the vicar after his sister jilted him?'

'I think I can trust you not to put it quite like that,' Archie said, amused. 'To avoid any confusion, at least call him a curate and not a vicar.'

Josephine laughed. 'All right. I'll see what I can do. If there was a different picture from the one we know, it's something that she might in all innocence be happy to tell me about. She loved them both, after all. Is she at their cottage?'

'Yes. Do you know where it is?'

'Ronnie pointed it out to me on the way in from Penzance. I'll call there later this afternoon. I don't fancy my chances of getting past Morwenna, though. She'll know immediately that you've told me, of course – are you prepared for that?'

'She won't necessarily guess that you know everything.'

'She's not an idiot, Archie – far from it.'

'I know, and I'm sorry to ask you to lie for me.'

'That doesn't bother me, particularly. But I know she's important to you, and I don't want to be responsible for destroying your friendship or making her feel any more betrayed than she does already.'

'To be honest, I think she's past caring. She told me nothing else could hurt her.'

'Yes, but when that's how you feel, something can come from nowhere and destroy you completely. Don't underestimate the effect that the smallest thing could have on her state of mind at the moment.' He said nothing, so she left it at that. 'William's asked me to have dinner with him and the girls tonight. Will I see you there?'

'I'll do my best, but it depends how the rest of the day turns out. I'm at the house at the moment, but there's a lot to do this afternoon.'

'You haven't stolen my thunder with Ronnie and Lettice, I hope?'

'No, a promise is a promise, and your reputation is still intact. Which is more than will be said of my young assistant if I don't get back to him.'

'Is Ronnie still on the prowl?'

'Yes, but she's having problems getting past his dog.'

He heard her laugh again and realised how glad he was to have her to talk to – now more than ever. 'I'd better let you go, then,' she said. 'I don't suppose there's any news on Christopher Snipe, is there? It would be nice to tell Loveday something positive.'

'No, I'm afraid not, but you might find out gently from her if she has any idea where he could be – without worrying her, obviously. We're off to Jago's now – I'm sure there's something he's not telling us, and it might help.'

'You know, he strikes me as a man who wouldn't let anything get in the way of a principle.'

'Jago?'

'Yes. They probably call it honour here, but it still sounds remarkably like violence to a Scottish ear.'

She was gone before Archie could ask her what she meant, and he walked thoughtfully back to the hall. Trew was there on his own, waiting patiently. 'Mr Motley asked if there was anything he could do, Sir, so I told him about the search. He's going to sort out some manpower for us. You're just to let him know where you want them – he's down by the stables.'

'Our lads are going to start by the church, aren't they?' Trew nodded. 'Then William's men should do the woods on the other side of the lake. We'll tell him on the way out, and I'll ask him to oversee it for the next day or two. Have my cousins gone?'

'Yes, Sir. Miss Motley offered to look after Treg for me, but he didn't seem too keen. I hope she wasn't offended. It was kind of her to think of it.'

'Very kind,' said Archie, smiling as he led the way back out to the car. 'She's good like that.'

Chapter Fifteen

Jago Snipe lived on the western side of the Loe Pool, half a mile or so along a narrow track which formed the boundary of William's land. The house – a modest, stone-built cottage with a rain-slicked slate roof – had its back turned to the estate's woodlands and looked out across cultivated fields to the village, just a ten-minute walk away. Penrose let Trew get out of the car, then parked close in to the hedge to keep the track clear. There was no sign of Jago's van. In fact, with the exception of the rabbits which scuttled to left and right – delighting Treg, who stuck obediently but reluctantly to Trew's heel – there was no sign of life at all.

'At least, being the undertaker, he'll be straight with us,' Trew said as they walked up to the door.

'You think so?' Penrose asked, raising a cynical eyebrow at his companion. 'He's a Cornishman, Trew, and what was it someone said about us? Beware the fluency of the Celts – it makes their lies more convincing than a Saxon truth.' He knocked smartly at the door, and lowered his voice. 'The first time he talked to me about Christopher's disappearance, he was certainly holding something back, but it wasn't official then and I couldn't press him. This is different. It's a murder inquiry now and it's up to us to make *sure* he's straight with us – but I don't think he'll do it as willingly as you might suppose.'

There was no sound from inside the house. Penrose

knocked again, but without any real hope of a response. 'He's obviously not here either,' he said after a moment.

'Looks like we've had a wasted trip, Sir.' Trew sounded disappointed, but Penrose's attention was fixed on a group of tumbledown shacks a couple of hundred yards further down the track.

'Not entirely,' he said, 'although it's not the man we were after. I'd forgotten that Caplin lives down here as well. He's having a good look at us, so we might as well satisfy his curiosity and find out why he wasn't where he should have been last night.'

As they walked over to the cluster of outbuildings, the man standing at the door to the nearest one made no attempt to look away or pretend he was otherwise occupied. 'Afternoon, Joseph,' Penrose called, and, when they were close enough, held out his hand. The other man hesitated, then shook it guardedly. 'We were after Jago, but he's not in.'

'Been gone an hour or more,' Caplin said.

'Don't suppose you know where?' The older man shook his head. 'Perhaps while we're here we could have a word with you about last night?' Caplin shrugged, as if to say that it made no odds to him what other people did with their time, and Penrose could trace the slow progress of alcohol in the lines on his face and the redness around his eyes. It was the face of someone who had long ceased to care how his days were filled, and that was hardly surprising; the tragic accident which killed his daughter – it must be fifteen years ago now, or more – had shocked the whole estate; it would have been a miracle if he had recovered. Penrose remembered how surprised he had been yesterday to see Caplin at the Minack at all; he wondered why the man had bothered to take part in something so alien to the solitary life he chose, and asked as much.

'Same reason you did, I suppose,' he said gruffly. 'Mr Motley asked me to.' He must have sensed Penrose's disbelief, because he added: 'God knows I've got little enough to be grateful for, but what I have got is down to him – a job, and a roof over my head. If you've spent as many years as I have thinking about how you've been wronged, you remember when someone plays fair by you – and he's always done what he could, for me and for a lot of other people. We might fight among ourselves, but you won't find many around here who'd wish him ill.'

Touched, Penrose glanced involuntarily across the yard at the roof to which Caplin referred. He remembered that William had found the farmer somewhere else to live after the tragedy, knowing it would be torture for him to remain on his own in rooms which held such appalling memories. The house was small – barely bigger than one of the squatters' cottages, built between sunrise and sunset all over the west country – but, although it showed signs of neglect, it was structurally sound and obviously regularly maintained, due more to William's efforts than Joseph Caplin's, Penrose guessed. Nevertheless, there was a bleakness about the property which depressed him, and he marvelled at how different the reality of a rural existence was from the way in which it was frequently depicted. Often, in London, his work would take him into the homes of clerks and shop assistants and rent collectors, and invariably there would be a picture of the yearned-after country cottage somewhere on those optimistic middle-class walls – one of those romanticised images by Allingham and her contemporaries, specialists in creating houses which existed only in their imagination. He found the smug cosiness of it all particularly offensive today; no landlord worked harder than William, but even he could only do so much.

'Do you want to come inside?' Caplin asked reluctantly.

'No, thank you. We won't keep you for long,' said Penrose, who could only imagine what the interior of the house was like and had no intention of humiliating the man by forcing him to make it public. 'I'll come straight to the point. I'd like to know where you were last night when Nathaniel was killed.'

'Over by the rocks on the other side of the stage, waiting for the next crowd scene.'

'You didn't have a more specific role?'

'No. I'm not what you might call the theatre type.'

'We've been told that you were supposed to be on the backstage path, making sure that nothing went wrong when Nathaniel jumped from the balustrade.'

Caplin smiled, but there was no humour in it. 'Ah. I see what you're getting at. You think I gave him a shove while I was down there.'

Penrose met his stare. 'It's a possibility I'd like to discount.'

'Well, your information is a bit out of date. It's true – the woman who owns the place did tell me to stand there throughout the performance.'

'Miss Cade?'

'That's her. It was early on, when I first got there. She was having some sort of tantrum about making sure everything was safe, and I happened to be in the firing line. She made me go down there with her and showed me where I had to be. It could have been anyone, though – I don't kid myself that I had any special qualifications.'

'So why weren't you there?' Penrose asked, ignoring the sarcasm.

'Because as soon as Morveth Wearne arrived and heard

about it, she changed things round. Said she'd do it herself, and I should go back to where I was.'

That made sense to Penrose. Morveth would never have trusted Nathaniel's safety to someone as unreliable as Caplin, although it didn't explain why she had not been in the recess later on. 'Did you see Morveth at all once the performance was underway?'

'No. Did you? You had the best view going from what I remember.'

'And when the play was stopped – did you notice anyone leaving the theatre or acting strangely?'

'If you ask me, we were all behaving strangely by being there in the first place – how would I know what was supposed to happen and what wasn't? I just did what I was told and, as far as I could see, everyone else did, too.'

'When you went down to the path with Miss Cade in the afternoon, did you actually go into the recess or did she just show it to you?'

'I went in, and stayed there until Morveth fetched me. It was nice to be out of the way for a bit, if I'm honest.'

'Did you see Nathaniel talking to anyone during the rehearsals?'

'You. And Morveth.'

'And you didn't speak to him yourself?'

'About what? God and I haven't really been on the best of terms over the last sixteen years, and if I've nothing to say to the organ grinder, I'm hardly likely to strike up a conversation with His monkey.'

'Would you mind showing us the soles of your boots?' Penrose asked. He recognised the futility of the question – Caplin had admitted to being in the recess and, even if his

boots matched the imprint perfectly, it got them nowhere –
but he asked it anyway. Caplin lifted his leg up behind him,
apparently amused to see the so-called sophistication of
Scotland Yard reduced to such pedestrian measures, and Trew
went round to examine the pattern. He shook his head at
Penrose, but added a valiant attempt of his own. 'What about
your other boots, Sir? Could we see those?'

'How many pairs do you think I've got?' Caplin asked scornfully. 'You've seen all there is to see. Now, can I get on with
some work?'

Penrose nodded, then thought better of it. 'Just one more
thing,' he said. 'You weren't sorry about Harry's death, were
you? That toast you made at his wake didn't seem like a slip to
me.'

For the first time, Caplin looked genuinely interested in the
question he had been asked, but he responded in the same flip-
pant way. 'Why should I shed tears over someone like Harry
Pinching?'

'I didn't say you should, but drinking to his death suggests
you hated him, and I just wondered why that was?'

'I hated him because he had no idea how lucky he was,'
Caplin said simply. 'He had his whole life ahead of him, but he
treated it like a game. I watched him in the bar of the
Commercial on the night he died, drinking and gambling,
fighting and playing with women's affections just because he
could.'

'Any woman in particular?' Penrose asked.

'Any woman he saw. Men like him have no idea of the lives
that stand to be ruined by their cheap talk and their easy smiles
– I should know, I lost my wife to one of them. I hated Harry
Pinching because he had no respect for anything – and I'm not

ashamed of hating him, either. Christ, the stupid bastard even cared so little for himself that he rode his horse into a lake. Those years he had and wasted could have been better used by someone else – someone who might have valued them.'

He turned back to his cottage and Penrose let him walk away, unable to defend Harry against the charge of recklessness which must seem so justified to a man who had lost everything through no real fault of his own.

'What was all that about, Sir?' Trew asked.

'Grief,' said Penrose, 'and guilt, but not the sort that involves us. He doesn't need any cell that we could offer him – he carries his own around with him. Come on,' he added, 'I thought I heard a car engine. Let's see if we can salvage something from this afternoon.'

Jago's gate was open when they retraced their footsteps past his cottage, and they knocked again, this time with more success. The undertaker, still wearing his hat and coat, answered immediately. 'Is it Christopher?' he asked before Penrose had had a chance to speak, then glanced anxiously at Trew's uniform. 'It's bad news, isn't it?'

'No, no,' Penrose said quickly. 'It's not bad news, but I'm afraid we haven't got anything positive to tell you either. We would like to talk to you, though – about what happened yesterday and about Christopher. I need to know anything that might help us find your son – any small detail, no matter how irrelevant it seems.'

'And last night?'

'We're questioning everyone who was there – anything you can remember about the evening might help us piece together what happened. Can we come in?'

Jago nodded, and stood back to allow them into a small,

neatly kept but functional front room. 'Sit down,' he said, gesturing towards a table which was still laid with breakfast crockery. 'I've only just got back from Nathaniel's family,' he explained, carrying what he could over to the sink, 'so I haven't had a chance to tidy up.' Penrose was moved to see that he had bothered – out of habit or longing – to lay a second cup and plate for Christopher. As Jago returned it unused to the dresser, he tried to imagine the effort it must have taken for the undertaker to comfort parents who were mourning their son when he was frantic with worry for his own child's safety. 'I never thought there'd be another tragedy so soon after Harry's death,' he said, more to himself than to his visitors. 'Please God, let it stop there.'

'We've got as many men as possible out looking for Christopher,' Penrose said gently. Jago sat down heavily in the chair opposite and rubbed his hand wearily over his eyes. 'It's going to be a long job and I'm not promising miracles, but if he's still on the estate, or if he's left any clue as to where he might have gone, we *will* find out. In the meantime, my sergeant is organising a national alert from London, just in case he's ventured further afield.'

'Are you looking for him alive or dead? Tell me honestly, Archie.'

'I really don't know – and that's the truth,' Penrose insisted as Jago looked at him doubtfully. 'If Christopher has run away of his own accord, then he won't be able to lie low for long with the kind of resources that we have available to us. I've found nothing to suggest that any harm has come to him but, in light of Nathaniel's murder, I don't want to give you false hope.' He paused, wondering how best to break through Jago's stubborn refusal to be completely open with him, and decided to take the most direct approach. 'Look, Jago – I give you my word that I won't keep anything from you in this investigation if it's relevant to Christopher's disappearance. We'll do everything possible to find him, but how can I do that efficiently if you're holding something back?' Jago began to protest, but Penrose refused to let him interrupt. 'With what happened last night, the time for secrecy and half-truths is long gone. Shall we start again?' The undertaker hesitated, then nodded. 'You told me you had no idea where Christopher might have gone – was that the truth?'

'Yes. I've asked round the rest of the family, just in case, but nobody's seen him. I can't think of anywhere else to try.'

'What about his friends in the village?'

'He didn't really have any friends,' Jago admitted. 'The sort of work we do – it gets respect from people of a certain age, but it's hard when you're young. The people Christopher went to school with – they don't want to hang around death all the time. He tried to keep in with them at first, went out for a drink at the weekends, that sort of thing, but they teased him about what he did for a living. He brushed it off and said it didn't matter, but I know it upset him. In the end, he just stopped going.'

'What about Loveday?'

Jago looked up sharply. 'I told you the other day – I put a stop to that before it started. Christopher didn't have anything to do with Loveday, except at Harry's funeral. They hadn't seen each other for weeks.'

Perhaps not to Jago's knowledge, Penrose thought, but he had no doubt that the friendship between Christopher and Loveday had continued in spite of any rules laid down by his father. 'On Monday, you told me that Christopher's disappearance might be some kind of punishment. You must have had a reason to say that, and it's not a word that just comes out of the blue, so I'll ask you again – what did you mean by it?'

Jago looked uncomfortably at Trew, and Penrose realised that whatever he was hiding would only be brought out into the open if it were just the two of them. 'While we're talking, would you mind if Angus took a look at Christopher's room?' he asked. 'We'd like to see if there's anything there which might help us find him.'

'Of course. It's the one on the left as you go up the stairs.'

Trew thanked him and left them to it, and Penrose knew he could rely on the constable to take his time and allow Jago to share whatever confidences he needed to. He seemed unsure of where to begin, and walked over to the fire to give himself time to think. In the silence, Penrose could hear the rhythmic sound of someone chopping wood in the trees behind the cottage and the approach of boots along the lane outside; through the small sash window, he saw Joseph Caplin walk past, head down against the weather. Jago stared after him for a moment, then brought a taper over from the grate and lit an oil lamp. The light fell in a yellow pool on the table.

'It's a long time ago now,' he began hesitantly, 'but it feels like yesterday and some things just can't be forgotten, no matter how hard you try. These years I've had with Christopher – they've given me the greatest happiness of my life, but it's been at someone else's expense and that's not right.'

Penrose knew how devastated Jago had been when his wife died giving birth to Christopher, and it was only natural that the joy of the child they had both longed for should be tinged with guilt. 'Sarah wouldn't want you to feel like that, though,' he said gently, hiding his disappointment that Jago's confession had such an innocent explanation. 'You've brought him up well and it's nobody's fault that you've had to do it on your own. It's certainly not something that anyone could say you needed to be punished for.'

'What?' Jago looked at him, confused. 'No, no, you don't understand,' he said, nervously brushing some crumbs from the table as he tried to find the words to explain. 'It's not Sarah I feel guilty about, although God knows I should. It's someone else. You see, she didn't die giving birth to Christopher.'

It was Penrose's turn to look bewildered. 'Then how did she die?'

'In childbirth, but not with Christopher. Christopher's not our son. Our child – a little girl, she was – died at the same time. There was nothing Morveth could do for either of them.'

'Then where did Christopher come from?' Penrose asked, but he knew the answer as soon as he had asked the question. 'He's Joseph Caplin's son, isn't he? The child he gave up after his daughter died.' Jago's head was in his hands and the nod was barely perceptible. 'What happened, Jago?' he asked quietly.

'We always knew it was risky – Sarah's pregnancy, I mean. It was late for her to have her first, but we'd wanted a child for so long that we ignored all the advice and kept trying for one. When we found out she was expecting, it was like a miracle. I've never seen anyone as happy as she was during those first few months, and the longer she carried the baby safely, the more confident we were that it would all be fine. Stupid of us, of course, because it wasn't. Sarah was so brave, but it was torture to her. Hour after hour that labour went on, and all for nothing. The baby was dead when she was born, and Sarah died a little while after her. Thank God she was too weak to know much about it. Morveth told her she could hold her daughter when she was a bit stronger, so at least she never knew that pain as well.'

'And this was around the time that Joseph Caplin decided he couldn't cope with his own baby?'

'Yes. He'd taken the child to the Union just a day or two before. Morveth knew about it. She thought she was helping, I know that – she meant well.'

'So it was her idea?'

'At first, but I went along with it – don't think she forced me into anything. I didn't know what I was doing with Sarah and the baby gone, and she took care of it all. She did the last for both of them, then brought me in to sit with them while she went out for a bit. She told me not to leave the house or talk to anyone until she came back.'

'And she brought you a son.'

'Yes. Beautiful little thing, he was – barely a month old and already abandoned twice by his own parents. I was terrified at first, but Morveth talked me round and persuaded me that I was his best chance of a decent start in life.' He looked at Penrose for the first time since making his confession. 'I'm ashamed to say that I didn't need much persuading. Loneliness drives you to things you wouldn't normally consider.'

'What happened to your little girl?'

'I'm an undertaker,' Jago said. 'Do you really need to ask? My God, how could I do that to Sarah? I loved her, but I shut her soul in with the dead and took the living for my own – and denied that poor baby a decent Christian burial.'

'Did Joseph suspect what had happened?'

'No. He started drinking badly around then, and anyway, I kept the child to myself for a while. Morveth told everyone that I needed to be left alone with my grief for a bit – which was true, but that's not why she said it. We didn't want people putting two and two together, you see, and Morveth helped me at first, took care of everything I couldn't do for the child. And then, as the months went by, it seemed that Christopher grew bonnier while his father – his real father, I mean – grew more wretched. I've watched him slowly destroy himself these last few years, while I've gained from his grief like a bloody parasite.'

'He gave the child up, though. You didn't force him into anything.'

'No, but he regretted it. I remember him coming to me once, when the boy was about five. He told me he'd always thought that a man on his own shouldn't be bringing up children, but if he could have seen me with Christopher earlier, he might not have been so hasty about giving up his own son. Can you imagine how that made me feel? So don't try and tell me I don't deserve some kind of punishment.'

'But punishment from whom, Jago? If Joseph had found out the truth, surely he wouldn't hurt his own son just to get back at you?' Jago just shook his head, as if he had lost the ability to make sense of anything. 'Did anyone else know about this?' Penrose asked. 'Apart from Morveth, I mean.'

'Some of the people at the Union knew, of course, but they turned a blind eye – partly out of loyalty to Morveth and partly because they could be sure that the boy would have a good home with me. Nobody from around here knew, at least not at first. Then a couple of months back, Nathaniel started doing some pastoral care at the Union.'

'Did he find out what had happened?' asked Penrose, relieved at last to find some sort of link between Nathaniel and Christopher.

'I'm not sure. Morveth told me not to worry, but I could see she was afraid. You'd be a fool to trust people to keep their mouths shut for ever, and it would only take a loose word from someone for the whole thing to come out.'

Penrose could imagine the fear that Morveth must unwittingly have put into the undertaker's head. He remembered the way in which Jago had brushed Caplin away from him backstage at the Minack on Tuesday night; he had thought at the time it was because Caplin's drunkenness disgusted him, but he knew now that it must have felt like retribution staring him in the face. There were many ways to break a man, and Penrose guessed that Jago and Caplin were not as far apart emotionally at the moment as they seemed from the outside. It was easy to believe that desperation would be enough to make Jago panic and do something drastic, but that didn't explain Christopher's absence. Unless, of course, the boy had found out the truth and been angry or confused enough to run away. In that case, Jago would understandably feel bitter towards the person who had brought it about. 'Did Christopher suspect he wasn't your son?' he asked.

'No.'

'You're sure of that?'

'Yes. I would have known. We didn't have secrets from each other.'

He realised the ridiculousness of the statement as soon as it was out, but Penrose let it pass. 'You must have been worried that he'd find out, though?'

'What are you getting at, Archie?' Jago asked suspiciously.

Penrose spoke softly, but his words were frank and unmistakeable. 'Did you kill Nathaniel, Jago?'

'No. Absolutely not.'

Penrose said nothing, knowing from experience that such a flat denial was often followed by an expansion of detail which exposed the lie. It was an old trick, but – unlike most people – Jago felt no need to fill in the silence, so Penrose went on. 'Where were you when he went over the cliff? I know you weren't on the stage because you were seen coming back into the auditorium shortly afterwards. Did you push Nathaniel over, then leave by one of the hidden paths?'

'No! Archie, for Christ's sake – what are you thinking?' He stood up from the table and went to walk away, then thought better of it and looked straight at Penrose. 'Look, I know I've done wrong, but I could never, ever take a man's life – not for anything. I've seen too much, and I know how easily people leave this world. You can't do my job without respecting life – you have to believe that.'

On the whole, Penrose did believe it but he had no intention of backing off until he'd learned everything he could. 'Then where were you when Nathaniel died?'

Jago sighed and sat down again. 'It'll sound like I'm losing my mind, and maybe I am. I keep thinking I see him – Christopher, I mean. Since he disappeared, I've hardly had a moment's peace. He's everywhere and nowhere. I made a fool of myself at the fair the other night – there was a lad walking away from one of the stalls, same sort of age as Christopher and looked exactly like him in the dark. Stared at me as though I was mad when I ran after him. Then last night, at the theatre, I thought I saw him at the back of the auditorium, but when I got there, it was just my imagination playing tricks again. I went out to look round the cars, though, just in case, and that's when I noticed my van was missing. Then I saw people starting to leave and went back to find out what was happening. By that time, Nathaniel was dead.'

It was a typical reaction from a parent whose child had gone missing, but Penrose couldn't help wondering if it really was Jago's imagination or if Christopher had in fact been there for reasons of his own. Just suppose that Nathaniel had said something to him in private, unbeknown to Jago; it was difficult to guess what Christopher's reaction would have been, but the undertaker had painted a picture of a lonely boy, whose most important relationship was with his father. What might he be capable of if he was in shock and feared that that bond was about to be taken away from him? He could have faked his own disappearance, then come to the Minack in secret to get rid of the problem once and for all. He was young and strong, and certainly fit enough to have got away from the scene without being caught. 'Christopher was supposed to help you at the Minack, wasn't he?'

'Yes. He was going to give me a hand with the scenery.'

'Was he in the play as well?'

'No, he didn't want to be.'

'So he didn't have a costume?'

Jago looked bewildered by the question. 'No, he didn't need one.'

But he *was* in the churchyard the last time he was seen, Penrose thought, and the vestry – where Nathaniel's costume had been kept – was never locked.

'You don't think he had anything to do with Nathaniel's death, do you?' Jago's horror was obvious, but Penrose could not tell if it was because he believed Christopher to be capable or incapable of such a thing. 'It's because of what Jacks told you about that business with Harry, isn't it?' the undertaker continued. 'That's why you think he could do something like that. It's completely different, though, Archie. You said it yourself – that was a childish tantrum gone wrong. This is cold-blooded murder, and Christopher couldn't do that any more than I could.'

'Was there any animosity between Christopher and Nathaniel? Any obvious change in their relationship?'

'No. They didn't see a lot of each other and, after what Morveth told me, I kept Christopher away from him as much as possible.'

Morveth again, Penrose thought. It was odd that she seemed to be in control of everything, and he had no doubt now that she had removed Caplin from that post under the recess for reasons other than safety. Nathaniel was naive and desperately wanted to do the right thing by his parishioners; Morveth would not have risked leaving him on his own with Caplin if she thought he knew the truth about Christopher's parentage and was tempted to reveal it. He remembered how she had interrupted his own conversation with Nathaniel, and how she and Jago had seemed so wary of him at Harry's wake. Until this visit, he would have believed Morveth incapable of anything but kindness and wisdom, but he also knew how strong she was; if Nathaniel had made one discovery too many, she might act quickly to save the families she loved from harm, and it was just about feasible that she could have committed the murder and melted back into the performance. After all, the crime relied more on surprise than on strength, and Nathaniel would certainly not have expected her to turn against him. But where did that leave Christopher? It was time they paid Morveth a visit, Penrose thought; he and Trew would head into the village as soon as they'd finished with his uncle Jasper. He had heard all he needed to from Jago for the time being.

With good timing, Trew cleared his throat tactfully from the door to the stairs and Penrose signalled for him to join them again. 'I'd like you to give PC Trew a full description of what Christopher was wearing when he went missing,' he said to Jago as he stood up to leave. 'And a recent photograph if you've got one. It would be helpful if we could borrow a piece of Christopher's clothing – something that he's worn.' He could tell from the look on the older man's face that he didn't need to explain why such an item was needed. 'It's still early,' he added, 'and we won't give up hope of finding him alive until we have evidence to the contrary. I meant what I said – we'll do every-thing we can.' Jago nodded, but Penrose could see that he was on the point of giving up. He could hardly imagine a greater torment for the undertaker than the uncertainty of it all. His whole life had been dedicated to giving people some sort of finality in the midst of their grief – some sort of hope, even. The rituals of burial brought comfort if you were lucky enough to believe in them, and Jago had looked after a whole community – the living and the dead – for forty years or more. It seemed a very cruel twist of fate that he of all people should be denied that solace. 'While you're fetching those for us, do you mind if I have a look at your van?' he asked gently. 'I gather Morwenna borrowed it last night and Morveth returned it to you this morning.'

'That's right,' Jago said. 'Help yourself – you know where it is.'

He went through to the next room, and Penrose looked at Trew. 'We'll talk outside when you've got the description. Don't forget . . .'

'The boots, Sir,' Trew said before he could finish, and smiled. 'Don't worry – I won't.'

Penrose went out into the lane and opened the door on the passenger side of Jago's Ford. There, on the seat, was a small trace of blood – very faint, but unmistakeable if you knew what you were looking for. The case had moved on, but he was still relieved to find something that bore out Morwenna's account of Loveday's troubles and their hurried departure from the Minack the night before. He looked carefully over the rest of the car but found nothing of any interest, and went back to his own vehicle to wait impatiently for Trew.

Chapter Sixteen

Josephine sat at the desk in the Lodge, wondering how best to approach the unenviable task with which Archie had left her. Even if she managed to see Loveday, she felt uneasy about probing the girl for information behind a mask of friendship; there was a Greeks-bearing-gifts quality to it which she felt sure that Morwenna would see straight through. Still, at least it gave her something to do. She had struggled her way through a brief first chapter, and the unfortunate blonde on the beach was now in the safe hands of the coastguard; with the police on their way, she felt happy to leave it there for now. She was long practised at recognising the sort of day when words were hard to come by, and she knew that staring at a blank sheet of paper would simply make things worse; it was better for her – and for those around her – if she walked away and did something else. If only by the law of averages, the work would be less bloody tomorrow.

Reprieved by her own arguments, she took off her glasses and stared out across the lake. Today, with the deterioration in the weather, the Loe was a different creature altogether, its surface rippled by the wind and its beauty much less at odds with the legends that surrounded it. The wildfowl which had previously bathed in sunlit open waters chose to carry out their business around the edges of the water, sheltered by reed beds or by the tangles of willow and alder which punctuated the bank at regular intervals. Observing them, Josephine was distracted by a movement near the boathouse. How long had Morwenna been there? She must have been too engrossed in her work to notice her arrival, but she watched now as the figure stood alone and pensive in the place where she had unwittingly said a final goodbye to her brother. It began to rain softly – the sort of misty rain that feels so insignificant and soaks to the skin within seconds – but Morwenna did not turn to leave or make any attempt to find somewhere more sheltered, and Josephine saw her chance: it would seem far more natural to ask her about Loveday here than to turn up unannounced at their cottage and demand admittance. She edged a disgruntled Motley Penrose gently off her lap, collected a pair of umbrellas from the rack in the hallway and went outside, wondering what on earth she was going to say.

Morwenna must have heard the sound of footsteps on the gravel behind her but she did nothing to acknowledge Josephine's approach, and Josephine hesitated slightly, caught between her promise to Archie and her natural reluctance to intrude upon someone's solitude. She could, of course, take the coward's way out; Morwenna showed no sign of hurrying back to Loe Cottage and Josephine might easily be able to see Loveday now without her ever knowing, but she did not want to risk getting the girl into trouble and she needed time to talk to her properly. It was tempting, but she rejected the underhand route and made her way down the grass bank to the water. 'I've brought you this,' she said, tentatively holding out the umbrella. 'It looks set in for the day now.' Morwenna ignored her, and even Josephine acknowledged that such a ridiculous comment wasn't worthy of a response: what difference could a spot of rain possibly make to this woman's landscape? She dispensed with the small talk, which was as alien to her as it was unwelcome to Morwenna, and tried again. 'How's Loveday? Archie said she wasn't well.'

At last, Morwenna turned round. 'If you know that, then I'm sure you know everything,' she said with a disquieting matter-of-factness, 'including why I'd like some time here on my own. If you want to visit Loveday, be my guest. She's at the cottage, and I'm sure she'd love to see you. Let's face it, she'd love to see anyone who isn't me, and if you can keep her occupied for a bit, I ought to be grateful to you.'

It was exactly what Josephine had wanted to hear and she could have left triumphant, but her pride was reluctant to be so easily dismissed. She had told herself that she didn't much like Morwenna when perhaps the more truthful way to put it was that she was intimidated by her – by her looks and her self-possession, by the closeness of her relationship with Archie and by the twelve years between them which separated youth from approaching middle age. Morwenna had a knack of making her feel as though she'd been caught out in a lie which she wasn't even aware of telling – and she resented it more than she would have cared to admit.

'Do me a favour, though, if you do go to see Loveday,' Morwenna continued, looking back out over the lake. 'Don't insist on reading too much into what she says. It's hard enough to get some peace round here, and telling everyone that I'm a battered woman isn't helpful. If you're going to spy, at least do it properly.'

'You'd rather everyone knew the truth, then?' Josephine asked, stung more by the justness of the rebuke than the abrupt way in which it was delivered.

'I'm past caring what anyone knows.'

'Even Loveday?'

'Especially Loveday. She'll be all right – she knows how to look after herself.'

Josephine had already allowed herself to be dragged further into the conversation than she had intended, and she had no wish to antagonise Morwenna by trying to tell her how to look after her own sister, but it seemed to her that Loveday was the most overlooked casualty of all that had gone on in the Pinching household. 'Surely you don't blame her for what's happened?' she said.

Morwenna looked at her sharply. 'What do you mean?'

'Well, I can see that bringing her up must have put a strain on you and Harry, but it didn't have to be for ever, did it?' Morwenna seemed to relax a little, and Josephine wondered what she had expected her to say. 'Why didn't you just wait a bit longer and start the relationship again once Loveday had left home? It was only a matter of time.'

'Like I said to Archie, it was different after the fire. And anyway, who's to say that Loveday *will* leave home? She's hardly ideal marriage material.' Morwenna gave a bitter laugh. 'At least we have that in common.'

Christopher would have been more than happy to remove the inconvenience, Josephine thought, almost allowing her sarcasm to get the better of her, but she remembered in time that Loveday would not thank her for betraying that particular secret. She remained unconvinced by Morwenna's explanation, though; if the fire had been the only reason for her rejection of Harry, surely the tension between them would have emerged much sooner? 'What did Harry do that seemed such a betrayal of everything you had?' she asked.

Morwenna was quiet for such a long time that Josephine

wondered if she had even heard the question. A strong breeze rustled through the nearby reed beds, revealing the white undersides of the leaves on the low-hanging willows and driving the water against the floor of the boathouse with a muffled, persistent thud. She was about to repeat herself when Morwenna answered her with a question of her own. 'You don't think that killing our parents was a betrayal?'

'Of Loveday, perhaps, but not of you. If you wanted to romanticise it, you could even say it was the ultimate act of love.' She knew as soon as the words were out that she had gone too far; privately, she was sickened by the violence and selfishness of Harry's behaviour and her opinion of him had changed very little since the first time she had discussed him with Ronnie, but making that obvious was hardly the best way to get anything out of someone who loved him.

'How could you even begin to understand that love?' Morwenna asked in a tone which made it clear that she had no intention of wasting any more time by talking.

'Just because he was your brother . . .'

'No, no – that's not what I mean.' She lifted her hand dismissively before Josephine had a chance to finish. 'You can't understand because you didn't know Harry. This isn't about some abstract question of right or wrong; it's about him, only him, and how he made me feel. You never met him, you never heard his voice or saw him smile or felt the touch of his hand on your face, so you can never understand what it means to be without him.'

There was no argument to this, and it struck Josephine as ridiculous that she should be envious of Morwenna, but the emotion she felt as she listened to this simple declaration of love – a declaration all the more powerful for its ordinariness

– could not be fooled into calling itself anything else. She had experienced it before – not a jealousy of anyone in particular, but a vague, unsatisfiable longing for a passion which she had never truly known and which she had now seen too much of the world ever to experience. How she wished she had been given the luxury of first love in peacetime, free from fear and believing that anything was possible rather than resenting the war which had taken away so many choices.

'Look, go and see Loveday now,' said Morwenna, surprising Josephine by moving forward to take the spare umbrella from her hand. 'I can't get through to her any more, so you might as well keep her happy. At least it's one hour of the day when I don't have to worry about her. Take her your book – she's always been easily distracted from the real world.'

'Is that such a bad thing?' The comment had been made without malice, but Josephine – unsettled by the rest of the conversation – reacted more sensitively than was necessary.

'It depends how far you take it, and what price you're willing to pay.'

'Price? That's a bit strong for a harmless bit of escapism, isn't it?'

Once again, she felt like a child whose ignorance was being tolerated under sufferance as Morwenna smiled and said: 'I remember Archie telling me a few years ago about someone he loved who used books and make-believe to keep the world at arm's length.' Too surprised to speak, Josephine stared down at the redundant barge, where the rain was making a valiant but forlorn attempt to revive the wilting flowers, and tried not to resent the fact that she was being placed in opposition to Archie by someone who had no idea about the relationship they shared and who was a complete stranger, to her at least.

300

'He called her his Lady of Shalott,' Morwenna added, 'because she only ever looked at life in a mirror. He didn't mention any names, but I'm assuming that was you?' Still, Josephine said nothing; she was too busy trying to take in what she had just heard. It was stupid of her to be hurt: she knew how Archie felt – he had accused her of being an escapist often enough to her face – and she had never assumed that he wouldn't discuss her with other people, but somehow – perhaps because it was with Morwenna, perhaps because she had not expected to have it thrown back at her like this – it felt like a betrayal.

'It hurts when someone destroys your trust, doesn't it?' Morwenna said. 'When you find out that some sort of bond has been formed behind your back, and suddenly you're on the outside, looking in. Perhaps that answers your question about what Harry did to betray everything we had.'

She walked a little way up the bank, but stopped when Josephine called her back. 'It's funny, but when Archie was talking to you about me, I don't suppose he realised how similar you and I are.' Morwenna looked questioningly at her. 'Harry was your way of keeping the world at arm's length, wasn't he? As long as you could believe in the fantasy of that relationship, you hardly had to engage with reality at all.'

She was rewarded with a nod of acknowledgement and an ironic smile. 'That's the trouble with mirrors, though, isn't it?' Morwenna said. 'They break far too easily, but perhaps that's just as well.' This time, it was Josephine's turn to wait for an explanation. 'Well, aren't you sick of shadows?' Morwenna asked, turning to go. 'I know I am.'

Morveth Wearne stood under one of the vast pine trees that formed the thickest plantation on the western side of the Loe and watched the two women on the opposite bank, safe in the knowledge that she could not be seen – by them, or by anybody walking behind her along the track which led to the church and on to the sea. She found it hard to believe what she was seeing: one conversation at the Minack last night had made it clear to Morveth that Archie's London friend was far too sharp-witted to be safe company for any of them at the moment, and she would have thought that Morwenna had more sense than to engage. In any case, Loveday shouldn't be left alone for long; anyone could drop by the cottage and talk to her, and both Archie and his friend were perfectly capable of piecing together more than they needed to know from a carelessly made remark. More anxious than ever, Morveth decided to finish what she had set out to do as quickly as possible, then go and sit with Loveday until Morwenna returned.

Still she watched, though, unable to tear herself away. Her left hand picked nervously at a loose piece of cotton which dangled from the garment in her arms; the coarse brown fabric felt rough against her skin as she tried to gauge the tone of the exchange from the women's body language, but it was impossible from this distance. Perhaps she should walk round and interrupt, but it would take her a good twenty minutes to reach them and by that time the damage might be done. Anyway, she thought, looking down, she could hardly carry this about the estate in full daylight; it had to be disposed of immediately. Burning it would be too risky – the police were bound to comb the area sooner or later, and a fire would leave traces behind; no, it had to be put out of sight in a place where no one would ever find it. When she looked up again, Morveth saw that Morwenna had left the boathouse and was now walking off in the direction of the Helston Road; Josephine watched her go, then turned and went back into the Lodge. Relieved, but still wondering what had been said, Morveth made her way quickly along the bank, through the bluebells and moss-covered tree trunks, and round to the deepest part of the lake.

The group of jackdaws sitting sociably on the roof of Loe Cottage seemed to Josephine to be an unfittingly high-spirited reminder of the night before. She watched their activity as she walked up the lane to the gate; one bird was perched on the rim of the chimney pot, periodically thrusting its head downwards until a puff of black smoke sent it to join its friends on the ridges of the thatch. Their characteristic doglike yap filled the air, high-pitched and insistent. She had read somewhere that jackdaws were once regarded as omens of doom; if that were true, they had chosen their meeting place well.

Loveday was looking out of one of the upstairs windows. Her face brightened as soon as she saw Josephine and she waved, then beckoned her inside. Feeling distinctly uncomfortable about letting herself into another woman's home, Josephine put her head round the door and called a tentative greeting. 'Loveday? Is it all right if I come up?'

'Of course it is.' The voice was too close to have come from the bedroom, and a few seconds later its owner appeared at the bottom of the stairs, dressed in a white cotton nightgown with her long blonde hair tied back in a single plait, and looking even younger than her fourteen years. She was paler than usual, but Josephine was glad to see that there were no other signs of illness. 'It's lovely to see you,' Loveday said, smiling broadly. 'I'm so bored of lying in bed, but Morwenna says I've got to stay there.'

'Quite right, too. Your sister told me I could come and keep you company for a bit,' she added, keen for Loveday to know she wasn't doing anything wrong. 'Personally, I can't think of anything more idyllic than lying in bed all day and doing nothing, so think of it as a treat and make the most of it while you can.'

Loveday protested good-naturedly, but led the way back to her room. The stairs, which went up from the ill-fated kitchen, came out on to a long, dark landing, and Josephine could not decide whether the claustrophobic feeling it gave her was due to the physical structure of the cottage or to her knowledge of what had gone on there; probably the latter, she thought, because the house itself was surprisingly spacious inside. Three doors led off the landing, and Loveday headed for the one at the very end, giving Josephine a perfect opportunity to glance into the other rooms on the way. The first was obviously Morwenna's and was notable only for being slightly untidier than the rest of the house, but the second – stripped completely bare, even down to the curtains at the windows – stopped her in her tracks. Of course grief affected people differently, but this utter eradication of Harry from the sisters' lives only strengthened her belief that he was guilty of something more terrible than his parents' murder – more terrible in Morwenna's eyes, at least. An image flashed into her mind of Harry and Morwenna by the boathouse on that last morning; it was not something that she could ever have seen – she didn't even know what Harry looked like – but it held the intensity of a memory, and she wondered again about his death. How or why was beyond her, but – having glimpsed this emphatic denial of a life – she had no doubt that Morwenna would certainly have been capable of her brother's murder.

'In here,' Loveday called impatiently. Her room was small

but cheerful, with ceilings which sloped almost to the ground and shiny black floorboards, covered in rugs worn so thin that the animals embroidered lovingly on to them were barely recognisable. On the mat nearest the bed, a horse peeped out from a hot-water bottle which had been cast aside onto the floor. The bedclothes themselves were entirely white, giving a pure, almost virginal quality to the room which was straight out of the stories of romance and adventure that filled the shelf above the bed. Clearly, Loveday's tastes inclined towards the heroic: Malory, Kipling and Rider Haggard rubbed shoulders with Ouida and Stevenson, and Josephine was pleased to see dog-eared editions of Conan Doyle and *Trent's Last Case* – her own offering might pale in comparison, but at least Loveday found the genre entertaining. Apart from the book jackets, the only other colour in the room came from a bowl of bluebells which stood with a water jug on the white bamboo table by the bed, the delicacy of their lavender flowers belied by the strong, green scent which filled the room.

Loveday patted the bed, and Josephine sat down. 'Here – I've brought you something to read,' she said, handing over Archie's copy of *The Man in the Queue*. *Kif*, she had decided, was a little too bleak in its outlook for an impressionable fourteen-year-old; there would be plenty of time for Loveday to find out that the world was rarely a fair place. The girl took the book eagerly, but her face fell as she looked at the jacket. 'Is something wrong?' Josephine asked, concerned by Loveday's obvious disappointment.

'No, no – of course not,' she said, smiling bravely. 'I just hoped it might be one of yours, that's all.' Realising that she must sound ungrateful, she added: 'I'm sure Gordon Daviot's very good, though.'

Josephine laughed. 'That's one of *my* secrets – except it's not much of a secret any more. It *is* mine – I just had it published under a different name.' She opened the book and showed Loveday the title page, where there was an inscription to Archie, signed in her own name. 'There – that proves it.'

'Won't Mr Penrose mind you lending me his book?'

'Of course not,' said Josephine, who had no qualms whatsoever about raiding Archie's library, particularly today. As far as she was concerned, he could curl up with his bloody Tennyson and leave her alone to polish her mirror. She smiled sweetly at Loveday. 'He'd be pleased to know you were enjoying it.'

'I'll keep it safe for him,' Loveday promised, tracing the lettering on the jacket thoughtfully with her finger. 'Why wouldn't you want people to know you've written a book?' she asked. 'I think it's a wonderful thing. If it were me, I'd have my name as big as possible on the front.'

'Not if you lived in Inverness, you wouldn't,' Josephine said, smiling.

'Why? Aren't the people very nice?'

'It's not that. It's just that as a family we've always preferred to keep ourselves to ourselves, and that's not necessarily the best way to make yourself popular in a small town. Everyone already thought I was a little odd because I refused to take part in the endless round of going out to tea, and I didn't want to make it worse for myself by being seen to do anything as queer as writing a book. It was stupid of me, really, but I thought I could keep the two things entirely separate.'

'But they found out?'

'Yes. The play I wrote was a bit of a hit, and that scuppered me completely. And you're right – calling myself Gordon Daviot wasn't the best idea I've ever had. It seemed a nice tribute at the time, but it gets me some very strange looks and I dread to think what they'll be saying about me in fifty years' time.'

'Who was it a tribute to?'

'Someone I used to know. It was a long time ago now – I was only a few years older than you. Daviot is a small village a few miles from where I live now – about the same distance as Penzance is from here. I used to go on holiday there every summer with my parents, and that's where I met him.'

'Where is he now?'

'Oh, he's not around any more.'

'Did you jilt him?'

Reluctant to start a conversation about the war and what it had meant to her, Josephine smiled. 'No. In a manner of speaking, I suppose you could say that he jilted me.'

Loveday looked petulant. 'I've jilted Christopher,' she said.

'Oh? Why's that?'

'Because he's ignoring me. He hasn't spoken to me since Sunday.'

'Does he know he's in your bad books?'

'Of course not. I haven't had a chance to tell him.'

Had she not realised the seriousness of Christopher's disappearance, Josephine would have been amused by Loveday's indignation: a girl was never too young to resent being denied the chance to air her grievances first. 'So you haven't heard from him at all?'

'No, not a thing.'

'And he didn't say anything to you about having to go away? To see some friends, perhaps?' Loveday shook her head. 'Not even as a secret? You don't have to tell me the details if you *do* know where he is – I'll just be impressed you found out.'

307

'No,' said Loveday sulkily, and Josephine could tell from her frown that she was speaking the truth. 'I was hoping to see him at the theatre, but I had to go. I don't suppose you saw him?'

'I'm afraid not.' She decided against worrying Loveday by telling her that Christopher had not shown his face at the Minack – or anywhere else, for that matter. 'I didn't even see much of you. You left in such a hurry – are you feeling better now?'

'Much better, thank you – not that Christopher cares. He made such a fuss of me at first when I didn't feel well, and I thought he was sure to come and see me today, but he hasn't as much as sent a message.'

Josephine was confused. 'I thought you hadn't seen him?'

Loveday looked at her as if she were a little stupid. 'I haven't.'

'But if he was concerned last night when you felt ill . . .'

'No, not last night. When I was *first* ill, I said – that was weeks ago.'

Surprised, Josephine said: 'Loveday, how did you feel back then, when Christopher was so worried about you?'

'Horrible,' she said, shuddering. 'I was sick all the time – just like I was once when I ate some berries I found in the woods, except this went on for longer.'

'And last night? Were you sick then?'

'No, that's stopped now, thank goodness. Morveth gave me something to make it go away. Last night was just the curse, but it hurt more than usual. Morwenna said it was so bad because I hadn't had one for a while. I suppose that makes sense, but I'm glad it's better today.'

Josephine was torn between relief that Loveday remained blissfully ignorant of her obvious miscarriage, and horror at this latest example of the way in which the girl was so easily manipulated by those around her. 'It sounds as though Morveth looked after you well,' she said. 'What did she give you?'

'I don't know exactly, but it smelt funny. Morwenna was angry with her for making me drink it yesterday when I wanted to go to the play, but Morveth said something about it having to be right with the moon, and if she waited another month it would be too late.'

Reminding herself that this was 1935, Josephine said: 'And Christopher knew you were being sick?'

'Yes. He was really nice to me about it, but I could tell he was worried.'

I bet he was, Josephine thought. She could imagine how Jago Snipe would have reacted to the news that his son had got Loveday pregnant. Running away – if that was indeed what he had done – must have seemed by far the lesser of two evils. 'Did anyone else know you were ill?' she asked.

'No. Morwenna said we should keep it to ourselves, and I was to stay at home as much as possible until I felt better. That's why she got so angry whenever I ran off – but it's so boring, being stuck in the house all the time.'

'What about Harry? Did he know you weren't well before he had his accident?' If Harry had found out that Christopher was taking advantage of his little sister, that would explain the animosity between them.

Loveday considered the question for a moment. 'No – he would have done something to make me feel better,' she said. 'He always knew how to cheer me up.'

It was the first time that Josephine had heard Loveday use the past tense with regard to her brother. At least she seemed to be coming to terms with that tragedy, although the news of Nathaniel's death – and possibly Christopher's – could surely not be kept from her for much longer, and she was bound to be deeply upset when she heard. 'I know he's made you cross – I would be, too – but you and Christopher are very good friends, aren't you?' she said gently. Loveday nodded, and she looked so sad that Josephine was tempted to try to explain the situation to her: was allowing her to believe that Christopher had betrayed her affections really any kinder than being honest with her about the danger in which he might have found himself? In the end, she decided against it; she could only guess at what had really happened to the boy, and telling Loveday something which she subsequently discovered to be a lie would only make her as insensitive as everyone else. Instead, with the unpleasant taste of treachery in her mouth, she did as Archie had asked. 'Did Harry ever have a special friend, like you have Christopher? One person with whom he was particularly close?'

'No. He had me and Morwenna.'

'Of course he did, but I mean someone different.' The irony was not lost on her as she added, 'Someone outside the family.'

This seemed to be a new idea to Loveday. She thought about it, but eventually shook her head. 'Definitely not. I would have known.'

'Even if he didn't want to tell you?'

'Oh yes. Sometimes I used to follow him, you see, just for fun.'

'And he didn't meet anyone, or go anywhere in particular? With Nathaniel, for example?'

'Into the village, usually. And he did meet people, but not

someone to be alone with, not like . . .' She left the sentence unfinished and looked down at the sheets, embarrassed. 'Anyway, Nathaniel wouldn't be like Christopher, would he?'

Josephine was saved the embarrassment of further explanation by the sound of someone opening the back door. Morwenna had returned sooner than expected, perhaps having had second thoughts about leaving her sister alone to talk to a stranger, and her time with Loveday was clearly about to be curtailed. Footsteps stopped halfway up the stairs, as though Morwenna were trying to listen to their conversation, and Josephine said brightly to Loveday: 'Would you like me to read you the first chapter before I have to go?'

Loveday nodded enthusiastically, and handed her the book. She had barely got halfway through the first paragraph before she was interrupted, but the voice was not Morwenna's.

'I'm sure you mean well, Miss Tey, but I think Loveday needs some rest now.' She turned to see Morveth Wearne standing in the doorway, her face resolute and brooking no argument. 'Perhaps you could come back another day.'

It occurred to Josephine that the same offer might have been made to a condemned man with more hope of its being allowed to come true, but she resisted the temptation to jump up as though she were one of Morveth's pupils. 'Oh, we've been taking it easy, haven't we?' she said casually, glancing conspiratorially at Loveday. 'And it's good to know that your patient is so much better than she has been of late.'

This last comment could hardly have been more blatant, but Morveth did not even flinch. 'Then let's make sure it stays that way,' she said, opening the door slightly. It was a subtle gesture, but somehow harder to disobey than an outright order to leave.

'I'll come and see you again,' she promised Loveday defiantly. 'Enjoy the book, and don't be too careful with it. When you're better, I'll let you read some of the new one.' She bent down to kiss the girl's forehead, and whispered in her ear so that Morveth could not hear what she was saying. 'You never know, I might find a role for you in it. But that's *our* secret.'

Loveday beamed at her and she left the room, glad that Morveth at least refrained from seeing her off the premises like a poacher discovered trespassing on estate land. As she closed the door behind her and walked down the path, Josephine could feel the eyes burning into the back of her head. She resisted the temptation to turn around.

Chapter Seventeen

Beth Jacks got up from where she had been kneeling on the cold stone floor of the church, and turned away while Jasper Motley tidied his clothes. Such modesty was hardly necessary, he thought, as he watched her wipe her hand quickly across her mouth, but at least she was getting better at masking her revulsion. If anyone had a right to be disgusted, it was he: her face was rarely without the marks of her husband's fist these days, and that purple stain of shame made it almost impossible for him to take any satisfaction in their sex – if what they did now was even worthy of the name. He had long since abandoned any attempt to force himself on her as he would have liked to; her compliance made no allowance for the sense of power which had first awakened, then guided, his sexuality, and she ought to be grateful that he was willing to continue the arrangement at all.

She took a seat at the vestry table, while he lifted the lid on the panelled oak coffer and removed a black bag. It was an elaborate piece of furniture to store so little that was of value, but he tried not to dwell on its emptiness as he put the money on the table in front of her. He saw an expression of disappointment cross her face as she picked the coins up, one by one – he had not been as generous as usual, but she had more sense than to complain. Instead, she pushed the Bible hesitantly towards him and waited. Impatiently, he chose a passage at random and began to read, keen to get this part of the business over and done with. He had laughed the first time she asked him to do it, scornful of the idea that the humiliating sin of which she was guilty could somehow be absolved by the person who had demanded it, but she had shown a rare moment of strength by insisting on a reading from the scriptures every time, and he obliged her because it cost him nothing. The understanding they shared had, of course, been his idea, and she had looked at him in horror when he first suggested it, but it had not taken her long to come round to the idea. Years of ill-treatment from her husband had dulled her self-respect but sharpened a streak of pragmatism which saw the sense in being paid for her shame, and it was not his place to strip her of the illusion that money would eventually buy her freedom. He had seen men like Jacks before and understood what drove them; there were no lengths to which the gamekeeper would not go to keep what was his, whether he valued it or not.

When the reading was over, he stood at the door in the north porch and watched Beth Jacks walk away through the gravestones, leaving the churchyard by the lych gate and heading back into the estate. The rain had stopped now, and the air felt young and fresh again – cleansed, he would have said, if he were the type to seek regeneration. Looking across at the rectory opposite, he noticed that there was a dark car parked by the hedge; as he watched, his nephew got out from the driver's side and gazed intently after Beth Jacks, then back at the church. Absentmindedly, Motley rubbed his temple, where a headache had been building all day. He had expected a visit from the police since this morning, when his wife had returned from the village full of the news of Nathaniel

Shoebridge's death. The curate's obvious antagonism towards him was bound to require some sort of explanation now, but never for a moment had he considered that the police might arrive in the shape of Archie Penrose, and he was suddenly uneasy: he feared Penrose's intelligence and his integrity – they were so like his mother's. He had never got to know his nephew – Lizzie made sure of that – and none of the family were regular churchgoers, so he had not even watched Archie grow up from a distance, but he was aware that an unspoken bitterness existed between them which stretched back to the war. Then, like many other preachers in hundreds of pulpits around the country, Jasper Motley had considered it his duty to encourage the young men of his parish to fight for their country, and he had done so with a dedication and a passion which did not usually characterise his sermons. On one such occasion – a harvest festival, he thought it was, right at the beginning of the war – the Penroses made a rare appearance in the family pew, more out of solidarity for William than anything else. He remembered the expression of sadness and scepticism on Archie's face when the preaching turned to the glories of war, and it had seemed so out of place in someone so young; two years later, having witnessed the horror for himself, his nephew returned to the church, on sick leave after an incident in which his closest friend had been killed. By then, the congregation had dwindled considerably and Archie sat alone in the front pew, directly in line with the gothic Victorian lectern, staring up at his uncle with hatred and blame in his eyes, as if the fighting were somehow his fault. Nothing had been said, but there was such an intensity in the moment that Jasper Motley had, ever since, harboured a secret fear that Penrose would eventually find something for which he could make his uncle pay, no matter how many years it took.

If he had had any doubt that the visit was official, it would have been dispelled when a uniformed police constable got out of the passenger seat. Motley met them halfway up the path, reluctant to talk in the vestry in case the sordid nature of his encounter with Beth Jacks remained somehow tangible there. Penrose came straight to the point, refusing to acknowledge any family connection between them. 'We need to talk to you about Nathaniel's death,' he said, with the easy politeness of a man talking to a stranger. 'I presume you've heard what happened?'

Motley nodded. 'I'd left the theatre by then, as I'm sure you know, but my wife told me this morning. Everyone was talking about it in the village, she said, and I telephoned William to get the details. He said it wasn't an accident.'

'We're treating it as murder, so I'd like to know more about the incident between you and Nathaniel just before he died.' He smiled, but there was no warmth in it. 'To eliminate you from our inquiries, as they say.'

'You'd better come up to the house,' Motley said, realising that he was not going to be able to get this over with as quickly as he would have liked. Penrose looked again at the church and, for a second, Motley thought he was going to argue, but he nodded his agreement and stood aside to let his uncle lead the way. 'You can't bring that thing in with you, though,' the vicar added. 'Edwina hates dogs.'

Apparently unoffended, the constable smiled good-naturedly and left the terrier in the car. As Motley opened the door to Bar Lodge, he heard his wife coming down the stairs. She stopped on the first landing, deciding against whatever she

316

had been about to say as soon as she saw that he was not alone; for a moment, she looked curiously at the small group in the hallway, then turned and went back upstairs without a word, but not before he noticed satisfaction in her eyes. It would amuse her to stand by while he lost everything; more than ever, he was determined not to let it happen.

He led the policemen through to the drawing room and stood by the fireplace, determined to maintain some sort of authority in his own home, even though his legs ached and he desperately needed to sit down. Penrose looked around with interest, and Motley realised that this was unfamiliar territory to his nephew, who had never set foot in the house before. His manner was relaxed and unhurried, and he glanced leisurely around the room before speaking, taking in the French-style walnut settee and the fine mahogany longcase clock, and noting, no doubt, the discrepancy between the luxury of the vicar's domestic space and the neglected professional arena which was supposed to be his first concern. 'Some of my men will be conducting a search of the churchyard and the church itself,' he said eventually. 'I'm sure they can rely on your co-operation.'

'Is that absolutely necessary?' Motley asked, genuinely surprised. 'Surely it can have no bearing on Shoebridge's death?'

'I'll be the judge of that,' Penrose said, and Motley detected the first note of irritation in an otherwise faultless performance. 'Christopher Snipe is missing, but he was last seen in the graveyard on Sunday night. Did you notice him there? Or anybody else?'

'No. Sunday was a busy day, and I was tired. We had an early supper after Pinching's funeral, and I went to bed. I certainly wasn't in the mood to wander round the churchyard in the dark.'

'I'm not suggesting you were, but there's a perfectly good view of at least half of it from here. You might have noticed something from the window.'

Motley shook his head. 'I was asleep from eight o'clock, or just after. Edwina will confirm that.'

'Nathaniel kept his original costume for the play in the vestry, ready to bring to the Minack for me to wear on Tuesday night, but it was already missing when he went to fetch it. When was the last time you noticed it there? It was one of the brown habits.'

'I remember seeing it on Monday afternoon.'

'What time?'

He thought for a moment. 'Well, I went to the church after lunch and stayed there for a couple of hours. The cricket match was just finishing when I left, and the costume was still there then. Listen, I hope your men are going to be careful,' he added, still thrown by the idea of a search. 'Make sure they show some respect – there are people at rest there.' He knew how hollow his concern for the souls of his dead parishioners must sound after all these years. Penrose laughed – a sarcastic, dismissive gesture which reminded Motley so much of his sister that he had to turn away for a second to keep his composure. He remembered how often Lizzie had laughed at him like that when they were children. She and William were always caught up in their rituals and their private jokes, and for years the only acknowledgement he ever received from them was rejection – until he realised that there was a way to make Lizzie notice him, late at night, when she was alone in her room with no one else to turn to. The first time he crept along that long corridor at Loe House, he had only intended to frighten her. Her room was in darkness, but she was sleeping so soundly that he was able to walk softly over to the bed without any risk of discovery. He listened to her slow, regular breathing for a moment, then put his hand roughly over her mouth, meaning to give her the shock of her life and bring this smug, untroubled rest to an abrupt end. She awoke in fear, which turned to anger when she saw who it was, but he was older and stronger and her small body was no match for his; he felt her struggle beneath him, and the excitement which he experienced for the first time in that moment was fleeting but so intense that he knew he could not leave it there. What surprised him most was how easy it had been to make his sister believe that his nightly visits were all her fault, to crush her vitality and independence under the weight of a secret shame. In the end, his pleasure was psychological as much as it was physical: isolating her from the rest of the family, making her fear her parents and even William, was a triumph, and he was amused to notice that she soon began to get herself into trouble deliberately, as if being punished for other sins would somehow assuage the deeper sense of guilt which festered inside her. Jasper knew it could not last for ever, but he had desperately needed someone to belong to him and, for a while, Lizzie did. Nothing else in his life had ever quite lived up to the potency of those three brief years.

With a start, Motley realised that Penrose was waiting for him to speak, but he had been too caught up in his own thoughts to hear the question. 'What did you say?' he asked, pulling himself together and trying to look at his nephew as a policeman rather than a dangerous reincarnation of his past.

Impatiently, Penrose repeated himself. 'I just wondered where you got your passion for theatre from?'

'What? I don't have a passion for theatre. I've left that to your side of the family.'

'That's what I thought. And yet you made sure of a front-row seat on Tuesday night.'

'They're the Winwaloe Players and I'm the vicar of St Winwaloe's – what's so suspicious about that? Aren't I allowed to support my own community?'

Penrose smiled again. 'There's a first time for everything, I suppose,' he said, and Motley felt a violence rise within him which, had he been ten years younger, he doubted he would have been able to control. Instead, he said nothing, but noticed with interest that even the constable seemed surprised by his superior's approach. 'You left the auditorium immediately after the incident with Nathaniel,' the inspector continued. 'Did you leave the theatre altogether?'

'I went to my car, which was parked at the top of the hill, and waited there for my wife. She arrived about ten minutes later, and we drove straight home.'

'You knew she'd come after you?'

'Of course.'

'Did anyone see you while you were waiting?'

'Not that I know of.'

'And you didn't meet anyone else by the cars? Jago Snipe or Morveth Wearne, for example?'

'I saw Snipe as we were driving off. He was standing on the edge of the lawn to Minack House, bent over with his hands on his knees, trying to get his breath back. I'm not surprised – that place isn't built for people our age. I doubt he saw us, but he must have heard the car. Morveth Wearne wasn't there, though.'

'Let's go back to the moment when Nathaniel departed from

the script. Do you know why he did that, and what he was trying to suggest?'

'I've no idea. He had a vivid imagination, and was prone to grand gestures. Theatricality suited him, particularly in the pulpit, but don't expect me to be able to tell you what was going on in his head.'

'He wouldn't be the first person to accuse you of certain financial irregularities, though, would he?'

'People talk in any small community. It's a substitute for something meaningful in their otherwise futile lives. I don't listen to gossip, and I would have thought that someone in your position would know better than to make accusations which have no substance.'

Penrose glanced around the room again, then continued. 'It's not so much the coins that interest me, though, as what Nathaniel chose to do with them. He poured them from a collection bag into your lap, and that struck me as a very sexual gesture. Would you agree?'

Motley shrugged, but he knew that his nervousness must be obvious to the two men looking at him. How much did his nephew know? he wondered. He suspected that his curate had put two and two together, but surely he hadn't had a chance to tell Penrose? 'I'd advise you to ask Shoebridge,' he said defiantly, 'but of course you can't.'

'No, but it seems fairly obvious to me that Nathaniel was making a point about certain excesses of the clergy. The question is – was he talking generally or specifically?' Motley watched as Penrose walked casually over to the window and looked back along the coastal path in the direction of the Loe. 'Perhaps I should ask Beth Jacks if she can throw any light on what Nathaniel meant. Of course, if I did that, her husband would want to know what I was talking about. I can only imagine how he'd take the news of his wife's infidelity, even if it was for the greater good of the Church. He strikes me as a man who values exclusivity.'

The specific threat of Kestrel Jacks's violence formed a very small part of the humiliation which suddenly faced Jasper Motley, and he took a gamble. 'There's no proof . . .'

'Now Nathaniel's dead, you mean?' Penrose jumped in quickly. 'I'm afraid these are my conclusions, not his. Beth Jacks doesn't work for you – well, not in any official capacity. So why would she be walking away from your church, counting money?'

'Why the hell do you think?' Motley shouted angrily, clutching at the only straw he could think of. 'She's been stealing from the vestry. I've had my suspicions for some time, but I've never been able to prove it.'

'So today, while she was in the church right under your nose, you just stood calmly at the door and watched her walk away with the collection?'

Somehow, Penrose's anger only served to emphasise his authority, while Jasper felt increasingly diminished by his own fury. His heart was racing and he tried hard to concentrate on what he was saying, but he could not clear his head of the fuzziness which had started to cloud his thoughts. 'You're surely not going to take her word against mine, are you?'

'Careful, Reverend – you're showing your true colours. Would you really stand there and accuse that woman – who has more wretchedness in her life already than you could ever imagine – of something she hasn't done just to save your own miserable skin? Hasn't she lowered herself enough for you? My mother was right,' he added, referring overtly at last to the personal

322

resentment which had run as a subtext to their whole conversation. 'There isn't a word to describe the extent of your hypocrisy. No man should wrong his brother – isn't that what you preach? And yet you can hurt your sister as often as you like.'

The shock of how much Penrose knew left him speechless for a second, but then his rage and his guilt got the better of him. 'She asked for it,' he said. 'Your mother was no better than a common whore, and nothing she said to you about her perfect marriage to your father can change the fact that I had her first.' Too late, he realised that his nephew had been speaking generally and his words did not, in fact, reveal any knowledge of the sin to which he, Jasper, had inadvertently confessed. He tried to retract what he had said, but he could not get the words out properly and anyway, he had gone too far. Before he knew it, Penrose was across the room and Motley felt strong hands at his throat. As he gasped for breath, he was dimly aware that the constable was telling Penrose to stop and pulling him away. His wife entered the room, too quickly to have come from upstairs, and he realised that she must have been standing outside the door all the time. Her smile was the last thing he noticed before everything went black.

Harry took the strip of cloth from around his neck and soaked it in a small pool of water which the obliging rain had created in the hollow of a sycamore tree. Gently, he removed one of his socks, wincing with pain as the rough wool, matted with blood, clung stubbornly to his foot in the places where the skin was broken. Days of wearing boots which were too small for him had taken their toll, and it would need more than water to repair the damage, but he did what he could. His whole body felt broken, exhausted. Last night, he had been so tired that he literally had had to drag his feet along the ground. The nails in his boots made sparks against the granite, reminding him of the hours he used to spend watching his father shoe the horses. If he closed his eyes, he could still feel the steam rising from the metal as it cooled and now, with the boot in his hand, the smell of leather did its best to take him somewhere he could not afford to go. He bent down and put it roughly back on, using the pain to blot out an image of the past which was as unwelcome as it was unreal.

It took every ounce of the willpower he had, not to give in to his tiredness and simply lie down – right here, on the floor of the woods where he and Morwenna had made love for the first time. It was autumn then, and the bluebells which now stretched out in front of him lay hidden and forgotten under the death of summer. He had kissed her once – the usual reward for whatever game they were playing – but this time she turned her face towards him at the last minute, making sure that he found her lips. As she held his shirt and pulled him tentatively down with her on to the leaves, he realised that what he felt for her – what he had always felt for Morwenna – was love. Eager, nervous, disbelieving that this could ever be his, he explored her body, noticing how the leaves tangled in her hair seemed to reflect the shades of red and gold which he had always loved. In the distance, someone had lit a bonfire and, for Harry, the pungent, melancholy smell of wood smoke would always mean Morwenna and home. Later, as they grew up, he felt like that child of twelve whenever they were together. He remembered the peace of those first moments alone with her – here, before the noise of life continued – and wondered if he would ever know it again. It was the only thing left which could make sense of all that had happened.

Harry looked through the trees towards Loe Cottage, his shelter and his prison. As he watched, trying to reconcile pasts which refused to belong to the same person, he saw Morwenna come out from the kitchen with a basket of laundry, her face ghostly in the strengthening sunlight, her weariness mirroring his own. For a moment, Harry had to turn away. His greatest fear had always been of looking back over his shoulder to find that she was happy without him, but seeing her like this – with all the life beaten out of her because of what she believed he had done – was much worse. He wanted to go to her, but he knew he couldn't – not in daylight, when someone might see him. Being anywhere near the cottage was dangerous now, even though he knew the Loe estate and its secrets better than anyone. Still, Harry took the risk because he no longer trusted himself to be away from Morwenna. He was losing himself, and she was his only hope. Without her, it was too easy to believe in his own death.

Penrose watched the ambulance pull away from Bar Lodge and gather as much speed as the narrow track would allow. Wearily, he leaned against the boot of his car. The stroke had been a serious one, and the ambulance men – while polite and efficient – had refused to commit themselves to Jasper Motley's chances of surviving it. In spite of their assurances that the attack had not been brought on by his questioning, Penrose could not help but feel a certain amount of guilt – professional rather than personal – for having given it every possible assistance.

A noise from the back seat drew his attention, and he opened the rear door to give Treg the opportunity for some exercise. The dog licked his hand gratefully and found plenty to amuse himself with along the hedgerow, and the two of them waited for Trew to finish talking to Edwina Motley. She had refused the offer of a lift to the hospital, preferring instead to wait at home for news of her husband, and Penrose guessed that his fate was of little concern to her, other than materially. He had never liked what little he knew of his uncle's wife, and had no intention of allowing the afternoon's events to make him feel guilty for that, but he had to admit to a grudging respect for the way that she refused to manufacture a grief for appearance's sake.

As for his own behaviour, he could only imagine what might have happened if Trew had not stepped in. It had all taken place so quickly, and yet he seemed to have experienced a lifetime of emotions in those few seconds – incredulity, disgust, loneliness and – least forgivably of all, perhaps – a selfish foolishness that he had never discovered the family secret for himself. He thought back to how he remembered his mother – or rather how he thought he remembered her – and no longer trusted what he saw; it was almost as if the unease he felt at Harry's funeral had been some sort of premonition that the foundations of his own life were about to shift unalterably. How easily the images you relied upon most could fall apart, he thought, although he was honest enough to recognise that the sense of betrayal which should have been for his mother was in fact for himself. Try as he might, he could not connect his outrage to her suffering; instead, he was shocked to realise that he blamed her – not for the violation itself, but for dying before he understood, before he had a chance to help.

Trew came over to the car, and Penrose was grateful to him for his businesslike attitude: if he felt either pity or concern for his superior's mental health, he was sensible enough not to show it. 'I'll have to go and tell William about his brother,' Penrose said. 'He'll probably want to go to the hospital, or at least see Edwina. And I need to talk to him,' he added, more to himself than to Trew. He looked at his watch. 'It's six o'clock now. I'll run you into Helston, and you can get a car back to Penzance from there.'

'There's no need, Sir. I'll take the path by the lake and get to Helston that way. Treg could do with a walk, and I'd like to have a look along that side of the water, remind myself what we're dealing with before the search.'

'Are you sure?'

'Absolutely, Sir. It won't take me long, and it's a pleasant enough evening now. You've got things to do.' He called Treg, who – with uncharacteristic disobedience – just looked back at him from the south porch of the church and refused to move. 'What's got into him?' He called again, a stricter note in his voice this time, and Treg reluctantly did as he was told. 'I'll make sure that everything's in place our end for first light tomorrow,' he said, when the dog was by his side again. 'We'll get the boys started here, then they can make their way through the woodland on this side while your uncle's men work along the other bank. Will he still be able to oversee that after what's happened?'

'Yes, I'm sure he will but I'll telephone you at the station later,' Penrose said. 'It's going to be a long job, so the sooner we can get started, the better.' The constable nodded and set off at a brisk pace, his dog at his heels. 'And Trew?' Penrose called after him.

'Yes, Sir?'

'Thank you for what you did this afternoon.'

'There's really no need, Sir.'

'Yes there is. I'm sorry you were put in that position.'

'It's forgotten, Sir, honestly.'

By Trew, perhaps, thought Penrose as he got back into his car, but certainly not by him.

Josephine called in at the stables on her way back from Loe Cottage, and spent a peaceful half-hour talking to Violet and getting to know one or two of the other horses. While she was there, one of the stable lads – not the man she had met on Monday night, but someone just as affable and respectful of the animals in his care – came to fetch Shilling from his stall for some exercise. She watched as he led the grey out into the yard and saddled him carefully, talking gently to the horse all the time. There was a nervousness in Shilling's eye as the man eased himself smoothly on to his back, a look which suggested that arrogance had been made to doubt itself for the first time, but the creature seemed soothed by his rider's calm confidence and, by the time they reached the parkland in front of Loe House, where tree trunks had been carefully positioned to form a series of jumps, man and horse seemed to have reached an understanding, albeit a fragile one.

'Getting better, isn't he?' She turned, pleased to see William, and the two of them watched in admiration as Shilling effortlessly managed each jump that was asked of him. 'I only wish I could be sure that patience and good care would have the same effect on everyone Harry left behind,' he said. 'It was kind of you to spend some time with Loveday, though. It obviously made her day.'

'You've seen her?' Josephine asked, relieved. She couldn't bring herself to believe that Morveth would harm the girl;

nevertheless, it was good to hear that her visit had not simply brought Loveday more trouble.

'Yes. I called in on the way back from seeing Nathaniel's parents. Actually, she was a breath of fresh air – I hadn't realised how much I needed to see someone smile. And I don't want to put any pressure on you, but you're going to have to write a lot faster to keep that young reader happy.'

Josephine laughed. 'She's started it, then?'

'Oh, she's nearly halfway through. It would seem that you *are* capable of a real shocker after all. She made me promise to tell you who she suspects, but I'm afraid I've forgotten what she said.'

'Don't worry. She can tell me herself – I'll call again tomorrow.'

'She'd like that.'

'Did you see Morwenna?'

'Yes.' He looked grave again, and Josephine realised that Ronnie was right to be worried about her father – the sadness on the estate was taking its toll on him as much as anyone. 'It's like talking to someone who's only half there. Any mention of the future, and she just retreats further into herself.'

'What will happen to them?'

'I ought to be able to answer that, but it's not a simple question. Financially, I'm happy to take responsibility for them until they get back on their feet – no matter how long it takes.'

'It's more than that, though, isn't it? They need a reason to look forward.'

'Exactly. And maybe I'm doing the wrong thing by taking care of all the practical worries for them – perhaps they'd find a focus more quickly if they were forced to fend for themselves, but I'm afraid cruel to be kind doesn't sit easily with me. There must be something which will make them happy, and I'd rather let them find it in a gentler way if I can.' He looked at her, a little embarrassed. 'Does that sound absurdly naive?'

'No, not at all. But it does sound like a long-term occupation.'

'It's easier with Loveday, I admit – partly because she's still so young, and partly because she's interested in everything. She adores the horses, you know – she's very like her father and her brother in that way – and I want to encourage Morwenna to let her help out a bit round the estate when she's better. She never had the patience to stick with school, although she's bright and Morveth did what she could – but Loveday's an independent spirit, and just the sort that this place needs.'

'You must be used to patching this estate together by now,' Josephine said, as they walked down the drive which divided the parkland from some marshy reed beds and the lake. 'Doesn't it ever get you down? The responsibility, I mean – for the people, as well as the land. Don't you ever hanker after an easy life?'

He smiled. 'Is there such a thing? Look,' he said, pointing across to the farmland which lay beyond the water. 'You can trace the history of our landscape for hundreds of years just in this one view – all those winding lanes and tracks between the farms, cut by the passage of people and animals through the centuries. Can you see how some of the layouts differ from others?' Josephine nodded, noticing that groups of oddly shaped fields with sinuous boundaries were interspersed here and there with more regular patches of land. 'There are different ways to manage somewhere like this,' William continued. 'Sometimes a new broom sweeps clean because it's easier than taking the time to repair what was there before. But that doesn't work with people.'

330

'I suppose the war was the ultimate broom,' Josephine said as they turned and walked back towards the house. 'It must have changed a way of life that had been undisturbed for years.'

'Yes, although I think those old ways were winding down, and perhaps a lot of the changes would have happened anyway. And not everything changed for the worse – the war did, at least, bring us together a little. Hating the next village always used to be a point of principle down here.'

'Co-operation isn't a Cornish trait any more than it's a Scottish one, then?'

'No. I suppose in that respect we're quite similar.'

'Much more so than I'd realised – the clan spirit is very much alive and kicking here. In some ways, I suppose I find that easier to understand than Archie and the girls do, even though they're born to it. Where I grew up – where I live – everyone knows everyone unless they arrived the night before, and sometimes even then.'

'And you're afraid to flirt with anyone in case he's your fiancé's cousin?'

Josephine laughed. 'Well, it's not quite that bad, but nearly.'

'So a Cornish life might suit you?'

She hesitated, unsure of what was meant by the question and feeling suddenly cornered, the way she always did when a conversation became too personal. 'I've got responsibilities at home,' she said, a little more abruptly than she intended, 'and it might feel similar, but there's a long way in between.'

'Yes, of course – you have your father to think about. The girls told me.'

Aware that she had been too defensive, Josephine tried to soften her explanation. 'I used to think about it a lot,' she said.

'What it would be like to set up home somewhere different, and where I'd go if I did. I remember walking along the Moray Firth one day – all right,' she laughed as she saw him raise a sceptical eyebrow, 'I know it's not exactly the other side of the world but I thought I'd start gradually. Anyway, I was walking along, wondering where to build the hypothetical cottage, and I realised I was fooling myself. Two minutes from a cinema and three minutes from a railway station is my idea of perfection.'

He held up his hands in defeat. 'All right – who am I to argue with perfection?' and then, more seriously, 'I'm glad it suits you, though.'

'How well do you know Morveth?' Josephine asked when they had been silent for a minute or two.

He looked at her curiously, intrigued by the sudden change of topic but too polite to say so. 'I've known her all my life, but it was Lizzie – Archie's mother – who was really close to her. You should ask Archie about Morveth – she was very good to him when his parents died.'

Josephine had every intention of discussing Morveth with Archie, but she said nothing. 'The other day – at dinner on the first night I was here – you were going to say something to Archie about Morveth and his mother, but you changed your mind.' She wasn't going to tell William what Morveth had revealed to her, but she was keen to find out if he really did have no idea. 'I was intrigued by what that might have been.'

'You don't miss anything, do you?' William said, impressed.

'Oh, believe me – I do, and the wrong end of the stick is absolutely covered in my fingerprints, but I did notice that.'

'Well, it's not really a secret – just something that Archie might find difficult to understand. You know the talents we were talking about with Morveth – the clothes, the healing . . .'

The convenient miscarriages, Josephine added silently, but only nodded. 'Well, Lizzie had those powers, too. She and Morveth – they believed in the same things. I thought at first that she was doing it to spite our dear pious brother, but it ran deeper than that. Like I said, there's no great darkness in it – even Wesley believed in the power of an acorn to heal a broken bone – but Archie has a very analytical mind, and his life revolves around evidence. That's a difficult combination, particularly since the war. The idea that death is just one stage in a continual cycle of renewal – which is what Morveth believes – is very difficult to accept for people who have seen that sort of suffering – and rightly so, I think.'

'And you? Where do you stand between brother and sister?'

'Oh, I believe in whatever gets you through – as long as it doesn't harm anyone else.'

Burdened with yet another secret from Archie, Josephine looked at her watch and saw that it was later than she thought. 'I'd better go and change for dinner,' she said. 'Ronnie and Lettice will be waiting.'

'There's really no need,' William said. 'You look lovely as you are, and standing on ceremony for the sake of it seems rather futile after the last few days. Wouldn't an extra cocktail before dinner do you more good than a change of shoes?'

She had to agree that it would, and they went inside. Ronnie and Lettice were already in the library, and Josephine was not surprised to see that they had found time for drinks and perfect footwear. Reminding herself that it was their job to look good, and that fashion was anathema to a decent plot, she sank into one of the comfortable chairs by the fire and watched the creation of the perfect Martini.

'Good day?' Ronnie asked, pouring her triumph into a glass.

333

'No,' said Josephine, 'most definitely not one of my best.' She accepted the drink that was offered and was surprised to realise how much she needed it.

'Is the book going badly, darling?' Lettice lit a cigarette for each of them and passed Josephine's over to her.

'It would be an exaggeration at this point to say that it was going at all,' Josephine replied tartly. 'I've managed eighteen hundred words, seventeen hundred of which will almost certainly be thrown away tomorrow, and Grant's had to up sticks and move along the coast. I can hardly set a shocker here after everything that's happened – it wouldn't be right. All that, and I've had to put up with a wigging from Morwenna Pinching into the bargain.'

'Really? What on earth for?'

'Oh, just something that Archie wanted me to talk to Loveday about.'

'Is there anything you'd like to share with us?' Lettice asked hopefully.

'No, I'd better not. Let's just say that I'm sorely tempted to tell Archie what he can do with his investigation *and* his Cornish holidays.' Was this the moment? she asked herself as she sipped her drink, and decided that it probably was. 'Anyway, I certainly wish I'd never asked him to move in with me,' she said casually, and was pleased to see that she had chosen well. Lettice choked on her olive, and Ronnie's astonishment made its way slowly out from behind a cloud of cigarette smoke. William, to his credit, simply smiled.

'Archie's moving into the Lodge?' Lettice asked, when her sister had finished hitting her on the back.

'Yes – didn't he mention it?' Josephine asked nonchalantly. 'I asked him to tell you.'

'And you're not moving out?'

'Of course not. Don't be so provincial.'

'Then none of us will be safe in our beds except you,' Ronnie said, a wicked glint in her eye.

'What do you mean?' she asked, bewildered.

'Well, with his mind on other things, I doubt that Inspector Penrose could run a fuck in a brothel, let alone a murder investigation,' she explained.

Josephine glanced – provincially – at William, but he seemed unperturbed by his younger daughter's choice turn of phrase. 'Don't be silly,' she said, beginning to feel that the joke had backfired somewhat. 'You know he always puts his work first. I only wish I could say the same.'

'Well, I think it's lovely,' Lettice said, beaming. 'I'm sure you'll get on like a house on fire.'

'Which brings us full circle to the Pinchings,' Ronnie quipped, and this time she did get a frown from her father. 'Is that why Morwenna's been stamping her foot? Because she caught Archie smuggling his pyjamas past the boathouse?'

Josephine handed Ronnie an empty glass to give her something else to think about. 'By the way – I've been meaning to ask,' she said to Lettice. 'Do you know anything about the Fowey woman? She's causing quite a stir up in town.'

The clumsy change of subject was greeted by a loud scoff from the cocktail cabinet but Lettice – starved of gossip for at least a week – took the bait, as Josephine had known she would. 'Daphne, you mean?' she asked eagerly. 'What's she been up to? We've never met her, but if she takes after Gerald du Maurier, I'm not surprised there's talk.'

'Oh, it's nothing like that,' Josephine said, conscious that she was about to be a disappointment. 'It's just that I had lunch with Victor Gollancz before I came down here – you know he pinched her from Heinemann last year, just after he started publishing – and he's very excited about the new novel. Full of smugglers and adventure, apparently.'

'Sounds like any night at the Ship Inn,' William said.

Josephine smiled. 'Well perhaps that's where she's done her research. Anyway, he's so pleased he's thinking of taking out full-page advertisements in the papers.'

'Oh, how vulgar,' Lettice said, in a tone that most people reserved for American divorcees.

'There speaks a woman who's never looked in disappointment at her royalty cheque.'

'Yes, I know, but I really do think that . . .'

The rest of the sentence was lost in the slamming of the front door, and they heard the sound of quick, purposeful steps across the hallway. 'Forgotten your toothbrush?' Ronnie called but the joke died on her lips when she saw the expression on her cousin's face. Without a word of greeting, Archie walked straight over to the drinks table and poured himself a large whisky, which he drank down in one. His glass refilled, he turned to face them.

'Jasper's had a stroke,' he said, looking at his uncle. 'It happened late this afternoon, while I was questioning him about Nathaniel's murder.'

'Good God,' William said, 'what a terrible thing to happen. How is he? Is he . . . ?'

Josephine got up to go over to Archie but something in his face made her stay where she was. 'I'm sorry to say that yes – he is still alive,' he said bitterly. 'But it *was* serious, so there's every reason to hope that he may take a turn for the worse in the next few hours.'

'I know he's done some despicable things, Archie, but surely you don't mean that.'

'Oh, I mean it. And do you know why?' he asked. 'No? Well, I'll tell you. Just before he collapsed, he admitted to raping my mother.' Josephine glanced at William, who was staring at his nephew as though he were speaking a foreign language. Ronnie moved protectively over to her father's side. 'How could you let something like that happen?' Archie continued. 'And how long did she have to put up with it before someone did something about it?' William's silence seemed only to increase his anger. 'Didn't it ever occur to you that it might be something I should know about?'

'Archie . . .' Josephine began, but he cut her off.

'Don't, Josephine. I know this is nothing to do with you, and I'm sorry you have to be caught in the middle of it, but there are things that need to be said.'

'William couldn't tell you, Archie,' she said, ignoring him, 'because he didn't know himself.'

'Don't be ridiculous. They were all under the same roof – how could he not know?' Suddenly, the significance of what she had said dawned on him and he turned to her, horrified. '*You* knew?' he asked in disbelief.

She hesitated, unable to see a way of vindicating William without betraying her own unwilling collusion in something that had never concerned her. 'I found out last night,' she admitted. 'Morveth told me when we were at the Minack. Your mother told her years ago, but no one else knew except your father.'

'So that's what all those questions were about this morning at breakfast?'

'No – that was to do with . . .' She tailed off, unable to

337

continue without exposing another family lie, and unwilling to use Morwenna's plight to defend herself. 'You know what that was about,' she said quietly, uncomfortably aware that all eyes in the room were now on her.

'Yes. It was about you being as bad as the rest of them,' he retorted sharply. 'Worse, in fact, because this isn't your secret to keep. You don't belong here, and you have no loyalty to anyone on this estate except me. So why keep quiet? What sort of thrill did you get out of knowing more about my life than I do?'

'Archie, it was never like that.' She tried to explain, but he was in no mood to listen.

'Or is it more serious than that? Are you still trying to punish me for Jack's death?'

'Don't you dare accuse me of something like that,' she said, her fury suddenly matching his. 'And stop bringing Jack into our relationship – I thought we'd put that behind us. Anyway, while I was grieving for him, you were busy having your cosy little chats with Morwenna. Does the Lady of Shalott ring a bell?'

'That's hardly the same thing.'

'No, it isn't. I didn't ask to be told about your mother and Jasper – Morveth told me out of the blue. From what I gather, though, you didn't need much encouragement to talk about *me* behind *my* back.'

Archie started to answer back, but stopped himself. 'I won't compete with you for grievances,' he said. 'I don't need to. You know in your heart that you should have told me. I could have taken it from you. Instead, I had to find out like this.'

He turned and left the room. She made a move to go after him, but William put his hand gently on her shoulder. 'Let him calm down first,' he said. 'If you go after him now, you'll both end up saying things that are impossible to forget. But will you tell me what Morveth said? I need to understand, just like Archie does.' Reluctantly, Josephine nodded, wondering yet again how far she should go with the truth.

Chapter Eighteen

'I'm sorry.'

Josephine looked round, startled. Caught up in her own thoughts, she had not heard Archie come back to the Lodge. He stood hesitantly in the doorway to the sitting room, obviously uncertain of his reception. 'Don't be silly,' she said, relieved to see him. 'It's me who should be apologising. I let you down.'

She started to get up, but he held his hand out and came over to join her by the fire. 'You were in an impossible position,' he said, sitting down on the floor next to her. 'You've been burdened with other people's secrets from the moment you got here, and I started it with Morwenna and Harry's suicide. I still can't imagine why Morveth said anything to you about my mother but, whatever her reasons, it's hardly your fault.'

'In her defence, she seemed to be trying to protect you from something, but it rather backfired. Look, I really did want to tell you, you know, but this morning wasn't the right moment and I thought I had plenty of time to wait until you'd finished the investigation. It never occurred to me that you'd find out another way – Morveth wasn't going to say anything to you, and I could hardly have foreseen that you'd get it from the horse's mouth. I suppose I shouldn't have underestimated your professional powers of persuasion.'

He grinned, and added some more coal to the fire to bring the dying embers back to life. 'You don't have to explain,' he said, paying more attention to the selection of a log than was strictly necessary and avoiding her eye. 'And there was no need for me to start summoning up our ghosts just because I'd found some more of my own. What I said about Jack was unforgivable.'

She took the poker out of his hand and forced him to look at her. 'You were in shock. Anyway, I doubt there's anything you could say to me that I wouldn't forgive you for eventually. But that's not a challenge,' she added, as he raised a questioning eyebrow.

'It's a bad sign, you know – bringing the bottle over with you,' he said, lifting the Dalwhinnie which stood in the grate.

She laughed, and stood up to fetch another glass. 'Well, that *is* your fault. I was worried about you. Where have you been?'

'Once I'd calmed down, I had to go back and talk to William. I expected you to be there still.'

'No. I wasn't really in the mood for company, so I left soon after you did.'

'Yes, they told me,' he said. 'Obviously, I needed to apologise, but I also wanted to know more about their childhood – to try and understand what relations were like between the three of them when they were growing up.'

'And has it helped?'

'A little, I suppose. He couldn't really tell me anything I didn't know – what Jasper did to my mother was as much of a shock to him as it was to me. More so, perhaps, because he was there with her at the time. Now he's having to reinterpret what he thought was happiness – and he feels guilty, of course.'

'For not being able to protect her?'

'Partly that, but it's more complicated. He feels bad about the way he and my mother used to shut Jasper out when they were children. There was no malice in it, but you can never tell what effect you're having on somebody's emotions in private, can you?' He sipped his whisky thoughtfully. 'I have to say – William's much more generous than I am. All I can think about is how the bastard must have made her suffer.'

'Do you know how he is?'

'William telephoned the hospital. There's no change.'

'Trouble seems to come in threes – look at Harry, Morwenna and Loveday. And if I'm honest, there were the same sorts of rivalries in our house when I was growing up. My youngest sister and I got on splendidly – but there was always a sense of duty in any time I spent with my middle sister, and I know she was aware of that. Things have always been rather forced between us. I'm not saying it's the same thing at all, but it's all about a balance of power. You're lucky to be an only child.'

'I'm beginning to agree with you. I used to think about what good friends William and my mother were as adults, and how Lettice and Ronnie always stuck up for each other no matter how much they argued in private, and I felt like I was missing out on something. Now, I'm not so sure.'

Josephine realised that this was the first time she had ever heard Archie talk about his childhood in any depth. They had regularly discussed the war and their shared past – probably discussed it too much – but he had only ever referred in passing to his life before she knew him. Thinking about it, that was probably because he had always genuinely believed it to be happy and trouble-free: the urge to analyse and reconstruct your past tended to come only with the realisation that things were less than perfect, and she sensed that he would be eager to talk now if she gave him the right encouragement. 'Morveth said your mother told your father about Jasper,' she said. 'He must have been a very special man for her to trust him with what she was most ashamed of. It's one thing to tell another woman, but trusting a man – especially a man who loves you – not to make things worse by how he reacts must have been quite a risk.'

'Yes, he was special.' Archie offered her a cigarette, and lit one for himself.

'I've never asked you about him, and I don't even know what he did for a living. Was it something on the estate?'

'I suppose you could say that he shaped the estate – or a lot of it, anyway. He was a plantsman, and he knew everything about the land here. There wasn't an acre of it that he wasn't intimately familiar with. It was almost as if he felt he had a duty to it because his family had given it away – like he had to prove it wasn't personal.' He looked long into the fire, remembering. 'When I was young, he took me everywhere with him – through the woods, round the formal gardens, into the hothouses, and he'd tell me the name of every plant that he'd grown and cared for. You've seen all the shrubs that screen the outbuildings near the house and the vineries on the walls?'

'Only in the dark.'

'I must show them to you – they're still very much as he created them, although on a much smaller scale. You know, we used to have fourteen acres of apple orchards alone – but I suppose William's told you how magnificent the estate was before the war?'

'Not really. He said that the war changed a lot, but some things were on the decline anyway.'

'Maybe that's true. I suppose my memories are bound to be different – I was young and I didn't have the headache of keeping it going – but I think William's doing himself an injustice. Loe was in its prime back then. He took it over about ten years before the war, and he and my father made it pretty much self-sufficient. Except for coal, it looked after its own community and more besides – we had crops for food, wood for building, even our own brewery at one stage, although I gather it was much safer to buy your ale over the bar.' He leaned forward and topped up their glasses. 'Then suddenly there was no one left to run it. We lost more men every month until we were down to a skeleton staff. I was at university by then, and every time I came back the place seemed more deserted. It wasn't just the men, either – the horses disappeared, even the trees. Teddy wasn't the only thing that the Royal Navy took from William,' he added dryly. 'Acres of oak went to them as well – hundreds of years of growth. It changed the whole character of the landscape in places. I know it's not the same thing as losing a son, but it broke William's heart.'

'So he threw himself into the war effort instead. He told me that much.'

'Yes, and my father was ill by that time, so there was really no one left to stand Loe's corner. She suffered along with the rest of us.'

Like Ronnie, he spoke of the estate as a woman, she noticed. As interested as she was in this new aspect of the war's impact, though, she tried to steer Archie back to a more personal history. 'It's a tribute to what your father achieved that anything managed to survive that,' she said. 'He must have had an extraordinary vision.'

'He did. The sort of vision that comes from respecting the

345

past, I suppose. He had hundreds of opportunities to move on – people were always coming to him for advice, offering him work on country estates that were a lot grander than this one. He could have been a rich man, but there was never any question of his leaving Loe. He was tied to it by something very powerful – so was my mother. But you're right – he did look to the future. He was always experimenting, and his knowledge was extraordinary. Even in later life, I can remember him sitting by the fire, exclaiming with delight over some new discovery he'd made. He never lost that childlike excitement.'

'You have that, you know – when you let yourself forget about work for long enough.'

'Once or twice a year, then,' he said glibly, but she could tell he was pleased.

'And that explains the books. I've been having a look through, trying to guess what belongs to whom. Who's the Trollope fan?'

'That was my father. The Lodge was always crammed with books. I've kept his favourites, but lots of the more specialist volumes have gone to a library in Penzance. It seemed a shame to keep them here, unused. My mother had lots, too, but her interests were less scientific.'

Josephine looked at him. 'Less scientific? In what way?'

He smiled. 'Morveth's not the only person round here who put her faith in unconventional remedies – at least, she wasn't when my mother was alive.'

'You knew?' she asked before she could stop herself.

'Was that another secret I'm supposed to be oblivious to?' Josephine blushed, but he made light of it. 'It was never an issue for her – just another way of looking at things. And she did share things with me,' he added, more seriously. 'That was

346

one of the things I loved most about her – and why I was so shocked this afternoon. I thought I knew her inside out, but I suppose some things were outside that understanding – and I have no choice now but to accept that. Her belief in folklore wasn't one of them, though.'

'But you were so dismissive of Morveth the other night at dinner.'

'No, not at all. I was – I am – dismissive of the idea that people have certain powers that are beyond our understanding – for good or evil. I don't like it whether it comes under the name of religion or magic or quackery. But as far as healing is concerned – people have managed for hundreds of years without some of the things we know now, and who's to say that their ways are no longer valid? Both Morveth and my mother chose to put a spiritual importance on their learning which I can't accept, but that doesn't detract from the facts. It's knowledge, just like my father's, and when I chose to study medicine, it was down to both of them – the healing and the science. But it wasn't to be.'

'The war again,' Josephine said bitterly. She knew the reasons for Archie's change of career but – privately – had always believed it to be a change for the better, the one precious thing to have come out of the sadness. Now, though, she was not so sure, and felt for the first time the loss of direction which Archie must have experienced on leaving that tribute to his parents behind.

He hesitated. 'The war was part of it, but it really only confirmed what I knew. In my heart, I'd already decided that medicine wasn't for me. Or rather, that I wasn't for medicine.'

'Why? It sounds to me as though you were born to it.'

There was a long silence, and Josephine poked the fire

unnecessarily as she waited for him to speak. 'Can you take another secret?' he asked eventually.

'As long as it's yours. I'd much rather share one with you than know something you don't.'

'Everything I told you about my father – all the learning and the knowledge – it made the way he died so cruel. He suffered from dementia for the last few years of his life. It was gradual at first, and still quite mild by the time I went up to Cambridge, but the estate wasn't the only thing I noticed a change in whenever I came home. I wanted to put my degree on hold for a bit but my mother wouldn't hear of it – she said my father would never forgive himself if he realised, and I suppose that was true. But it was hard on her, that sort of steady decline. Sometimes he'd go missing for hours and she'd find him in the gardens, desperate because he couldn't find something he'd planted or remember the name of a flower. He'd get so angry – with himself and then with her. Then, of course, it got worse and it was my mother and their marriage that he had no connection with.'

'I can't imagine anything more difficult. My mother's illness was terrible for my parents, but at least they faced it together and took some strength from each other. She must have felt completely isolated from all she loved most.'

'Yes, that's exactly how she felt. It wasn't so much the physical strain of caring for him – that was bad enough, but William and Morveth were a great help to her; it was the loneliness that nearly destroyed her, being taunted with a physical presence which was so familiar to her and yet having no emotional connection. For someone like my mother, that was a living hell.'

'Lizzie died soon after your father, didn't she?'

'That's what I'm coming to. She was actually diagnosed with cancer a few weeks before his death.' Josephine said nothing, unable to articulate a response which would do justice to the series of events that had transformed Archie's life. 'She hadn't felt well for a while, but she ignored it because of how things were at home. By the time she did something about it, it was too late. They gave her six months. She was absolutely devastated when she found out.'

'Worried about what would happen to your father?'

'Yes. It was the beginning of the summer holidays, thank God, so at least I was there. That was the first and only time I ever saw her completely lost. It wasn't the natural way of things, you see – my father was several years older than her, and she should have been able to care for him until he died. She accepted her own fate, but not at the expense of his. I couldn't bear to see her like that. At first, I refused to believe her diagnosis. I tried to persuade her to see other doctors, but we both knew it was a waste of time, and my not accepting the situation was just making things more difficult for her. Anyway, by that time she'd already faced up to her responsibilities – at least, that's how she saw things. She had vowed to look after my father until the end, and that's exactly what she did.' He paused, obviously trying to find the right words to explain. 'There's no easy way to say this.'

By now, she knew what Archie was going to say, and tried to make it easier for him. 'She restored the natural way of things – would that do?' He nodded, unable to look at her. 'Did you know what your mother had done?'

'Yes. He died peacefully one night and she was so calm about it. She knew I'd guessed, but we never spoke of it – I suppose she didn't want to involve me, just in case someone else found out, and I didn't want to make it any more difficult for her than it already was.'

'Did Morveth know, do you think?'

'No. I think it was something private between the two of them, the last intimacy they shared.'

'It was brave of her not to share it more fully. She could have saved herself a lot of pain if she'd chosen to die with him.'

'But that would have implicated my father in some sort of pact, and she wouldn't have wanted anything to tarnish his memory. For my sake, apart from anything else. She stayed around as long as she could to help me through his loss – I can see that very clearly now.' At last, he looked up from the fire. 'Are you shocked?' he asked.

She thought for a moment, knowing how important it was to both of them that she gave an honest answer. 'No, not shocked. Surprised, perhaps – but only in the sense that I'm always surprised when someone does something utterly selfless. It doesn't happen very often.'

'You think it was selfless?'

'Of course it was. She protected the people she loved from further suffering and unbearable guilt without any thought for how it would damage her own emotions – her peace of mind, if you like – during the last few weeks of her life. I can't think of anything *more* selfless. I'd call it heroic if it didn't come out of such bloody misery, and I only hope that someone would have the courage to do the same for me if it were necessary.' It was hard to tell what effect her answer had on him, if any. 'It doesn't matter what I think, though,' she continued. 'You obviously felt it was wrong in some way, or you wouldn't have abandoned the path you set out on.'

'No – that's just it. I was so sure it was *right* – that's why I

350

couldn't go down that path. I wish it hadn't happened, of course I do – but never for one moment have I doubted that she did the right thing. I'd have even done it myself if she'd asked me, and that's not the attitude to have if you hold someone's life in your hands. I was afraid of that certainty. It's more than just making a decision and sticking to it – it can so easily become arrogance, and I've seen that in too many other people to think that I'm immune to it myself. Policing is different – you have to have evidence and it's never just down to you, no matter how good you are. You can't play God.'

'Is that really what you think she did?'

'It's what I was afraid *I* might do, given the opportunity.'

'And do you regret the decision, if not the act that led to it?'

'Not very often these days. I love what I do, and I'm good at it, but . . .'

'But what?' she prompted.

'I don't know. I've been thinking about everything that's been going on here lately, and perhaps I was wrong ever to go away at all. William could do with some support now, and God knows what it's going to be like when he's older. Lettice and Ronnie are hardly likely to take over the reins. Perhaps I should come back here, after all.'

'Is that really what you want?' Josephine realised suddenly how much she depended on Archie's being in London, and tried to fight a selfish impulse to influence him. She could hardly expect him to base his future on their friendship while she remained free to walk in and out of his life as she pleased, but it occurred to her now that much of the pleasure she took in her visits south was down to him, and her earlier words to William came back to trouble her: Cornwall was a very long way from Inverness. 'Would it make you happy, do you think?'

'No, probably not, but sometimes living your own life feels like a very self-centred thing to do.'

'You have to answer to yourself for *not* doing it, though.'

'Is that what you've done? You gave up your freedom to go back to your father when your mother died.'

'No I didn't. I gave up a reasonably satisfying job as a physical training instructress, which would have given *me* up eventually anyway. All right, I resented it at first simply because it was expected of me, but it didn't take me long to see that it would work for me. I have as much freedom as I want, with time to write, time alone, and the financial means to come and go without feeling guilty. And I've never been tied to my father – he's not an invalid, just a man.'

Archie laughed. 'I know you get on well.'

'Yes, most of the time, and he respects what I do. I might complain about a few domestic chores but it suits me, this life – you know it does. So don't make me a martyr, for God's sake. I couldn't bear that.'

'All right. I take it back.'

'And don't be one yourself. I know how this sadness affects you, particularly where Morwenna's concerned, but distance isn't the same thing as detachment. Do you think Morwenna would have found such comfort in talking to you if you weren't to some extent an outsider?'

'No, I suppose not.'

'Anyway, from what I've seen, William's got a while to go yet before he's ready to ask for help. Perhaps in a few years' time, when you've got your feet under the chief superintendent's desk and you're tired of pushing papers. Think about it then. In the meantime, we should get some sleep. I expect you've got another early start?'

'Yes. Listen, before you go to bed – did you manage to find out anything from Loveday?' He looked sheepish. 'I feel rather hypocritical about asking you to act as my spy when I've set up camp on the moral high ground, but now I've done it, I may as well reap the benefits.'

'Well, I didn't get anywhere with what you asked me to find out. Loveday didn't say anything about Nathaniel that you don't already know, and there was nothing to indicate that his love for Harry was ever reciprocated.'

'But?' he asked, sensing that there was more.

'I might be able to throw some light on Christopher's disappearance. Loveday was pregnant, and there's no doubt the baby was his. She thinks he's abandoned her, and I wouldn't be surprised. He's not the first boy to make a run for it rather than face his father's wrath – and if I were him, I wouldn't want to face Morwenna, either.'

'You said Loveday *was* pregnant.'

'She had a miscarriage – not that she understands any of this, of course, but it was obvious from what she said. That's why they left the Minack in such a hurry.'

'That makes sense. Jago was concerned about Christopher's relationship with Loveday, although he insisted it had never got that far. Poor Loveday – she's another one who's had more than her fair share of grief lately. Still, perhaps this latest blow is for the best. A child would only complicate things – for her and for Morwenna.'

'Mmm.'

'You don't agree?'

'About the child, perhaps. But I don't see why everyone should be so sceptical about Loveday and Christopher making a go of things – it seems to me that they stand as good a chance as any of us. But that wasn't really what I meant. We're back to playing God again.'

'Go on.'

'From what Loveday said to me, I'd put money on the fact that Morveth found a way to bring on the miscarriage.'

'Really? God, I hope you're wrong, for Loveday's sake *and* mine. It would put me in an impossible position – professionally and morally.'

'How would you ever prove it? And what good would it do Loveday if you did? It's just someone else she can no longer trust.'

'You don't like Morveth, do you?'

'No, and not just because she chose on a whim to tell me something which could have destroyed my relationship with you, or because she frightened me to death by catching me pumping Loveday for information. Morveth is the worst kind of criminal, if you really want to know what I think. She manipulates people's lives because she thinks she knows what's best for them, without ever putting her own emotions on the line, and walks through the wreckage unscathed. It's exactly what you said about certainty leading to arrogance: she's so used to taking things into her own hands that she never questions herself any more – if she ever did. Hubris is as dangerous as cruelty or ignorance. In fact, when you find out who killed Nathaniel, I've no doubt you'll come across Morveth's handiwork in there somewhere. She won't have pushed him over – that sort of direct approach isn't her style – but she might as well have done.'

'There was a time when I would have argued,' Archie said. 'Her kindness kept me sane when my parents died.'

'I'm sure, but you were never as vulnerable as most of the people whose lives she shapes, for want of a better word – not even then, when you were grieving. And I'm not saying she does it maliciously. I'm sure she genuinely believes she's doing good, but that only makes her more dangerous. I can't tell you how relieved I was when William said he wanted to take charge of Loveday's future. Morveth isn't a good influence for someone like her.'

'No, I agree,' he said, and told her everything he'd learned from Jago Snipe about Christopher's unofficial adoption and the tragic circumstances that made it possible. 'There's no doubt that it was Morveth's idea to give the child to Jago,' he finished gravely. 'I need to go and see her first thing in the morning. Will you come with me?'

'Me? Why? Won't Ronnie's constable go with you?'

Archie smiled. 'No. I spoke to him earlier and he'll be busy getting the search underway. I think you may be right about Christopher, but I'm not leaving anything to chance. I owe that much to Jago – or to Joseph Caplin, whichever way you want to look at it. And part of the conversation I need to have with Morveth is personal. We have to talk about my mother, and she made that your business by telling you what happened. I'd like you to be there. After today, I don't entirely trust myself to behave well. Will you come?'

'Of course,' she said, getting up and putting the guard in front of the fire, much to Motley Penrose's disgust, 'and I'll try to keep my dislike to myself.'

He kissed her goodnight and walked through to the hall, but stopped on the bottom step. 'About Morwenna and that bloody poem,' he said, looking back. 'I only meant . . .'

She put her finger to her lips. 'I know what you meant, Archie, and I overreacted. It's actually a very good metaphor for what I do.'

'Anyway, it was a long time ago. I've learned to live with it.'

He matched the lightness in her tone, but she sensed that they were both trying a little too hard. 'What happened to her, by the way?' she asked. 'The Lady of Shalott, I mean – I don't know the poem.'

'She died,' he admitted reluctantly. 'She walked away from her work to face the real world, and it killed her.'

'I rest my case,' Josephine said wryly, but could not fool herself that it was anything other than a hollow victory.

Chapter Nineteen

Loveday lay in bed and watched as the oblong of thatch which hung over her bedroom window began to define itself in the early morning light. She loved the stillness of this part of the day, before anyone else was awake, when she could pretend that she was alone in the world, free to make of it what she could, but this morning she was restless and the darkness seemed obstinately sluggish and slow to retreat. Softly, she slipped from the bed, reaching back under the covers to find the clothes that she had pulled in beside her to warm. She dressed carefully, taking time to make sure that the buttons on her cardigan were fastened correctly, then climbed on to a chair in front of her tiny mirror to make sure that the end result met with her approval. With a critical eye, she examined every inch of herself, square by reflected square, then sat back down on the bed to tie her laces. Impatiently, she spat on her hand and wiped a fleck of mud from her left shoe. If they found Christopher today, she wanted to look her best, to let him know what he was missing by running off and leaving her.

Avoiding the steps which creaked was second nature to her after years of furtive comings and goings, and she reached the bottom of the stairs as silently as if she had been carried by the draughts which persistently defied any attempts to block their entrance through the cottage windows. She shivered – whether from cold or excitement she could not say – and went over to the pantry, where she chose a bread roll, two apples and a large piece of cheese to see her through the day. She was on her way back over the flagstones to the door, when she realised that her luck had run out.

'Where are you going?' Reluctantly, Loveday turned round to face Morwenna. Her sister was at the bottom of the stairs and, as she stood there in the shadows, dressed in a long white nightshirt with her hair untidy and dark circles around her eyes, she reminded Loveday of a ghost, one of those lost, reckless women who haunted all her brother's best stories. The similarity was so uncanny that she wanted to laugh, but something in Morwenna's expression told her not to. If she wanted to get her way now that she had been discovered, she would have to be cleverer than that.

'I'm going to look for Christopher with the others,' she said, deciding that Morwenna could surely not object to something that involved everyone.

'How do you know about that?'

'I heard Mr Motley telling you when he came round yesterday. I think it's a bit silly of them not to have asked me to help,' she added, unable to prevent a note of petulance entering her voice. 'I know all the secret places, after all, and I'm more likely to find him than anyone.'

'But Loveday, you haven't been well,' Morwenna said in the exasperated tone that her little sister had grown so familiar with over the last few months. 'Why don't you go back to bed and read your book?'

'I've finished it.' Loveday looked sulkily at the floor. 'You never want me to have any adventures of my own. Just because you're stuck here all the time, you want me to be miserable with you. Well that's just not fair.'

358

'Oh, do what you like,' Morwenna said, holding her hands up in defeat. 'Why should I care, anyway?'

She turned and went back upstairs, and Loveday stood in the hall for a moment, confused. She had expected a longer battle, and was surprised to find that it irked her to have won so easily. Having settled into a relationship of confrontation with her older sister, she was disoriented by the sudden shift in power, and she had to fight an impulse to be contrary and stay in the cottage after all. She forgot it as soon as she was out in the garden, though. A delicate veil of mist hung low over the ground and, by the time she reached the gate, her legs were wet with dew from the unkempt lawn, but the freshness of the morning was exhilarating and the scent from the trees so strong that there scarcely seemed room for anything else in the world. She cut across the lane which led down to Christopher's house, wondering if he would be back there by the end of the day, and ran down into the bluebell woods.

'Loveday?'

The voice came from behind her and she stopped instantly, not daring to look back in case she had made a mistake. Then it was there again, and this time she was sure – no one else said her name with so much joy, not even Christopher. She turned and threw herself into Harry's arms, almost knocking him over.

'Steady,' he laughed. 'You're not as little as you used to be.'

Loveday buried her face in his neck, taking in the rich, sweet smell of tobacco which always hung around Harry and talking unintelligibly all the time. Eventually, she lifted her face and looked intently at her brother. 'You're dirty,' she said, grinning.

'And you're cheeky, but I still love you.' He laughed, and ruffled her hair. 'What sort of greeting is that after all this time? And where are you off to so early, anyway?'

'To find Christopher,' she said, and regretted her frankness the second she saw the cloud pass across Harry's face. In her joy at seeing him again, she had quite forgotten how much the two people she cared most about disliked each other. 'I've missed you,' she said, matter-of-factly. 'Everybody has, but me most of all. I looked everywhere for you. Where have you been?'

'I missed you too,' he said, and she suspected he was avoiding her question. 'You *and* Morwenna. How is she?'

'Cross. She's always cross these days. And don't tell me she's got a lot to worry about,' she added as he opened his mouth to speak. 'Everybody tells me that, but it never makes things any easier for me.'

'I know, and I'm sorry,' he said gently. 'It's all my fault for having to go away, but I'll make it up to you – to both of you. Is she at home now?' Loveday nodded. 'Then shall we go and see if we can stop her being so cross?'

'Do we have to go right now?' asked Loveday, disappointed. She resented having to share Harry so soon. It wasn't fair when she was the only one who'd believed unquestioningly that he would return to them – she ought to have longer to savour her triumph alone. 'Can't we go for a walk first?' she pleaded, taking his hand and trying to pull him away in the opposite direction.

'Later,' he said firmly. 'We can do that later. But I need to talk to Morwenna first. It wouldn't be fair if I saw anyone else before I saw her, would it?'

'Suppose not.' She glanced further into the woods for a moment, remembering Christopher and torn between her loyalty to him and to her brother. Then she reminded herself that it was Christopher who had left her, and decided he could wait; it would serve him right to wonder where she was, just as she had lain awake thinking about him.

Harry was quiet as they walked back to Loe Cottage together. No doubt he was worried that Morwenna would be cross with him, too, and Loveday squeezed his hand reassuringly. It would be all right when the three of them were back together again. She led the way round to the back and pushed open the door, longing to see the look on Morwenna's face when she realised what had happened. She must try not to show off too much about having been right all along; it was Nathaniel who had convinced her, and she would have to go and thank him as soon as possible. People never died if there was someone left to care for them. Love brought them back. That was as it should be.

Quietly, they walked down the corridor to the kitchen. Morwenna was fully dressed, now, and standing at the sink. 'Found him already?' she asked without turning round. 'Or have you just changed your mind?'

'I've found *someone*,' Loveday said. 'I told you I would.'

Impatiently, Morwenna turned round and Loveday looked on, fascinated, as all the colour drained from her face – something which she thought only happened to people in books. The plate which Morwenna was drying fell to the floor, and Loveday watched the pieces scatter across the blue slates. She stepped forward to pick them up, but Morwenna raised a hand to stop her. 'Loveday, go outside,' she said, and there was something strange and tight about her voice, as if invisible fingers around her throat made it difficult for her to breathe.

Horrified at the thought of missing the reunion which she had longed for, Loveday started to argue. 'No, I want to stay with Harry,' she said. 'You can't make me . . .'

'Get out,' Morwenna screamed.

Loveday looked desperately at her brother. 'I can't leave,' she said, realising she was about to cry and furious with herself for being afraid. 'What if you go away again?'

Harry knelt down and took her hands in his, and she caught the strong, dark scent of earth on his fingers. 'I won't go anywhere without you – I promise,' he said, in that special voice that he used only for her, and she shot a triumphant look at Morwenna, who turned away. 'But your sister and I have some things to talk about and we need to sort out what the three of us are going to do now. Will you do something for me?' She nodded. 'Go outside for a bit, and don't tell anyone you've seen me. It's the most important secret that you and I have ever had, and you've got to promise me to keep it safe. Will you do that?'

'Of course,' Loveday said, offended that he'd even had to ask. 'You know I will.'

'Thank you,' he said. 'Now, give us some time and then, when we've finished, you and I can get back to the way we were.'

Reluctantly, Loveday left them to it. Halfway down the corridor, she turned round to have one more look at Harry, and was a little miffed to see that he and Morwenna already seemed to have forgotten about her, so absorbed were they in their silent contemplation of each other. Suddenly, she thought back to how she felt when she was growing up and Harry and Morwenna had ignored her, and the jealousy which she had all but forgotten in more recent years returned with a vengeance. Why should she be sent away? She was grown up now – even Harry had said so – and she refused to be excluded any longer. At the end of the corridor, out of sight of the kitchen, Loveday opened the side door and closed it again as loudly as she could, then crept quietly up the back stairs to her room, trying hard not to feel like that lonely child of six again.

An eclectic mix of uniformed policemen and locals had already begun to gather when Archie and Josephine left the Loe estate. To save time, they took the car into the village rather than using the coastal path and Archie parked against the harbour wall, below a row of smart Edwardian houses with bay windows and a coat of arms on each gable. The terrace, which curved gently round, following the horseshoe outline of the harbour, culminated in an attractive granite building with a Welsh slate roof and square clock tower – three black faces and one white, Josephine noticed as they walked past.

'What an unusual building,' she said, admiring the quiet, unostentatious way in which the tower stared solidly out to sea, providing a focal point for the harbour no matter where you stood. 'What is it?'

'That's our literary institute,' Archie replied with mock grandeur, 'although the arrival of a billiards table has rather changed the nature of its use. In fact, I believe they've had to bring in a second table to satisfy the current demand for learning.' She laughed. 'I thought it would be better if we left the car here,' he added. 'I don't want to announce our visit any more loudly than I have to, and Morveth's cottage is only a few minutes away.'

They walked up the cliff road, past a handful of fishermen's cottages, and then a small tea room. Rather than object to the exercise, Josephine was pleased to see something of the village at last, and she realised that, in spite of its wide open spaces and many wonderful landscapes, the Loe estate had become a little claustrophobic because of its sadness – a little intense, even, in its beauty. A sizeable net-making business stretched back from the road on the left-hand side and, as they walked past, Josephine heard the rattle of machines and buzz of friendly conversation, and smelt the tar from the tanning factory opposite, where a donkey and cart stood waiting to drag the nets into nearby fields to dry. It was merely a glimpse of ordinariness, which echoed what had happened yesterday and would no doubt be repeated tomorrow, but it reassured and cheered her nonetheless.

Archie seemed to feel a similar respite from matters of life and death. He spoke very little on their way up the hill, but nodded warmly to several people, often using a nickname which was utterly incomprehensible to Josephine. 'That's Morveth's house,' he said, pointing ahead to a beautiful thatched cottage, separated from the sea by nothing more than the narrow road and a single-storey net loft. 'It's the oldest house in the village – the houses either side were built on much later – and it used to belong to the estate. Veronique – William's wife – absolutely adored it. They'd come here together, just the two of them, before they had the children, and he left it to her in his will – he knew she wouldn't want to stay in the big house after his death. Of course, it was never an issue. As soon as Veronique died, he sold it to Morveth – he couldn't even bear to have the responsibility of it any more.'

'It's glorious,' said Josephine, and meant it. 'I can see why Veronique was so captivated by it.' The cottage, though smaller than Morwenna's, was not dissimilar except that it was immaculately kept, with gleaming white walls and a neat straw roof. It could scarcely have changed at all since the day it was built, but she could imagine how different it must have looked – how proud and aloof – when there were fewer buildings on this particular stretch of cliff. Even now, with its ridges raised slightly higher than the rooftops around it, the cottage still maintained something of its former superiority, as if years and pedigree counted for more than square footage.

Archie knocked firmly on the dark-blue door but the only response it brought was from the neighbouring house, which doubled as a small shop – one of those sitting-room affairs where wives added to the household income by selling things from their front rooms. The face of a woman in her sixties appeared at the window and hovered over a pair of brass scales which shone like a dollar through the glass; she looked curiously at Morveth's visitors for a moment, then nodded to Archie and moved back into the house. Frustrated by the possibility that Morveth herself might be out, Archie peered through one of the sash windows, then raised his hand to someone inside. 'It's all right – she's coming through from the back,' he said, and a moment later the door opened. Morveth's expression changed when she saw Josephine, but she stood aside politely to let them both in.

The front door opened straight into one of the most chaotic sitting rooms that Josephine had ever seen. The room had a stone-flagged floor and whitewashed walls, but very little of either was visible beneath the detritus of a long life, lived in contact with many rather than devoted to one. There were photographs everywhere – some showed successive groups of smiling children, lined up outside a small school building; others were less formal images of Morveth with boys and girls of varying ages – and the surfaces were cluttered with trinkets and mementos which she guessed were presents from former pupils. Taken together, the collection was a meaningless jumble, but Josephine had no doubt that each individual item carried a memory and a significance for Morveth.

A large oak dresser stood against the only straight wall; its shelves and cupboards were crammed with bottles, jars and books, and Josephine recognised some of the titles from the Lodge, together with a selection of classic novels and poetry and an old prayer book, so well thumbed that even to remove it from the shelf seemed to threaten its existence. She was interested to see how easily Morveth's loyalties blended Christianity with folklore, and wondered cynically where the woman's belief in her own powers sat in relation to either. What was more fascinating still, though, was the fact that – in spite of the disorder – Josephine instantly recognised the peace that Archie had described to her from his past visits. The air was scented with herbs, bunches of which were nailed to the beams, and the fresh, sweet smell of rosemary drifted across from the adjoining kitchen, where a range gently infused the herb with its heat. It was curious, but the room offered a sense of calm found rarely even in spaces which were much less muddled.

There were only two chairs, so Josephine sat on the stairs, keen to distance herself from the conversation that Archie needed to have with his friend. Morveth's first words, however, were addressed to her, and they were blunt and accusing. 'You've told him, then?'

'No – did you want me to? Was that why you singled me out for your confidences?'

Archie interrupted. 'Josephine hasn't told me anything,' he reiterated, 'although I don't understand why you chose to put her in that position. I'm afraid that I had to hear it from the horse's mouth.' Succinctly, he explained what had happened during his visit to the rectory, and his tone was gentle but professional. 'So now I hope you might be able to tell me yourself what happened to my mother. We can't deny it any more, not even to ourselves.'

Morveth was silent for a long time, although she did have the grace to glance apologetically at Josephine. 'What good would it do, Archie? What good does raking up the past ever do? I could sit here and tell you everything that Lizzie told me in confidence, but how do all those shameful, miserable details help you or serve her memory?'

'That's too easy, Morveth, and it's not your decision to make.'

'But I know how desperately she wanted to save you from it – I won't betray her like that. You're right – I should never have said anything, and I wouldn't have if it weren't for the shock of what happened to Nathaniel. But I did it because I care about you, Archie. I can't look out for you any more – you've moved away from us now and you have a different life, and that's how it should be – so I told the one person you might take help from if you ever needed it.' She looked at Josephine, who wondered again how Morveth knew so much about her friendship with Archie. 'Anyway, your mother had the last word on the subject of Jasper Motley in her will.'

'Taking his piety with a pinch of salt, you mean.'

'That's one way of looking at it, yes. Or it could simply stand for nature's way of healing a wound. Whatever she meant, it sounds as though someone has done her work for her at last – and someone with a much higher authority than you.' She smiled at Archie with genuine compassion, and Josephine guessed that he was beginning to see the sense of what Morveth was saying: there really was no need for him to know anything more about his mother's pain. Morveth picked up a photograph in a plain wooden frame from where it stood on the small table next to her chair, and passed it to Archie. 'That's the relationship you should be remembering,' she said. 'It's the one that made her strong enough to face her demons – no matter what form they took. Leave it there.'

He stared at the picture for a long time before speaking. 'All right,' he said at last, handing the image of his mother and father over to Josephine to look at, 'but we are going to have to talk about some aspects of the past, Morveth. When Nathaniel died, he took everybody's right to secrecy with him – and I mean everybody's. You've held lots of those secrets safe for years, but it's time to let go. Right now, I do need some help, but it's not the sort that Josephine can give. Can you?'

'I don't know anything about Nathaniel's death.'

'Not directly, perhaps, but don't fool yourself that his murderer is a stranger. He or she is somewhere on the Loe estate, I'm convinced of that much, and you know more about that community than any of us. Let's start with the Snipe family, shall we? Jago told me about what happened to his baby daughter and what you did to get him another child – did Nathaniel find out from the records at the Union what had happened, and who Christopher's real father is?'

Morveth was clearly unsettled by Archie's question, but she was not stupid enough to deny the truth of what he was saying. 'Why did Jago tell you that? We swore to each other we'd never tell a soul.'

'He's worried sick about Christopher, and rightly so. The boy's been missing since Sunday night, and that's too much of a coincidence coming so shortly before Nathaniel's murder. Perhaps he's been hurt himself, perhaps he's got something to hide – either way, he's in trouble. So did Nathaniel know that Christopher was Joseph Caplin's son?'

'Not to my knowledge, but Nathaniel had begun to keep a lot of things to himself lately. He didn't talk to me as readily as he used to.' Wise man, Josephine thought, but said nothing. 'The information's there at the Union if you know where to look,' Morveth admitted, 'but I don't know if he found it.'

'And you haven't mentioned it to someone who might have told Christopher? Morwenna, for example – could Loveday have overheard something that she thought Christopher should know?'

'I've never broken that promise to Jago,' Morveth said indignantly. 'It's not the sort of thing you casually "mention".'

'Of course, there is one more thing that might have made Christopher run away,' Archie said. 'Am I right in thinking that Loveday was pregnant?' Suddenly, Morveth looked genuinely frightened. 'We've been friends a long time,' he continued, 'and, because of that, I'm not going to ask you if you did anything to ensure that she would lose the baby. But I will ask you this: why were you so against her having a child?'

'You obviously know a great deal more than I thought, Archie,' Morveth said, recovering a little of her composure. 'And if that's the case, I don't know how you can even ask why I'd be against that girl's pregnancy.'

'I know she's young and the circumstances are hardly ideal, but a child at her age isn't unheard of and it wouldn't have been the end of the world. Anyway, Christopher clearly cares for her. He would have stood by her if people had been a little more understanding, and he's got – or at least he had – a solid future.'

'Christopher?' Morveth said, surprised. 'Why should he have to take that on? None of this is his fault, and Jago would never have put up with that.'

'But you're surely not suggesting that it was entirely

Loveday's fault? The baby was Christopher's and he would have faced up to his responsibility once he'd had time to come to terms with it.'

'No, no – you've got that wrong,' Morveth said. 'Jago swore there was nothing going on between Christopher and Loveday, and I believe him.'

'That was wishful thinking, I'm afraid. For some reason, Jago objected very strongly to Loveday, but there's no question in my mind that the child she lost was Christopher's.'

So whose baby did Morveth think it was? Josephine wondered. Loveday knew so few people. 'But Morwenna said . . . she seemed so sure,' the older woman whispered, confused, and suddenly Josephine knew exactly what was in her mind.

'My God,' she said, horrified, 'Morwenna thought it was Harry's baby, didn't she? She thought it was history repeating itself.' She turned to Archie, who was staring at her in disbelief. 'That's why she felt so betrayed – when Morwenna ended her relationship with Harry, she thought he'd turned to their little sister, either to spite her or – even more unbearable for her – because he had never genuinely loved her.' As Archie continued to look doubtful, she spoke more forcefully: 'That's what she said to me – a bond had been formed behind her back, and now she was on the outside. What else would destroy her so completely? Or make her so resentful of Loveday?'

Archie turned to Morveth. 'Is this true?'

Slowly, Morveth nodded. 'She was devastated when she came to me – sick with worry about the effect it would have on Loveday, and hardly able to believe that Harry could do such a thing to her – but she knew the signs. If anyone knew them, Morwenna did.'

'What signs?' Archie asked impatiently. This complex web of misplaced certainties and false logic was beginning to irritate him as much as it did Josephine.

'They were spending lots of time together, disappearing into the woods for hours at a time. And Loveday started being spiteful towards Morwenna, taunting her with the fact that she and Harry had their own secrets now, saying that Harry loved her best.'

'Surely she had a lot of time to make up for?' Josephine suggested. 'Harry and Morwenna had shut her out for so long that you can't blame her for wanting to get her own back. Do you have brothers and sisters? No? I thought not. Trust me – it's what siblings do. Nobody takes more triumph from the small victories than a scorned younger sister.'

'But Loveday was growing up,' Morveth insisted, determined to justify Morwenna's reading of the situation. 'Morwenna couldn't deny her sexuality any longer.'

'I suppose it never occurred to anyone to ask Loveday who her baby's father was?' Josephine demanded, her sarcasm getting the better of her. 'If she was so grown up, a straightforward question might have saved a lot of heartache for everyone.'

'There was no need – Morwenna was so sure,' Morveth repeated desperately. 'And when she told me what her suspicions were, it seemed so obvious.'

'Her suspicions? So she wasn't sure – not until you'd encouraged her to believe it.'

'But it seemed so logical – there must be something in it, surely?' Morveth looked pleadingly at Archie, but Josephine was incensed and in no mood to let the subject drop easily.

'Why? To salve your conscience? All because you'd rather

believe in some kind of genetic sickness than face up to emotions that frightened you and a love you didn't understand? Because no matter what anyone else thinks about it, that's what Harry and Morwenna had – a deep, lasting love, the sort that very few of us ever know. I can see why Morwenna was capable of getting it so wrong – she was obsessed with Harry and jealousy distorts everything – but what's your excuse?'

'How do you know about Harry and Morwenna?'

'Morwenna told me,' Archie said, 'and she also spoke to Josephine about Harry.' The latter was a slight exaggeration of the truth, and he was surprised to find a champion for the older Pinchings in Josephine, but he had no intention of relinquishing the moral high ground so early in his conversation with Morveth. 'Morwenna had the sense to realise that Nathaniel's murder demands the truth from everyone, no matter how preferable silence may be.'

'And do you condone it so easily, this love that I don't understand – whatever its consequences?'

'I don't easily condone anything that's against the law,' Archie said carefully, 'but I do consider the consequences of *my* actions before I condemn it.' Morveth flushed at the pointed reminder of the blind eye which Archie had just turned to her own departure from the legal path.

'Is that why you were so concerned about my spending time with Loveday?' Josephine asked. 'You thought I'd find out that Harry was taking advantage of her?'

'Among other things. The family's had enough to worry about without that sort of shame getting out.'

'Other things?' Archie repeated, conscious that he was being sidetracked yet again from the murder investigation which he had come here to pursue. 'Do those other things include anything that Loveday might have let slip about Nathaniel's death?'

'No. I just meant Harry and Morwenna – I wasn't to know you were already aware of what had gone on between them. And as far as I know, Loveday doesn't know what's happened to Nathaniel. Morwenna thought that she should be allowed to get better first, and I agreed. They were quite close.' She turned to Josephine. 'If you don't mind my saying, you seem very sure of what you know for someone who's only met Loveday once or twice.'

'I'm afraid I can't lay claim to any great feats of perception,' Josephine said, refusing to be intimidated. 'I only listened to her, just as you advised me to. You were right, though – few people *are* wise enough to do that. Most of you are so caught up in your secrets and your intrigues that you miss what's right under your nose. Loveday adored her big brother, as most young girls do; she was competitive with her sister, as women of all ages are; and she experimented sexually with someone she liked who paid her some attention – again, that's hardly unusual. So yes, I am sure of that much.'

Josephine's reference to Christopher reminded Archie of his own conversation with the undertaker, when he had referred to Loveday as damaged goods. 'Did you tell Jago what you suspected about Harry and Loveday?'

'Yes. He knew what had gone on before – between Harry and Morwenna, I mean. Sam Pinching was his best friend, so he knew what Harry was like.'

'The sins of the brother, you mean? So easily repeated with the next sister in line?' Until now, Archie had managed to maintain a professional detachment, but Morveth's unwitting

373

manipulation of the lives around her – and the willingness of others to be so easily led – suddenly disgusted him. 'No wonder Jago was so determined to keep Christopher and Loveday apart, and I'm not surprised he denied any relationship between them – he wouldn't want his son lumbered with the product of an incestuous relationship.' He thought about his promise to Morwenna to keep her past out of the investigation, and questioned now that he would be able to stay true to his word: how far had the myth of Harry and Loveday actually travelled, he wondered? 'Do you think that Jago would have gone as far as saying something to Christopher to put him off Loveday?'

'No – he'd never do anything like that. He knew he had to keep it to himself.'

'Really?' Archie said sceptically, wondering how a woman as intelligent as Morveth could be so oblivious to the irony of what she was saying. 'Did anybody tell Nathaniel?'

'Absolutely not. He would have done something about it.'

Like give Harry a chance to defend himself, Archie thought, remembering that the curate's first response to Loveday's account of the fire had been to ask the accused man for the truth. 'Did Harry know what you were all so ready to believe him capable of?'

'Not at first, no. But Morwenna confronted him with it eventually. She couldn't help herself.'

'She told me that she'd accused Harry of never really loving her on the night he died – that was about Loveday, wasn't it?'

'I suppose it must have been.'

'Jesus – no wonder he killed himself,' Josephine said. 'The woman he loved – the only woman he could ever love – accused him of turning to their little sister?'

'But why didn't he deny it?' Archie asked, bewildered. 'Why

would he just accept it and say nothing?' It was, he realised, exactly what Nathaniel said Harry had done when asked about the fire – except then he had been guilty as charged.

'Perhaps the knowledge that Morwenna could even think that of him was enough to make him want to die,' Josephine suggested.

'But they saw each other again after the argument,' Archie said. 'And Harry was kind to her – like his old self, she said. He ought to have been indignant with her – furious, even. Why would he make his peace and ride into the lake because of something he didn't do? It just doesn't make sense. Something else must have happened in between.' He looked questioningly at Morveth.

'That wasn't the only reason he might want to take his own life,' she admitted reluctantly. 'He might have tried to make Morwenna see the truth after he'd calmed down, but by then it was too late.'

'Why? What happened?'

'He'd done something that couldn't be denied.'

'Will you please stop talking in bloody riddles and just tell me what else you know? When was the last time you saw Harry?' Morveth hesitated, so he asked again. 'Did you see him on the night he died?'

'Yes.'

'At last – we're getting somewhere,' he said. 'Tell me what happened.'

Hesitantly, Harry took a step towards Morwenna and went to touch her face, trying to blot out the memory of the last time the two of them had stood here together, when he had raised his hand to her in anger.

'Don't touch me,' she said, taking a step backwards. Her voice was barely more than a whisper. 'Don't come anywhere near me.'

The combination of shock and loathing in her eyes almost made him falter, but he carried on, desperate to make her understand. 'At least let me explain,' he said.

'Has someone kept you away from here until now? Held you prisoner, and prevented you from popping home to tell me that you weren't actually dead?'

'No, of course not . . .'

'Then how can you possibly explain what you've put me through? Do you know what it was like waiting by that lake every day, dreading the moment they found you and yet hoping against hope that you really *were* dead? Of course you don't – if you had any idea, you wouldn't be here now. You left me alone to pick up the pieces of the mess you ran away from. And what about Loveday? All right, so you could do it to me, but how could you make her suffer? Unless . . . oh God, no – have I really been that stupid?' Blindly, Morwenna felt behind her for the door handle, then turned and left the house.

'Unless what?' he shouted, following her out into the garden. He grabbed her by the arm and made her turn back towards him. 'Morwenna, tell me what you mean.'

'Did she know all along? Is this something you made up between you – one of those precious secrets she kept telling me about? She must have known. How else could she have been so sure?'

'No – I swear Loveday didn't know. No one knew. I did this for you – only for you. For us.'

'There is no us, Harry,' Morwenna said, looking at him, and

the quiet certainty with which she spoke frightened him more than her anger or her scorn. 'There never really has been, has there? We were a sickness, you and I – that much was obvious to me when I found out that you could move on so easily. Everything I thought I was – every honest feeling I've ever had – was twisted and warped beyond all recognition when you betrayed me with Loveday. What sort of life do you think that left me with? Now you walk back in here and start talking about us – with God knows who in your grave and some other poor woman going through the hell of not knowing what's happened to the person she cares about. And do you know what the most priceless thing of all is, Harry? You honestly thought I'd be pleased to see you, didn't you? Well, didn't you?' she shouted, infuriated by his silence.

'Not straight away, perhaps,' he lied, trying to ignore the emptiness in her voice whenever she spoke his name, 'but when you'd had a chance . . .'

'A chance to what? Calm down?'

'To understand.'

'You just don't get it, do you? Do you really want to know what I felt when I turned round and saw you standing there, holding Loveday's hand? Nothing. Absolutely nothing.'

'That isn't true,' he said, more defiantly than he felt. He had played out his meeting with Morwenna a thousand times in his head, anticipating her anger, her horror, her disbelief. Not once, though, had he imagined that she could be indifferent and, even to his own ears, his insistence that she would eventually understand felt hollow and ridiculous. He remembered now how tongue-tied he always became whenever they argued as children, how her spirit made everything he said sound slow-witted and insensitive, and suddenly, standing in front of her, his despair was greater than it had ever been in those long weeks apart.

'There's nothing left here, Harry, where it matters,' Morwenna said, holding her hand against her chest. 'You made sure of that. Ironic, isn't it? Both of us back here, alive and dead at the same time.' She laughed bitterly and took his face in her hands, forcing him to confront the darkness in her eyes that he had tried so hard to ignore. 'Look at me – look at what you've done. We were two parts of the same person, you and I – locked together, for better or worse. What you've done has tainted us both. When you ceased to exist, so did I. But there's no coming back for me – not any more. That's the difference between us.' He felt her fingers trace the thick growth of stubble, searching for the familiar contours of his face as if she could somehow find their past there. 'Why didn't you let me die when I wanted to?' she asked. 'It would have been so much kinder than this.'

In the distance, Harry could hear the sound of a car engine. Quickly, he pulled Morwenna into one of the stables next to the house, out of sight of the road. The threat of the outside world seemed to renew his sense of urgency. 'Because I couldn't let you die believing that of me,' he said, and now it was his turn to force her to look at him. 'It isn't true. Whatever you think and no matter why you believe it, I've never loved anybody but you. Loveday's a child, for God's sake – she's our little sister. How could you ever think I'd hurt either of you like that?' She tried to pull away, but he refused to let her. 'You know me. The most intimate moments of my life have all been spent with you. Every physical and emotional instinct I have has been shaped and guided by you. Is that honestly what you think you've created? A monster?'

'You're lying, Harry – otherwise, you'd have denied it straight away. Has it taken you all this time to think of a convincing story? Well, don't waste your breath. I've had enough.'

'How did you expect me to react? You'd just accused me of never loving you and fucking our sister, who we've brought up like our own daughter since she was six years old.' She flinched as though he'd struck her again, and he tried to stay calm. 'I was angry when you told me – angry and frightened and dazed, and I didn't know what I was doing. Then I hit you, and suddenly I no longer trusted myself to be near you. I had to get out before I really hurt you.'

'But what about later – at the boathouse? You were calm enough then.' There was a long silence as Harry wondered how to go on, and he sensed a change in Morwenna: for the first time, she wanted to believe him. 'Don't play with me, Harry,' she said, as if reading his thoughts. 'Loveday reminds me of everything I hate most – the thrill of you, the knowledge that I can't have you – and I know what it means to fear the violence in yourself. You're lucky I didn't kill you both back there.'

He risked a smile. 'You can't kill a ghost.'

'If you knew how often I'd died since you left, you would never say that.' She sat down on a bale of straw, and asked him again. 'Why didn't you even *try* to convince me the last time I saw you? Weren't we worth saving?'

He pretended not to have heard the past tense. 'Of course we're worth saving – that's all I've ever tried to do. But something happened that night after I left you, Morwenna, something I never planned. By the time I saw you again at the boathouse, things were different. I'd done something I couldn't undo, no matter how badly I wanted to.'

'Could there really be anything worse than what I was already thinking, Harry?' she asked sadly. 'You're right, though – I do need to understand.'

'I met him on the coastal path,' Morveth said, and she spoke so quietly that Josephine had to lean forward to hear. 'It was one of those nights when the mist comes in from the sea more quickly than you'd think possible. I'd been up late, talking to Beth Jacks while her husband was out looking for poachers, and by the time I got to the edge of the lake, I was beginning to wish I'd taken the road through the village home – I could hardly see a step in front of me and the torch I had was next to no good. But it seemed such a long way to go back and I was already tired, so I pressed on as quickly as I could. I thought the mist would be better away from the Bar, but I was wrong – it was tenacious, so bad that even the sea sounded a long way away. I heard the horse before I saw Harry – just a quiet nicker, nothing more than that, a warning to his master, I suppose – but it seemed so loud in the stillness that I stopped, just in case someone was about to run me down. Nothing happened, so I carried on for a bit and there he was, sitting by the side of the path. I didn't know it was him straight away, of course – all I could make out was a man's figure – but I recognised Shilling, and then it was obvious. I said his name and he looked up, but he barely seemed to know what he was doing. When I got close enough, I could see how terrible he looked. At first, I thought he'd had an accident – come off Shilling in the mist or some-thing – and it might be my imagination playing tricks on me now, but I could smell the blood on him. When I looked harder in the torchlight, I could see he'd been fighting; his left eye was badly swollen and there was a nasty cut on his lip, and more, I guessed, that I couldn't see. I made him come back to the cottage with me. He didn't want to but I insisted, and he was in no state to argue – he looked as though all the fight had been knocked out of him at last. I think holding on to that horse's reins was the only thing that kept him upright along the last bit of path. When we got in, I sat him down by the range, bathed his cuts and tried to sponge the worst of the blood off his shirt, and all the time he was crying.

'When I'd done the best I could, I tried to find out what had happened to him. As I thought, he'd been at the Commercial Inn all night. He'd had a terrible row with Morwenna earlier in the evening – I could guess what about, but I didn't say anything – and he'd tried to drink himself into oblivion. It was a trick he'd learned from Caplin and his friends just lately, but that night it got out of hand. There was a group of young men from up country at the bar, all office workers down here on holiday, and you know what it's like – they have a week's worth of drink in one night and think they're invincible. Anyway, there was a fight – not just Harry, a lot of the local lads got stuck in – and they were all thrown out. Harry thought that was that, and he started to walk home with Shilling – he was too drunk to ride – but one of the visitors went after him. Before he got far along the path, he heard footsteps behind him and somebody tried to wrestle him to the ground. He pushed him away easily enough – Harry was so strong – but the lad wouldn't let it go. He followed him, goading him a bit – pointless, infantile stuff, really, and nothing Harry couldn't handle, but then the man started hitting Shilling. Well, that was it. Harry was close to breaking point anyway, but you know how he loved that horse. He said he couldn't explain what happened next; it was like he was standing outside his own body, while this person he didn't recognise picked up a rock and started hitting the stranger with it, over and over again, until he stopped struggling. When the anger subsided and he came to his senses, Harry knew he'd killed the man – he literally beat him to death. He was sickened by what he'd done and horrified at the thought of what might happen to him. His first instinct was to get as far away as possible and he started to walk away, but he knew in his heart there was nowhere left to run. That's how I found him – lost, scared and hurt.

'He asked me what he should do, and I told him there was only one option left open to him. His first instinct was right – he had to leave, and go for good. I know it was wrong of me, but I couldn't tell him to give himself up – not when there was so much at stake, and not when Morwenna was already sick with grief for what he'd done to her. I couldn't put her through watching him hang – it would have put a rope around her neck, too. And I saw a chance to give her some peace, so I took it. I knew the only way she'd ever break this hold that Harry had over her was if she thought he'd deserted her, so I told him that if he valued his own life *and* hers, he'd get as far away from the Loe estate as possible and never come back. He argued, of course – said he couldn't leave like that without a word, but I managed to persuade him that it was for the best. He left in the early hours of the morning. I didn't know he intended to see Morwenna one last time to tell her what he was going to do; if I had, I'd have advised him not to in case it weakened his resolve. But as it turned out, he knew he couldn't stay. Things had gone too far for that. But that's what happened in between. When he went back to Morwenna, he had another man's blood on his hands.'

The room was unnaturally quiet when Morveth finished speaking. 'So what happened to the body?' Archie asked.

*

'Morveth told me it was the only way you'd ever find peace.' Harry tried to gauge what Morwenna was thinking as he talked, but her face was impossible to read. 'She's always known how to play us, hasn't she? She knew your happiness was the only reasoning I'd ever listen to.'

'I think happiness is a bit ambitious now. Too much has happened.'

'To spare you from even more pain, then.' He sat down beside her on the straw, and took comfort from the fact that she didn't move away. 'If I stayed, I knew it wouldn't stop at what I'd done to that man. The fire would come back to haunt us, and everything that led up to it – and once everyone knew about that, no one would have believed me about Loveday. People don't differentiate between evils – bad is bad, and that's all they see.' He rubbed his eyes, determined not to give in to an overwhelming tiredness before he finished what he had to say. 'And as I sat there in Morveth's kitchen, with that man's blood on me, I began to think they were right – I'd blighted your life from the moment we were born, and it was time to stop. That sounds like self-pity, I know, but it's not meant to – I honestly wanted to do what was best for you.'

She looked sadly at him. 'I believe you, but I meant what I said about feeling nothing, Harry. This is going to hurt you, but it would have been the same for me whatever you'd chosen to do.' Saying nothing, he stood and walked over to the empty stall which had once been Shilling's, and she watched as he touched the familiar things that belonged to a happier time – bridles, a saddle and the long leather leading rein she had given him on their eighteenth birthday. 'He's all right, you know – Shilling, I mean. William Motley took him – I just couldn't bear to look at him after what happened. I know it wasn't his fault, but he was too great a reminder of you. He'll be well looked after where he is.'

'I know. I've been to see him.'

'You've been to the stables? What if someone had seen you?'

'I was careful, but I had to go. You're not the only one I've let down.'

Suddenly Morwenna smiled, a genuine expression of warmth which seemed to surprise her as much as it did him. 'My God, you've got a nerve,' she said. 'How could I have forgotten that about you? It was always one of the things I loved most.'

He brushed the moment away, wary of investing too much hope in it. 'Shilling wasn't any more pleased to see me than you were, as it happens. I've a long way to go to rebuild his trust.'

'What happened after you left Morveth?' she asked, and he sensed that she was shying away from the future that his words had hinted at. 'Did you go back to the body?'

'No, not straight away. When it first happened, I panicked and hid it as best I could in the undergrowth on the edges of the wood by the pool. It wasn't very well concealed, and I knew it was only a matter of time before it was discovered, but I couldn't face going back to it again and seeing what I'd done. Anyway, I'd made up my mind to disappear, and it didn't seem as important as getting out as soon as possible. The mist had cleared by then, so I got back here quite quickly to collect some things and say goodbye to you, but the cottage was empty.'

'Loveday wasn't in bed?'

'No, there was no one here and I couldn't think where you'd gone. I was frantic because I couldn't leave without seeing you, but I knew time was against me, so I forgot about the clothes and everything else except finding you. I got back on Shilling and went to all our special places, one by one. Then I saw you from the woods on this side of the pool, sitting by the boat-house, and I knew instantly what you were going to do – what I'd driven you to. I had to stop you, even if it meant risking my get away.'

'And yet you still didn't talk to me about Loveday? You didn't even mention her name, as if you were glossing over the whole thing. The easiest way to talk me out of killing myself would have been to convince me that I'd misunderstood. Why didn't you try, Harry? Things could have been so different.'

'Some things would *always* have been the same. I've never done anything but care for Loveday, but I did kill our parents and I did kill that man.'

'We could have said it was an accident – he provoked you, for God's sake. And Nathaniel would have kept quiet if you'd begged him to – he'd have done anything for you.'

He looked away from her. 'No one would have believed it was an accident. I didn't just hit him once, Morwenna – I smashed his face to pieces. And Nathaniel . . .' He paused, thinking about his friend. 'Nathaniel would always have done the right thing,' he said eventually, a note of bitterness in his voice. 'Morveth was right – there was no going back.'

'But I gave in anyway. I couldn't argue with you any longer, and the more you talked, the more you said you loved me, the more I hated myself for what we'd done and what it had led to. You thought you were bringing me back from that water by giving me hope, while all you were really doing was proving to me that I had to pay for everything that had gone wrong. And I couldn't do that by taking the easy way out.'

'So I persuaded you to punish yourself by living?'

'Yes. We've always been selfish, you and I, and I've never

really felt any great impetus to make amends for what I've taken – but I did then. I looked at your face, and it was cut and bruised and ugly – and that seemed to say everything about the way I'd loved you. Nathaniel would have said that I was paying for my sins, I suppose, but there was nothing noble about it, nothing good, and I don't expect any great reward for it in another life. This one has been more than enough for me. I thought you'd tricked me, you know.'

'Tricked you? How?'

'By persuading me to live and then going into the pool yourself. It was one more thing that I could never forgive you for.'

'I didn't plan it that way – you have to believe that. After I left you, I had to get away. Turning my back on you for good was so hard, and I didn't trust myself to stick with what I'd resolved to do, so I wanted to get out before I weakened and changed my mind. I rode Shilling as hard as I could along the Bar, partly to do just that and partly to feel the exhilaration of that ride one last time, but something got in my way. That idiot Christopher threw something at the horse and frightened him to death. He shied away and started making for the pool, and there was absolutely nothing I could do except hang on. We hit the water, and it was as though I'd suddenly come to my senses. Everything that had happened in the last few hours suddenly seemed more real. I suppose I'd been in shock until then, but everything came into focus and I knew that I was fooling myself. I couldn't run away from what I'd done, and I couldn't live without you. You're right. Death is the easy way out, but I didn't have your courage and I decided to take it. I knew Shilling was strong enough to make it to the other shore, especially without me to weigh him down, so I just let go.'

'I don't understand – why would Christopher do something like that?'

'Because I'd given him such a hard time over Loveday, I suppose.'

'But there was nothing going on between him and Loveday. Morveth checked with Jago to make sure.'

'What would Jago know? What do fathers *ever* know? Of course there was something going on. I caught them together one evening at the boathouse, told him to keep his hands off the living and gave Loveday a telling-off she'd never forget.'

'Why didn't you tell me?'

'Because I promised her I wouldn't as long as it didn't happen again – not for a few years, anyway. I thought that would make her think twice before going behind our backs.'

Without a word, Morwenna got up and put her arms round him. Surprised, and hardly daring to believe what was happening, he returned the embrace. When she raised her face to him, he saw that she was crying. 'You didn't believe me until just now, did you?' he asked gently. 'Why, Morwenna?'

'Because of how she was with you. When things changed between us, you shut me out – you and her.'

'I missed you, and it felt like Loveday was the only family I had left – but not like that. Never like that.'

'I'd see you coming back into the house with her after you'd been out somewhere together. She always looked so happy, and I remembered – how could I ever forget? – that was exactly how I used to feel when I'd been with you. Like nothing could touch me, like the whole world was mine for the taking because I had you, and nothing and no one else mattered. So when I found out she was pregnant . . .'

'Loveday? Pregnant?'

'Not any more – she lost the baby, thank God, but I thought it was yours.'

'Is she all right? She didn't seem ill.'

'Yes, she's fine. She'll soon forget about it – her big brother's back and all's well with the world. I wish it were that simple for all of us.' She sat on the straw again and pulled him down beside her. 'What made you change your mind once you were in the water?'

'Fear. Nothing more honourable than that. I let myself sink deep down into the lake and it was so cold, so dark. I'd never thought about the darkness before – it was the loneliest moment I'd ever known. If I'd weighed myself down or allowed the sea to take me instead, it would have been different – I'd have left myself no choice. But it's very difficult to stay down there when all your instincts are to live. I don't know how long I was under the water. It can only have been seconds but it felt much longer. I could tell you that I came back up to punish myself like you did, or I could say that it wouldn't have been fair to die after persuading you to live – but the truth is I just couldn't do it. I reached the surface close to the shore, by that tangle of low-hanging branches on the western side, and I was disgusted with myself for not even having the decency to die properly. That's when it came to me – if everyone thought I was dead, I could start again as someone else. *We* could start again.'

'So you used the other man's body to fake your own death?'

'Yes. I knew I didn't have long because it had been light for some time, so I went back to where I'd left it and carried it to the thickest part of the wood. I was exhausted, and sick to the stomach at what I was doing, but I tried not to let myself think of him as a human being. I put my own belt and boots on him, and took his money – he had enough on him to get me out of the area for a bit and to see me through until I could find some casual work in a place where I wouldn't be recognised. Then I carried him to the bank where the water's at its deepest. I knew the body would be unrecognisable if I made sure it was in the lake long enough – I remember overhearing Jago Snipe talking to Dad once about a drowning he'd brought out of the pool – so I weighed it down as best I could and pushed it in.' For the last few minutes, Harry had been afraid to look at Morwenna but he could not avoid it any longer. 'Aren't you horrified by what I've done?' he asked, surprised to see how calm she looked.

It was a long time before she answered. 'I know what you're capable of, Harry. You killed our parents and it didn't stop me loving you, but it put a distance between us. Now, I don't know what I feel. Numb, I suppose, and frightened of the violence.'

'But I'd never hurt you.'

'I know you wouldn't. But you would hurt – you have hurt – because of me, and that's worse. This darkness in you – I have to carry it inside, too, and it frightens me that I'm prepared to do that, simply because it's better than having nothing of you at all. What does that make me?'

'Would you rather I'd stayed away?'

'No, of course not. I told you – I'm too selfish for that. But it's not straightforward like it is for Loveday.' She leaned over and touched his cheek. 'And like it seems to be for you. You really do think we can start again, don't you?'

'Yes, if we went away somewhere. It could be straight-forward if nobody knew us, if we could forget about the past.'

'And what about Loveday?'

'She can come with us.'

'Don't be so bloody naive, Harry. We can't drag her away

389

from a place she loves and expect her to act out our lies for us – that isn't even feasible, and it certainly isn't fair.' She must have seen the desolation in his face, because her next words were softer and he knew she was trying to be kind. 'I can be your sister, but I can't be your lover – here, or anywhere else.'

'So it's all been for nothing?'

'Is that really nothing? You could still have a family, Harry – even here. We could find a way, make something up to explain it.'

'Here? Now who's being naive? Haven't you heard a word I've said? I'm a murderer, Morwenna – I can't just turn up again from nowhere without people asking questions. I've killed someone and let you bury him thinking it was me.'

'But there's no proof.'

'He was wearing my belt, for Christ's sake. And there's Nathaniel.'

'My God, of course – you don't know, do you? Nathaniel's dead, Harry. Someone killed him the other night at the Minack. I'm sorry – I know you cared about him and I know this will sound heartless, but he can't tell anybody anything. He's no longer a threat to us.'

Sadly, he stroked her hair, then held her face in his hands for a long time. 'But he is, Morwenna – more so than ever.'

'For the last time, Archie, I've no idea what happened to the body. I keep telling you – I never saw it, and I never asked Harry where it was. That way, I couldn't be lying if someone came asking. If he had any sense, he'll have let the sea take it. It's probably been washed ashore by now – I wouldn't have heard about it. I've had too much on my hands with Morwenna and Loveday.'

390

'It hasn't come ashore, Morveth. When we started looking for Christopher, I asked the coastguard about recent drownings at sea along this stretch and he told me that the only bodies washed ashore in the last two months have been elderly men, women and one child – nobody who tallies with what you've just told me about Harry's victim.'

'Oh, I don't know then. He could have hidden it anywhere on the estate – it's a big enough place.'

'True, but there are very few places on it that wouldn't have been worked or at least looked over during the time that's passed since that night.'

'It's possible, though.'

'Yes, it's possible, but even you don't sound very convinced. I think there's something you're not telling me, Morveth, so I'll ask you again. But first, let me tell you something: a clerk from up country was reported missing several weeks ago,' he said, repeating what Fallowfield had told him. 'He came down here on holiday and hasn't been seen since. I'd put money on the fact that he was the man who got in Harry's way that night, and that he has a family and friends who are worried sick and waiting for someone to knock on their door with the worst possible news. Can you look me in the eye and tell me that you feel no sense of responsibility for what those people have been going through? Do I have to fetch Jago Snipe and get him to tell you how it feels not to know what's happened to your son before you'll be completely honest with me? All right, so they're strangers to you but they've done nothing wrong and they have a right to any help you can give – a right, I might add, which Harry Pinching forfeited the moment he took another man's life.'

'You make it sound so easy, Archie,' Morveth said sadly. 'I

wish I still had your certainty. I only ever wanted to protect them.'

'Morwenna and Loveday?'

'Yes – and Harry, too, I suppose, even after everything he's done. I've looked out for them all their lives – it's hard to break the habit. But you're right – that other family's grief is on my conscience, and more besides, and I don't trust myself to do the right thing like I used to.'

'Then I'll appeal to your conscience now,' Archie said, more gently this time. Morveth was one of the proudest women he had ever met and, whilst he recognised the truth in Josephine's opinion of her, he sympathised with how difficult it must be for Morveth to acknowledge her own fallibility – to him but more especially to herself. 'I'm here to investigate Nathaniel's death but things have been going wrong in this community for much longer. Please tell me anything you can that might help me piece it together.'

'All right, but you have to understand – I don't know anything for sure. I can only tell you what I think – although it's actually what I've been trying *not* to think.'

'Go on,' Penrose urged.

'It's going to sound ridiculous, but the longer all this goes on, the more certain I am that Harry didn't die after all.'

For the first time in many years, Morwenna was afraid. It was an emotion which she always associated with the early days of her relationship with Harry; back then, the fear that someone would discover their secret had been mixed with excitement; now, she felt it in its purest form – paralysing rather than exhilarating, and stripped of all the heroic illusions that had fooled her when she was young. 'What else have you done,

Harry?' she asked, trying to keep her voice level. 'Not Nathaniel – please, tell me that wasn't you?' As he continued to say nothing, refusing even to look at her, her plea became a scream. 'Tell me it wasn't you, Harry.'

'I had no choice,' he said, his words barely audible. 'I'd already killed – what difference could it make?'

Morwenna stared at him in disbelief. 'How can you say that? There's no comparison. The other man was a stranger – and anyway, he provoked you. Nathaniel's death was cold-blooded murder, something you must have planned – why would you do that?'

'I don't know – nothing made sense any more. I did it for us – so we could be together.'

She slapped him, hard, and tried to focus on the stinging in her hand to keep herself from losing all reason. 'No, Harry – you got away with that when you killed our parents but it's not good enough any more. Don't pin this on us – you owe me more than that, and you certainly owe Nathaniel something more. He was your friend, for God's sake – he loved you. And you've just exchanged his life for a fantasy – wiped him out because he got in your way. What's happened to you? If you can do that, you can do anything. Where's this going to end?'

'Oh stop pretending, Morwenna. You've known what I'm capable of since we were eighteen. It didn't bother you then, when it was our parents, so why all this grief now? You didn't even particularly like Nathaniel, so why choose his life over mine?'

'It's not a choice. Why is everything so black and white with you? What you did to our parents was an act of despair, Harry – you wanted oblivion for yourself, and you didn't care who you took with you. I understood that, and I can understand the type of rage that led you to go too far with a stranger who was stupid enough to push you. But Nathaniel wasn't in the wrong place at the wrong time – what you did to him was pure hatred. Can't you see there's a difference?'

'All I can see is that I couldn't be parted from you, and Nathaniel was in the way. He knew too much – we could never have been happy.'

'Like we are now, you mean?'

'Don't mock me, Morwenna,' he said angrily. 'I did hate Nathaniel – and with good reason. I hated him just like I hated that man when he hurt Shilling, only this didn't pass.'

'But why? Nothing that's gone wrong between us was Nathaniel's fault. He didn't ask to be told about the fire, and we've been perfectly capable of tearing each other apart without any help from him.'

'How can *you* say *that*? I've been watching you, Morwenna . . .'

'What do you mean? How could you have been watching me? How long have you been back here?'

'A few days. I read the announcement in the paper, and I could hardly miss my own funeral, could I?'

The sarcasm sounded strange coming from Harry, and the realisation that he was capable of shocking her hurt Morwenna far more than anything he had to say. 'Where have you been hiding?' she asked.

'There's a tunnel under the church that no one knows about. I've been there most of the time, but I had to see you, even if it wasn't safe to let you know. So yes, I watched you and I saw what it had done to you – the belief that I could forget you and turn to Loveday, and everything else that had happened. All the life in you had gone.'

'But what's that got to do with Nathaniel?'

'No matter what you say, you'd never have believed that of me if he hadn't put it in your head. You know, I stood under that church, listening while he stumbled his way through that pathetic eulogy, and all I could think about was how none of this would have happened if it weren't for him – we could still be together. You talk about love, but he was a coward and a hypocrite. Yes, he loved me, but not in the way you think; he wanted me just like I want you, and he couldn't deal with it. I went out of my way to be friendly to him, to show him that it made no difference, and it really didn't – not until he had the nerve to preach to you about forbidden love and tell you that I was fucking my little sister.'

'Harry, he . . .'

'Don't try to defend him, Morwenna. Why would he make up those lies about me? Was it some sort of spiteful revenge for everything he couldn't have or was he just worried about my soul? If that was it, he should have saved his counsel for himself, because I showed him what damnation really means. I showed him that dead men do come back and they get what they're owed.'

'Listen to me, Harry. He didn't put anything in my head. I told you why I jumped to the wrong conclusions about you and Loveday, and it had nothing to do with Nathaniel.'

'But that night, when we were arguing – you accused me of turning to her and never really loving you. Then when I was leaving – when I'd hit you and I couldn't bear to stay – you called after me. You said that Nathaniel knew everything anyway and it was only a matter of time before he said something to someone else.'

'I was talking about the fire.'

395

'What? You mean he hadn't talked to you about Loveday and me?'

'No, of course not, and I would never have said anything to him about it – I was too ashamed.' The horror of Harry's misunderstanding hit Morwenna like a physical blow. She got to the stable door just in time and, as the sour smell of vomit rose from the hard earth, she retched again, as if she could somehow empty herself of her grief and her guilt. She felt Harry's hand on her shoulder. 'What have we done?' she asked eventually, turning to look at him. 'What have *I* done?'

Her devastation was reflected in Harry's face. 'I thought he'd lied to you to spite me,' he said. 'I was so sure.'

'He'd never have done that – not to you, no matter what he felt. He would never have talked about you behind your back.'

'But he came to you about the fire.'

'That wasn't spite, Harry – that was sorrow. Couldn't you see that in his eyes? He didn't want to believe it and he hoped you'd tell him it wasn't true. If you'd denied it, he'd have let it go – even if, in his heart, he didn't believe you. But you wouldn't deny it, so he came to me.'

'The look on his face, Morwenna,' he said, and she could tell from his eyes that he was reliving that moment with a new sense of horror. 'I didn't even have to push him, for goodness' sake. He was so frightened when he saw me – all I had to do was take a couple of steps towards him.'

'He thought he'd driven you to suicide,' Morwenna said quietly. 'I put that in his head – I was so angry with him.'

'After everything he'd been through, all the confusion over what he felt and what he knew – he must have thought a dead man had come to take him to hell. It's what I wanted him to think. What must that be like when you believe what Nathaniel believed?'

Throughout the misery of the last few weeks, Morwenna had, she realised now, been nurturing a vague, elusive hope that there was a way out of the wretchedness, and, as she looked at her brother, she saw it with a clarity which both frightened and astonished her. 'You're right,' she said calmly, knowing that her certainty would reassure him. 'We do have to go away – I see that now. We've got no choice.'

'Really? But how can we after . . .'

The look of hope in his eyes almost made her waver. She had always wondered if a day would come when she would destroy him completely, and she realised now that this was it. 'Don't argue, Harry,' she said, putting her finger to his lips. 'We both need to be strong. We'll go away, the three of us, and start again, but you need to rest first. You're exhausted. Let's go inside and get you something to eat, then I'll go and find Loveday and tell her what we're doing.'

At the thought of her sister, Morwenna felt a stab of regret but she pushed it quickly from her mind and led Harry back into the kitchen. She built the fire up and made him sit down next to it, then went into the pantry to fetch some food. When she came back, he was unlacing his boots, wincing with pain as he did so. 'Here, let me,' she said, bending down to help.

He smiled gratefully at her. 'They're not my boots,' he explained.

'They'll have to do for now,' she said. 'We buried your best ones with you.' Gently, she washed his feet while he ate, noticing how badly blistered and cut they were and trying not to think about the man whose boots had done such damage. 'Go to bed and rest now,' she said when she had finished. 'I'll bring you a drink up. I think there's some whisky left over from the wake – it doesn't seem right that you missed it.'

When she took the glass upstairs, Harry was standing in the doorway to his room. 'You've cleared my things out already,' he said. 'There's nothing left. It's as if I never existed.'

'It was all I could think of to do,' she said, wishing she'd told him to take her bed. 'The one thing I could control in the middle of so much that I didn't understand. I'm sorry.'

He shook his head. 'Don't be – it's all right. After all, I don't exist any more, do I? Harry Pinching's dead. Neither of us can be who we were before.'

'Use my room,' she said, opening the door. She watched as he undressed and got into bed, then sat down next to him and handed him his drink. 'This will help you sleep.'

He downed it in one. 'God, that's good. You'll come back as quickly as you can?'

She took the empty glass from him and went over to the door. 'Of course. You won't even know I've gone. Then the three of us can leave.'

'Do you know where you'd like to go?'

'I don't mind. As far away as possible, as long as we're together.'

'And you'll fetch Shilling?'

'Yes, I'll fetch Shilling.' She turned to go, but thought better of it and went back to the bed. As she bent her head to kiss him, the taste of the whisky on his tongue – mixed with the familiar feel of his hand on the back of her neck – almost overwhelmed her. 'You do know I love you, don't you?' she asked, when she eventually pulled away.

'You wouldn't be doing this if you didn't,' he said, and smiled.

398

'You're right,' she said sadly. 'I wouldn't.'

'So it hasn't all been for nothing?'

'No, Harry – not for nothing,' she said, and left him to sleep.

Loveday listened as her sister moved about downstairs. She had been furious when Harry and Morwenna went outside, leaving her alone in the cottage, unable to hear what was going on. Her anger had soon disappeared when they returned, however: at last, it seemed as though everything she had ever wanted was about to be hers. Harry was back, and the shouting had stopped. Perhaps the three of them could be happy together after all. She would miss the Loe estate – and Christopher, of course – but going away would be an adventure. The adventure that Harry had always promised her.

She sat down on the narrow bed, feeling suddenly quite tired. If she were honest, Morwenna was right – she still wasn't completely better. Like Harry, she ought to get some rest. Quietly, Loveday crawled between the sheets and waited for Morwenna to fetch her.

There was a long silence in the room. Archie looked at Josephine and saw the shock and disbelief in her face. Rather than share her surprise, though, he felt that something had suddenly fallen into place which would explain everything. He could not begin to imagine yet how Harry had achieved such a complex illusion, but his instinct was to believe that Morveth's suspicions were correct. 'You're saying that Harry put the other man's body in the Loe Pool to fake his own death?' he asked.

'I'm saying it's possible.'

'But surely someone must have identified the body?' Josephine said, still incredulous.

'It's not as simple as that,' Morveth replied impatiently. 'A body in the water for that long barely seems human. Morwenna identified the belt as Harry's and Jacks had seen him going into the lake – that was enough to satisfy the authorities.'

'But wouldn't the undertaker be able to tell? Is it really that bad?'

'It can be,' Archie said. 'It depends on the temperature of the water and, to an extent, on predators, although most of the decaying organisms come from the body itself. I'll spare you the details but a month would be long enough to make visual recognition impossible, or at least very difficult – and don't forget how badly the man's face was already beaten.' He turned back to Morveth. 'And I suppose that certain people were quite relieved to bury Harry Pinching after everything that had gone on. The world was a far more convenient place with him dead.'

'I can't speak for Jago, although he's never given me any indication that he suspected the body wasn't Harry's. I certainly didn't know.'

'But now you seem quite sure. Is that because of what happened on Tuesday night? You realise, I suppose, that if you're right, and Harry is still alive, he's a prime suspect for Nathaniel's murder? Did you see him at the Minack?'

'Not exactly.'

'What the hell does that mean?' Archie asked, exasperated. 'I'm beginning to lose patience here, Morveth. If Harry Pinching is alive and somewhere on this estate, I need to find him before someone else gets hurt. I haven't got time to sit around here all day playing word games with you, so I'd be grateful if you would tell me as quickly as possible everything you know about Tuesday night, starting with why you weren't where you were supposed to be when Nathaniel jumped from the balustrade.'

'Loveday and Morwenna needed me,' Morveth said. 'Loveday was ill and Morwenna came to find me. I suggested they take Jago's van to get home – it was quick and it meant no one else had to be involved. I helped Morwenna get Loveday up the hill and settled into the van, and I watched them drive off.'

'But that was earlier in the evening, wasn't it? Morwenna told me they were away from the theatre before Nathaniel died.'

'Yes, but I couldn't bring myself to go straight back. I sat there for a while in the darkness, thinking about everything that had happened to that family over the years, all the sadness and the lies and the guilt. It should have been a wonderful night, with Harry on stage and his sisters watching him proudly in the audience – but it was a mockery of everything that was normal and right. Harry was dead – or so I thought – and his fourteen-year-old sister was pregnant with his child, and Morwenna – well, who can say what grief and insanity she's been fighting. So I was mourning them, Archie, when Nathaniel died – not just Harry, but the whole family, Sam and Mary too. And suddenly all that artifice and play-acting on stage seemed so wrong. I just wanted to put a stop to the whole thing, but someone else did that for me, and in the most terrible way imaginable.'

'But can you say for certain who that was?' Archie persisted.

'Not for certain, no, but I knew I couldn't stay away from the play for ever, so I started to make my way backstage by the steps that run alongside the auditorium, and before I'd got very far,

I found the cloak – one of the brown habits. It wasn't hidden – just cast aside, like someone had taken it off in a hurry.'

'But you hadn't seen anyone?'

'No. I picked the cloak up and went further down, and by that time, of course, the play had been stopped and everyone was just standing around, wondering what had happened.'

'You must have realised that the two things were connected. What did you do with the cloak?'

'I took it backstage and put it with the rest of the costumes as people were taking them off, next to the bishop's outfit so that I could find it again.'

'And it didn't occur to you to hand it over as evidence?' Archie asked angrily.

'I was going to say something, but then I met Jago. He was upset, because he thought he'd glimpsed Christopher in the auditorium but he couldn't find him anywhere – and I was horrified.'

'You thought that Christopher might have left the cloak there? That he killed Nathaniel because of the business with his parents?'

'Yes, and I couldn't put Jago through that – he's never really forgiven himself for what we did all those years ago – so I kept quiet until I could find out more about what had gone on. But then I went back to the cloak and, when I picked it up again and held it closer to me, I knew it wasn't Christopher who'd been wearing it.'

'How?'

'Because of the smell. Harry always took a pipe – do you remember?' Archie nodded. 'He used to smoke his father's tobacco – one of those childish acts of rebellion that he indulged in until he found something much more serious to get himself into trouble with – and he never lost the habit. It was always one of the first things you noticed about him – that and his smile. There's nothing quite like it when you've lost someone – the smell of them, I mean. On their clothes, in their books – but that cloak had never been near Harry while he was alive. Yet he might as well have been standing there in it.'

'And Christopher doesn't smoke?'

'No. He might have the odd cigarette to act like a man, but not like this. Pipe tobacco's very different, and Harry's brand was quite distinctive.'

'It still seems odd to me that you'd leap to that conclusion – to pin a murder on a dead man.'

'Not after what I'd heard that afternoon. I knew about the fire and I heard Nathaniel telling you how he panicked when he found out, so there was no question in my mind that Harry would have good reason to make sure Nathaniel kept his mouth shut. And I couldn't get the words Nathaniel used out of my head – something about Harry standing beside him and taking him to hell. That's what he looked like that night on the cliff path, you know – a man in a living hell.'

'I don't suppose there's any point in my asking where the cloak is now, is there?' Archie said, knowing full well what the answer would be. 'Destroying evidence is serious, Morveth, and *not* something I can turn a blind eye to.'

'I know, but I *did* get rid of it,' Morveth said. 'I thought it was for the best. You see, I didn't want to believe that Harry had done it.'

'Or that you made it possible for him,' said Josephine sharply.

Morveth looked at her sadly. 'Do you think I could ever forget that?' she asked. 'My own conscience is far more ruthless than a stranger's tongue.'

'But instead of doing anything about it, you've just been waiting for him to turn up, haven't you?' Josephine continued, ignoring her. 'That was another reason for driving me out of Loe Cottage yesterday – you think he'll come back for them, and you're keeping watch.'

'Have you said anything to Morwenna?' Archie asked, standing up ready to go.

'No – like I said, I'm not certain of any of this, and it's better that she believes him dead until we know otherwise.'

'I'm afraid I beg to differ there. She may be in danger.'

'No, Archie – he'd never hurt them.'

'Are you sure about that? Eight years ago, Harry was desperate enough to wipe himself out and take most of his family with him. If you're right about what he's done now, he's got even less to lose – and this time, he won't leave without Morwenna.'

When Morwenna went back upstairs, Harry was sleeping soundly. She watched him for a moment, taking a last look at his face against the pillow, then took the matches from her pocket. The piece of material which she carried – a scarf that Harry had been wearing the first time they made love and the one thing of his which she could not bear to destroy – was faded and worn now, and smelt overpoweringly of petrol; still, if she closed her eyes to blot out the present, she fancied she could still catch the faint scent of earth and leaves and a fourteen-year-old autumn that felt so recent. Who could have predicted then that she would finish what Harry had started, and that this would be her final gift to her brother? An oblivion which she longed for herself, free of the fear and pain that had filled Nathaniel's last conscious seconds.

As the fire took hold, she shut the bedroom door behind her and locked it, thinking about all the times that she had closed it from the other side, desperate to keep Harry out and deny everything that he had ever meant to her. She paused, glancing towards Loveday's room, and wondered if she should take something with her to remind her of her sister – but there was really no need; the guilt she felt over the way that she had treated her was more than enough to carry. She locked the side door and removed the key, then went out through the kitchen and back to the empty stable where she had made her decision. Quickly, she took the reins from their hook and ran down through the garden and out into the woods. She had to get away before her resolve weakened and sent her screaming back into the house to save Harry and damn herself.

They saw the smoke long before they were anywhere near Loe Cottage. Archie drove faster, forcing the car down the narrow country lane, and Josephine sat silently beside him, willing them to be in time – for what, she could not honestly have said. Morveth's conversation with Archie had left her searching for an outcome which could conceivably be described as for the best, and so far it eluded her.

When they pulled up outside, the fire seemed confined – so far – to the first floor and could not have begun long ago. Nevertheless, the flames were making short work of the thatch and a small crowd had already gathered at a safe distance in the garden to watch this new assault on such an ill-fated cottage. Instinctively, Josephine looked up at Loveday's window, remembering the girl's face pressed to the glass the day before; please God, let her be all right, she thought. It was an uncharacteristic appeal to an authority in which she did not believe, but that Loveday should be spared seemed to her the only certainty in an unimaginable sequence of events, and she was willing for once to lend her faith indiscriminately.

For want of a better explanation, Josephine realised with a mixture of astonishment and relief that her prayers had been answered. As she and Archie got out of the car, she saw beyond the front row of onlookers to where a group of women had gathered around a small figure – a living and breathing figure, albeit one whose face was blackened by smoke and stained with tears. 'Loveday – thank God,' she said, acknowledging her own hypocrisy but feeling it was the least she could do. Mrs Snipe was amongst the women, and Josephine went over to speak to her.

'She's not hurt, Miss Tey,' the Snipe said, her arm still reassuringly around Loveday's shoulders. 'But she's scared half to death and very confused. She keeps saying that Harry's in there, but she must be getting it mixed up with the last time. It beggars belief, doesn't it? This happening twice, I mean – it scarcely seems possible.' She lowered her face and placed a comforting kiss on the top of Loveday's head. 'I'll look after her, though – don't you worry.'

'Who got her out? Was it Morwenna?'

'No, Miss – it was Jacks, of all people. He was working in the woods and saw the smoke. Morwenna's nowhere to be seen. Loveday swears she's not at home – keeps saying something about her going to get Shilling, but I don't think the poor kid knows what's what at the moment.'

'And where's Jacks now?'

'He's gone back into the fire.' She looked up, and Josephine knew exactly what she was thinking. 'He wouldn't have it that Morwenna was safe.'

406

Archie was talking urgently with two men, one of whom turned and left as Josephine approached. 'The fire brigade's been called,' he said, 'but Jacks has gone back inside. I've told Joseph Caplin to go and fetch William – the last thing he needs is to stand here and watch a fire after what he's been through. Is Loveday all right?'

'Shocked and upset, but not hurt,' Josephine said. 'But Harry *is* in there. No one else believes her, of course.'

'Shit. What about Morwenna?'

'Loveday says not. She went to fetch Shilling, apparently.'

'Shilling? Why would she do that?'

Josephine shrugged. 'You're asking me for logic? Just be pleased she's not in the cottage. That neither of them is. It looks like Harry made sure this time.'

'Do something for me – go and speak to Loveday, and try and make sense of what happened. If she insists that Morwenna went to get Shilling, take the car to the stable block and see if there's any sign of her or the horse.'

'What about you? You're not thinking of going in there, I hope.'

'I don't have any choice.'

'Archie, you can't – it's not safe. I won't let you do that – leave it to the fire brigade when it gets here.'

'Who knows how long that will take? Look, I'm not going to be stupid about it, I promise. If there's no chance, I'll come out straight away, but two men are in there and I have to try.'

'Why? Just so you can hang one of them if he's not already dead and let the other one carry on beating his wife? Do you have to be a hero, Archie? Just because we got here too late and there's nothing else you can do? Can't you see how selfish that is?'

'Go and speak to Loveday,' he repeated, and turned towards the cottage before she could say anything more. Angry and upset, Josephine did as she was asked.

The back door was already open, and Archie headed for the stairs. Before he was halfway up, though, thick, black smoke drove him down into the kitchen again. Realising that he had even less time than he thought before the whole cottage was alight, he went quickly through the sitting room and along the corridor to the back stairs. If anything, the smoke was even worse here: already, his eyes were smarting and he found it difficult to breathe, but, as he climbed the steps, he could see Jacks halfway along the landing, bent double and choking with the fumes, but still inching slowly forward. He called out, but Jacks either couldn't or wouldn't hear him, and Penrose had no choice but to follow. He grabbed the gamekeeper's arm and tried to pull him back towards the stairs, but was pushed roughly aside.

'Fuck off, Penrose. I need to find Morwenna.'

'She's not here, Jacks. There's nothing more you can do.'

'You're lying. That door's locked – there must be someone in there. I can't just leave her.'

'It's not Morwenna,' Penrose insisted, still trying to force Jacks back downstairs.

'Who else would it be? You just want to play the hero.'

'Don't be so bloody ridiculous,' he said, already tired of an accusation that he had heard twice in as many minutes. 'That isn't Morwenna and this isn't a game. Look at those flames – whoever it is, he's beyond our help. Come with me – now, before the roof collapses.' The sound of exploding glass from the nearest bedroom served to underline Penrose's warning, although he suspected that the thought of another man in Morwenna's bed was more influential in Jacks's decision. Reluctantly, the gamekeeper turned and allowed himself to be pushed towards the stairs.

Help arrived sooner than Penrose could have hoped for. By the time he and Jacks emerged from the cottage, choking and gasping, an ambulance driver was wrapping Loveday in a blanket and the clanging of a fire engine's bell could be heard across the fields. He brushed aside any medical assistance for himself but made sure that Jacks was in safe hands, then walked back to the road. There was no sign of Josephine or the car.

'Sir?' Penrose turned and saw Trew hurrying over the lawn. 'I got here as quickly as I could. What's happened?'

Penrose explained succinctly, impressed – as he had been at the Minack – by the calm and intelligent way in which Trew absorbed information and wasted no time on questions that could wait until later. 'Tell the firemen what they'll find inside and clear everyone away before they bring the body out, especially his little sister – make sure she's looked after. I don't know how long she was in there with the fire, but the shock alone will need some care. I'm going to look for Morwenna.'

Trew nodded and went to greet the fire brigade, and Penrose headed for the woods which offered the quickest route to the house and stables. Within a matter of minutes, it was as though he had entered a different world. A density of new summer growth cushioned him from the pall of smoke and commotion that clung to Loe Cottage, and he looked with a mixture of astonishment and sadness at the extraordinary beauty which could exist so close to death. The flowers

409

stretched out in front of him, as if someone had taken a brush and covered the ground in a delicate, vein-blue wash, and he had the illusion of walking through water – a continuation of the lake which could be glimpsed here and there through the trees, first lavender, then cobalt, as the light played different tricks on its surface. He picked his way through the bluebells, and their faint but unmistakeable scent brought back his childhood and something else besides – something universal, something lost. The woods were quiet, unnaturally so, and suddenly Penrose knew what he would find. How strange, he thought, that he should feel such a calm acceptance as well as regret; that even he, it seemed, could acknowledge that this was the best – the only – way.

Morwenna had chosen a sycamore tree to mark her death. Her body was hanging from its lower branches by a narrow rope – a lone, dark figure, one for sorrow, certainly, although the grief was no longer hers. A soft breeze ruffled her skirt and the sleeves of her blouse, and the image was so familiar to Penrose that he wondered if that moment all those years ago – that pairing of beauty and death which had affected him so deeply – had, in fact, been a premonition, a sign that it was already too late to save her. There was a pile of logs close to her feet and, as he got closer, Penrose could see that the rope was actually a long leather rein – one of Harry's, no doubt. Her head was tilted to one side, away from the fatal knot, and the only mark that he could see on her skin was the imprint of a metal ring at the front of her neck. Otherwise, her face was pale and uncongested, suggesting a merciful cardiac response rather than slow asphyxiation. She would probably only have suffered a few seconds of consciousness, but she had left nothing to chance: as he walked around her body, he noticed that her wrists were tied clumsily together behind her; it was a poignant sign of her resolve, and something which he had occasionally seen in those bent on self-destruction who feared they might lose courage at the final moment. Every human impulse in him wanted to raise his arms and lift her gently down, but he knew that he should not touch anything, and he felt the conflict between his job and his heart more sharply than ever.

There was no note that he could see, but then he would not have expected to find one. Morwenna had nothing left to say to the living – she had made that perfectly clear at their last meeting. But on the ground, too close to the place of her death to be a coincidence, Penrose noticed something which was as eloquent an expression of atonement as any suicide note he had ever read. A dead bird lay among the bluebells – a jackdaw. He knelt down and parted the hanging flowers to take a closer look, and saw that there was a piece of rough twine around its neck. Its small, serpent-like eyes were clouded and lifeless and, if Penrose had ever doubted Morveth's story, he did so no longer. Whatever had gone on between Harry and Morwenna that morning, this was her response to the realisation that their love had killed Nathaniel. This was an end to it.

Josephine got back from the stables to find that Archie had left the cottage and was headed towards Loe House. She left the car this time and hurried off in the direction pointed out to her, keen to catch up with him and make sure he was all right; he might have escaped the fire without harm, but she knew that his emotions would not be similarly unscathed by what had happened.

She saw Archie first, and Morwenna a split second later. He

was kneeling on the ground, his head bowed, and she knew that he was examining the scene, but, from where she stood, the action held a much deeper poignancy: it was a moment of great peace and respect and, at the same time, an acknowledgement that however hard Archie had tried to save Morwenna, in the end, it had not been enough. The sun shone through the leaves, gentle and diffuse like light through stained glass, and she stood for a second, caught between an instinct to go to him and a horror of intruding on this most private of scenes. Morwenna was beautiful, even in death – still isolated, and more distant than ever, but suddenly immune to the shadows that had cursed her for so long. Slowly, Josephine walked forward through the bluebells.

'I'm so sorry, Archie,' she said.

He had been too deep in thought to hear anyone approaching, but he turned now and walked quickly over to her, shielding her as best he could from the sight of Morwenna's body. 'Come over here,' he said gently. 'You don't need to see this.'

She allowed herself to be led a few yards away, and they sat down for a moment on a fallen tree. 'I went to the stables. Shilling's still there – but you obviously know that.' Archie nodded. 'This must be a shock for you . . . are you all right?'

'I don't know how I feel,' he said. 'Morwenna and I have known each other for so long but I didn't really understand her until yesterday, when she talked about Harry – and part of that understanding was accepting that there'd be no happy endings. So I suppose it *is* a shock, but not really a surprise.'

'So much love and so much misery. How on earth did it all come to this?'

It was a rhetorical question, but Archie surprised her by his answer. 'I think Morwenna knew she had to be strong enough for both of them,' he said, 'and I think she started the fire this time, not Harry. He must have told her that he killed Nathaniel – I found a dead jackdaw over there by her feet. There's a group of them strung up on the fence.'

'Yes, I saw them.'

'They're Jacks's trophies. She knew all this had to stop and she took things into her own hands. If she needed a sign to justify her decision, I can't think of anything more appropriate.'

Josephine tried to imagine the utter desolation that Morwenna must have felt when she realised what she had to do – and the strength that was required to see it through. 'I told her she was using her love for Harry to keep the world at arm's length and to hide from reality,' she said sadly. 'I could hardly accuse her of that now.'

Wearily, Archie rubbed his eyes. 'At least it's over for her now – her *and* Harry.' He stood up and held out his hand. 'Come on – I need to get some help to take her down and seal this part of the wood off.' She followed his gaze as it took in the glory of the woods around him. 'It's always the beautiful things that death taints for the living, isn't it?' he said, with anger in his voice.

Josephine hesitated, remembering all that Morveth had said to her about protecting Archie and wondering if his acceptance of Morwenna's death was as final as he thought it was. 'Shall I fetch someone while you stay with her?' she asked.

He smiled at her gratefully. 'Thank you. At least I can make sure that she's looked after now. It's ironic, isn't it?' he added sadly as she walked away. 'You always said that Morwenna had killed Harry, and I'm sure you've turned out to be right.'

Chapter Twenty

Josephine sat by her bedroom window, looking out into the darkness. Loe House was not visible from the Lodge but she imagined that, had she been able to see beyond the curve of the lake, several lights would be in evidence despite the lateness of the hour, mirroring her own restlessness across the water. The jumble of lives and events in her head weighed her down with a claustrophobic intensity, and she was glad of the cool night air and the sense of absolute peace, disturbed only now and again by the screech of an owl from the woods behind the house. Most of all, though, she thought about Loveday – safe at Loe House, with the best of care from William and his household, but with her own demons still to face: Harry and Morwenna dead; Christopher's fate still uncertain; and no more hope of refuge in her friendship with Nathaniel. When the harsh sound of the telephone cut through the stillness, Josephine welcomed the distraction.

'Did I wake you?'

'No, Archie, of course not. Where are you?'

'Still at the station. I'm waiting for some reports from the fire and the post mortems, and I know I'll get them quicker if I'm here to breathe down people's necks. Are you all right?'

'I'm fine. I was just thinking about Loveday and everything she's got to come to terms with.'

'And there's something else, I'm afraid.'

'Oh God – Christopher. Is he . . . ?'

'No, no – he's absolutely fine. The Falmouth force picked him up this afternoon from the description we circulated. He'd got himself a job on the docks, of all things.'

'So he did run away – but why now?'

'You know he was in the churchyard on Sunday night?'

'Yes.'

'So was Harry. Christopher saw him come out of the church and go off into the woods.'

'Good God – I'm not surprised he decided to disappear, then. He must have known how Harry would react to finding out that his little sister was pregnant. But surely this is good news for Loveday?'

'What? That Christopher deserted her? There's not much comfort in that. I can't help thinking that Christopher could have saved everyone a lot of heartache if he'd been just a little bit braver.'

'Oh Archie, he's young – you can't blame him for that. And let's face it – being brave might have got him killed. Who knows what sort of state Harry was in? At least this way he's still around to make it up to Loveday.'

'Not exactly. From what the sergeant who questioned him told me, he's got no desire to hurry back home. I think Harry Pinching unwittingly gave Christopher a taste of freedom. Falmouth's hardly the other side of the world, but it must feel like it to someone who's never been away from the Loe estate. And that will be such a blow for Loveday on top of everything else.'

'She's stronger than we think, though,' Josephine said after a moment's consideration. 'And this could be the making of Christopher. There may still be a time for them to be together, but, if there is, I've no doubt it will be on her terms. If anyone's going to be destroyed by Christopher's new life, it'll be Jago rather than Loveday.'

'I know. And he blames himself, of course. I spoke to him earlier, and he's torn between relief and regret. If he hadn't been so set against Christopher and Loveday, things might have been very different – but he was making too many assumptions.'

'Do you think he'll ever tell Caplin or Christopher the truth?'

'I've no idea, and that's between them now. I feel I've interfered enough in the lives of people here.' He spoke drily but it did not quite mask the tiredness and sense of regret in his voice, and Josephine wondered again how difficult he would find it to get over what had happened; unlike Loveday, Archie did not have the resilience of youth on his side. 'Anyway, I've let William know about Christopher and he's going to tell Loveday in the morning,' he continued. 'She's sleeping now and she needs to rest.' He paused for a moment and Josephine heard someone else in the room with him; when he spoke again, the vulnerability had vanished. 'Sorry – I've got to go. I'll see you later if you're still awake – if not, we can talk in the morning.'

Josephine left the hall lamp on and went back upstairs. Determined to be awake when Archie finally got home, she settled down in a chair to read. When a faint smell of smoke drifted in through the open window, she thought at first that it was her imagination, the result of a traumatic day which still weighed heavily on her mind, but it only took a second or two to convince her that she was not mistaken. Please God, not more tragedy, she thought, hurrying over to the window, but the blaze was real enough. There was a circle of flames a few yards in front of her, floating on the water, and she realised that someone must have set light to the barge, creating a parody of the ceremony which was supposed to have taken place that night. In the glow from the fire, she could just make out that the figure standing by the boathouse was Morveth Wearne.

Quickly, Josephine pulled on a coat and went downstairs. As she walked across the gravel and down to the edge of the lake, Morveth turned to greet her. 'Hasn't there been enough destruction for one day?' Josephine asked. 'What exactly is this supposed to achieve?'

'A fresh start,' Morveth said simply. 'Sometimes things have to be destroyed to begin again. Morwenna knew what she was doing when she set that fire.'

'Of course she did. She wanted to obliterate everything, just like Harry did eight years ago. But that was about the past, not the future, so don't try to give it a meaning which it could never have.'

'There's a meaning in everything, if you look hard enough,' the older woman replied, still staring into the flames.

Josephine looked down on to the barge. The fire had not yet taken hold of the collection of objects which were piled up in the bottom of the boat and she recognised some of the photographs and trinkets from Morveth's sitting room, as well as a bridle, and some clothing that might well have belonged to Morwenna. Clearly, this strange act of atonement held some meaning for Morveth as she struggled to come to terms with her own part in the tragedy, but Josephine remained unconvinced. 'Tell that to Loveday while she's trying to cope with losing the rest of her family,' she said.

'So what will your story be to get her through this?' Morveth asked, her voice barely louder than a whisper. 'First we die and then we rot?'

'Of course not,' Josephine said angrily. 'But filling her head full of false hope is hardly going to help her in the long run. She needs to understand that there are no second chances – that way, she'll make the most of the one life she has got.'

'There *are* second chances if you're willing to search for them,' Morveth insisted, more to herself than to Josephine. 'There have to be. Otherwise, how could you ever go on?' Bending down, she took the rope from one of the poles on the landing stage and threw it into the water. The barge floated slowly out across the lake. 'I'm not going to argue with you, Josephine,' Morveth said. 'You must believe whatever brings you comfort.'

She walked slowly away. Unsettled, Josephine watched her go, staring into the darkness long after the figure was out of sight. She looked back at the Lodge. It might be hours before Archie got back, and she was reluctant to return to the silence; unusually for her, she felt in need of company. William and the girls would probably still be up, so she left a note on the kitchen table and set off to Loe House. Several lights were still on, as she had guessed they would be, but she was surprised to see the soft glow of a lamp coming from the stables as well. Who would be there at this time of night? she wondered. Perhaps one of the horses was ill. Curious, she decided to stop there first and went quietly over to the door. At first, she thought there was no one there; then she saw Loveday, curled up on a pile of straw by Shilling's stall. The girl glanced up, and smiled with relief when she saw who it was.

'Loveday, what on earth are you doing here?' Josephine asked, going over to her. 'You should be tucked up in bed.'

'I know, but I wanted to see Shilling so I pretended to be asleep and then slipped out. Mr Motley's very trusting.' She grinned, and Josephine had to admire her spirit. 'That's all right, isn't it?'

'I suppose so, but only for a bit. Shilling needs his rest, and so do you.' She sat down on the straw next to Loveday, and put her arm around the girl's small shoulders. 'But as you're here, I've got some good news for you. The police have found Christopher, and he's absolutely fine.' Loveday hugged Josephine in delight; when she eventually pulled away, Josephine was both touched and concerned to see the joy in her eyes. 'He's not coming home straight away, though,' she said, anxious not to give the girl false hope. 'I'm sure you'll be able to see him when you're better, but you'll have to be patient. You've both been through so much.'

'That's all right – I'm used to being patient with Christopher,' Loveday said. 'But Morveth was right – she said I shouldn't give up hope.'

'Oh?' said Josephine cautiously. 'You've seen her, then?'

'Yes. Mr Motley brought her up to talk to me this evening. It was Morveth who told me I should come and see Shilling. She meant when I was better,' Loveday added, misinterpreting the concern on Josephine's face, 'but I couldn't wait. She said that Shilling and I had lots in common because we'd both be missing Harry, so we should stick together and keep each other company.'

'That sounds like good advice,' Josephine said, surprised. 'What else did Morveth say to you?'

'She explained that people have to carry on with their lives even when they're sad, and that's when they need their friends around them most. She told me that I must never forget Harry and Morwenna, or be too upset to talk about them, and that everything they meant to me is still here even if they're not.' Josephine listened, wondering if she'd done Morveth an injustice after all; the advice – which seemed to have given Loveday some genuine comfort – was a long way from the false hope of which she had just accused her. Suddenly, she felt ashamed of the criticisms which she had handed out so readily: someone who viewed the world through a mirror was hardly in a position to judge other people's methods of dealing with reality. 'And she gave me this to remind me of them,' Loveday added. Josephine took the book which was held out to her, but failed to see how *Ivanhoe* could possibly remind the girl of her brother and sister. 'No, not that – this,' Loveday explained impatiently, pulling out the photograph which she had been using as a bookmark. 'It's the only one she had of the two of them together.'

It was not a physical likeness which would have told Josephine that the man with Morwenna was Harry, even if she'd come to the picture without Loveday's explanation; there was a resemblance around the mouth and chin if you looked closely, but that was all. No, it was the expression of joy in Morwenna's eyes that gave it away – a declaration of love as eloquent as the verbal description which had had such an impact on Josephine during their conversation outside the boathouse. With a shock, she realised that she was not looking at Harry Pinching for the first time: she had met him before – in the stables on Monday night, when she went to find Shilling. She remembered how struck she had been by the young man's passion for the horses and the gentleness with which he had treated them; it was a rare and powerful combination, and she acknowledged the truth of Morwenna's words: you had to meet Harry to understand their love. Aware now that the dead man was not in fact the stranger she had assumed him to be, Josephine felt his loss with a new intensity.

She gave the photograph back to Loveday. 'Morveth's right, you know – about your friends, I mean. They'll take care of you, just like you'll take care of Shilling.'

'Yes, I know. Morveth's promised to look after me – her and Mr Motley. And if Christopher does come home, I'll be able to look after him.'

Josephine smiled at Loveday's unconscious recognition of her own strength. 'We should go back to the house,' she said, 'or you won't be in a fit state to look after anyone.'

'All right,' Loveday agreed reluctantly, 'but will you come and see me tomorrow? Miss Motley read me a story this afternoon, but she's nowhere near as good as you. It was kind of her to bother, but I don't think she really believed in what she was saying. You have to *believe* in a story to make it a good one, don't you?'

'Yes,' said Josephine, getting up and holding out her hand. 'Yes, I suppose you do.'

Author's Note

Angel With Two Faces is a work of fiction, inspired by real places, real lives and, in some cases, real events, and is a tribute to the unique beauty of Porthleven, the Loe Pool, and the Penrose Estate, as well as to the people who live and work there. It's a community that I love being part of – one which does indeed turn a face to the past as well as to the present, and is all the more special for that.

Josephine Tey was one of two pseudonyms created by Elizabeth Mackintosh (1896–1952) during a versatile and successful career as a novelist and playwright; the other, Gordon Daviot, was reserved for plays, historical fiction and a biography. Unravelling her life through her work and her letters continues to be a fascinating journey, and the Josephine Tey who appears in *Angel With Two Faces* blends some of what we know about Elizabeth Mackintosh with the personality which emerges so strongly from her eight crime novels – novels which have always been widely regarded as some of the finest and most original to emerge from the Golden Age period.

In reality, Tey did, of course, finish the book we see her writing here, although it was not set in Cornwall. *A Shilling for Candles* was published in 1936, and went on to be the basis of Hitchcock's film, *Young and Innocent*. In her book, Tey's murder victim – the actress Christine Clay – leaves her fortune 'for the preservation of the beauty of England', something which the author herself would do less than twenty years later, when, after her premature death at the age of 55, she left her estate and the royalties from her writing to the National Trust for England in a special Daviot Fund.

I'm sure she would be delighted to know that the Loe Pool and the Penrose Estate are now in the safe hands of the National Trust, and some of the author's proceeds from *Angel With Two Faces* will go to support the Trust's work on the Estate.

Acknowledgements

I owe a great debt to my Cornish friends – to Victor and Monica Strike for their generosity in sharing stories of their family trades in matters of life and death, which have shaped the book more than they can know; Oliver Allen for bringing 1930s Porthleven to life with his own family history; George Snell for his legendary tales and for memories of Loe Bar and Gunwalloe; Brian Stephens for the loan of his library and his name, and for keeping an eye on us whenever we're there; Motley Penrose (or Lynford) for making Helston Lodge more glorious than it is already; Lynda Green for happy times at the Galley and at Motley & Co., and Sheila Toy, Michael Crowle, John Strike and all the Motley regulars; and Sandy and Russell at the An Mordros Hotel for their constant support and encouragement, and most of all for their friendship – without which, there would be no Cornish novel.

I'm forever grateful to the Rogers family for allowing people to enjoy the beauty of the Loe Pool and Penrose Estate, and to the staff and touring companies at the Minack Theatre, who continue to keep the spirit of Rowena Cade very much alive with magical performances each summer. My apologies go to the artist Hilda Quick, who actually designed the costumes for the Minack's 1935 production of *The Jackdaw of Rheims*; to my knowledge, the performances went off without a hitch.

My thanks go to Arts Council England, East, which funded part of the research for this novel; Claire Wachtel, Julia Novitch and everyone at HarperCollins for their continued support of the series; Jennifer Joel and Karolina Sutton; Walter Donohue for his passion and insight; Dr Peter Fordyce for devoting so much of his precious time to advising on nastiness, and for his love and knowledge of horses; Alastair Cameron from the National Trust for providing information about the history of the Penrose Estate; Margaret Westwood, Dr Helen Grime and Anne Fraser of The Highland Council for continuing to unravel the past; Professor Harriet Jump for the gracious loan of her mother and aunt; Carol Carman for all the inside information from the Yard; and Cambridge University Library for holding the answers to so many questions – I don't know how anyone writes a book without it. Special thanks go, once again, to Irene for her magic and blessings, and to St Anthony of Holland Park for so much more than finding the title.

Love and thanks – as always – to my family, in particular to my father for his love of the woods and a good game of cricket, and to my mother for her passion for a good story and her eagle eyes during the early stages of this one.

And to Mandy, who drove 380 miles in the snow to start *our* Cornish adventure in Morveth Wearne's cottage – this book is precious to us for lots of different reasons, but none more so than the fact that we've done it together.

Turn the page for a preview of
Nicola Upson's next novel

TWO FOR SORROW

A Mystery Featuring Josephine Tey

Available soon from

HARPER

NEW YORK • LONDON • TORONTO • SYDNEY

Holloway Gaol, Tuesday 3rd February, 1903

Morning arrived, cold and frosty and defiant, as unwanted as it was inevitable. Celia Bannerman looked up at two thin rows of glass, seven tiny panes in each, and wondered again why anyone had bothered to go through the motions of letting daylight into such a godforsaken place. Even if the dirt from the world outside had not made it all but impenetrable, the window would have been much too high to see from. Soot from the Camden Road was left to accumulate peacefully on the glass, shielding those inside from a life which continued without them. The cell was airless and oppressive. In the absence of adequate natural light, a lamp burned throughout the day and on into the night, denying the prisoner even the comforting anonymity of blackness. Like many other things about prison life, the brightness of the room was a compromise – never truly light and never truly dark, as if a denial of such extremes could somehow keep their equivalent emotions at bay.

From her chair in the corner, Celia watched the shadows dance over the cell's familiar contents: a wooden wash-stand, with its pathetic ration of yellow soap, and a single filthy rag, meant to clean both mug and chamber pot but fit to touch neither; a corner shelf with a Bible for those still able to find comfort in its pages; and an enamel plate and knife, made from folded tin and sharp as a piece of cardboard. A low black iron bedstead took up most of the room's thirteen feet by seven. The woman in the bed had turned her face resolutely to the wall, but Celia knew she was not asleep. As she thought of what lay ahead, she felt the customary tightening in her stomach and, for a moment, she was a child again, remembering the mornings when she herself had pulled the blankets over her head and prayed for time to stand still so that she did not have to face what the day held. At the time, those young fears had seemed terrible enough, but surely nothing could compare with what was going through Amelia Sach's mind in the hours before her death.

Quietly, Celia stood up and walked over to the far side of the cell, where a dark blue serge cloak hung on a hook, placed halfway down the wall to discourage those who might be tempted to take fate into their own hands. The bottom of the garment lay crumpled and dusty on the floor, and Celia rearranged the folds and smoothed the rough material as best she could, recognising the futility of the gesture but anxious not to let any opportunity for kindness go overlooked, no matter how small it seemed. In the three weeks between Sach's sentence and her execution, she was watched over constantly by two women at a time – strangers at first and then, as the days passed, allies, even friends. There was a peculiar intensity about the bond between wardress and prisoner: as she sat through her shifts, eight hours at a time, Celia shared every second of Sach's miserable existence, watching her as she washed and dressed, ate and cried, getting to know her habits and her preferences as she would have come to know a husband's in the early days of marriage. She had lived with Sach, and now she would see her to her death. Two warders had been brought in from another prison in case the distress of the execution proved too much for their female counterparts, but there was an unspoken determination amongst Celia and her colleagues to see this through to the bitter end: not because of suffrage or professional pride, not even – if she were honest – because they wanted to comfort the prisoner in her final moments, but simply because it was too late. The emotional damage had already been done. By the time the final week came, all but the most hardened of hearts found themselves counting the days as desperately as the condemned woman herself.

Long periods of sitting had created a numbness in her legs and back which she would willingly have shared with her other senses. She stretched her cramped limbs and wriggled her foot to get rid of the pins and needles, and her colleague – asleep in the other chair – sensed the movement and opened her eyes. The two women looked at each other, and Celia nodded. It was time. She walked over to the bed, holding her keys to stop them jangling – ridiculous, she thought, to suppose she could eliminate the reminders of incarceration, but it was another flicker of humanity to clutch at – and noticed Sach's body stiffen in anticipation of the hand on her shoulder. As Celia drew back blankets which were far too thin for the time of year, the smell of stale linen, sweat and fear rose up to greet her. Sach moved closer to the wall and tried to pull the covers back over her, but the hand was firm and she eventually allowed herself to be cajoled to her feet. In vain, Celia tried to reconcile the tall, gaunt woman in front of her with the arrogant, unfeeling creature who had filled the pages of the press since her arrest back in November. Sach looked much older than her twenty-nine years. Her face was grey with exhaustion, and her body looked barely strong enough to get her to the scaffold. How different she was from the woman who had entered prison with an incredulity bordering on indignation, who had believed that this could never happen to her. Right now, crowds would be gathering outside the prison gates, waiting for the customary announcement, but had any of them come face to face with Amelia Sach, Celia doubted that they would recognise her as the monster who lived in their minds.

She encouraged the prisoner to dress, trying not to adopt the expression of pity which she had noticed in every other visitor to the cell, from the chaplain to the governor. Most of Sach's clothes were already on, worn in bed to fight the cold, but Celia helped her pull the standard blue shift – faded, and sufficiently shapeless to smother any sense of individuality amongst the Holloway women – over her head. Kneeling down to guide Sach's feet into shabby, ill-fitting shoes, she noticed holes in her stockings where the nails which held the shoes together had snagged the black wool and punctured the skin beneath. The feet felt so small and vulnerable in her hands that, for a few seconds, Celia found it difficult to breathe; the jury had been right, she thought – it must be so much worse for a woman to be hanged than a man. Or was that unfair? Did male warders feel this same raw despair when the time came for their prisoner to die? Too shaken to stand, she felt Sach's fingers rest briefly on her head; whether the gesture was a benediction or a silent plea for strength, she did not know, but it was enough. Pulling herself together, she began to scrape Sach's once-pretty auburn hair – now lank with neglect – back into a ponytail and fixed it in a bun, away from her neck, where it would not catch in the noose. It was a simple act, but it seemed to affect Sach more deeply than anything else and Celia took the cloak quickly from the hook, trying to blot out a sound which was more like the whimper of an animal in pain than anything she had ever heard coming from a human being. As she wrapped it round Sach's shoulders, she wondered if terror – like dirt – could find a way of weaving itself into the fabric, accumulating with each poor soul who wore it. She turned the prisoner round to face her, desperate somehow to stem this outpouring of grief, but the woman's cries only grew louder and more coherent. 'Don't let them do it to me. I haven't done anything,' she repeated over and over again, drawing Celia into her hopelessness until the other wardress was forced to intervene.

'Come now, Mrs Sach,' she said, gently but firmly removing the hands that clung pitifully to Celia's dress. 'You haven't touched your breakfast. Try and eat something.'

'Can't we give her something stronger than bread and tea?' Celia asked angrily. 'What use is that to her now?'

The older woman shook her head and glanced quickly at her watch. 'There's no time,' she whispered. 'It's nearly nine.'

As though to prove her point, there was a noise in the corridor outside. Like most prisoners, used to spending so much time waiting and listening to events which could not be seen, Sach was quick to hear the approaching footsteps and eager to guess at their meaning. As they stopped outside the cell, then moved on again, the flicker of hope on her face was unbearable to Celia, who knew that only half the execution party had walked past; the other half would be just outside, waiting for the governor's nod. Staring at the door, she saw the slightest of movements as the hangman moved the peep-hole cover to one side to assess the mental state of the prisoner and then, after what felt like an interminable wait, the chime of the bells from the church next door signaled nine o'clock. Celia counted two strokes before she heard the rattle of the keys in the lock, three before the heavy iron door opened, and then the small group of men was in the cell, setting in motion a relentless sequence of events from which there was no escape, which could never be undone.

The hangman moved swiftly across the cell and began to pinion Sach's hands behind her back. As soon as she felt the leather straps against her skin, she seemed to lose what little strength she had left. Celia stepped forward to prevent her falling to the floor, whispering words of comfort, but they seemed to have the opposite effect and Sach had to be half led, half carried out into the corridor. A few feet to their right, at the door to the adjacent cell, a similar scene was being played out, but the contrast between the prisoners could not have been more marked. Annie Walters was a short, grey-haired woman in her early fifties, as sturdy and homely looking as Sach was delicate, but it was their demeanour that set them apart, not their build or their age. The sight of the other woman only increased Sach's distress until it bordered on hysteria, but Walters remained cheerful and talkative, swapping casual remarks with the second

432

hangman as if oblivious to the fact that these were her final moments. Looking at the two women now, brought face to face for the first time since their sentencing, it was hard to believe that they were conspirators in the brutal murders of babies – as many as twenty, some said, and most only a few days old.

Everything happened quickly from then on. The first hangman steadied Sach and prepared her for the short walk to the gallows. With a wardress on either side, the prisoners followed the chaplain towards the double doors at the end of the wing and into the newly built execution shed. It was only a dozen steps or so, but far enough for Celia to notice that the prison seemed unnaturally quiet, almost as if a collective breath were being held. For three weeks now, the Holloway women had been restless and uneasy; the inevitable mixture of distress and sensationalism which greeted the sentence had been replaced by an angry helplessness, and everyone was touched by it, staff and prisoners alike. Celia knew she was not alone in longing to move the clock forward or back, to exist anywhere but in this present moment.

And then they were inside. Two nooses hung straight ahead of them, one slightly higher than the other, and the prisoners were led swiftly onto the trap. The executioners dropped to their knees to fasten the leg straps, their movements perfectly synchronised. Celia looked at Sach through the oval of rope, willing her ordeal to be over and refusing to look away in the face of death; it was the only help she had left to offer, and she held the woman's terrified gaze as a white cap – kept like a foppish handkerchief in the hangman's top pocket – was placed over her head and the noose adjusted. All the time she could hear the low, steady voice of the chaplain chanting out the service for the dead, but the words were indistinct. As the executioner moved across to the lever, the only thing she could focus on was the small circle of cloth moving in and out over Sach's mouth.

Afterwards, Celia could not say for certain if she had heard Walters calling out a goodbye to Sach shortly before the trapdoor opened, or if it had just been her imagination. But what she did remember of the seconds that followed – and she was sure of this because it came back to her sometimes, even now, in the early hours of a winter's morning – was the silence.

* * *

Josephine Tey picked up an extravagantly wrapped hatbox and used the perfect Selfridge bow to hook it on to the rest of her parcels.

'Are you sure you wouldn't like me to have that delivered for you, Madam?' the assistant asked anxiously, as if the hat's independent departure from the shop were somehow a slur on her standards. 'It's really no trouble.'

'Oh no, I'll be fine,' Josephine said, smiling guiltily at the group of young girls behind the counter. 'Carrying this will stop me going anywhere else today, and that's probably just as well – if I send many more packages round to my club, they'll be charging me for an extra room.'

Balancing her recklessness as best she could, Josephine took the escalator down to the ground floor. Its steady, sedate progress gave her plenty of time to admire the vast, open-plan design of the store, a look which was still so different from what most of London's shops had to offer. The whole building seemed to sparkle with an innate understanding of the connection between a woman's eye and her purse; even the prominent bargain tables were neatly stacked with beautiful boxes that gave no hint of their reduced price. December was still a week away, but staff were already beginning to decorate the aisles for the festive season and the familiar department store smell – plush carpets and fresh flowers – had been replaced by a warm scent of cinnamon which only the drench of perfume from the soap and cosmetic

434

departments could keep at bay. As a ploy to make Christmas seem closer than it really was, it seemed to have worked: even this late in the afternoon, the shop was packed with people and Josephine had to fight her way past the make-up counters to the main entrance and out into the bustle of Oxford Street.

She turned left towards Oxford Circus, following the long stretch of glass frontage to the corner of Duke Street. The shop windows were full of wax models, each a variation on the theme of Lot's wife, forever stilled in the midst of a gesture. Some beckoned to the curious to step inside, others carried on with their imaginary lives, oblivious to the flesh-and-blood women who studied every detail, but all were arranged against a background of light and colour which had been as carefully designed as any stage set. Josephine paused by a particularly striking bedroom scene. A ravishing wax figure, dressed in a crepe-de-chine night-gown, stepped out of a nest of silken sheets and pillows. Her pink foot rested lightly on the floor, and she stretched a perfectly manicured hand over to her bedside table, which held a morning paper, a novel – *The Provincial Lady in America*, Josephine noticed – and a tea tray with the finest bone china. Her dressing table – a magnet for feminine extravagance – gleamed with crystal, gold-stoppered bottles. It was a powerful image, but its message – that a life of comfort and intimacy was available to anyone who knew where to shop – was as painful for some as it was seductive to others. There was a whole generation of women for whom this would never be a reality, whose chances of happiness and security, even companionship, had been snatched away by the war, and no amount of satin could soften the blow of what they had lost. Glancing at the spinsters on either side of her – she used the word half-heartedly, aware of her own hypocrisy in treating them as a race apart – Josephine knew that the troubled look on their faces was about more than the lingerie's ability to withstand the November cold.

The pavement was only just wide enough to accommodate a double flow of pedestrians, and Josephine walked on slowly, recognising herself in the women from provincial towns who seemed utterly engrossed in their business, determined not to miss a thing. It was after five o'clock and, in the last hour, the pinks and oranges of a winter sunset had quickly given way to a sky the colour of blue-black ink. An unbroken line of street-lights stretched ahead of her like pearls on a string, drifting into the distance and relieving the mile-long stretch of shops – ladies' mile, as it was known – from the ordinariness of the day. Some of the smaller branches had already closed, emptying more workers out onto the streets, and a few shop-girls stopped to gaze wistfully into the windows of the larger stores, a long day on their feet having strengthened their desire to stand for once on the other side of the counter; most, though, headed quickly for the underground or for bus queues which grew longer by the second, muttering impatiently to themselves and keen to make every second of freedom count before the daily routine began again tomorrow.

As impressive as its sequence of huge stores was, Oxford Street was one of Josephine's least favourite parts of London, something to be endured for the sake of a weakness for clothes but never for longer than necessary. Gladly, she left its crowds and its clatter behind and cut through into the more select surroundings of Wigmore Street. There was something about the anonymity of walking through London in the early evening that never failed to delight her, a sense of freedom in the knowledge that – for as long as she chose – no one in the world knew where she was or how to contact her. She had travelled down from Inverness ten days ago, but had so far managed to keep her presence a secret from all but a few casual acquaintances at her club. It couldn't last forever; there were several engagements booked for the fol-lowing week and she would have to pick up the telephone soon and open a floodgate of invitations, but she was in no hurry to socialise before she had to. A world in which there were no time-tables to be followed or deadlines to be met, and where messages left were never for her, suited Josephine perfectly. She was determined to enjoy it for as long as possible.

Even so, the sort of undemanding companionship offered by an afternoon of dedicated shopping was a relief after the solitary morning she had spent in her room – just her and a typewriter and a series of shadowy figures from a past which felt utterly alien to her. She was still not sure about the novel she was working on and wondered if her desire to write something other than a detective story had been wise after all. When her editor suggested a book with a historical slant, a fictionalised account of a true crime seemed a good idea, particularly one with which she had a personal connection, but the claustrophobic horror of Holloway Gaol was starting to depress her and she had only just begun. Summer – both the real summer she had spent in Corn-wall and the imaginary version which she had recently delivered to her publisher – seemed a long way away, and she found herself craving the warmth of the sun on her back and the comfort-ing presence of Detective Inspector Alan Grant, hero of her first two mysteries. These early stages of a book, when all the charac-ters were unfamiliar, were always the hardest to write. Getting to know them felt like walking into a room full of strangers, something from which her shyness made her recoil in horror; she would be pleased to get further on with the story, even if the world she was creating was unlikely to get any cheerier.

Across the street, the Times Book Club was still open and she was amused to see that books never failed to bring out the dormant shopper in a man. A lamp under the blind threw a welcoming yellow glow onto the shelves, where faded covers of popular novels and obscure political pamphlets were brought together as randomly as the people who browsed them. She considered going in, but decided that she was too laden with shopping to manage the sort of rummaging that books required, and pressed on instead to Cavendish Square. Here, the streetlamps were more forgiving, their pools of light interspersed with longer stretches of darkness, and there was a restful elegance about the area. The Square had been more fortunate than many of its London counterparts, where residential buildings were asked to rub along with modern offices, and it still consisted principally of beautifully proportioned old houses. It was home time, and as she made her way round to number twenty, Josephine watched the lights coming on in the upper stories, imagining doors opening and voices calling up the stairs while life moved from the office to the sitting room.

The Cowdray Club occupied a particularly handsome eighteenth-century town house on the corner of Cavendish Square and Henrietta Street, at the heart of what was once the most fashionable area of Georgian England. The house had been bought from Lord Asquith – the latest in a line of distinguished owners – and, in 1922, established as a social club for nurses and professional women by Annie, Viscountess Cowdray. Lady Cowdray – whom Josephine had never met but who had been, by all accounts, a formidable fundraiser and loyal supporter – had also paid for a new College of Nursing headquarters to be built in Asquith's old garden; thanks to some ingenious architectural thinking, the two buildings now functioned happily together, one providing for a nurse's working needs and the other for her rest and relaxation. Just over half of the Cowdray Club's membership came from the nursing profession. The rest were from all walks of life – lawyers, journalists, actresses and shop-girls, attracted by stimulating conversation, comfortable surroundings and the cheapest lunches in town – and Josephine was pleased to call it home whenever she wanted her time in London to be private and free from obligations to friends. Since Lady Cowdray's death a little over three years ago, the members had not lived together quite as harmoniously as the buildings: nursing was a political profession, and those left to run the club in its founder's absence had different views on its priorities and future. It was the same when any natural leader died or moved on, she supposed, but things were bound to settle down eventually; in the meantime, she kept her head below the parapet and tried to avoid the bickering.

Outside the main entrance, she balanced her parcels precariously on one arm but the door flew open before she could reach it, and a young woman – one of the Club's servants – rushed out, nearly knocking her to the ground.

'Am I missing the fire?' Josephine asked, a little more sarcastically than she meant to.

'Crikey, Miss – I'm so sorry,' the girl said, bending down to pick up the boxes that had skidded across the pavement and into the street. 'I wasn't looking where I was going.'

'Obviously,' Josephine said, but softened as she noticed how upset the girl seemed. 'I don't suppose there's any harm done. None of this is breakable.' She held out her hand to take the last of the parcels. 'What's the rush, though? Is everything all right?'